"Corrigan's second Jack Austin mystery features deft prose, clean plotting, and enjoyable subject matter and will appeal to golf fans."
—*Library Journal*

"Corrigan commands a wealth of technical detail to make Jack's every round vivid and exciting . . . Highly recommended for golfers, golf widows and widowers, and everybody who's ever wondered what the fuss is about."
—*Kirkus Reviews*

"[A]uthentic and exciting . . . Corrigan's second Jack Austin novel, starring a PGA touring pro struggling to hold on to his playing credentials, gets a lot of things right. There's plenty of on-course action . . . Corrigan comes up with a decent premise that doesn't involve bodies in bunkers . . . [and] an affecting subplot about Austin's dyslexic caddie."
—*Booklist*

"[T]rust us: it's another fun read with an interesting finish."
—*New England Journal of Golf*

"Imagine a wisecracking Tiger Woods as Sherlock Holmes. That's the sort of lovable hero John Corrigan has created in this new mystery series. Witty and intriguing, *Snap Hook* will delight every mystery reader who loves golf—and every golfer who loves mysteries."
—Tess Gerritsen, author of *The Sinner*

"How does a golfer spend an ideal day? Eighteen holes on the links and the evening spent reading John Corrigan's new mystery, *Snap Hook.* Corrigan's Jack Austin is a grand, new hero—sensitive, smart, loyal, and one hell of a fine golfer!"
—Roberta Isleib, author of the Agatha- and Anthony-nominated Golf Lover's mysteries

"From sand traps to kidnapping, money laundering to murder mystery, John R. Corrigan is a brilliant story teller. With *Snap Hook,* he hits a hole in one."
—Ridley Pearson, author of *User: Unknown*

"John R. Corrigan accurately portrays life on the PGA Tour, and throws in a wonderful twist by adding a mystery and an interesting sleuth in Jack Austin. Anyone who likes golf and mysteries will find the two here."
— PGA Tour player J. P. Hayes,
winner of the 2002 John Deere Classic and 1998 Buick Classic

"*Snap Hook* exposes its readers not only to the glamorous, slippery-putt tension of the PGA tour but to the fast-paced drama of crimes, high and low, local and international. A natural read for lovers of golf and suspense."
— Billy Collins

PRAISE FOR *CUT SHOT*

"*Cut Shot* is a riveting novel, with characters you care about, well conceived and gracefully presented."
— Robert B. Parker

"Corrigan, a Maine writer (and dyslexic), moves murder into a new field with this first novel about blackmail and murder on the fairways. Mystery fans have bought into Dick Francis's novels set in the world of horse racing, and Corrigan could well make a killing of his own with his player-detective on the PGA Tour. Crime goes hand in golf glove with the game."
— *Kennebec Journal*

"*Cut Shot* deftly combines life in professional golf's sunny top tiers with the dark world of life-or-death sleuthing. The first of a planned series, this debut novel is a fun, relaxing read. Beyond that, it's a fresh attempt to link a major sport to mystery in much the same way Dick Francis has linked mystery to horse racing . . . Good people, a good game and a good mystery add up to a score worth repeating."
— *Portland Sunday Telegram*

"I kept thinking I was reading a golf version of the Dick Francis novels . . . I'm looking forward to enjoying another evening or two with the next Austin mystery."
— *Hole by Hole*

"[A] very promising debut . . . [Jack] is also constantly trying to improve his game (do you know someone like this? If so, this book is for them!) . . . I have a hunch we shall see more blood on the green and look forward to it."
— Kate's Mystery Books Newsletter

CENTER CUT

OTHER BOOKS BY JOHN R. CORRIGAN

Cut Shot (Sleeping Bear Press, 2001)
Snap Hook (UPNE, 2004)

HARDSCRABBLE BOOKS—FICTION OF NEW ENGLAND

Laurie Alberts, *Lost Daughters*

Laurie Alberts, *The Price of Land in Shelby*

Thomas Bailey Aldrich, *The Story of a Bad Boy*

Robert J. Begiebing, *The Adventures of Allegra Fullerton: Or, a Memoir of Startling and Amusing Episodes from Itinerant Life*

Robert J. Begiebing, *Rebecca Wentworth's Distraction*

Anne Bernays, *Professor Romeo*

Chris Bohjalian, *Water Witches*

Dona Brown, ed., *A Tourist's New England: Travel Fiction, 1820–1920*

Joseph Bruchac, *The Waters Between: A Novel of the Dawn Land*

Joseph A. Citro, *DEUS-X*

Joseph A. Citro, *The Gore*

Joseph A. Citro, *Guardian Angels*

Joseph A. Citro, *Lake Monsters*

Joseph A. Citro, *Shadow Child*

Sean Connolly, *A Great Place to Die*

Ellen Cooney, *Gun Ball Hill*

John R. Corrigan, *Center Cut*

John R. Corrigan, *Snap Hook*

Pamala S. Deane, *My Story Being This: Details of the Life of Mary Williams Magahee, Lady of Colour*

J. E. Fender, *The Frost Saga*

    The Private Revolution of Geoffrey Frost: Being an Account of the Life and Times of Geoffrey Frost, Mariner, of Portsmouth, in New Hampshire, as Faithfully Translated from the Ming Tsun Chronicles, and Diligently Compared with Other Contemporary Histories

    Audacity, Privateer Out of Portsmouth

    Our Lives, Our Fortunes

Dorothy Canfield Fisher (Mark J. Madigan, ed.), *Seasoned Timber*

Dorothy Canfield Fisher, *Understood Betsy*

Joseph Freda, *Suburban Guerrillas*

Castle Freeman, Jr., *Judgment Hill*

Frank Gaspar, *Leaving Pico*

Robert Harnum, *Exile in the Kingdom*

Ernest Hebert, *The Dogs of March*

Ernest Hebert, *Live Free or Die*

Ernest Hebert, *The Old American*

Sarah Orne Jewett (Sarah Way Sherman, ed.), *The Country of the Pointed Firs and Other Stories*

Raymond Kennedy, *Ride a Cockhorse*

Raymond Kennedy, *The Romance of Eleanor Gray*

Lisa MacFarlane, ed., *This World Is Not Conclusion: Faith in Nineteenth-Century New England Fiction*

G. F. Michelsen, *Hard Bottom*

Don Mitchell, *The Nature Notebooks*

Anne Whitney Pierce, *Rain Line*

Kit Reed, *J. Eden*

Rowland E. Robinson (David Budbill, ed.), *Danvis Tales: Selected Stories*

Roxana Robinson, *Summer Light*

Rebecca Rule, *The Best Revenge: Short Stories*

Catharine Maria Sedgwick (Maria Karafilis, ed.), *The Linwoods: or, "Sixty Years Since" in America*

R. D. Skillings, *How Many Die*

R. D. Skillings, *Where the Time Goes*

Lynn Stegner, *Pipers at the Gates of Dawn: A Triptych*

Theodore Weesner, *Novemberfest*

W. D. Wetherell, *The Wisest Man in America*

Edith Wharton (Barbara A. White, ed.), *Wharton's New England; Seven Stories and* Ethan Frome

Thomas Williams, *The Hair of Harold Roux*

Suzi Wizowaty, *The Round Barn*

CENTER CUT

JOHN R. CORRIGAN

University Press of New England

HANOVER AND LONDON

Published by University Press of New England,

One Court Street, Lebanon, NH 03766

www.upne.com

© 2004 by John R. Corrigan

Poetry on pages viii, 33, 104, 126, and 247: From *New Selected Poems* by
Philip Levine, copyright © 1991 by Philip Levine. Used by permission of
Alfred A. Knopf, a division of Random House, Inc.

Printed in the United States of America

5 4 3 2 1

Library of Congress Cataloging-in-Publication Data

Corrigan, J. R. (John R.)

Center cut : a Jack Austin mystery / John R. Corrigan.

   p.   cm. — (Hardscrabble books)

ISBN 1–58465–405–8 (alk. paper)

1. Golfers—Fiction.   I. Title.

PS3603.O773C46   2004

813'.6—dc22   2004009402

This novel is set in the world of the PGA Tour, and while a number of real players
are mentioned, the characters and incidents in this book are solely the product of
the author's imagination. Any resemblance to actual persons or events is purely
coincidental.

This is for my father,
John Walter Corrigan,
who taught me everything I know
about being a father and a man.

Thirty years will pass before I remember
that moment when suddenly I knew each man
has one brother who dies when he sleeps
and sleeps when he rises to face this life

—Philip Levine, "You Can Have It"

ACKNOWLEDGMENTS

First, thanks to the home team: To my wife, Lisa, who, as always, provided me with time and emotional support as I worked on this novel. Additionally, one summer morning, when I needed to hear it, she uttered a key phrase regarding not only this book but writing in general. My debt of gratitude extends far beyond what is said here.

To my mother, who refused to listen when a teacher, failing to understand dyslexia, said, "Face it. Some kids are just slow." Thank you for fighting for me. And thanks to my sister, for her love and friendship. To my in-laws, Keith and Bev McBurnie, thanks for believing in me and for all you've done for me.

Thanks also to the following people, who generously fielded my research questions:

David P. McClure, president and CEO of U.S. Internet Industry Association, for offering Internet statistics and insight into on-line business ventures;

Andy Pazder and Allison M. Vogt, both at PGA Tour Headquarters, for taking time to answer question after question and offering details into PGA Tour player groupings, statistics, and other fascinating insights I literally could never acquire elsewhere;

Chief of Police Naldo Gagnon, of Presque Isle, Maine, and private investigator Sheila Cantor of Sleuth, LLC, in Washington, D.C., for their respective insights into missing persons procedures, from varying perspectives;

Doug Van Wickler, director of golf at the Woodlands Club in Falmouth, Maine, for sharing his knowledge of the club, offering access, and even a great swing tip on a late-October day;

Jon MacDonald, my cousin and a former Secret Service agent, for insights into the legal system;

Professors Linda Graves of the University of Maine at Presque Isle and Irv Kornfield of the University of Maine at Orono, for sharing knowledge of DNA and how blood evidence is uncovered;

Attorney Frank Bemis and Carl Flynn, M.D., of Presque Isle and Caribou, Maine, respectively, for answering legal and medical questions.

A special thanks to two friends who have been in the business a lot longer than me and never stop lending wisdom—Rick DeMarinis and Les Standiford. Thanks for sharing your knowledge and for your friendship.

As always, thanks to my agent, Giles Anderson, who closes deals and thinks of the future.

To my editor John Landrigan and the University Press of New England, thank you for offering Jack Austin a home and for all your assistance.

To everyone else at UPNE—Barbara Briggs, Johanna Hollway, Sherri Strickland, Sara Carpenter, John Lyman, Elizabeth Rawitsch, and Mary Crittendon—I appreciate all you do behind the scenes for my books.

CENTER CUT

*W*hen you live out of a suitcase and travel city to city, strangers enter your life daily. Some appear like a brilliant moon rolling from behind cloud cover only to fall back into the distance as time passes. Others, however, like Lynne Ashley, stay with you forever.

The eighteenth hole at the Colonial Country Club in Fort Worth, Texas, is a 427-yard par four, a true test requiring complete focus. The tee shot requires a draw, but the fairway is lined with trees to catch draws that don't listen. The green is guarded on both sides by bunkers. A lake shimmers just left of the putting surface. It was a Friday in May, and the temperature was eighty-five—only slightly higher than my score—as I stood on the tee box at the Bank of America Colonial with my caddie, Tim Silver. Our playing partners stood behind us.

"Wish you'd have told me you just planned to screw around this week," Silver said.

His head was the color of a dull penny and shone beneath the Texas sun. Built like a gymnast, he toted the fifty-five–pound bag with ease over hilly tracks in the most humid conditions.

"'Screw around'?" I said.

"Yeah. Could've saved myself a trip."

We were out of earshot, waiting for the group ahead to hit respective second shots then clear the fairway. Silver leaned on the bag and wiped his forehead with a towel slung over his shoulder.

"Screwing around is what we're doing, Jack. Maybe I'm doing more—sweating my balls off lugging the bag, reading greens, giving yardage—but you're not playing golf."

"Never got into rhythm this week."

" 'Rhythm'? You haven't gone low in a month."

I walked to a corner of the tee box, away from Silver, away from the other players, away from spectators. There was no getting away from my thoughts. Silver was right. Going low was something I had not done. Hadn't shot in the sixties for five consecutive tournaments. Golf is a game of numbers (not always a good thing for a dyslexic prone to reversals), and survival on the PGA Tour revolves around low numbers. Nevertheless, my career choice and my dyslexia have always gone hand in hand: Dyslexics are often single-minded and driven, qualities that are my trump cards—or, until recently, had been. As a professional golfer of the Tiger era, focus and drive are prerequisites, and I usually lead the field in those categories.

"You're a grinder, Jack Austin." Silver was back. "You and Vijay Singh usually close the range. You're up at five in the morning to lift weights."

I stood looking at him.

" 'Rhythm,' my ass. You practice last time you were home?"

"Let's get something straight," I said. "I don't need you in my face. When I say I can't find my rhythm, I can't find my rhythm. Period. On a given day, I can beat anyone out here."

Silver smiled. "Welcome back." He handed me the driver. "Now hit a nice draw."

I shook my head, moved away from Silver, and took two well-controlled practice swings. They were identical to the motion I always used and offered no hint of turmoil. However, when I conducted the mental aspect of my pre-swing routine—visualizing my drive moving right to left, landing in the middle of the eighteenth fairway—I heard sounds from the gallery: faint voices, and the slap of sneakers against paved cart path. Then I was reviewing my score, thinking even a hole-in-one wouldn't allow me to make the cut.

I fought the mental demons. *One shot at a time.* Next, though, I thought of home, my wife and newborn.

My drive settled in the right rough, leaving a mid-iron to the green. I slammed the driver into the bag.

Silver slid the head-cover on it. "Let's finish this off right," he said.

We watched Tripp Davis hit his drive to the center of the eighteenth fairway.

"Never a good thing when your caddie says, 'Finish this off' and it's only Friday."

The drive of the third member of our group, a rookie named Newsome, four under on his round, landed beside Davis's in the fairway.

"We both know the facts, Jack." Silver smiled.

He got a kick out of *facts, Jack.*

Rhyme or not, Silver spoke the truth. He knew the game and my place in it. I'd shot seventy-five Thursday; even a birdie on this hole would give me a second-round seventy-nine. I wasn't going to make the cut. I still sought my first pro win, but I'd always earned enough to retain my Tour card, a rare feat for a winless player. I'd done so by working my tail off. Silver had a master's in journalism and had written a book about life on Tour, based on his time working for me. The book was accurate—if not always flattering—and told of our trials and tribulations. Most of all, I thought the book was fair. In that regard, the book was an extension of Silver—he always told you what he thought.

We moved to my ball in silence. The fairway was lined with spectators of all ethnic backgrounds. When I'd been a twenty-four–year–old rookie, there'd been primarily one type of fan, the country club set: he, taking an afternoon away from the office; she, skipping a spa treatment. Times had changed. Indeed, so had I. Back then, during long delays, I noticed females in the gallery, paying particular attention to those of the attractive and apparently single persuasion. Now I was older, wiser, and happily married. Maybe even more mature. However, the gift I attributed to dyslexia, the one I had long believed set me apart—my focus— was wavering. I didn't understand that. And it scared me.

"Maybe you should take next week off," Silver said.

We paused across the fairway from Davis and watched him prepare to hit.

"Playing the Memorial," I said. "It's Nicklaus's event."

"Haven't made a cut or a pay check in six weeks, Jack. Just thinking the rest might do you good."

"I told you, don't worry about me. Take care of yourself."

"That's what I'm doing."

I turned from Davis's ball, airborne and heading toward the green, to Silver.

He shrugged, and said, "Being honest," then flashed a wide grin. "But least your butt looks great in those khaki pants."

We were quiet. He'd always been able to deflate on-course tension.

"If there weren't laws against it," I said, "I'd fire you. Having a gay caddie hurts my concentration."

"My being gay has nothing to do with it. It's my obscene comments that hurt your concentration."

I nearly smiled. "Thanks for clarifying that."

. . .

A choke-down eight-iron put me on the green, within birdie range.

Standing behind my ball marker, I examined the line. I had all of eight feet for seventy-nine, straight, and slightly downhill. The putt would probably be slower than it looked.

The number "eighty" bothered me. Always had. I was more consistent than that. My bad rounds didn't lead to eighties. I took my time. Four practice strokes. Glances at the line from behind the ball marker, then from each side of the green to review the slope.

"I see it about six inches, left-to-right." Silver wiped the ball with his towel, then tossed it back to me.

I only nodded, trying to stay in the moment. I replaced the ball and pocketed my coin. Then I went into my pre-putt routine: crouched to get one final read, then addressed the ball, took two more practice strokes, and pulled the trigger. It was probably my best stroke of the day, yet I played too little break.

The ball darted left hard, missing on the low side.

I tapped in for eighty, shook hands with Davis and the rookie, Newsome—both of whom would be around for the weekend— then tossed my putter to Silver.

"Want to talk about whatever the hell is on your mind?" he said as we walked off the green.

"Nothing's on my mind."

"Been with you twelve years, Jack Austin. Don't bullshit me. Something is. It's pretty damned obvious."

I didn't say a thing.

"Last time you shot eighty it was drizzling, wind was blowing like a bastard."

I still didn't reply. Maybe I didn't know what was going on. Or maybe I just couldn't put it into words.

That spring we had moved to southern Maine, something I never envisioned my wife, Lisa Trembley-Austin, doing. The move from Rockville, Maryland, was a big one for her, but Maine was an excellent place to raise children. For me, southern Maine was vastly different from central Maine, where I'd grown up during the 1970s and 1980s. There was an arts scene, and, of course, there were the "weekenders," out-of-staters who purchased property near the ocean to serve as a "getaway."

If it had been realistic, I'd have preferred down-east Maine, farther up the coastline. However, that might have been too far from Rockville for Lisa. Given my occupation, it was also too far from the Portland International Jetport. We still had my small Orlando condo, where I could practice during winter, and the fishing cabin I'd long owned in northern Maine, but we were residing in an oceanfront home, only a couple hours from Boston. Besides, southern Maine had Land Rovers and Starbucks, so Rockville didn't seem that far away.

The move to Maine had been the second major change of the year. At 9:15, Saturday morning, I held the first major change as I entered the living room.

Lisa sat across a coffee table from three Tour wives. The wives had agreed to be interviewed for an article Lisa was writing, and they now sat on the sofa facing Lisa. Weekend or not, Lisa was working—so she wore Talbots. All her work outfits came from Talbots. In fact, if Talbots sold automobiles, we'd probably be driving something apple green. Usually, her black hair was shoulder-length. Now, though, she was growing it out and it hung past her collar.

Lisa clicked off the recorder and walked to me. "What time did you get in?"

"After midnight."

Beyond the picture window, the ocean ran to the end of the earth. I smiled at the ladies, who *Oooed* at six-week-old Darcy. Or maybe the *Ooo* was for me. I was unshaven, wearing a T-shirt and shorts. By contrast, Darcy lay wrapped in a pink blanket, asleep in the crux of my arm. She was the safe bet. She looked just like her mother. My blue eyes, but the dark hair, facial features, and long lashes were all Lisa.

Lisa kissed me. "Welcome home. Thought you were going straight to Ohio to practice for the Memorial."

I didn't know what to say to that. It was closing in on June. I routinely play thirty or more events but I had wanted to see Darcy. Fatherhood was affecting me, off the course and on, in ways I hadn't imagined.

"You're not sick, are you?" Lisa took Darcy.

I shook my head.

"Just wanted to be home?"

"Yeah."

"This," Lisa said, smiling proudly, turning to face the women, "is Darcy Ann."

"Hey," I said, "and your husband, Jack."

The women laughed. Rather, the two I knew did. The third, a young attractive blonde with big brown eyes, who I assumed to be Lynne Ashley, stood rubbing her open palm on her thigh as if drying a sweaty hand. Her husband, Grant, was a good friend. He'd emerged three seasons earlier—with a thick accent and a swing nearly as classic as the late Payne Stewart's—from the University of Georgia, where he'd been a three-time All-American. But I knew next to nothing of Lynne. Married in the off-season, she'd not traveled with Grant. I'd heard she'd been a football cheerleader at UGA.

I was married, happy, and in love. But I am human. Lynne Ashley looked the part of a cheerleader—cover-girl-quality jaw-bone, thin straight nose, wide mouth, stylish short blond hair, art-fully applied makeup, and the physique of one who worked out regularly. There was something else there, too, something sug-gestive, as if sensuality, for her, would never require silk sheets or candles, but was something she carried with her. She was the tallest woman present, maybe five feet ten, in her mid-twenties, and wore diamond earrings worth a top-five finish.

Lynne Ashley also looked nervous, as if being interviewed—even in our home, amid normal weekend life—bothered her. Dressed nervous, too. The Saturday interview was obviously in-formal, yet she wore a porcelain-blue blazer with matching skirt. Compared to the others, she looked as if she were con-ducting the interview. She watched from the sofa as the two other wives gathered around Lisa and Darcy.

"There's a plumber here looking at the garbage disposal," Lisa said.

"What happened to it?" I said.

She only shrugged, but I knew her focus was on the interview and that I was to handle domestic issues until she finished ques-tioning. In fact, I could picture Lisa before my interruption, seated, her posture absolutely perfect, yellow pad in her lap, feet together on the hardwood floor, smiling—but asking serious questions.

Strong perfume mixed with the aroma of Lisa's newsroom-strength coffee. Bright morning sunlight slanted through the picture window across from the fireplace. On the mantel, two baseball-sized crystals signified my participation in past U.S. Opens. The cedar-shingled house had been built in 1928 and had four-inch floorboards and thick molding near the ceiling. My father, a carpenter, had fallen in love with the place immediately. Glass-paneled French doors offered a view into the den. Lisa's office was upstairs; the den was mine. The walls were lined with books, poetry collections and golf history. I read there or reviewed tapes of my golf swing. Or mused over my oft-mal-behaved putting stroke.

"Sorry for the interruption," I said.

"Time for a break, anyway."

"I thought everyone just arrived."

"When there's a baby in the house," Angela Davis said, "everything functions on baby time." She spoke from experi-ence, mother to four. She had participated in six Boston Mara-thons and wore faded jeans and a nylon warm-up jacket. She was petite with short brown hair.

"And," Lisa said, "Darcy needs to be fed. Please excuse me for a few minutes. Jack, here, can entertain you, I'm sure."

"Undoubtedly," I said. "I've been working on some new jokes."

"Oh, God." Lisa left with Darcy.

The interviewees returned to their seats and talked amongst themselves. That might have bothered me, but my ego found solace in my disheveled appearance. When I had heard Darcy stir, I'd been on my way to the basement for what, for me, was to be a late-morning workout. Now I poured a cup of Lisa's deadline coffee and stood near the door. Through the open window along the east wall, the rich earthy odor of the sea en-tered. The ocean scent was one of Lisa's favorite aspects of coastal living.

"Finding the baby to be a big change?" Angela Davis said. She sat on the loveseat. I knew her husband, Tripp Davis, well. When traveling, Lisa and I ate dinner with them occasionally.

"Not unless you consider getting zero sleep, revamping your entire practice schedule, and realizing a simple glance from her makes you happier than almost anything."

Angela smiled broadly. "Welcome to fatherhood, Jack."

Tripp had just been named captain of the next United States Ryder Cup team. His had been a storied career: two major championships, fifteen Tour titles. Angela had been there all the way. Their four children now in middle and high school, she had recently become very active in the Tour's daycare facility and Wives' Association.

"Is Grant coming up tomorrow after the Colonial?" I said to Lynne.

She looked startled. She'd been staring into the den. "Oh, uh, no—no. I'll be flying back tonight."

"To Atlanta?"

"Of course. Where else would I go?" Her tone was sharp, her chestnut eyes suddenly vivid and direct. "Why do you ask?"

"Just curious."

A man with a pitted face, a receding hairline, and wearing oil-stained blue jeans, a white T-shirt, and engineer boots, entered the room. He looked around.

"I'm the owner," I said. "You can talk to me."

He nodded. "The garbage disposal," he said, his eyes scanning the room, "needs . . ." His eyes stopped and focused on Lynne. He stood staring for three full seconds. "Don't I know you from somewhere?"

Lynne turned away and stood staring out the window.

"The garbage disposal needs what?" I said.

"Oh, right." He glanced at Lynne once more, than back to me. "A couple of parts I don't have in the van. I'll bring them by Monday."

"Sure," I said.

He turned and left.

"Guess he thinks you're cute, Lynne," Michelle Goode said.

"He's a disgusting slob," Lynne said.

Angela Davis cleared her throat. "You should take those glass panes out of the French doors."

My gaze swung to her.

"A young child could break one, Jack, cut herself. We replaced ours with Plexiglas."

"Plastic?" Lynne said.

"Yes, it's much safer."

Lynne shook her head sadly. "And uglier."

I refilled my coffee and spooned in sugar. The morning air seemed cold after Texas. The ocean provided a breeze on even the most uncomfortable days. As a Maine native, I knew it also took care of the state's official bird, the black fly. The silence seemed to intensify. Had I missed something, maybe an earlier insult for which Lynne had just gotten even?

"When you have kids," Angela said, "you'll understand."

"Motherhood isn't for me." Lynne turned and stared at the ocean again, chin jutting proudly.

"Not yet," Angela said.

"Not ever," Lynne said. "I enjoy exercise."

Michelle Goode chuckled. It was faint as if a distant echo. She sat next to Lynne. About my age, Michelle leaned back, legs crossed. She wore designer jeans and a navy blue blazer over a white top. Long, wavy, brown hair. She smiled at me. (Maybe I'd underestimated my appearance.) Michelle was relaxed and confident. Husband, Bob, I knew vaguely from rounds together. His career paralleled mine: We'd gotten Tour cards the same year. He had one victory, one more than I had.

Lynne's head turned very slowly, her eyes, narrow and intense on Michelle. Her voice was not distant. It was firm. "Don't laugh at me. Exercise is my life, my outlet."

Dead silence.

I drank some coffee and revised my earlier desire to be this crowd's focal point.

"You might change your mind about having kids," Angela said to Lynne.

"No. I won't."

"Anyway, would you be interested in doing some charity work for needy children? I'm president of the Wives' Association and we need—"

Lynne waved her hand as if stopping a sales pitch. "Forget it."

Lynne had been curt before, but Angela was trying to help kids. This reply was rude. I shook my head and exhaled slowly. They heard me and looked over, so I drank my coffee. This wasn't my battle. I was home to play with my daughter, lift some weights, then go to Ohio.

Angela leaned back on the couch, glanced at me, and rolled her eyes.

"I'm too busy," Lynne said, trying to rebound, "but, thank you, um, anyway."

As if she'd hit a switch, I noticed a southern accent.

"I don't travel much. I'm a homebody." *Body* was dragged to *boudy.*

Michelle shifted on her end of the sofa and sighed. "Traveling is a way of life. It can be fun, too. If you want to know about things to do in each city, just call. I'd be happy—"

"I'm certain you would," Lynne said. "No, thank you."

"Lynne," I said, "it *is* a way of life. Take her offer. Grant'll be playing another twenty-five years, then the Champions Tour."

She looked at me for a long time. I stared back. In the distance, a foghorn's low rumble was heard as a boat passed. One of the others took a deep breath.

"Can I have a differing opinion? Is that allowed?" The accent had vanished.

"Have any opinion you want," I said.

Lynne shifted, shoes scraping the hardwood floor. Michelle shifted on the sofa. We waited for Lisa's return. After a few moments, the quiet seemed heavy.

"Anyway, I didn't like to fly, at first," I said. "Traveling will get easier, Lynne."

"Did you travel with Grant last year?" Angela said.

"Why do you ask?" Lynne said.

Angela glanced at me. I shrugged. I was procrastinating, but a long hard workout was looking better.

"We can't all be perfect little Tour people. I have my own life, apart from Grant's golf."

"Most of those 'little Tour people' are pretty good folks," I said.

"If you buy into this all-for-the-husband mentality. I don't."

"A lot of people buy into a *partnership*," I said.

"No one's trying to take your independence," Angela said. "I'm a CPA. After tax season, I take most of the summer off and travel."

"How quaint."

I couldn't just leave them. This was Maine. Even the rudest guest should be treated well, my mother always said. I had to wait for Lisa, but this was grating. I dragged my thumb and forefinger down my cheeks, where they met at the point of my chin. "Lynne, please be civil."

"I'm certain I am." The genteel overtone was back. I thought she even batted her lashes at me, a southern belle once more. Then her eyes locked on mine. "If this lecture is over, I'd care to use the bathroom, Jack."

I let that go and told her where the bathroom was. She grabbed her purse and left. We watched her in lingering silence. I have said many times, I am nowhere near smart enough to understand women. Thus, I was greatly relieved by the sound of Lisa's shoes clicking on the hardwood floors. She entered, handed Darcy to Angela, and regained her seat across from the two remaining wives.

"What's wrong?" Lisa said.

Angela and Michelle were quiet.

Although not bright enough to understand women, I'm not stupid. I know to stay clear of anything that might impede a Lisa Trembley interview. I kept my mouth shut.

"Jack?"

I pretended not to hear.

"She's just nervous," Michelle said to Angela.

Angela kissed Darcy's cheek, straightened, and shook her head. "I don't buy that. She's the typical cheerleader-type. I know some sweet ones, but she thinks looks mean everything. I've got no use for it."

"Jack," Lisa said, "what is going on?"

I shrugged innocently. Hadn't I just rolled out of bed?

"Is it Lynne?" Lisa said. "What is it?"

"Poor Lynne," Michelle said. "I think, underneath it all, she's a sweet kid."

I let my thoughts on that observation pass and freshened my coffee. Three cups would have me thoroughly caffeinated for the workout.

"What happened while I was gone? Did Lynne say the inter-view was making her nervous?"

"No," Michelle said. "She didn't say that."

"But something is making her difficult as hell," Angela said, "and rude, too. I've had enough of it."

I had always liked Angela.

Lynne was gone several minutes. Lisa was back to asking Angela and Michelle questions. I was working on my third coffee, waiting to get Darcy back. Angela, however, looked as if she'd fight me if I made a play for the baby. Besides, I was curious to see what Lynne would pull next.

Lynne brushed past me and sat on the sofa.

"Michelle and Angela just told me how they met their husbands," Lisa said.

"How wonderful," Lynne said.

Brown eyes narrowing, Lisa ran her tongue along her upper lip. She only did that when she was angry. I sipped my coffee slowly.

"Let me tell you how I met Jack."

I'd heard her recite the tale many times. It usually made me grin, but at this point, Lynne had offended everybody, excluding Darcy. As I listened, I wondered where in hell Grant picked this one.

"I was assigned a piece on putting. And"—Lisa smiled widely—"being an honest journalist, I thought I should show all sides of the topic—good strokes, and this is where Jack came on the scene, and bad ones, too."

Angela and Michelle chuckled. Lynne wasn't laughing. In fact, she sat with her hands beneath her, staring at the floor, the posture bizarre—a scared school kid waiting outside the principal's office. She began to rock back and forth slowly.

Lisa finished the story: She'd been live with Brad Faxon, having him demonstrate his putting motion, telling viewers how to emulate it. Next, she played a clip of a flawed stroke and pointed to breakdowns, never showing my face. Didn't have to. I knew the stroke and approached her afterward to protest. The argument did not go as I intended. She systematically rebuked each comment. Worse, when I finished barking, she looked me in the eye and offered a lesson. I stormed off, but, unable to get her out of my mind, made a peace offering—a dinner invitation—three nights later.

"How'd you meet Grant?" Lisa said, turning to Lynne.

"Huh?" Lynne looked up. She stopped rocking, then sniffled, and sneezed.

"God bless you," Lisa said and repeated her question.

"Oh, college."

Lisa sipped her tea and smiled. "I mean, tell us about it. Was it in a class?"

All eyes were on Lynne. I was leaning against the doorjamb.

"Nothing to tell."

"Come on," Michelle said. "We all told our stories. I admitted to meeting my husband at a driving range. How boring is that?"

Lynne shrugged. "I didn't pick up my husband at some driving range. I met him in a class at UGA."

Michelle's face reddened. "I'm not some goddamned groupie."

"Didn't say you were," Lynne said, the charming accent returning.

I guessed that was how young Grant had fallen for the act. I glanced at Lisa. She considered atmosphere essential to a quality interview. I could tell she was thinking about ways to re-establish a pleasant setting here. I had a suggestion, but it involved the words *door hit you on the ass,* so I kept my mouth shut.

"What was the class?" Lisa leaned back in her seat, smiling like a long-lost friend, but her voice had lost its energy. It sounded like a final try.

Pressed for an answer, Lynne sighed. "I don't know— *calculus.*"

"Were you a math major?" Angela said, smiling at Darcy. "I love math."

"Well, I don't."

Angela looked up quickly.

"I won't give up everything just because Grant wants to play golf. You may not understand that, but I have my own life."

"Lynne," Lisa said, "there's no reason to get offensive."

"Offensive? When I get offensive, you'll goddamn well know it."

"Look," Lisa said, "this doesn't seem to be working. Maybe—"

"Maybe I should leave? Yes, I should."

Lynne breezed past me again.

Lisa was on her feet. I fell in behind as she followed Lynne to the kitchen.

"Lynne," she said, "when I asked you, you were eager to be interviewed."

"I thought things would be different."

"I don't understand," Lisa said. "If I said something—"

"Forget about it. Just forget it," Lynne said, dropping her head and looking down. "It ain't . . ." She froze, quickly looking up at Lisa and me to see if we'd heard her. "I mean, it's not you."

Lynne flung the front door open and walked out. Lisa and I watched her go, neither making a move to stop her, because we had no way of knowing what was to come.

We had received two surprise houseguests. They arrived mid-afternoon on the heels of Lisa's interviewees, all of whom had not left with the commotion of Lynne Ashley. On Sunday morning, both guests had awakened before me. As I descended the basement stairs holding Darcy, I knew the guests would mention my late wake-up.

I had finished the basement myself, over the winter. It was a full cellar, two thousand square feet, the size of a very friendly green. Son of a carpenter, the moment I laid eyes on the eight-foot ceiling, I mulled over options, eventually settling on a workout room. I had framed and sheetrocked the walls and hung ceiling tiles. It had been enjoyable work. In fact, I'd spent many a summer vacation alongside my father doing similar projects, noting the care and diligence with which he worked, as if each project were being done to our own home. He'd called it "Maine pride." It was old-fashioned New England work ethic.

Beyond payment, the effort he put forth each job was acknowl-edged with handshakes received entering our town post office or eating at the local diner. Workdays had begun at 5 A.M. and ended as late as 9 P.M.

Reaching the bottom of the stairs, the sight of my carpentry work reminded me of my father, of those summers, of the un-spoken lessons. As it would follow, on Tour, my workdays often began at sunrise, lifting weights or jogging before heading to the course. The last two months, admittedly, had been different, and looking around the basement, guilt hit me like a spike.

"About time you got your ass down here." Perkins was sit-ting on the bench press, breathing hard, a towel over one shoul-der. "Last night you said we'd run at five, then lift. I did six miles, candy ass." He pointed to the stair climber, which stood on a rubber mat in the far corner.

"Overslept."

Darcy woke and lay smiling in my arms.

"You must be sick. Usually you get five hours and you're good to go. Anyway, I did the damned stair machine, then watched *SportsCenter* three times."

"Why didn't you run outside?"

"Didn't want to get lost in Prettyville, U.S.A.," he said.

Chandler, Maine, was quiet and convenient, but Perkins had grown up next door to me in rural central Maine. The small towns we knew were Carhartt work clothes, my father's Chevy pickup with 190,000 miles on it, and engineer boots soiled with oil or cow dung. Conversely, Chandler was a commuter town for Portland, Portsmouth, even Boston. Carhartt gave way to business suits.

Perkins leaned back on the bench and did a set with what looked like every weight I owned. On black rubber mats around him were chrome-plated dumbbells. I had four hundred pounds of free weights, a military press, and two thirty-five–pound Olympic bars.

Across the room, stood a man whom I had idolized as a child. Now he was a father figure. Peter Schultz, eighty-three, had a deep tan and thick hands that belied his 140 pounds. He stood on my prized creation, the makeshift putting green I'd devised using two-by-fours, plywood, and green indoor-outdoor carpeting. I had stood the two-by-fours on edge, then set the plywood atop to construct an indoor putting surface. A thirty-two–inch television and a loveseat rounded out the room. With the exception of a bar and steaks, my basement had everything a man needed.

Schultz glanced at his watch and shook his head. "I got up, didn't find you, so I called the golf course. They said you weren't there. Thought we were going to have a lesson."

"We will," I said.

"First thing," Schultz said, "is these new putters are overrated. This 'White Hot' putter"— he shook his head contemptuously—"the old Bullseye is still the only putter."

Who was I to argue? The guy had won the Masters many years earlier.

Darcy cooed. Her eyes flickered and closed. The basement was cooler than the upstairs. Rectangular windows on the east and west sides of the house were open. The heavy, earthy scent of the ocean was present.

I heard the bar clang against bench and looked over. Darcy woke but didn't cry.

Perkins sat up. "Thought you said Lisa stopped working." He was gasping.

"Out of shape?"

He gave me the finger. Perkins was six feet five, 275 pounds, with naturally white-blond hair and pale blue eyes. He'd played line two seasons for the Patriots and, before that, UMaine, where we'd roomed. He hadn't let himself become the fat mass some ex-football players become. Rather, he got into bodybuilding and now had legs the size of my waist, biceps thicker than my eighteen-inch neck.

"She's doing some freelance for the *Washington Post*."

He grinned. "Small-town rag, huh?"

"Yeah. Small time."

"If she's going to do something," he said, "she's going to do it big."

"That's Lisa."

Lisa had walked away from her full-time job as a head golf

analyst for CBS, a decision we'd discussed at length, one that still concerned me. Motherhood or not, Lisa was a journalist. Since beginning her career more than a decade earlier, she'd eaten, slept, and breathed her work. I guessed the transition to stay-at-home mom would not be easy and was glad she was freelancing.

"You've got a good one, there, Jack," Schultz said.

"Too good for him," Perkins said.

Schultz laughed.

Darcy was out again. I moved to the electronic swing and set her in it. Then I went to the bench and did some pushups on a rubber mat.

Perkins leaned back to do his next set. "If you're going to lift," he said, "just let me know. I'll blow up some balloons and tie them to the bar. 'Bout all you can handle."

"Cute." When he was done lifting the house, I shooed him off the bench and did a warm-up set: twenty-five reps with 135 pounds. I got off the bench, letting him take over.

Schultz had a Bullseye putter now—one I had once used, now retired—and made a silky stroke from eight feet. I'd always envied his slow rhythmic motion. Given my play of late, I'd have arm-wrestled him for that stroke.

The ball dropped, center cut.

Schultz smiled broadly and clenched his fist. Catching himself, he looked around, embarrassed. I pretended not to have seen his mini celebration, but it made me smile: The eighty-three–year–old former Masters champ still found excitement in the game. Golf did that to people. I felt even guiltier and more confused.

On television, ESPN's *Sports Reporters* was on. Not golf. I was glad. I didn't want a tourney update. I hated hearing scores after missing the cut.

Schultz had told me he'd come to offer a lesson, having given Hall of Fame swing tips and putting insights a year earlier. However, my problems now weren't mechanical. The approach to the eighteenth green two days before told me as much. I felt that if I talked about what I was thinking, allowing my internal thoughts to be known, they'd become recorded or in some way official, and I'd be trapped, unable to get back to where I wanted to be. Maybe that was ridiculous. But I play a game where three-quarters of a single stroke separates Tiger Woods and forty places on the PGA Tour money list. Superstition means a lot.

Schultz went to the television and clicked to The Golf Channel, which constantly updates scores of the PGA, LPGA, Nationwide, and Champions tours. "Let's see how the tournament's going." He looked at me. "What's wrong?"

"Nothing. What do you think I should do with that empty corner over there?" I pointed to the far wall.

Schultz shrugged.

Perkins clanged the weight down again and sat up. He had four twenty-five–pound plates on each side. If I didn't know better, I'd have thought the bar would bend. The sound didn't stir Darcy.

Perkins stood and waved his arms in large circles. "Lisa growing her hair out?"

I said she was. She hadn't mentioned it, but I sensed the alteration had to do with staying home with Darcy and was not just a cosmetic change.

"Looks great either way." Schultz turned from the television, his voice carrying a fatherly overtone.

Perkins and I smiled.

The television showed Justin Leonard leading.

"Longhorn fans must be going nuts," Schultz said. "Either of you want to put ten bucks down? Best-of-five from eight feet?"

"You want Jack to pump his fist," Perkins said, "like in the pictures?"

"He'd have to beat me to do that, and neither of you can do it."

Perkins grinned at the old man half his size.

They were speaking of Lisa's decorating job in the living room. To my embarrassment, she had placed several action photos of me on the walls. In one, I was pumping my fist as a distant golf ball began its tumble into the hole. The pictures made me feel like I was in a self-indulgent shrine. Worse, they gave

Perkins endless pleasure. Twice he'd paused, returning from the kitchen to his post in front of the television, to imitate the fist pumps.

"Get up here and choose a weapon, you two." Schultz pointed to a line of nearly thirty putters on the wall. "That flight yesterday took a lot out of me—security checks, three-hour layover—but I'll still take your money."

Schultz wore khakis, a white golf shirt, and a sleeveless V-neck sweater. The house was seventy-five degrees, but he complained about "Maine being so damned cold, even in the summer."

I grabbed an Arnold Palmer blade, the same make and model I'd been using, albeit poorly, of late.

Schultz crouched behind a ball, lining up his putt carefully.

"Peter," I said, "it's turf carpet. It won't break."

He looked at me indignantly, not for a moment considering advice from the enemy.

Perkins smiled. "Security checks are a pain now, but I'm glad for tighter security. New job has me on the road a lot."

"Must give you a whole new respect for my annual grind," I said.

Perkins tilted his head, thinking it over with care. "No."

Schultz waved for us to stop. He was over the ball now, eyes running from it to the cup, and back. The first putt looked to be on line, then darted left near the hole.

"What the hell was that?" He turned to Perkins. "A damned break. Did you hear him tell me it wouldn't break? Over ten bucks? These guys play for millions nowadays, and Jack's trying to squeeze ten bucks out of me."

Perkins laughed.

I smiled. "Local knowledge pays."

"You guys are fun," Schultz said. "And at my age, fun counts for everything."

"My age, too," Perkins said.

"So you're with the Tour full time now?" he said to Perkins, as he lined up the second ball.

"Special consultant to PGA Tour Security Office."

"The sport of integrity," I said, "hiring you. Hard to imagine."

Schultz smiled. Perkins pretended not to hear.

"I've got a private investigations business in Boston, but"—Perkins pointed to me—"helped his ass out a couple times, and the Tour commissioner wants to step up security. Said I could basically name my price."

"And you did," Schultz said, positioning the second ball. Then he paused to look at Perkins, making a realization. "You're the one who shot Nikoli Silcandrov."

Perkins nodded somberly. It had been a bad episode. Silcandrov laundered money through the Tour's charity office, then forced Perkins to shoot him, dead. It was suicide. To Perkins, though, it felt like murder. Perkins's actions saved my life, however, and we named Darcy after him. He hated the name and had gone by his surname as long as I could remember. Now I smiled each time someone said her name and he mistakenly looked up.

Schultz hit the second putt. It caught the left edge, tumbling in. This time he didn't hold back—a full-out fist pump. His eyes locked on mine, and he glared, issuing a challenge.

He made two of the next three, finishing three of five.

"Let's see what you're made of," he said to Perkins.

The sight of Schultz, who weighed as much as one of Perkins's shoes, an elder statesman of the Tour, jawing at Perkins, and of Perkins simply taking it, nearly made up for the mocking fist-pumps in the living room.

Perkins hunched over, his knuckles white on the putter.

The first attempt ran past the cup, off the putting surface, and thumped my sheetrocked wall.

"This isn't croquet," Schultz said, slapping his thigh, openly enjoying his joke.

"Stop talking, so I can concentrate." Perkins went one for five.

"Candy from babies," Schultz said as I readied to putt.

Following two slow practice strokes, I sunk the first attempt, dead center.

"Even a blind squirrel trips over a nut," Schultz said.

I made the second.

"Both were dead center," Perkins said.

So was the third.

"Two putts to make one. Pressure makes the player, Jack."

Schultz's voice had changed slightly. He eyed me as my father had years earlier when challenging me to do better, and I now knew Silver had called Schultz and asked him to visit.

I brought the putter back slowly on my fourth attempt. The follow-through was solid. The putt looked good, catching the left edge, before spinning 180 degrees and rolling off harmlessly, stopping two feet right of the hole.

"One more shot," Schultz said. "You miss and we tie. And I was eight and one in playoffs."

Using the blade, I dragged a ball to my set-up position, carefully aligning the word "Titleist" so that if struck properly, it would blur into a tight spiral.

It did. The putt fell into the heart of the cup. Schultz smiled and handed me his money.

"I'm an amateur competing against pros," Perkins said.

"Pay up, Darcy," I said.

"Don't call me Darcy."

Perkins was still explaining his amateur status when I heard the cellar door open and Lisa's quick footsteps on the stairs. She reached the bottom in a hurry.

"Grant Ashley's on the phone. He wants to speak to you, Jack. He called home all last night and again this morning. Lynne never answered."

"What do you mean?" I said.

"Lynne never went home."

"I'm supposed to tee off in a while," Grant Ashley's voice came through the phone. "Lynne's not home yet."

"What time was she supposed to arrive?" I said.

"Don't know, exactly. Yesterday."

His Georgia twang was ever-present, but I didn't hear it now. Instead, I heard the sincere concern of a scared kid.

"I called 'til three a.m.," he said.

Lisa, Perkins, and I sat around the kitchen table. I was on the wall phone; Lisa held the cordless. Schultz had Darcy in the living room, rocking her like a grandfather. Perkins sat like a dog watching someone eat steak, eavesdropping as Lisa and I spoke.

"She left early, Grant," Lisa said. "Is there any place she'd likely go?"

"Give me a phone." Perkins's expression said amateur hour was over. "This is what the Tour's paying me for, Jack." His gray T-shirt pulled tightly at his shoulders. There was a sweat ring around his collar.

"There's a speakerphone upstairs," Lisa said. Perkins stood, and the two dashed upstairs.

"You're certain she said she'd be home yesterday?" I said to Grant.

"Yes."

"Maybe she knew you were playing the weekend"—just saying it made me think of missing the cut and something flickered inside—"and she took a shopping trip, figured she'd meet you at home tonight."

"Not going home," he said. "I'm playing the Memorial. We

23

were supposed to talk last night. Her idea. She said it might be a night when she needed to talk."

There was a burst of static on the line, then Lisa shouted from upstairs that she had him on speakerphone. I hung up the wallphone. As I climbed the stairs, my mind raced. Lynne certainly had stressed her marital independence. Yet I found myself wondering, if she had simply changed plans, why not notify Grant? Could she be that self-centered?

Lisa's office was pale yellow. On her desk was a photo of her asking a question at the White House, another of her guest-lecturing at Georgetown. The walls held her master's degree and several awards.

"Lisa"—Grant's voice was shaking when I entered—"how was she?"

"She seemed distracted."

We listened as Grant pushed out a large gulp of air.

"Grant," I said, "what did you mean by 'a night when she needed to talk'?"

"Nothing."

Perkins introduced himself and summed up his relationship to the Tour. "What makes you sure she isn't on a trip?"

"I just know."

It wasn't much of an answer, and I wasn't alone in that observation. Perkins stared at the phone and spread his hands. Lisa was sitting rigidly, thinking something but remaining quiet.

"You said she was supposed to fly to Atlanta," Perkins said. "That's where you live?"

"Yes."

"She have family in other parts of the country?"

There was silence.

"Look," Grant said, "I've got to get ready to play. Maybe I'm overreacting. Hell, she's probably sitting home right now. I'll try again."

I looked at Perkins, who continued to stare at the phone.

"Lisa," Grant said, "how distracted was she?"

She furrowed her brows in contemplation, tiny wrinkles appearing at the corners of her eyes. "What do you mean?"

"I mean, she seem okay? Not nervous, or, or distant?"

"I think both," Lisa said.

"Oh, Jesus."

Lisa had hit on something. The three of us sat as if listening for a clock's tick.

"Grant," Lisa said, "Lynne left in a hostile rush."

"What's that mean?"

"She got pissed and took off," I said.

Lisa shot me a look.

"That's what it means," I whispered and shrugged.

"Does that mean anything to you?" Perkins said. "She get nervous a lot?"

"Huh? Course not. Just a question. I'm concerned about my wife. You understand that?"

"What time was her flight supposed to arrive, exactly?" Perkins said.

"I don't know."

"Flight number?"

"I said I don't know any of that."

"Why not?"

"I'm in a hotel room. None of that stuff's here."

"Well," Perkins said, and shook his head, "some places have a twenty-four–hour waiting period to file an official missing-person's report. I don't know what Georgia's law is, but by the time you finish your round, it'll have been twenty-four hours. If she's still not home, call the Atlanta cops."

"Police?" Grant said. "No. No, I don't need cops. I don't want this public. Just wanted to call, see if she stayed an extra day."

"You said you called home until three a.m.," I said.

Lisa sat perfectly still, concentrating on the phone as if looking into Grant's eyes. "Grant, I know you don't want to think the worst. But protocol dictates you call the authorities."

"No police."

"I'm telling you," Perkins said, "they've got the man power. It's your best bet."

"I'll keep that in mind."

"Well, the Tour will probably send me down there, and the first thing I'll do is go see the local cops."

"No." The word seemed both forceful and stunted—a reaction he had not meant to let escape. He took a deep breath.

We waited.

"Why? Why would you go to the police when—when you got down there?"

Perkins looked at me, then at Lisa. She shrugged.

"They can give details about the area. Save me a lot of time. Tell me how far they've gotten. Plus, I'm not working independently. I'm representing the Tour, on the Atlanta cops' turf. I *should* tell them I'm there."

"Look," Grant said, "she's fine. Probably just missed her flight. Tough to get flights into Atlanta."

I'd probably spent three-fourths of the last decade on airplanes. I knew Atlanta was a hub for several commercial airlines. In fact, in 1999, Atlanta International was the world's busiest airport. A return flight hardly seemed a problem.

"Got to go," Grant said. "I'll call tonight to let you know everything's fine." He hung up.

The three of us sat looking at each other. It was Perkins who said what we were all thinking.

"He *will* call tonight and tell us that," he said, "whether it is all right or not."

By early afternoon, Perkins, Schultz, and I were at the Woodlands Club in Falmouth. The club is just north of Portland and less than a half hour from my home. The Woodlands is a relatively new golf course, having opened in 1988. It was designed by noted golf course architects Jim and (uncle) George Fazio. I'd sought membership at the Woodlands because, as four-time home of the New England Classic on what is now the Nationwide Tour, the club had the practice facilities I needed—two full-size practice greens and a range with three target greens.

The three of us now stood on the driving range, a place where I'd not spent enough time of late. Sun overhead, the seventy-degree air seemed chilled after nearly a week in Texas. I was loosening up, hitting wedge shots that danced around the hundred-yard target. Five or six others were on the range. Perkins had brought his clubs and was hitting next to me, spraying balls from one side of the range to the other as he and Schultz chatted.

"You play a lot?" Schultz said.

"Not much. Figure I'll play more golf now that I'm working for the Tour."

I held my follow-through and glanced over. "Please don't," I said. "We're trying to promote the game."

Perkins was leaning on a mid-iron, which looked like a twig that might easily break if he put all his weight on it. He grinned. "Bite me."

Perkins wore a collared golf shirt (club rules), navy blue slacks, and Nike running shoes. He'd said golf shoes hurt his feet; the leather wouldn't stretch like nylon over his tripled-E-wide pontoons. He wore aviator sunglasses. The unintended, yet overall, impression of Perkins golfing was something along the lines of Arnold Schwarzenegger flailing with a baton. When I'd brought my guests into the pro shop to meet the staff, Doug Van Wickler, director of golf, looked at Perkins as if this might be the first stickup in club history.

Schultz, however, was different. Peter Schultz was golf royalty and treated as such. He had on spikeless tan bucks, a flashy Tobasco shirt, and khaki pants. Aside from his Masters victory, he had fought in World War II and earned the Purple Heart. The staff—while keeping an eye on Perkins and the cash register—had all shaken hands with Schultz and insisted on a group photo.

"Your boy looks just like you," Schultz said, holding Perkins's open wallet.

"That's okay," I said, my head down, the club head of my five-iron waggling behind the ball. "Dating in high school is overrated anyway."

"Hey, the kid is goddamned good-looking."

I smiled and started the club back, rotating my torso, pausing when the club was at the top of my backswing, just short of parallel to the ground. The motion down was sharp, too quick. The result: a hook.

After contact, I looked up, watching the ball bend left and keep going.

"Judging from your stance," Schultz said, "that wasn't intended."

"Correct, professor."

He came closer. "Hit another."

I did. In the half second of contact, the club head struck the ball with a *click,* then cut through the range's rye grass, sounding like a heavy footstep. This shot was crisp and floated over the two-hundred–yard target, landed, and bounded out of sight.

"Beauty," Schultz said. "I watched last week. Every time they showed you, that's what I saw. Then the score ticker in the corner of the screen said you weren't even close to the cut line."

The amateur golfers on the range glanced covertly at us. It happens often when your name is on your bag. As the club's— and the state's, for that matter—lone Tour player, I was accustomed to it.

"When muscle memory is in place, inconsistency can stem only from poor concentration, Jack."

"Concentration, huh?"

He nodded and took Oakley sunglasses from his hip pocket and put them on. His intensity and energy were legendary. He had bungee jumped at almost seventy. When his wife had passed, he'd leaped into coaching headlong—reading, studying swing tapes, even taking sports psychology classes at a university. It was why he got $500 an hour, and why I knew I was damned lucky to have his help (for free) and his friendship.

. . .

A half-hour later, we were working on my driver. I hit three bombs, three-hundred–plus yards. My forth was a snap hook.

Schultz turned away. He turned back, opened his mouth to speak, then closed it, and walked to Perkins, who had sweat through his collared shirt and was grunting with each swing.

"You're a twenty-six handicap?" Schultz said.

"Yeah," Perkins said.

I coughed, as if choking.

Perkins gave me a look. "I am a twenty-six."

"When *you're* keeping score."

Schultz looked at me, tilted his head, and spoke in a fatherly voice. "I think you need to stop talking and think about what it is you're doing here, Jack."

I was silent.

He turned back to Perkins. "Anyway, a decent putting stroke can have you consistently breaking a hundred. Let's hit some putts."

Perkins shot me a look as they left. Schultz had flown in to see the baby and help me. Now he was frustrated. Nice, Jack. An eighty-three–year–old gentleman. Perkins hadn't missed it.

I hit another drive, making a good pass at this one, and watched the ball sail. It started low and rose gently, the way a plane ascends to flight, then seemed to splash against the crystalline sky and fall back to earth. The contact had been pure, the sensation running through my hands took me back in time.

I'd fallen in love with golf when other things had failed me. At nine, I flunked math. No one knew why, and school got worse before getting better. Declining grades led to meetings—my parents, teachers, school administrators, and I, discussing me.

Dyslexia. It's an information-processing affliction. Yet, for me, it was a strong and forceful hand. Long division was the mountain I attempted to climb each day. The hand appeared from atop the mountain and pushed me down, telling me to subtract when I should divide, shaking the sequence of steps like dice prior to the roll. I'd climb again, and the hand would shove once more. When long division turned to attempting to memorize Latin verb tenses, then molecular equations, golf provided solace. It also instilled confidence that daily school life stripped.

I was a scratch player by thirteen and won the Maine State Amateur after my freshman year at UMaine. I have often heard Tour players say they hadn't intended to play golf for a living, that as their game improved, they simply turned to it as a profession. By contrast, I had vowed to play the PGA Tour since age eleven.

I leaned into a drive, sending the ball long and straight, and over the net at the end of the range. I heard the ball crashing amid the trees.

I was doing what I'd dreamed of. I was married, with a beautiful healthy daughter. A legend had come to assist me with my game. Moreover, it was a perfect day to work, a day on which my father would have risen early, maybe had his first cup of coffee atop someone's roof and watched the sun rise before tacking shingles.

"Jack." It was Schultz's voice.

I turned to see him standing behind me.

"I wanted Perkins away from us for a minute."

The others on the range were out of earshot.

"The problem isn't your swing. That's never been something you've had to worry about. You don't have a Payne Stewart swing, but you've got a simple, repeatable motion."

His head was at my chin, arms folded across his chest. He looked me in the eye.

"And your putting average is actually in the top fifty on Tour. First time ever. This should be your best season."

"Still might be."

"You believe that?"

I watched two players hit at the far end of the range. "Of course."

"At the Buick Classic last year, you had a chance to win, went head-to-head with Phil Mickelson."

"Yeah."

"You finished second—after he hit a shot only two, three guys in the world could hit."

I was still watching the two players. They had finished, got in their cart, and drove off.

"You've been on the Tour almost fifteen years, Jack. Haven't won, but you got so close that week you could taste it. Then you fell a tiny bit short."

I looked directly at him. The Oakleys were off. His eyes seemed an extension of his will—iron colored, steady. I knew why he was eight and one in playoffs.

"You didn't blow that tournament," he said. "Oh, it happens. Guy misses a four-footer on the eighteenth, puts himself in a playoff, then loses. Never hear from him again."

I was holding his gaze.

"That isn't what happened, Jack. You stood there, toe-to-toe, and duked it out with a guy who has been ranked in the top three in the world. And damn near won."

"'Damned near' isn't the same," I said.

"What I think is you lost your confidence after that. Now you're questioning yourself."

My mouth was dry. I was sweating, despite the temperature.

"I've been your coach for a year or so now, but I'm your friend, too. Want to talk about it, let me know."

I stood staring. I said nothing. He turned and walked to the practice green, where Perkins was waiting. It had been a conversation I'd not anticipated.

The one I'd expected, the second call from Grant Ashley, never came.

$\mathcal{M}$onday morning, Perkins was out of the house first to begin the two-hour drive to Boston and his office. The night before, he had tried to leave a message on Grant Ashley's answering machine, but the machine was full—the result, probably, of Grant's efforts to reach Lynne until 3 A.M. Schultz had kissed

Darcy, then Lisa, and now sat waiting for me in the car. We would head to the airport together. A 9:05 A.M. Delta flight would have me in Columbus, Ohio, at 1:17 that afternoon.

Morning sunlight slanted into the kitchen, where I stood near the door, bags in hand. Lisa stood, wearing faded blue jeans and a white V-necked golf shirt, near the sink holding Darcy.

"Play well this week," she said.

"It's strange not having you there."

"No one to ask you embarrassing questions on national television?"

"You know what I mean."

She nodded and came closer. Her perfume smelled gently of berries. The aroma mixed with the rich odor of coffee. I put my arms around her and kissed her. The baby lay asleep between us.

"Give Darcy some time, Jack."

"I know," I said and sighed. "I love watching her sleep."

Darcy wore a pink T-shirt that snapped to form two leg holes.

"Jack, you don't want to go, do you?"

"It's what I do."

Lisa's new CD, Bruce Springsteen's *The Rising*, played softly in the background. Three empty coffee cups were on the kitchen table. The *Portland Press Herald* lay in scattered sections amid cereal boxes, a carton of milk, and a cardboard container of orange juice.

"It's what you love to do."

"Of course," I said.

"What is it? I've never seen this look on your face."

I shook my head. "Schultz is waiting. His flight leaves first. I love you, Lisa."

.   .   .

On the plane headed to the Memorial Tournament in Dublin, Ohio, I had a Philip Levine poetry book across my lap. I often read when I fly. The son of a substitute teacher, I had a B.A. in English and, since my rookie campaign, had read to pass down time. I'd spent more than a decade alone as a professional golfer.

Before Lisa, I'd been solo—cars, airplanes, hotels, often meals. I was solo again.

The coffee tasted bitter, as if left on the burner too long. The paperback was worn; its faded pages smelled the way an attic does when entered for the first time in years.

Dyslexia made me a slow reader, but my mother had made me a careful one. At my pace, a novel might take a month. Poetry, however, offered instant gratification. I knew putts more than I knew poems and probably missed subtleties, yet I loved Levine's poems. They were about people from my past. I saw myself in many. I read "Lights I Have Seen Before" and stumbled upon the lines:

> The children are off somewhere
> and when I waken
> I hear only
> the buzz of current
> in the TV
> and the refrigerator

I read the poem in its entirety, then drifted back to this section, to the man in search of his kids. I glanced out the window. In the kitchen, Lisa's point-blank question had taken me by surprise. She had asked me worse—on national television, no less—so I should have expected it. The plane jolted once with turbulence. Soft mounds of clouds rolled by like tumbleweed. Part of me couldn't wait to get to the Memorial, to compete against a great course, a world-class field. Yet Levine knew another part, a part of myself I'd only recently discovered. That part wanted to turn around, head home.

.   .   .

Seated near a window in the clubhouse dining room at 2 P.M., I was with longtime friend, Brian "Padre" Tarbuck. I was eating tuna salad. Padre was having a club sandwich. He had two Tour wins and exempt status through the following season. Oddly, he'd begun life as a priest. Now he was, ironically, the closest thing the Tour had to a sex symbol, which made him uneasy—but not to the point of being shy around members of the opposite sex. Padre seemed always to have a different—and stunning—woman at his side.

"Silver writing any more books about you?" Padre grinned.

"The book's not about me. It's about life on Tour."

"Tell him to put more about me in the next one." He drank some water. "You staying for Monday?"

"Unfortunately."

Padre had referred to the United States Open Sectional Qualifier, a thirty-six–hole event held on the heels of the Memorial Tournament. Anyone with a handicap of two can enter to qualify for a spot in the U.S. Open. There are two pre-tournament stages, but fully exempt PGA Tour players get to skip the first—Local Qualifying—and begin at Sectionals. Some pros don't have to qualify and are immediately eligible to compete—the top fifty on the Official World Golf Rankings, for example. I had to qualify and would give it my best shot on Monday.

"How many spots are open?" Padre said.

I shrugged. "I'm not thinking like that."

"A shot at a time?"

"That's all you can do."

"Yeah," he said. "In 2003, thirty-four guys from a full field made it in."

"Like I said, I'm not thinking like that."

We ate in silence for a while.

"Well, this is Jack's tournament," he said, motioning to the Golden Bear, Jack Nicklaus himself, who sat across the room.

"This is a big one." I sipped ice water.

"How have you been hitting it?"

I shrugged.

"Purse is close to five million dollars, Jack." He bit into his sandwich.

I had ranch dressing on the salad, which added kick to the tuna. I knew how much we were playing for. The winner's share was more than seven hundred thousand.

He paused and set the sandwich down. Then he looked past

me, like a nervous kid giving a speech, focusing on the wall above the teacher's head. "You know, Jack, you ever need a lesson, well, it's part of being out here. You gave me a tip last year, really helped my driving." He made eye contact again and drank some iced tea.

I nodded.

"We've been together out here awhile."

"Yeah," I said, "and I've missed more cuts in the last two months than in the last two seasons."

"You've also got a lot going on at home right now."

It was cool in the clubhouse. Outside, the air had felt warm, moist with humidity. Padre Tarbuck was someone who spoke his mind, someone I had talked to openly for years. There was still some part of him that was priestly; it made me feel like I was at confession.

I sighed. "Yeah, I do."

"That the problem, Jack?"

I ate some tuna salad and glanced out the window. Sergio Garcia was at one end of the practice green. At the far end, a player I didn't know wore khaki pants, a blue and white striped shirt, and a white Titleist hat. He had on headphones, and the cord ran to a gadget clipped to his belt. He was bebopping to music between putts. A long ponytail hung through the opening at the back of his hat. I could see a diamond stud in his ear. From short sleeves to his wrists, his arms were laced with tattoos, blending to a kaleidoscope of reds, blues, and blacks.

When he sunk a twenty-five–footer he turned the putter around and played it like a guitar. Several fans smiled and applauded.

"Who's that?" I said.

"His name is Kip Capers."

"What?"

He repeated the name. "A rookie, hasn't made a cut yet. That's why you haven't heard of him. Nice kid."

I nodded. "So that's who that is. Lisa was talking about this guy. Fits her description exactly. She said he might make for a feature article."

"Not real focused, but he's got his priorities in order."

"What does that mean?" I could feel someone standing next to me and looked up.

Grant Ashley was there, his face pale.

"I'm on the tee in a few minutes," he said, looking at me. "Want to play?"

.   .   .

Silver didn't like it, but ten minutes later, we were walking to the first tee.

"This is cutting into my nap." Silver grinned, the big Maxfli staff bag slung over his shoulder.

"This book publication's gone to your head."

"The next one's going to include how nice you look in khakis, Jack."

"If I fined you for every harassing remark, you'd be working for free."

"I'd be willing to work free." His grin widened. "Think about it. Me and a hundred fifty-six men dressing preppy? Heaven."

I shook my head.

"For real, Jack, I think we should be on the range, beating balls."

"All work and no play?"

"We need the work so we can play—for money on the weekends. We're oh-for-six lately. Or are you saying you found the groove on the range while you were home?"

"Tim . . ."

He heard something in my voice and stopped.

". . . Lay off the comments about my game and how much work it needs. I know where we are on the money list and how much you've made this year. And I don't feel good about it."

I walked onto the tee, where Grant was waiting with his new caddie, a kid I'd never met named Mike Easley. Easley looked about twenty-one and twig-skinny. When he heaved the bag over his shoulder, I expected him to topple backward. He had a bird's nest of curly black hair and a two-day beard. A silver star hung maybe half an inch from a chain off one ear.

You never know what you may find when it comes to caddies. Some players have their wives loop for them. Former Chicago Cubs second baseman Ryne Sandberg even caddied for a Tour-player friend once. Most players want established pros, guys who know the respective courses, but I'd had a college football player jockey for me the previous summer. I knew the player-caddie relationship encompassed many dynamics.

It was spring in Ohio, the sun bright above Muirfield Village Golf Club. Jack Nicklaus had conceived and developed the course. This was his baby. The layout could bite you—seventy-one bunkers; water hazards on eleven holes.

The first hole is a par four, 451 yards. Across the tee box, Grant looked at me. He took a practice swing, sunlight reflecting in a bright flash off his metal driver. I assumed he'd recruited me because he wanted to talk about his missing wife. Maybe that was wrong. Maybe he just wanted a money match and knew I was on a skid. Regardless, I had planned to practice all afternoon anyway.

Grant hit a short tee shot to the heart of the fairway.

I hit three-wood. My ball carried nearly 280 yards and left what I guessed would be a seven-iron to the first green. Grant's caddie told Silver he'd bought his book about life on Tour and planned to read it. The comment earned Easley best-friend status with Silver. They chatted as we walked down the first fairway.

I fell in line with Grant. "Any word from Lynne?"

He shook his head, staring at the ground.

"Perkins?"

He looked up. "Why would I hear from him?"

"I know Perkins. You *will* hear from him."

"I don't want to."

"He doesn't give a shit, Grant. He was there when you called. He's special consultant to the Tour Security Office."

"He can't just jump in the middle of this."

"Of what?"

He looked at me.

"We're talking about finding your wife, Grant. Have you called the cops? Anyone?"

"I told you. I don't want this public. Lynne knows what she needs to do."

"You didn't feel that way yesterday."

"You telling me I don't understand my own marriage?" He walked to his ball and went into his pre-swing routine—looked down at the ball, then toward the green, where a line of trees swayed in the distance. I knew he was judging the wind.

"What do I have from here?" he said when Easley and Silver got to us.

The Easley kid fumbled with the yardage book, attempting to pull it from his back pocket. It fell to the ground. When he bent to retrieve it, the bag fell over.

Grant sighed.

"Be 'bout a hundred and eighty or so," Easley said.

Silver's face went from jaw-drop to grin, then he laughed, full-out. He set the Maxfli bag down.

I don't know if Silver realized it or not, but Easley wasn't kidding. That was the figure he was offering. A guestimate. It wasn't a laughing matter. Silver had walked the course that morning and carefully documented distances in our yardage book. Tour pros know exactly how far each club will carry. It's why a change in equipment, ball or clubs, is such a large decision (or endorsement contract). Accordingly, yardage figures must be exact. Easley's response was blasphemous.

"It's one ninety-one from that tree," Silver said.

Easley glanced at the tree.

"Pace it off, from the tree to here, and give an exact distance," Silver said.

"First week doing yardage?" I said.

"Third," Easley said.

Grant looked at me. The look was not one of embarrassment but the expression of one who has said too much. The look vanished, and Grant pulled his four-iron and hit his approach shot to the back of the green.

I went to my ball, wondering about the look and what Easley may have said.

"One seventy-one," Silver said to me.

We were in the center of the first fairway. I was no longer thinking of Grant and his caddie, Easley. The pin placement had my full attention. The hole was cut behind the front right bunker, which meant I'd have to carry the ball past the cup and spin it back to the flag.

"A helping breeze," Silver said. "An easy six-iron."

I had pulled the seven. "A six?"

He nodded.

"Even with the breeze behind us?"

"Yeah. You need to spin it back, Jack." He grinned, loving his *back, Jack.*

I hit the six to within six feet. If I didn't think it would have inflated his ego, I'd have thanked him.

. . .

In the second fairway, Grant stopped short. We were thirty paces in front of the caddies.

"I only knew her two months before we got married," Grant said.

"Sometimes it doesn't take long."

He had just contradicted what Lynne told Lisa—that they met at UGA, which Grant left three years earlier. They married in the off-season. Therefore, they had met only eight, nine months ago.

He was shaking his head, smiling, staring off, recalling the past. "Partied a lot in college, you know?"

"Sure," I said. He seemed to be mixing their stories.

His legs were spread wide, arms folded across his chest. "Said she loved me more than anything. It's always been the other way around, I guess."

I stood looking at him. He didn't elaborate.

"Did she go to UGA?" I said.

He looked at me for a long moment. His eyes narrowed, and he took in some air. He turned and waited for Easley. We stood in silence for half a minute. He'd brought the subject up; now he was killing it.

Still twenty paces behind us, Easley was short of breath as

they approached. He walked as if carrying the bag across the Sahara, leaning so far forward he moved as if bracing against a fierce wind.

"Where'd you get him?" I said to Grant. "He's not going to make it seventy-two holes."

"Long story," Grant said. "He'll make it. Made it the last two weeks."

"How'd you do?"

He shrugged. "Made two of three cuts."

"Who am I to talk?"

"You'll turn it around," he said. "Besides, I'm learning there's more to life than golf."

That caught my attention. We looked at each other through another long silence. He had said something. I knew it, and he knew it. We stood staring at each other until the caddies reached us.

I was having dinner with Trip and Angela Davis. We'd found a tiny diner away from the hotel and, for Trip, the spotlight. As recently appointed captain of the next U.S. Ryder Cup team, every journalist, Lisa included, had requested a sit-down with him.

Davis had close-cropped hair and everyone called him "General." I'd always thought the name fitting. In fact, in the locker room, I'd once witnessed forty-eight–year–old General listening to a loud-mouthed and buffed rookie spout off about weight lifting. On a bet, General dropped to the floor and did 250 push-ups, non-stop. The kid stopped keeping up after eighty-five.

"Great place," Angela said.

"Kind of place where the coffee mugs are a half-inch thick," I said.

The diner smelled of grease and onions. It was a little after five, and the dinner rush had not yet hit. We were in a booth near the door, across from the counter. I could hear beef sizzling. A guy in a Cleveland Indians cap was cooking in the back. The chrome and black-and-white interior made me think of Maine, of childhood evenings with my parents, and of the joints where I'd eaten as a rookie, when I occasionally slept in my car.

My rookie campaign had been an endless struggle to earn money. I entered thirty-two tournaments that year, missing eighteen cuts. One top-ten finish; three other top–twenty-fives. I had stood over the final putt that season knowing my place on the money list's top 125, which carried an exemption for the following season, was riding on that stroke—and I had made the putt. It had been a gut-check, telling me I had what it takes.

A waitress garbed in blue jeans and a gray sweatshirt told us the specials and took drink orders.

Seated across from one of the most successful golfers of my generation, I thought of the current season and how, to date, it had been the second most difficult for me. At least my failures as a rookie had been due to ability. My current problem was between my ears, which made it all the more frustrating.

"Jack, I really enjoyed seeing the baby," Angela said.

"When are the ladies going to start traveling?" General said.

"Lisa wants to wait until Darcy's a little older."

"Understandable." Angela sipped ice water.

"Yeah, but tough, nonetheless." I turned to General. "Saw you in the commercial." I motioned to the Buick logo on the sleeve of his Ashworth shirt. "You know you've made it when you're on television with Tiger."

"Sure, Austin," he said. "Just call me Mr. Big Time."

I chuckled. Angela was grinning.

The waitress returned. General and I were drinking Heineken from bottles. Angela had iced tea. The waitress took our orders and left again.

"Let's just hope . . ."—General sipped some beer—"nobody

wants to do anything like that Nike commercial where Tiger bounces the ball off his wedge and baseball-swings it down the fairway. I'd foul it off into my face."

Angela laughed. I smiled and drank some beer.

I'd always thought that as parents the Davis couple must serve as great role models. They seemed to radiate with self-discipline. I felt like I should drop to the floor and do pushups to keep up. Instead, I drank more beer. Maine is known for its microbreweries, but, Mainer or not, I am loyal to Heineken.

"How'd you play today?" I said.

General shook his head. "I've been working on the Ryder Cup so much—reviewing the points race, thinking of potential match-ups—I haven't practiced."

"And we were late getting started today," Angela said. "The courtesy car got a flat. I missed a fieldtrip at the daycare."

I pointed to the Buick logo again.

"It's not Buick," he said. "That's the tire company."

"Loyal to your sponsor." I grinned.

"You blame your bad shots on Maxfli?"

"No." I smiled. "On Tim Silver."

"I can't fault you there." He shook his head. "Friggin' guy told me I 'had great biceps' for a man my age!"

I nearly spit my beer, slapping the table with my palm.

"Who's Tim Silver?" Angela said.

"Jack's caddie."

"Anyway"—Angela didn't know Silver, so she remained serious—"we love Buicks, have two LaSabres and a Rendevous."

General was still grinning. "Friggin' Silver."

.   .   .

General and I were having second beers when the food arrived.

"I won't be walking the course much this week," Angela said. "I'm volunteering at the daycare."

"She hasn't stopped talking about Darcy since she got home," General said.

"Your house sounds like a daycare," I said.

General cut a piece of his steak and onions. "Used to be a lot worse. The boys are all in high school now. Our daughter, Karen, goes to middle school next year."

I turned to Angela. "You always volunteer at the daycare?"

"Maybe once a month." She was having the soup and salad special and quietly sipped her soup. "It's only open Wednesday through Sunday. Lisa will love it. Three teachers. They give you a silent pager, so you can watch your husband play, and, if they need you—"

"To come get your screaming kid?"

"So cynical, Jack. But, yes, if they need to contact you"—she grinned—"about your child, they can page you."

"Well," I said, "my kid will take after her dad—and be a perfect angel."

"Sure she will," General said. "How'd you play today?"

I shrugged. "Pretty good on the front; thirty-eight on the back."

"Putting?"

"Inconsistent in all areas."

The place had filled. It was 5:34. Lisa had gotten me a digital watch when the Tour started tightening its five-minutes-between-shots rule. If your group is slow, officials put you "on the clock"—you get timed. It can lead to a $20,000 fine.

A guy walked in wearing engineer boots, a blue flannel shirt unbuttoned over a white T-shirt, and blue jeans. He had on a John Deere cap.

"Dresses just like my old man," I said. "We used to eat at a place like this after doing carpentry all day. Coffee was strong and cheap, and people would come for the free refills."

"My father was a greens keeper," General said. "It was how I could afford to play—got on for free in the evenings."

"What did your dad do?" I said to Angela.

"Pilot." She ate some of her salad. "Hey, did Lisa talk to Lynne Ashley after she left?"

I shook my head.

General looked at her curiously.

"Grant's wife stormed out of the Austins' home," she said. "It was pretty ugly."

"Yeah?" He looked at me.

I nodded. "It was ugly."

"She needs to make more of an effort," Angela said. "She's young."

I thought of Grant's comments earlier that day, and of my phone conversation with Lisa after my practice. She had told me Perkins was coming to see Grant and wanted to stay with me.

"More of an effort to do what?" General said.

"I don't want this to sound bad, but to fit in. She just seemed so self-absorbed and anti-Tour."

He raised his brows. "'Anti-Tour'?"

"Said she didn't want to give up her independence." I drank some Heineken.

"Actually, Jack, she said she didn't want to give up her *exercise*."

"She seemed very uncomfortable," I said.

"It's hard," Angela said. "I remember our first trip to the Mercedes Championships. You're there with only the winners from the previous season. They treat you like royalty. We ate with Tom Watson and Jack Nicklaus. I was twenty-four and thinking, *These people are famous. What am I doing here?*"

"I hope I don't make you feel like that now," I said.

General laughed.

"Funny, Jack," Angela said. "Do you get my point?"

"Yeah. But she has to let down her guard. It's a two-way street. Most people out here are down to earth. They know how lucky they are."

.   .   .

After dinner, we ordered coffee. It was early, and I wasn't in a hurry to get back to an empty hotel room.

"You know, she said something before you got there," Angela said.

"Who?" I said.

"What are you talking about?" General said. "Angela, we're talking about Ernie Els."

"I'm still thinking about Lynne Ashley. She said something before you got there, Jack, something about having no place to go." She shook her head. "I just thought it was odd."

I set my coffee down. "What did she say?"

"I forget how it came about." Angela sipped coffee and made a face.

"Coffee bad?" General said.

"Strong," she said.

"What did she say?" I said.

"We were talking about what we were going to do after the interview. When I said I was coming here, Lynne made a strange comment—I remember we all turned and looked at her—about having no place to go."

"'No place to go'?"

She nodded. "Yes. I said, 'Is work being done to your house?' And she shook her head."

I shrugged. Lynne Ashley's disappearing act hadn't hit the papers yet. I wasn't going to mention it.

"If she didn't have a place to go, where the hell do they live?" General said.

"Atlanta," Angela said.

I kept my mouth shut but looked at him and thought it a very good question.

At the sound, I sat bolt upright. The door to my hotel room had opened, slamming the inside wall. A bar of light from the hallway was blinding. The digital clock read 2:33. Perkins had entered the hotel room in typical fashion.

Back when we'd roomed at UMaine, the scenario was often similar—except I usually entered with him, and, although both of us were stumbling, back then darkness had nothing to do with it.

"I left you a key at the goddamned desk so you could enter quietly," I said.

He hit the wall switch. After six hours' sleep, light struck my eyes like a streak of lightening.

"Don't give me any shit," he said. "You've been walking fancy lawns with preppies. I've been in Atlanta, sitting in a library, which you know I hate, and calling in a favor in Boston."

"A favor? You have a friend besides me?"

"I'm too tired for your jokes. A friend of a friend of a friend ran a NCIC on Lynne Ashley and got zip."

"What does NCIC stand for?"

"It's the Interstate Identification Index, through the National Crime Information Computer. Searches someone's criminal history, nationwide. It's a big-time background check—a cop has to log his goddamned badge number to get the report."

"So you do have one other friend."

"A friend of a friend of a friend—I have no connection to the cop and won't. You don't build a contact list by getting people in trouble. Whoever the cop was that ran the check connected it to a case they're working on—and never heard of me. And I never heard of him."

I wiped sleep from my eyes, stood, and went to the bathroom. I drank water from the faucet, then returned to bed. For Perkins, unpacking consisted of walking to a corner, unzipping his duffel, and dumping. Jeans, sneakers, a leather belt, a black attaché case, even a navy blue blazer fell to the floor. He took the sports jacket to the closet and hung it.

"So you learned Lynne has no record," I said.

"Yeah. It's hard to get a lot of background on her because I haven't mentioned her husband or the connection to the PGA Tour yet. Plus, I had to come back early. Peter Barrett and I met with Grant Ashley tonight."

That woke me more than the burst of light. Barrett was PGA Tour commissioner. "Jesus, what did Grant say to Barrett?"

"First, you got anything to drink?"

"It's two-thirty in the morning."

"A beer would be nice right now," he said. "You playing early or late tomorrow?"

"Late. How's Linda and Jackie?"

"Haven't been home, but called. They miss me."

"Hard to believe," I said.

I could see him grin. He gave me the finger. We'd been through a lot together, and the best friendships are brotherhoods requiring no words. Perkins preferred hand gestures anyway.

When Lisa had been making a six-figure CBS salary, we'd shared a suite. I was alone, so I had a hotel room now. There was no fridge, so I had filled the bathroom sink with ice. The ice had surely melted, but from bed, I heard Perkins rummaging. He emmerged with a green bottle of Heineken.

"Why don't you get Heineken to sponsor you?"

"Don't you watch the ads?" I said. "It's only about the beer."

"Not golf?"

"Hard to imagine, but no."

He pulled the straight chair away from the desk, turned it so he faced me, and sat, sipping his beer. Then he held it up, examining the bottle like a guy tasting expensive wine. "Grant ever say anything about his sister-in-law?"

I shook my head.

"Had one."

"'Had'?" I said.

"Lynne's sister died. Nine-eleven. She was on that plane to L.A."

Wasn't much to say to that, but I knew he didn't mention things for the hell of it.

"And?"

"And, I don't know." He drank some beer. "I didn't waste time going to the Atlanta cops. Grant hasn't notified them, so there'd be no file six—missing person. And southern cops have no reason to drop what they're doing to help my northern ass. So I kicked around the Atlanta-Fulton Public Library and went through the archives of the *Atlanta Journal-Constitution*. Found the wedding announcement from the fall. If it's legit, Lynne's maiden name is Meredith."

"Those UMaine research skills come in handy."

"The wedding announcement was strange. Very little on Lynne—no parents named, and 'of Atlanta' for residence.

Mentioned her late sister. The rest of it was on 'PGA star Grant Ashley.'"

"In Maine, Lynne said she didn't want to be known as a Tour wife," I said, sitting up now, leaning against the headboard. "The announcement doesn't jibe with that."

"That's all I found out." He kicked off his shoes and stretched his legs. I had never known him to nap. He'd probably been awake more than twenty-four hours, but he looked as if he could go another twelve.

"What did Grant tell Peter Barrett?"

"Grant begged for a little time, said this was a family matter he could work out." Perkins shrugged. "Barrett wants this kept quiet for P.R. reasons anyway. But he's no fool. He realizes that if the Tour knows about a missing person, it has to give the info to the cops—eventually."

"If something happened to her, and the Tour had been sitting on it, next of kin would have a hell of a lawsuit."

"I can't locate any next of kin, but you're probably right. Anyway, Grant was absolutely devastated by the thought of this going public, for whatever reason. Barrett told Grant the Tour— meaning me—would look into this for another week or so. If I come up with zip, and Lynne doesn't appear, Barrett gives the whole thing to the cops." He shook his head slowly, recalling the talk, then lifted his beer and sipped. "You thought Grant was jumpy on the phone? Should talk with him in person about this."

"I have."

He had just pulled the pager off his cordovan belt. He sat back and stared at me, waiting. I told him about my practice round earlier that day with Grant and about our conversation.

"So, given Grant's timeline," he said, "Lynne lied about meeting him at UGA."

"It would mean Grant never met his sister-in-law, since he only met Lynne last fall."

Perkins finished his beer and sat staring at the empty bottle as if it reminded him of something. "Grant said he partied a lot, huh? You know him to be like that?"

"Never heard that before."

We were quiet, and there were no surrounding sounds now— the corridor was silent, no muffled television voices from adjacent rooms, the parking lot, too, was hushed.

"I have one other thing for you." I told him what Angela Davis had said at dinner.

A hand on each side of his face, he rubbed his temples. "I love cases that make no sense whatsoever. Lynne said she had 'no place to go'? Don't they have a house, Jack?"

"I assume so."

"For Christ's sake." He shook his head. "I should have been a preppy golfer, not an investigator."

"You're not graceful enough."

"If grace were all golf required, I'd be Tiger Woods, pal. It's garment discrimination—I don't own enough khaki."

"Not all of us are preppy," I said. "You'll like this new kid, Kip Capers. He looks like Bon Jovi."

"I'd like him better if he looked like the guys in Metallica. But at least Bon Jovi is a step above the khaki-and-collared-shirt crowd."

Ten minutes later, he lay on the far bed. Soon he was snoring.

. . .

Thursday, Perkins was gone before my 6 A.M. wake-up call. My tee times for the Memorial were afternoon-morning, meaning I played Thursday afternoon but Friday would get the putting surfaces before they were spike-pocked. Since I had the morning off, I was on a stationary bike in the Tour's forty-eight–foot fitness trailer shortly after breakfast.

The exercise was a continuation of my week: I had worked hard, and my game was showing signs of life. Tuesday, I had shot sixty-nine and taken $200 from Padre; Wednesday morning had been spent working on my short game—alternating between putting, chipping, and bunker work. Now, peddling against middle-aged mediocrity, I read a story by Associated Press golf writer Doug Ferguson. The story listed Phil Mickelson among the favorites this week, since Lefty was on a hot streak. My name wasn't mentioned.

The article made me revisit Schultz's comments and recall memories of the final back nine at the previous season's Buick Classic. The fitness trailer was busy with players working out— on Lifecycles, treadmills, lifting weights, or stretching, some with assistance from trainers. As I thought back to the Buick Classic, I knew the tourney's waning holes provided an experience I'd never forget. With the late-afternoon sun burning pink on the horizon, the championship had become a two-man race, a contest between Mickelson and me. Nobody had expected me to win. Except me.

Schultz was right on one count: When I lost, I had been crushed. Yet, the loss was not the cause of this year's poor play.

A bead of sweat fell from my forehead to the sports page. It turned the white paper momentarily gray, spreading to dime-sized on the text. Mickelson had driven one par-four hole. It had been the difference in the tournament. Moreover, it had been a shot I'd *chosen* not to attempt. I had the length to get there, but it would've been a risk. I played safe, a veteran decision based on odds. Nevertheless, I kicked myself for the decision afterward. Therefore, Schultz felt it was that day's back nine that was bothering my game and me this year.

Golf is a game of failures more often than a sport of successes. You try to minimize the failures, so you may capitalize on your small triumphs. I had always known that and had focused on something else to take from that day: I worked hard all these years to be in that exact position—in contention Sunday afternoon, in a showdown with one of the world's best. That day proved what I'd long known: I possessed a golf game that could win on Tour.

Folding the paper, I searched for my name on the money list: 188. A long way from the top 125. The past year had brought so many changes—marriage, Darcy, the house in Maine—that the Buick Classic seemed distant. Schultz was wrong. It wasn't the Buick Classic loss that was effecting my game.

Something was, though. Silver knew it. Schultz knew it, too. Lisa hadn't mentioned it yet, but surely she knew it as well. Only I, however, was finally beginning to realize what it was.

Silver did what he always does when we meet on the driving range: glanced obviously at his watch, shook his head, and grinned. "You're late," he said.

Silver wore khaki shorts and a white golf shirt. The shirt bore the same logo, Maxfli, that mine did. I'd given him a bunch of shirts and hats prior to the season. The shirts were big on him, but the fad in golf was to wear your shirtsleeves past your elbows anyway, so he looked stylish. Wrap-around Oakley shades rested atop his hat brim.

I took my five-iron from the bag, put it across my shoulders, held the club face with one hand, the grip with the other. I twisted my torso back and forth. It created flexibility and developed a wide shoulder turn. I had made this rhythmic, pendulumlike motion for hours since childhood, often indoors. It had been a drill even four feet of Maine snow didn't prevent.

"Poked my head in the fitness trailer," Silver said. "Saw you working your ass off, so I'll let your tardiness slide."

"How kind."

It was closing in on 8 A.M. The range was full. The sun burned high overhead, the sky surrounding it like a vast ocean, a smattering of clouds serving as distant whitecaps. Some players worked with coaches, some warmed up with only their caddies, others worked alone. Padre Tarbuck, two spaces from us, waved.

"Guy's gorgeous," Silver said.

I sighed.

"I just got here, myself. Mike Easley stopped me. Figured he needs more help than even you." Silver leaned forward, unzipped the front pocket of my golf bag, and took a quick inventory.

I knew what he'd find: three new gloves; three sleeves of balls and a felt-tipped pen to mark them; sun block; Oakley sunglasses I never wore; extra socks; my rain suit; a plastic bag with nearly a thousand tees; pencils; the tape recorder I used to note swing thoughts; Power Bars; Gatorade packets; and, finally, one item that sets me apart from probably every other professional golfer, a lucky book, *The Simple Truth,* by Philip Levine. Silver was meticulous, and the golf bag was our office. He had started caddying only in search of information. Now, however, he was a pro.

"What's Easley want?" I said.

"He ought to want to get in shape, but he asked about the pick-and-clean rule."

"It's sunny."

"Yeah. I know you took on a rookie when I was away writing my book—and that it showed you I'm irreplaceable—but Nash Henley was at least in great shape."

"And he studied the rule book I sent him."

"And he knew yardage."

I grinned. "And he could carry the bag three times as far as you."

"But, could he read greens?"

"He was getting it. He spent Thanksgiving with Lisa and me. He led the conference in rushing, as a freshman."

"He's a good kid," Silver said. "Easley, on the other hand, is a disaster waiting to happen. What was Grant thinking?"

"He told me Easley did fine the last couple weeks."

"We'll see. We're paired with them today."

"I saw that," I said. "And a guy who'll make your next book for sure, Kip Capers."

"The tattoo kid?"

I nodded.

"A hell of a threesome," Silver said.

. . .

I had showered after the workout and practice session and now sat in the locker room in a high-backed leather chair, a phone shrugged to my ear. It was lunchtime, and Lisa was detailing Darcy's morning: They'd gone for a walk, then Lisa worked on her Tour-wife article while Darcy napped. Lisa was hoping, during the baby's second nap, to take the baby monitor downstairs and work out.

"How do you feel, going into today's round?" she said.

"This is just like old times. All we need is a camera crew."

"Cute, Jack."

"Hitting it pretty decent this week. Putting's not bad either."

"Practicing hard?"

"Just came from the range."

The locker room had been packed at breakfast. Now it was 11 A.M., and only a handful of players watched television, read the paper, or rummaged through lockers. The door opened, and Grant Ashley entered. He saw me and looked away, continuing to his locker. He sat across the room and took a box of Titleist Pro V1 balls from his locker.

Everyone with a Titleist contract was playing the Pro V1. I was with Maxfli, but had broken my deal to use Pro V1s. In 2002, the ball had become a staple for Tour players. It added fifteen yards to my drive, and I wasn't alone. Since high school, I had tinkered with drivers—changing lofts and shafts, trying titanium and every other material—to add distance. Then, one afternoon, Padre had showed up on the range with a prototype ball and bombed past me for a half hour. It was no coincidence that in a single month tournament scoring records for the U.S. and European Tours had been dismembered by Ernie Els—playing the Pro V1.

Grant, however, wasn't thinking about the Pro V1. He glanced at me from the corner of his eye. He was maybe fifteen yards away.

"How's Tim," Lisa said. She never called Silver by his last name.

"Same."

"Meaning he's driving you crazy, but doing a good job at the same time?"

"He drives everyone crazy. Told General he had great biceps for a forty-eight year old."

"My God." She was laughing. It was nice to hear.

"I wish you and Darcy were here."

"I know you do. I thought you were going to withdraw the morning you left, Jack. I've never seen you like that."

I passed on that conversation. "Lynne didn't meet Grant at UGA."

"How do you know that?"

I told her.

"Is Perkins going to look into the UGA comment?"

"I think so."

"Why did Lynne tell Angela she had no place to go? I didn't hear her say that, but it makes no sense."

"I don't know," I said.

Grant stood and walked over, casually tossing a ball in the air. "Your fucking pal followed me around the putting green this morning. I'm trying to work."

"I'm on the phone, Grant."

"You hear me?"

I told Lisa I had to go. We said our good-byes and hung up. I stood. "I was on the goddamned phone, Grant."

"Did you hear what I said?"

"Who followed you?"

"The detective."

"Perkins probably wants to talk."

"No shit."

I stepped closer. "So talk to him."

Grant backed up and stood looking up at me. "You're missing my point, Jack. Tiger shot sixty-four. I was practicing."

The look on my face told Grant something. He took another step back.

"He's been hired to find your wife," I said. "Not by you, since you're not looking. By the Tour."

"I don't need to look."

"Your wife said she met you in college. Is that true?"

He looked at me.

"Where is Lynne?"

"I'm here to play golf." He cursed, then walked away.

I stood watching him go. "A sixty-four, huh?" I said aloud. I had to get ready, too.

9

I had the round off to a good start. My playing partners, however, weren't fairing as well. Kip Capers was three over after four holes; Grant was even par—impressive when you considered that his caddie seemed to walk the course in a daze.

We were on the tee at the 531-yard par-five fifth hole at Muirfield Village, a dogleg right, which, on paper, hardly sounds overwhelming. A stream, however, weaves through the fairway, and all second and third shots must be played with the water hazard given careful consideration. Three bunkers surround the green, which is small, undulating, and in recent years had been moved closer to the water, making the entire scenario more perilous.

We were waiting for the group in front of us to clear. I had the honor and stood next to Silver, arms crossed. Hale Irwin once called Muirfield's greens "some of the most beautiful in the world—but some of the toughest." And he putted well enough to win two U.S. Opens. For me, Muirfield's greens had been a constant migraine. This late-May afternoon, though, I was one under through four holes.

We'd gone off at 2:22 P.M. with an after-school crowd following us. Golf had done wonders for me as a kid. Where I struggled as a student, golf provided something to strive for academically (I needed a C-average to play) and athletically (the desire to stand out positively at something my school offered). A month earlier, in fact, at my new home course, the Woodlands, in Falmouth, I had offered a free clinic to kids, at which I gave golf tips, but also spoke about school and staying out of trouble.

"Nice to see so many kids," I said.

"Good to see black kids." Silver was leaning on the large Maxfli staff bag that had my name on the front. He had a towel over one shoulder to prevent the strap from chafing.

The kids following us ranged from elementary age with parents to high schoolers. Their garb varied, too: khaki shorts and collared shirts; a Metallica T-shirt; a Cleveland Cavaliers jersey.

Across the tee box, Kip Capers gave Metallica T-shirt a thumbs-up, and high-fived the kid. Capers had on a black turtleneck, the style Tiger had made popular. The sleeves were short and showed his tattoos. When Capers swung, the ropy muscles in his forearms made the tattoos move like purple snakes. Today's earring was a two-inch chain with a small cross. His ponytail hung well past his shoulders.

"Quite a sight," Silver said.

"If it turns out he can play, he'll be good for golf. Kids love him."

Silver pulled the six-iron from the bag, took a tee from his pocket, and cleaned the grooves of the club face. The club looked as if he'd polished it only minutes before. He was a neat freak.

"Hear about Capers's Nike deal?" he said, holding up the club face, examining it.

I shook my head.

"It's big. Kid isn't near the top hundred and twenty-five, either."

I shrugged. "Might take the game to the masses."

"You just like him because he calls you 'Mister Austin.'" He slid the six-iron back in the bag.

"You could take lessons from him."

Silver ignored that. "I want success rewarded, not tattoos."

"People pay to see us," I said. "Makes us, on some level, entertainers."

Amid the various teenage fashion statements, one guy didn't fit in. Ahead, near the ladies' tee, a man wearing a denim shirt, jeans, and scuffed black cowboy boots waved.

I waved back.

"Know him?" Silver said.

"You don't recognize him?"

Silver squinted. "Dempsey?"

Jim Dempsey wasn't your typical sports agent. He'd played outside linebacker at Texas A&M and had a long scar on his cheek, courtesy of a steer. He wore a Stetson and usually ordered Lone Star beer but would settle for Heineken if that was all there was. We'd met long ago in a Houston bar and still had a handshake agreement: He got 10 percent of any endorsement contract he landed me. He was my age and recently divorced. Although we e-mailed and spoke often, I hadn't seen him in more than a year.

The fairway was clear.

"Give me the driver," I said.

"Going down the right-hand side?"

I shook my head. The stream entered the fairway from the left. The right side offered a longer landing area, but the dogleg bent to the right. Therefore, if you didn't play to the left side of the fairway, your second shot would be blocked by the right-side trees.

"Going to flirt with the stream?"

"Hopefully not."

"You're going for everything this year," Silver said. "What happened to Steady Eddie? Conservatism?"

He offered the three-wood.

I waved that off. "Driver."

"Seriously, Jack, you're playing like Gregg Norman or . . ."—he looked at me, then away—"Phil Mickelson."

"I'm playing my game."

He shook his head. "You made nine hundred thousand last year. Why change?"

"We're not discussing philosophy mid-round," I said. "Give me the driver."

He did.

Next to us, Grant took his three-wood and waited. Capers looked at the kids, winked, and pulled a big 350–cubic-centimeter driver. A couple kids cheered.

I took two practice swings. A slight breeze was at my back. Silver was right: If I hit it too far down the left, the ball could end up at the bottom of the creek. I was coming off a birdie at the par-three fourth and was swinging well. More importantly, my head was in the game today. The Mickelson comment, though, bothered me—and I knew who planted the seed: Schultz. I was tired of being analyzed.

I teed the ball an inch off the turf, set the Pro V1 off my front instep, and made a smooth pass, catching the ball just as the club began its ascent. It was a high tee shot and stopped five yards short of the stream.

"Good call, boss." Silver held out his palm.

I slapped it, irritated. I paid him to caddie, which encompassed yardage, club selection, and many other things—serving as confidant and friend, even amateur swing coach. At times, we'd butted heads on the course, usually over club selection. This, however, was different. He'd questioned my approach to the game.

"You made the right call," he said. "You're back, Jack."

I forced myself to let it go. This was neither the time nor the place. "You love saying that, don't you—'back Jack'?"

"Keep making birdies. I love making money, honky."

"That's a racist remark."

"Isn't that better than sexual harassment?"

"Let's just keep the round going."

Grant's three-wood finished thirty-five paces behind my tee shot. When he handed the club back to his caddie, Mike Easley fumbled it, the three-wood falling to the ground. Grant shot him a look of disgust.

Capers hit his first drive into the water, then a three-wood, short and right. He hit his layup—his fourth shot—to the center of the fairway, at the corner of the dogleg. He was three over par on his round.

Grant weighed about as much as my golf bag and didn't have much of a choice to make. Unless he jumped out of his shoes when he swung, he couldn't reach the par-five in two. He hit four-iron to a spot in the fairway that left 110 yards—ideal wedge distance—to the pin. In the hour we'd spent playing the opening holes, Grant had not mentioned Perkins or Lynne. He was even par and swinging well. Golf was business, and we were at the office. I wasn't going to bring up his missing wife.

Grant glanced at me as he handed the four-iron back to

Easley, who seemed to clasp this club as if holding on for dear life. "Bombed that drive, Jack," Grant said.

"Thanks. New driver. I've been killing it."

"Last couple months," Silver smirked, "he's been killing it into the woods."

Grant grinned. "Got to love caddies."

"Woods?" Easley said. "I love the woods. Camp out a lot."

"Huh?" I scratched my head and looked at him.

Grant ignored Easley and started toward my ball. Silver talked to Easley as we walked up the fairway. Grant walked in front of us.

At my ball, I took the five-metal from Silver. The contact was crisp. The ball flew high and landed softly. I'd be putting for eagle.

"Nice swing, Jack," Grant said.

As he, Easley, and Silver moved to his ball, I veered toward Capers, who walked near the gallery, chatting with the fans. Some players can do it all the time and still score—Lee Trevino, for example. I, on the other hand, need all the focus I can stand. But I saw Dempsey following us. The temperature was low-eighties and everyone wore shorts. By contrast, in a long-sleeved denim shirt, Dempsey looked like a Texan dressed for a blizzard.

I shook his hand. "What are you doing here?"

"I'm your biggest fan. Came to see you play." The scar on his cheek bunched when he smiled. His twang made *play* sound like *ply*.

"Lisa's my biggest fan."

"Makes sense. How is your lovely bride?"

"Wonderful."

"I'm on business. Where are you staying?"

I told him.

"I'll call you for dinner. Got something you'll be interested in."

I said good-bye and caught up with Grant, Silver, and Easley. Capers was still working the crowd.

"Guy's three over after four holes," Silver said. "How do you think Nike feels about that?"

At his ball, Grant took his yardage book from his back pocket.

My estimate of 110 was off by four. Easley handed Grant a club that looked like a seven-iron.

"What the hell is this?" Grant said.

"Nine."

Grant stared at Easley for a long moment. I was looking at Silver, who watched carefully.

"It's a six." Grant shook his head and pulled a club with more loft, obviously a wedge.

"Want help understanding the yardage book," Silver said, "come see me."

Easley looked at him. "What for?"

"Shut up," Grant said to Easley.

He didn't sound angry; rather, concerned, as if trying to stop Easley from saying too much. I thought of his tone as Silver and I moved away to let them work out the club selection. We started toward my ball.

"Guy's baked out of his gourd," Silver said.

I looked at Silver.

He nodded. "He's high."

I still didn't speak.

"Pot, Jack. You hear me?"

I shook my head. It explained things.

"Look at his eyes," Silver said. "I know what I'm seeing. Bloodshot eyes. Kid's walking next to me, telling me he's a millionaire businessman."

I was staring at him. Charlie Rymer, ESPN's on-course commentator, approached. I motioned toward Rymer, and Silver stopped talking. Rymer paused to watch Grant hit, then moved toward us. I smiled, then, head down, went to my ball.

Silver was quickly at my side. "Keep your head in the game, Jack."

I didn't answer.

"It doesn't concern us."

"Doesn't concern us?"

"It's Grant's problem, not ours, Jack."

"Look around. Kids are everywhere."

"Mr. Save the World." Silver chuckled.

"You see nothing wrong?"

"I see a lot wrong with it, but I can let it go. I know you, Jack. I'm saying worry about golf, then do whatever the hell you want later."

"I plan to."

"You going to the tournament officials?"

"I'll handle it myself."

"That's what I was afraid of."

.   .   .

I played the front in thirty-three, my best front-nine score in more than thirty tournament rounds at Muirfield. It also had me on the leader board, a place where I'd not been of late. Given the distractions, I was more than pleased.

Grant was heading in the opposite direction. He'd gone out in thirty-nine and needed a drastic turn around. Capers shot forty-two, an embarrassing score for a pro, even worse considering the benign conditions. The flags hung straight down. The sun burst on and off through scattered clouds. Growing up in Maine, I had an uncle who'd been a game warden. He spent so much time outside he could predict changes in the weather by the feel of the air, the way leaves hung on trees, and other natural means I didn't understand. I wasn't that good, but today the air did feel heavy and humid. Rain had been predicted, and I trusted the forecast. It meant today was the day to make birdies.

We were on the par-four, 441-yard tenth tee.

"I've got to pull out of this," Grant said to me, "and make some birdies."

Easley stood alone to the side of the tee box. Silver was at the back of the tee. The spectators were twenty paces away. Capers, finally quieted, stood solemnly behind us, away from the crowd. It was 4:15, and the sun was low in the sky. A slight breeze had come up. The gallery had dwindled. Even my agent was gone now. I looked at Grant and smiled as if chatting about a lip-out.

"Tell your caddie if he's on something I'm going to kick his ass for him."

"What?"

"You heard me, Grant. It's a disgrace. There are kids following us."

"It's obvious?"

I didn't say anything.

"I don't do it, Jack."

"I don't give a shit." I smiled again. Then I turned away. I had the round to finish. I bent, teed my ball, and began my pre-swing routine.

"Jack," Silver said.

I looked up. Grant was waving for a PGA Tour official. A silver-haired man approached.

"I'm withdrawing," Grant said. "My back is hurt."

"I don't know if I could ever get used to eating dinner at eight-thirty," Perkins said.

We had just sat in a booth at the restaurant in the Courtyard in Dublin, Ohio. He and Dempsey arrived an hour before and had beers in the bar while waiting for me. Perkins's white-blond hair was gelled into place. He wore jeans, running shoes, and a blue blazer, which I knew concealed a shoulder holster. People at other tables glanced at him. It was hard not to notice someone with white-blond hair, who stands six feet five, and is built like Hulk Hogan. Perkins had been a homicide detective, not a covert operative.

"I don't mind eating late," I said. "Playing in the afternoon makes the evenings shorter."

"I'm a night owl anyway," Dempsey said. "Lonely alone in that hotel room all night?"

"Yeah. Best job in the world, but I still miss home."

"Never thought you'd get married."

I drank some Heineken.

"Never thought we'd find someone to take him," Perkins said.

Dempsey raised his bottle. Perkins clinked it. Both were drinking Lone Star.

"Last two seasons, Lisa and I've been inseparable." I wondered what she and Darcy had done that afternoon, what Darcy had eaten for dinner, if Lisa was giving her a bath before bed.

A young waitress came to the booth. She was mid-twenties, and Dempsey noticed the short skirt. Blond hair hung halfway down her back. She had a wide mouth and big blue eyes. She smiled at him.

"Good evening," he said.

"How are you doing?"

"Better, now that *you* ask," Dempsey said.

She blushed.

I looked at Perkins, who rolled his eyes.

"Can we order?" Perkins said and told her what he wanted.

I thought she'd go through two notepads: sixteen-ounce steak, baked potato, side salad, and something called "fire wings" for an appetizer. I got the chef's salad.

"Give me the twelve-ounce steak," Dempsey said, "still mooing."

She laughed and smiled at him once more before leaving.

"Cute, huh?" Dempsey said.

"Young," I said. "Sorry to hear about the divorce."

He drank some beer and waved that off. "Just didn't work out."

"How long were you married?" Perkins said.

"Twelve years. Just one of those things."

Twelve years seemed a large investment to me, contrary to Dempsey's light tone. I drank some Heineken, ate a roll, and listened to the cacophony of the restaurant: silverware chiming against plates and dishes; the low rumble of conversation; the occasional laugh. When you eat out thirty weeks a year, you long for PB&J on a paper plate at home in front of the television. Listening to Dempsey's uninflected description of his failed marriage made me long for that even more.

"I looked for you this morning," Perkins said to me. "Poked my head into the fitness trailer and saw you busting your ass, so I left you alone."

"That's what I pitch," Dempsey said. "Jack Austin has never been a Lietzke."

"Lietzke had a hell of a career," I said.

We were speaking of Bruce Lietzke. There are guys like Fred Couples and Lietzke who—due to injury or family commitments—rarely practice yet have the God-given talent to still win a million bucks a year. I'm not that gifted, but can, when I work my tail off, shoot the same scores. I had always practiced a lot. Won the New England Amateur before turning twenty-one and had made All-America twice at UMaine. One goal remained, however.

"Seems ironic, doesn't it?" Dempsey said. The hair on his forehead was pressed to his skull where the Stetson had been.

"What's that?"

"You work your ass off to stay with Lisa on the big tour, and now that you guys are finally married, you're apart."

"I work my ass off to win."

"I'm just happy he's not a bachelor anymore," Perkins said. "My wife, Linda, never thought it would happen."

"She told me," I said. "She thought my life revolved around golf too much."

"Not now," Perkins said. "Diapers, strollers, bibs."

"I still want to win on this tour—not the Nationwide, not the Champions Tour. On the PGA."

It took two members of the wait-staff to carry the plates. If you're easily embarrassed, don't eat with Perkins. He watched carefully as our young waitress set plates around him in a semi-circle. "Can you bring more rolls?"

"Certainly, sir," she said and left.

Dempsey watched the hem of her short skirt bob as she walked away.

"She's about half your age," Perkins said.

"Huh? Don't know what you're talking about."

I put ranch dressing on my salad. Dempsey had been a friend

for a long time. He was going through something he wasn't talking about. Whatever it was, it was sad to observe.

"Off to a good start," Dempsey said to me.

"Sixty-nine."

"Your first sub-seventy round in a while."

"You've been following me."

"Internet is a wonderful thing. You're my client. The second-place finish at the Buick last year had a lot of sponsors interested, but you stayed with Maxfli."

I shrugged. "I like the clubs." I put pepper on the ranch dressing and mixed it into the greens.

"I know, I know. But I have a second offer. Maxfli wants you to play a Maxfli ball again, too."

"I play the Pro V1."

"That's Titleist, Jack. You play Maxfli clubs. They'd like you to play the ball again, too."

"I can't give up that distance."

"It's a very nice offer."

"How much?" Perkins said.

Dempsey told us.

Perkins raised his brows and looked at me.

I shook my head, although it was a nice offer. Very nice. I sipped some beer and swallowed slowly. "I appreciate your work, but I can't give up that distance. We've got kids ten years younger than me who look like Hercules out here now. I need my power game."

Dempsey nodded. He ate his steak, glancing around the restaurant. He didn't push the issue and we ate quietly for a while. He was still a one-man agency, but growing. I was in the worst slump of my career and didn't believe he was here by accident. The offer had been one he could have conveyed via phone or e-mail.

"What really brings you from Houston?"

"The chance to dine with my favorite client, of course."

I grinned. "Cut the shit. I've known you a long time. You know why I switched to Titleist. I needed the extra length."

"Okay." He shrugged. "Got a new client. You played with him today."

"Grant Ashley or Kip Capers?"

"Grant. Too bad he hurt his back. Withdrew and went home."
He cut his steak and ate. He looked at Perkins and stopped
chewing. "What did I say?"

"He left?" Perkins said. Typically, Perkins wouldn't put his
fork down if someone yelled *Fire!* He'd stopped eating altogether now.

"Why?" Dempsey said.

"Where'd he go?" Perkins said.

"Home."

"What time did his flight leave?"

"I don't know, Perkins," Dempsey said. "What's going on?
The kid's a client."

"Tell me how you met him," Perkins said.

Dempsey looked at me. I nodded for him to answer.

"He was in Houston last year. The Tour Championship. Kid
led after the first round."

I remembered. Perkins took a quick bite of steak. I had nearly
finished my salad. The young waitress reappeared and offered a
second Heineken. I didn't want to be rude, so I accepted.

Dempsey watched her walk away again.

Perkins snapped his fingers.

Dempsey turned back to him. "What?"

"Tour Championship," Perkins said. "You were telling us
about Grant."

"I told him I could get him a nice corporate deal—Courtyard
by Marriott." Dempsey looked at me, eyes falling to his plate.
"Sorry, Jack."

"Don't be."

"Anyway, I got him the deal and was in town to check on
Jack, Grant, and a couple rookies I had meetings with."

"What do you think of his wife?" Perkins said.

"Lynne? Great lady."

"You think so?" I said.

"Sure. I guess. I mean I only met her once, but she seemed
supportive of Grant. Why?"

I shook my head and finished my salad. The waitress brought
my fresh beer. I stared at the bottle. Lynne Ashley, supportive?

"Grant mention Lynne recently?" I said.

"No." Dempsey finished his steak and pushed the plate away. "Will you two tell me what the hell's going on?"

We did.

.   .   .

"So what do you think?" Perkins said to Dempsey. We had finished eating.

Perkins's narrative had contained everything—Lynne's visit to Chandler, Maine; his brief stay in Atlanta; even Grant's caddie strolling the fairways kite-high.

Dempsey was shaking his head. He turned to me. "Today Grant's caddie walked the course stoned?"

"Yeah."

"Bullshit. Grant's not stupid. He wouldn't risk what I got him."

"You know Silver, right?"

He nodded.

"I take Silver's word," I said. "Guy's been places, lived places I know nothing about."

"What the hell does that mean?"

"Means I don't know much about it, but Silver does. If he tells me the guy is on drugs, I believe him."

The waitress cleared our table and asked if we'd like more beer. The restaurant had cleared out. Most players were in their rooms watching NBA or NHL playoffs. The Red Sox hadn't hit their annual late-summer slide yet, and the Bruins had made the playoffs, so, like every other New Englander, I was hopeful. A year ago, about this time, Lisa would have been returning from the course—leaders interrogated, interviews concluded, next day's notes prepared. She would order room service (usually a salad), then find the fitness room.

"Coffee," I said.

Perkins nodded.

Dempsey asked for another beer. It would be his fifth since I arrived. I didn't know how many he and Perkins had in the bar. At his size, Perkins could drink for hours, the alcohol seemingly having no effect. Indeed, I hadn't seen him drunk since college.

The restaurant seemed larger now, the empty room no longer offering background noise. The place was relaxed and comfortable. We all seemed to sit lower in the booth, relaxing. It was almost like old times. Except Dempsey was drunk, the whites of his eyes reddening, his speech thickening. Watching another person get drunk always made me uneasy, the equivalent to observing a man's weakness—something I did not wish to do, especially a friend.

"Sure you don't want coffee?" I said to Dempsey.

"No. No. I'm a swinging single now, brother." *Brother* came out thick: *broffer.*

The waitress returned and poured coffee.

Dempsey raised his fresh beer, looking at her. "Here's to beautiful Texas gals."

Her gaze ran awkwardly to Perkins and me.

"Well, then," Perkins said.

She raised her brows and walked away.

"What's her problem?" Dempsey said.

"For one," Perkins said, "this is Ohio."

Dempsey laughed and slapped the table with his palm. "Jesus, that's right."

Our coffees spilled. Perkins stared at Dempsey, annoyed, while Dempsey's laughter echoed throughout the room, and the waitress, standing with colleagues, gestured toward our table and nodded at him.

"He's a good kid, you know?" Dempsey said. "Just a little stupid. Thinks she loves him."

"Who?" Perkins said. "Grant?" He dipped his cloth napkin in his water glass and wiped the tablecloth, as if not concentrating on Dempsey's words.

"He *is* a good kid. I'm telling you."

I looked at Perkins with raised brows. "We know."

"Thinks who loves him?" Perkins said.

"Where's your beer, Jack?" Dempsey said.

"I've got a morning tee time tomorrow. Grant thinks who loves him?"

"Have another beer with me, *broffer,*" Dempsey said to Perkins.

"Sure." Perkins held his hand up. When the waitress looked over, he pointed to the Lone Star. She brought one.

"There's something 'bout being free," Dempsey said. "Isn't there? At first, I didn't know what I'd do. She *frew* me out on my ear. But now it's like college, like when I met Joan all over again."

"Sure." The beer sat before Perkins. He drank some coffee. "How does Grant get along with his wife?"

Dempsey paused mid-drink. "Fine—great."

"Grant got a girlfriend?"

"You hear that somewhere?"

Perkins shrugged then took a pull on the beer.

"That the word going around?" Dempsey said to me.

"I haven't heard that," I said.

Perkins kicked me.

Dempsey finished the beer on his third drink. "Might be good for Grant. Dinner's on me. Jack Austin's been a client a long time. Stuck with me. Now I'm going places. Hear me?"

"Sure," Perkins said.

I didn't know exactly how to take that. It sounded like the signing of Grant had taken the agency to another level. He had, however, drunk far too much. He waved, and the waitress returned. He gave her an American Express gold card.

"Grant a good client?" Perkins said.

"Yeah, sure. He loses this Marriott sponsorship I won't be saying that."

"So he's a good client, not a good husband."

Dempsey was signing the check and looked up at Perkins. "Never said that. He's a kid, and stuff is out of his hands."

"What is out of his hands?" I said.

Without looking up, he waved that off as if batting a fly. When he was finished with the check, he stood, and said good-bye.

We watched him go, neither of us speaking.

"He always drink that much?" Perkins said.

"No."

He thought about that.

"Grant is in a mess," he said.

"Yeah."

"So is your agent."

I didn't respond.

Perkins sipped some coffee. "You want some free advice?"

"No."

"I'd be looking for a new agent," he said. "You've got a wife and kid now, and Dempsey's drinking too much and hitting on women half his age."

Some things you can't control, and the sooner you learn that the better off you are on the PGA Tour. Friday morning, the weather turned to a scowl. My threesome changed, too—now it was a pairing.

Seated before my locker in stocking feet, I pulled Gore-Tex rain pants over my khaki Dockers. Titleist owns Footjoy, so standard operating procedure has those playing Titleist wearing Footjoy gloves and shoes. I put on new "Dryjoy" shoes and took three extra gloves from the top shelf of the locker; the rain could have me changing gloves every third hole.

I've heard it said playing professional sports extends adolescence. I'll go one step further: It's better than that—a ten-year-old's Christmas, every week. Upon arriving at a new venue, I open my locker to find a stack of new gloves in cellophane packages, two dozen Pro V1 balls, and whatever additional goodies Santa's Titleist- and Maxfli-bearing elves leave—demo putters, extra hats, the occasional umbrella.

This morning, the locker room was hopping. Some players arrived early to use the fitness trailer, others hit balls or putted. Now, it seemed, the entire 156-man field was in the locker room, sitting quietly before their lockers, reading the paper at card tables, or watching CNN's *Headline News.* Everyone seemed to be eating. The breakfast buffet smelled of bacon and onions. Idle chatter was heard—talk of kids, the course, even taxes and investments. Mixed with the bacon odor was strong flavored coffee, hazelnut or French vanilla.

I got a bowl of Wheaties and returned to my locker. No paper. No television. No chitchat. I was on the tee in just over an hour and into my pre-round routine. Minutes before, I had sat alone, visualizing several shots I knew I'd have to hit—for example, avoiding the water off the tee on the par-five fifth again. After eating, I'd go to the range, where Silver would meet me and ask why I was late. There, I'd hit thirty or sixty-one shots, one better than my respective tournament lows for nine and eighteen holes (a superstitious harbinger). I'd end with three drives using the club with which I planned to hit my opening tee shot. Lastly, before being introduced on the first tee, I would putt, getting a feel for the speed of the greens. I always finish with a two-footer, not looking up, listening for the clatter— pocket change into a tin can—as the Surlyn shell of the golf ball rattles the cup.

"Mr. Austin."

It was Kip Capers. He wore blue slacks and a white turtleneck today. Atop the turtleneck was a sleeveless V-necked windbreaker like the ones made fashionable by the late Payne Stewart when he'd torn the sleeves off his jacket at the 1999 U.S. Open. A cross hung from a chain on Capers's left ear.

"Sorry to bother you, sir."

"Mr. Nicklaus and Mr. Palmer are 'sir,'" I said.

He made a child's shrug—head tilted to his shoulder, eyes toward the floor. "Guess I'm old-fashioned."

The remark and his mannerisms sharply contrasted with his garb.

"What can I do for you, Kip?"

"I was wondering if I could pick your brain."

"Not much to pick." I grinned.

Grant Ashley's withdrawal left Capers and me playing a twosome. I anticipated a quiet round since, the day before, Capers and I literally did not speak following first-tee introductions. On the whole, Thursday's round had not been chatty. Grant hadn't wanted to talk, I had not brought up Lynne, and Capers had worked the gallery. Some playing partners fit you better than others. A chatterbox like Lee Trevino would have had D.T.s by our fourth hole. Some guys control their concentration as if with a switch—get to their ball, throw the "on" lever; yet others walk eighteen holes, game face painted from opening tee shot until the final putt. I usually fall somewhere between.

"You can call me Jack."

He smiled, still looking at his feet.

"Have a seat," I said.

He did, next to me on the bench. I set the bowl of Wheaties between us.

"You eat Wheaties every day?" he said.

"When I joined the Tour, I was the anomaly: a six-one, two-hundred-fifteen-pound golfer. Look around the locker room. Bunch of twenty-somethings my size now and leaner. I need my Wheaties."

"Can you tell me about the greens?" he said. "I won't bother you for too long. Just wondered what you expect from the rain. I know you've played here thirteen straight years."

I stopped chewing and looked at him.

Embarrassed, he shrugged again. "I read a lot."

"Worse habits."

Capers, I noticed for the first time, was in good shape. Despite the jacket, I could tell his shoulders were broader than I'd thought. Previously, I thought he was skinny, and he certainly was not fat, but he was thin and lean, like Charles Howell III. The locker room door opened, and Padre entered. His blue rain suit was wet and shone beneath the ceiling lights, rain pants sprinkled with mud.

"You shot your career best, sixty-two, here in 1998."

"You do read a lot."

"I like golf history," Capers said. "Majored in history in college."

"Where'd you go?"

"I got my B.A. from Boston University. I was enrolled full time at the Yale Divinity School. Taking a year off."

"Becoming a priest?"

"Episcopal."

Lisa was right. Capers would make a great feature article.

"Thought I'd go into ministry," he said, "but this might offer a larger forum."

I recalled the day before and wondered what he'd said to fans.

"You majored in English at Maine," he said.

"Thought I'd teach high school. Playing pro golf is probably less stressful."

He looked like he wanted to laugh but didn't, which was too bad. Would've been a reaction my jokes didn't typically evoke.

"As you can guess," I said, "the rain is going to slow the greens. But I think not as much as people expect. I'm not going to hit putts much harder than yesterday."

He sat perfectly still next to me, hands clasped in his lap.

Hours earlier, I had woken to rain tapping the hotel window. The room had been dark, Perkins's bed again empty. Where he went and when I never knew. My mind had been fogged with the edges of sleep. Yet I registered the sound of rain, and I had thought, momentarily, about the greens rolling slower due to the moisture. When the 5 A.M. wake-up call came, the rain had turned to drizzle. By 6:30 it passed, and morning tee times were slated to go as scheduled.

"You'll be surprised how fast they'll be," I said to Capers.

He nodded slowly. "Thank you, Mr. Austin."

And that was it. He stood and left, before I could tell him— again—to call me Jack.

.   .   .

The typical PGA Tour event uses a "split tee" start, meaning if you begin on the first hole Thursday, you go off the tenth Friday. Thus, Capers and I would open with the tenth, a par four, 441 yards. It might be an easier first tee shot than No. 1; however, there's enough there to get your attention. Off the tee, sand traps line the landing area, while bunkers also surround the green. In fact, the greenside trap on the right is shaped like a claw, fingers jutting out to snare wayward shots.

Capers looked ready to play. He stood quietly behind Silver and me, driver across his shoulders, rotating his torso slowly, his face a mask of concentration. He had fought back to shoot seventy-six Thursday. Woods's sixty-four had held up, giving Tiger the overnight lead and leaving Capers twelve shots back, after only eighteen holes. The top seventy scores and ties would make the cut and vie for the $5 million purse on the weekend. The estimated cut line was one under par, so Capers needed to make up five strokes. The course, however, was playing long, making sixty-seven a tall order.

We were on schedule: 8:12 A.M. The air felt heavy and moist. The vast Ohio sky, which yesterday seemed an upside-down ocean, was now a thick gray mass. Members of our gallery could be counted on two hands. The rain was back, if only a drizzle, but was a steady tap on my rain-suit, and I wondered if, at some point during the morning, I'd hear the horn halting play.

The tenth hole at Muirfield provided me a choice: Try to launch my tee shot beyond the bunkers guarding the landing area, or lay back with a three-wood, a more conservative approach. Similar to the first hole—where a triangle of three bunkers protects the dogleg's right side—some players can take the bunkers out of the picture, bombing tee shots past them. I had shot sixty-nine Thursday and wanted to begin Friday with a birdie.

Silver held out the three-wood.

I shook my head and pulled the cover off the driver.

"It's wet, Jack. Air is heavy. Why push your luck? We're three under par."

"We're six back. And Woods has a huge advantage today."

Silver nodded. "Yeah, the course is going to play long. But we can't go for everything, all day."

"Haven't we had this discussion before? Club selection is one thing, philosophy in non-negotiable." I took the driver, stepped away, and took two practice swings.

Silver ran a hand over his shaved head and moved to the side.

The turf was wet against the knuckles of my right hand as

I reached down to tee the ball. I set the ball high and slightly forward in my stance, nearly off my front toe, to help the fade. I brought the club back slowly, made a wide shoulder turn, paused just short of parallel at the top, and began the down-swing. My hips cleared. I powered the club down and through impact, my wrists rolling, snapping right over left. The contact was excellent. My best shots feel pure, as if no ball exists, nearly the same sensation as a practice swing. I held the follow-through.

Everyone has something that provides a rare sense of auton-omy. Hitting a golf ball with clean, precise contact is mine. The feeling of the ball leaving the club face, the sensation running through my hands, arms, shoulders, so crisp and clean, like tak-ing snow in your palm and feeling it melt against your flesh, the water running through your fingers. It was a sensation I first discovered at age nine and had sought continually since.

"Beauty," Silver said.

The ball moved slightly left to right, carried the right-side bunker, kicked hard to the left and rolled, leaving only a short-iron to the green.

.   .   .

My feelings about Capers were mixed. During my time on Tour, I'd seen lots of kids get caught up in outside distractions and get washed away. If Capers considered the Tour a secondary inter-est, however, it was because he valued religion more. Tough to find a flaw in that. So it was difficult to watch him struggle.

On our first green, I was putting from six feet for birdie; Ca-pers lay four, facing a thirty-foot bogey attempt.

"Kid's never withdrawn from a tournament," Silver said. He leaned casually against the bag, which stood between us.

The drizzle paused, then quickened, the steady tapping sound now a drum roll against my Gore-Tex rainsuit.

"Is that a compliment?" I said.

"He shot the season's highest score, eighty-seven, in Tucson. Q-School might have been a fluke."

Annually, more than a thousand golfers begin the PGA Tour Qualifying Tournament. Only roughly thirty-five earn Tour cards.

"Pretty elaborate fluke," I said.

We watched Capers roll his ball six feet past the cup. He glanced at me.

We had seemingly identical distances. Too close to judge, so I nodded. I'd go first, giving him time to regroup. Hale Irwin's line "beautiful . . . but toughest" greens came back. I wanted to get this round off the ground immediately, and a birdie was the way to do that. The line looked straight, but after thirteen tournaments and Lord knows how many practice rounds, I knew the ball would gain speed and dart left at the hole.

I crouched behind the ball, Silver leaning over my shoulder.

"You got the line, Jack?"

"Yeah."

"Quick and left at the hole. Three balls outside the left edge, and let the break take it."

I nodded and stood. I gently placed the putter's blade behind the ball. I aligned my shoulders to the hole, took two practice strokes, then pulled the trigger. At the hole, the ball broke hard, catching the left edge, and spinning out. I tapped in for par.

"The water is screwing up our speed," Silver said. "That was a good stroke."

I nodded. The hard rain was now scattered needles falling past the visor of my cap.

We watched as Capers made his putt.

"Nice stroke," Silver said.

Capers nodded slowly and, defeated, moved like an old man to the next tee.

.   .   .

I played my first nine—the back nine—in even par. So I was disappointed with a mediocre par on my tenth hole—No. 1— because the second hole is one of the tougher par fours on the course: 455 yards, a creek guarding the right side of the fairway for the final hundred yards, wrapping around the right and rear of the green. It was a hole to which I'd surrendered many shots over the years.

I hit my three-wood 265 yards to the center of the fairway.

Capers hit what looked to be a cut shot. However, the layout called for a straight drive. The result was out of bounds. He shook his head, the fits of inconsistency getting to him. He had been six over par. Next, he hit the fairway with a five-iron and would be hitting his fourth shot from there.

Our caddies walked the fairway together, chatting. I walked beside Capers. He moved slowly, head down.

"I wouldn't say this to just anyone," I said, "but you asked for advice earlier."

He looked up, then glanced around. No one was within earshot.

"When the wheels fall off, you've got to be stoic. Don't hang your head. These guys are the best of the best. You can't show a weakness."

It was something I had never done. It amounted to a pep talk. Tour pros don't need pep talks. Not from fellow players, anyway. Maybe a close friend might ask someone to dinner, see what is wrong. Capers wasn't a close friend, though, and, worse, my comments came mid-round. But I had said it, and now we stood looking at each other for a long moment.

I moved away, my footfalls splashing the wet turf. The silence and my thoughts were momentarily broken by a distant roar— something had happened, somewhere, with positive or negative implications. As I stood next to Silver and watched Capers hit a 190-yard approach with a four-iron, I thought I must have sounded patronizing and wished I had kept my mouth shut.

"What's wrong?" Silver said. He held an umbrella over the bag.

I pulled a club and wiped the grip with a towel.

"Something's wrong," he said.

"I told Capers not to hang his head."

"His head hanging your problem?"

"Damn it."

"Yeah," Silver said. "You see something, you always got to fix it. You ought to join the United Nations. Could use a guy like you."

"Shit," I said and walked to my ball with my six-iron.

．　．　．

On the green, I was crouched behind a fifteen-foot birdie attempt. I wanted to make sure I had the speed. On the first green, I hadn't hit the putt firmly enough to hold the line, and it died before the cup. However, fifteen feet was too far to get cute. I didn't want to roll the ball six feet past.

The gallery around the green was not large. Maybe a half-dozen people stood in clusters. I saw Dempsey standing alone and nodded. He waved and offered the thumbs-up signal. The drizzle sounded like pellets against my rain suit. Most spectators wore hoods, caps, or held umbrellas. The damp air felt thick as I inhaled. Dempsey wore a rain suit and a tan cap, patches of which were now brown. A tall, thin blonde approached and stood next to him. She wore sunglasses, despite the weather, and a navy blue windbreaker, white short-shorts, and sneakers atop ankle-length socks. She said something to Dempsey then turned to see what he was watching.

When I looked at her, she shifted and seemed to slide behind Dempsey. I realized two things immediately: The first was that she should wear short-shorts. And the second—that I had seen her before.

I addressed the ball, took two practice strokes, then hit the putt. Maybe distractions help my game—the putt fell, although I didn't celebrate. When Silver slapped my palm, I was staring at Lynne Ashley, who now stood alone.

12

It was nearly startling to see the two of them together. Yet, Perkins and Dempsey, each with a beer, sat in a booth near the one where we'd eaten the night before. Of course, seeing Osama bin Laden sitting next to Dempsey wouldn't have shocked me after recognizing his companion hours earlier. Now, however, Lynne Ashley was nowhere in sight.

I walked toward the table, attempting to hide any remnants of the stunned expression my face surely held on the second green. I had called Perkins on my cell phone from the locker room immediately after the round. After several tries, he'd reached Dempsey and made it sound like the two of them—only—were having a friendly dinner. Jack Austin, party crasher.

Dempsey did not look happy to see me approach. I smiled widely. He was, after all, my agent. And a guy can always trust his agent to tell him the truth, right? I felt bad about the breakup of his marriage, kids were involved, but much of the sympathy I felt the evening before had dissolved on the second green.

"The three amigos, again tonight," I said and slid in next to Perkins.

"How'd you play?" Perkins said.

"You don't follow my every shot on the Internet?" I said.

Perkins grinned. "Now that's ego."

It was 6:45 P.M. Around us, the restaurant was busy with the dinner crowd—business travelers and Tour players and families. Padre Tarbuck sat across the room with a blonde. He nodded, and I waved. A waiter walked past with sizzling fajitas, pungent odor of spices riding the air.

"I shot sixty-nine," I said.

"Here's to fourth place." Dempsey raised his beer.

We all clinked.

Based on his showing the night before, I was hoping Dempsey wouldn't drink so much we'd have to soak him up with a sponge and ring him out in his room.

"You didn't stay around long," I said to him.

"Left after the second hole."

"With Lynne Ashley," I said.

"Who?" His eyes ran to a group of Tour players at a table across the room. Two-time U.S. Open champ Lee Janzen was eating there. Dempsey waved and called, "Hey, Lee."

Janzen waved back.

Beside me, Perkins let out a long exhale. It summed up both of our feelings: How far would Dempsey take the charade?

"Lynne Ashley," Perkins said. "You were watching the golf tournament with her today."

Dempsey's eyes refocused on Perkins. Then he looked at me again. I saw the realization in his face. He knew why he'd been asked to dine. This wasn't a shoot-the-shit dinner.

"Oh," he said. "Yeah . . . I ran into her . . . there."

Perkins looked across the table at Dempsey and focused hard, two tiny lines forming between his eyebrows. It was a look that made people aware of the difference between Perkins and themselves. The difference was Perkins's possession of a primal state, a gear he shifted to, where he looked at things in terms of good and bad, right and wrong. When he hit that level all bets were off as to what he might do. He'd hit it years ago when he'd beaten a man to near coma, then "retired" from the Boston P.D. The incident had occurred after Perkins and his partner found a four-year-old rape victim, then located the perpetrator—the girl's father. The stare told you he was willing to hurt you. Not beat you up. Hurt you. Put you in the hospital. I had never been the recipient of the look but had seen it often. When the look surfaced, people were aware of it.

Dempsey was. He looked down, staring at his beer.

"Where is she now?" Perkins said.

"Lynne? I don't know."

"Where's Grant?" I said.

Dempsey shrugged as the waitress returned. We ordered dinner.

"Look," Perkins said, when she left, "with the Hutch Gainer thing you helped us out. I thought you were a stand-up guy." He paused to sip some beer.

Dempsey watched him.

Perkins smiled widely. "Either you fucking talk"—his voice carried no hint of anger—"and talk candidly, or you'll be eating through a straw for months."

"Jesus," Dempsey said.

"Yeah, 'Jesus,'" Perkins said. "I've been all over Atlanta. Now you tell me where the hell Lynne Ashley is."

Dempsey sighed and sat back. "You married?"

Perkins nodded once.

"How long?"

"Eight years."

"So you know what it's like."

Perkins didn't say anything.

"Jack doesn't know yet," Dempsey said. "He's a newlywed. But eight years . . . you know."

I sipped my beer. Dempsey was getting to something. I wanted to know what it had to do with Lynne Ashley. At the Janzen table, a round of drinks arrived. Three men wore suits. I guessed they were agents or corporate executives. The golfers drank water and iced tea. The suits had what looked like mixed drinks.

"My wife threw me out," Dempsey said and waited for a reaction.

Neither Perkins nor I offered one.

The waitress returned, set salads in front of us, and said, "Another round?"

Dempsey nodded, but Perkins said, "No. Three waters, please."

She went to get them.

"I can't order a beer?" Dempsey said.

"Not tonight." Perkins made a gesture with his hand that told Dempsey to continue.

Again, Dempsey leaned back, sighed deeply, and blew out a

long breath. "I fucked up my marriage. Did something stupid. Joan threw me out." The words came in rapid bursts, as if he wanted to get the confession over. He sounded sincere. Finished, he sat staring at his beer.

Perkins pushed. "What did you do?" He was interrogating, so past friendships were out. He was working now, looking for Lynne Ashley, determined to find her.

"It's personal. All you need to know is I'm not married now." He was looking at me as he said this, as if explaining something.

"What did you do?" Perkins said.

"Got nothing to do with you."

Perkins shifted in his seat and pinched the bridge of his nose with his thumb and forefinger. He was going to lose it.

I jumped in before he did. "Demps, he's hired to find Lynne. If you were still with Joan, I wouldn't have seen you with Lynne today." That wasn't necessarily true. She was, after all, married to his client, but we'd been told the client had gone home. And I needed to say something.

Dempsey held his beer on the table and sat staring at it, thinking.

"What happened between you and Joan?" I said. "You leave her for Lynne?"

He looked up at me, then at Perkins.

As if on cue, the waitress came back, this time with water and our meals. No one had finished his salad yet, but she didn't seem to care. She carried a thick brown tray over her right shoulder and set it down on a stand. Perkins received the twenty-ounce porterhouse and baked potato; Dempsey got a chicken sandwich; and she put spaghetti and meatballs in front of me.

When the waitress was gone, Dempsey was still looking at Perkins.

"I'm waiting," Perkins said.

"It's personal."

"I'm looking for Lynne Ashley. You knew that last night but said nothing to either of us. Now you're seen with her today. I want to know everything about everything."

Dempsey's eyes scanned the entire room, then refocused on Perkins. Dempsey exhaled and looked at me. No one spoke, but

I nodded encouragingly. Perkins did not. He sipped ice water and chewed the cubes, glaring at Dempsey the whole time.

Dempsey sighed again. "I cheated on my wife with Lynne. I'm in love with Lynne."

I set my fork down.

Perkins stopped chewing.

"I couldn't help it. It just happened."

"You had an affair," Perkins said.

Dempsey crossed his arms and leaned back. "That's how others might view it, but it's much more."

"Of course," Perkins said.

"You said you ruined your marriage," I said. "How can it be 'much more'?"

Dempsey sighed and shook his head sadly. "You don't understand, Jack. Neither of you do."

"Try us," Perkins said.

Dempsey shook his head.

"When did you move out?" I said.

"February. Divorce was final in March."

"When and how did you meet Lynne Ashley?" Perkins said. "Exactly."

Very slowly, Dempsey bit into the chicken sandwich. Perkins and I took the cue and ate as well. Padre and the blonde had gone. It was 7:30 now, and the crowd had thinned. The Janzen table was still there. Papers were in the middle of the table. A guy in a suit was pointing to the papers, talking to Janzen.

Dempsey set his sandwich down, drank some water, and sat looking at Perkins, who chewed slowly, looking back at him the way a shark would eye a wounded manatee.

Finally, Dempsey slumped in his seat. "Lynne said others wouldn't understand." He exhaled slowly. "Things happen for a reason. Now we've found each other. That's all that matters."

"You reading that off something?" I said. "What about your kids?"

Perkins wasn't getting sidetracked. "When and how did you meet Lynne Ashley?"

"I was at a sports and talent representation conference in Miami and there's this blonde model. It was Lynne. Something in my marriage had changed. I don't know what, but we were in a lull. And Lynne made—makes—me feel . . ."

Dempsey's facial expression resembled the way I must've looked twenty years earlier when a pretty girl accepted my invitation to the prom. I sat back, listening. Perkins put down his silverware.

"Lynne makes me feel powerful. These guys are there from the big agencies, IMG and those places. Tiger's managers were there, and Lynne shows up at *my* room, says she has questions."

"What kind of questions?" Perkins said.

"Do I represent actors? Says she was a cheerleader, wants to get into commercials. I tell her I don't. She says, Do I know anyone who does? I say, I do, and she wants me to introduce her."

"So what happened?" I said.

Dempsey took a sip of ice water. His face flushed. "You wouldn't understand. It's not like it sounds."

I waited.

Perkins's expression didn't change.

"I know I'm an adult," Dempsey said, "responsible for my actions and all that, but . . . " He spread his palms. "I fell in love."

"Were you in bed when you made that realization?" I said.

"I'm offended by that, Jack."

"You're not seventeen," I said.

"I've been with the same woman for almost fifteen years. Now I've found what I've always wanted." Dempsey stood, tossed his cloth napkin on the table, and walked away.

"We had him talking," Perkins said. "Nice going."

I drank some beer.

"You know how I suggested you seek alternative representation?"

"Big words," I said.

"When I need them. You don't need to worry about that now," he said. "I think Dempsey has moved on."

"Like he did with his wife and kids," I said.

"*Y*ou're early," Tim Silver said, sitting across from me at 8:30 P.M. "This must be a serious meeting."

After dinner, Perkins had dashed to see if Lynne Ashley was still a registered guest, and I had gone to the bar to wait for Silver. I chose a booth, away from a group of golfers seated around a circular table watching the NHL playoffs.

Silver was right. This was a serious meeting. Only two times before had I conducted formal employer-employee discussions with him. The first was when I hired him; the second, when Silver told me he wanted six months off to finish his book.

"Want something to drink?" I said.

"Coffee."

I flagged a waitress.

"I know why we're meeting, Jack."

"Yeah?"

His hands were in front of him, clasped on the paper place mat. His fingers were slender and graceful, the nails well kept. Ceiling light reflected off his onyx ring. He didn't look tense, but his face was serious.

"The two debates over club selection," he said.

He wore a black T-shirt beneath white overalls, a black cap with a white Nike swoosh, and Doc Martens, ever stylish. By contrast, I, too, had changed from work attire, khaki Dockers and a collared shirt, to civilian garb—fresh khaki Dockers and a collared shirt.

The wall that abutted our booth was lined with windows. Outside, people walked to and from cars. I'd played two of four rounds, my workweek only half over. To the rest of society, Friday concluded the week, provided a time of excitement, a release. You could see it in the way people moved, the carefree expressions. There would be dinner dates, down time, even parties. I hoped to be partying when my workweek concluded as well, on Sunday—in celebration of my first Tour win.

When the coffee arrived, Silver meticulously spooned in one and one-half tablespoons of sugar, then slowly poured in cream, stirring as he poured. It reminded me of our golf bag. He made Stone Phillips look unorganized.

"Tim, we've been together a long time," I said, dumping a sugar packet into my coffee, spilling some on the tabletop. "You know my game inside and out. You know my swing. Truth be told, you're a hell of a caddie."

"Jesus Christ," he said. "You're firing me."

"No, I'm not."

He waited.

I sipped coffee and chose my words carefully. Caddies offer advice, encouragement, swing tips, and assist golfers in major and minor on-course activities, from wiping mud and grass off balls prior to putts, to reading greens, to judging wind's potential affect on ball flight. Tiger Woods's looper, Steve Williams, plays bad cop to journalists and fans who click photos during Tiger's backswing. I was a husband and father, but after more than a decade on Tour, I knew my relationship with Silver to be nearly as crucial as my family ties.

"This has been a tough season for me, admittedly."

He nodded.

"Been slumping for almost two months."

"You're distracted," he said.

I let that pass. Certainly, he was right, but this wasn't a therapy session. "I don't know why I've played poorly. But I'm coming out of it, and we're in fourth place going into the weekend."

"I'm just trying to get you to play a little more conservatively," he said. "The way you've always played."

I shook my head. "You've been talking to Peter Schultz. And you both think I'm kicking myself for losing the Buick Classic, that I'm trying to reach every par four because I didn't try to drive one I could have reached, and the decision might have cost me the tournament."

He didn't speak, and his eyes focused on his coffee.

"That's not right, Tim. The Buick Classic was a good experience. A hard one, sure. But I learned something."

He looked up at me. "What?"

"I always knew I could hang with the best guys out here. But I hadn't finished top-three in two years."

"So the Buick Classic showed you still have game?"

"Not exactly. I've always believed I'm a world-class player."

He drank some coffee. "Wouldn't be out here if you didn't."

"Right. But at the Buick, I learned something about the Tour's elite. Phil Mickelson took a gamble—not all day, not every hole—but on a tee where he knew, if he made his best swing, he could pull off a shot that makes Tour players special."

Silver set the coffee down and leaned forward, hands resting quietly on the tabletop. He looked at me, head tilted slightly, and nodded. "He wasn't careful."

"Right. He wasn't *afraid to lose.*"

The guys around the table cheered. I glanced over. The Detroit Red Wings had scored against the Toronto Maple Leafs.

"A guy like me," I said, "spends a lot of energy, physical and mental, trying to keep his card. I don't have exempt status. Mickelson, with more than twenty wins, has the lifetime exemption."

"He can take risks you can't."

"No. That's the thing. He *takes* risks that anyone *can.* It's not like he either wins or misses the cut each week."

Silver drank coffee. I did, too. A brown liquid ring was on the tabletop where my coffee had sat, having sloshed over. Silver's side of the booth was spotless.

"After thinking about this all winter," I said, "over the course of a season, if I choose my spots, I'm going to be better off if I take some gambles that in years past I haven't taken."

Silver ran his tongue along his upper lip. "Run this by Lisa?"

"No."

"Why?"

"She's not my caddie. You're the one who needs to be on the same page with me."

He looked at me for a long moment. Then he drank some coffee. "You made nine hundred grand last year," he said, setting the cup down.

"It's not about the money," I said. "Never has been."

"Staying in the top one twenty-five is all about money, Jack."

"A win is a two-year exemption."

"There's that." He looked around the room, then back to me. "This have anything to do with Darcy?"

I held his look for a long moment. I shook my head and reached for my coffee. But he knew me very well.

"In my book, I say you can tell a lot about a person by how he plays golf," he said. "It's always been true of you, Jack. You're steady as a rock, on the course and off. Nothing flashy. Consistent as hell. Never indecisive. Always make the smart play. It's how you've lasted out here so long."

"I'm not making huge changes, Tim."

"But you're taking risks you haven't in the past."

"I want to win."

"At all cost—to both of us?"

I drank some coffee and looked at him. I knew what he was saying. If I made $900,000 last year, he'd made $45,000 plus $700 a week.

"We're a team," I said. "I'm doing what's best."

"You missed six straight cuts, Jack."

"That's unrelated to what we're talking about."

I knew it sounded ridiculous as soon as I said it. But my recent poor play was not the result of on-course gambles; rather, it was due to something I didn't even fully understand but knew it had a lot to do with Darcy, indeed, and Lisa and my home with the two of them.

"'Unrelated'?" he said. "How can it be unrelated? We're talking about your golf game here."

This discussion had begun with Silver on the eighteenth fairway at the Colonial in Fort Worth, Texas, had continued at the Woodlands in Falmouth, Maine, with Schultz, and here I was again with Silver, talking about what was wrong with my game.

I sighed. "I'm in fourth place. Let's go from here. What I want you to know is that, in certain situations—not constantly—but in some situations, I'm going to take more chances. You're my caddie. I need you to support that."

"You've made me good money over the years," he said. "And I know you always trust what your gut tells you."

I didn't speak. He was thinking aloud.

"And it's usually right."

I nodded.

"And these young kids are fearless," he said. "And you are getting older." He grinned.

"Not older," I said. "Better."

"If you think you can make bigger checks taking some chances, Meal Ticket, I'm in."

He raised his fist. I tapped it with mine.

"Now that we've got that settled," he said, "if I order a sex-on-the-beach and get two straws, will you share it with me?"

I rolled my eyes. "I'm going to bed." I stood, threw $5 on the table, and turned to go.

"Jack."

I turned back.

"I'm behind you, man. As caddie and friend." He held up his hand again.

This time we shook.

"Woods is minus twelve," General Davis said to me, motioning to the leader board and shaking his head.

It was Saturday at 12:22 P.M. We were on the first tee, waiting for the group in front of us to clear. At midday, the temperature allowed for short sleeves. A mild breeze blew, peppering the air with the scent of barbecued steaks from the clubhouse or the hospitality tents.

"Nothing Woods does surprises me," I said.

"Yesterday was a bitch. I was just trying to hang on." General looked from me to Silver. Given what he had told me about Silver's "biceps" comment, it was safe to assume Silver noticed the short sleeves General now wore. Silver said nothing, though. He kids me on the course, knowing it doesn't bother me. If anything, it keeps me loose. However, Silver would never make a remark to a competitor.

"Tiger shot sixty-four in the rain," I said.

"Let's hope he does that for me in the Ryder Cup. We're playing Carnoustie."

"Yeah," I said.

General walked across the tee box to where his caddie waited, took what looked to be a three-iron from the bag, and made several practice swings.

My Saturday tee time put me near hallowed ground. On Tour, the thirty-six–hole cut reduces standard tournament fields from 156 players (144 before daylight savings) to the top seventy (and ties). Players surviving the cut play the weekend in twosomes arranged according to score, teeing off in descending order—first place (and ties) plays last. On this day, Tiger headlined the final pairing, which was going off at 12:40. Fourth place had me in the third group, paired with General, with whom I was tied at six under.

Life was good. The sun shone brightly overhead. The gallery was large. I was playing with the U.S. Ryder Cup captain. More importantly, my tee time indicated to all that I was in contention, back from wherever I'd been. After the previous month, playing two tee times from the leaders was a treat. Hell, after missing six cuts, playing the weekend for a paycheck was glorious. Moreover, I knew Schultz would be watching.

General walked back to me, leaned the three-iron against his leg, and pulled on a new glove. "Let's put up a couple low scores, give Tiger something to think about." He opened and closed his fist, stretching the new leather. The white glove had black nylon material over the knuckles and a Nike swoosh on the Velcro tab.

"Couple of sixty-sixes would do that," I said.

He winked. "In the locker room, I told Tiger there's a lot of fight left in this old dog."

"This one, too."

He shook his head. "You're what, thirty-five, thirty-six?"

I nodded.

"Your best golf's still in front of you."

I was looking forward to my round with General. We enjoyed practice rounds together but rarely played tournament rounds with one another. On Tour, the opening two rounds, Thursday and Friday, have players categorized according to credentials, then randomly grouped in threesomes by a computer. General was a Category 1 player. Category 1 features tournament winners and players in the top twenty-five on the career money list. Category 1A consists of those players no longer in the top category but active on the PGA or Nationwide Tour, or who are past winners of major championships. I was a Category 2 player. This flight is for players currently in the top 125 on the money list, players who have made fifty career cuts, or those in the top fifty on the Official World Golf Ranking list. Category 3 is everyone else—Monday qualifiers, sponsor exemptions, and rookies.

Winless, I was never paired with General, Freddie Couples, or Tiger Woods for the first thirty-six holes. From a television standpoint, marquee plays with marquee. Why waste time showing Jack Austin trudging eighteen holes, when viewers can see Phil Mickelson walk the fairways with David Duval? I have no problem with this. In golf, fame is earned. Teammates never carry you. There's no place to hide in the batting order. If you can dunk but can't hit the outside shot, you'll be sent packing. In our sport, you play well or go home. I had played well this week and thus, this day, would get plenty of airtime.

General was standing near his caddie again, reviewing the yardage book. His wife, Angela, stood in the front row of the gallery, her pass, in a clear plastic holder, hung from a string around her neck. For a moment, I thought of Lisa and Darcy in Chandler, Maine.

"Slight cross breeze," Silver said to me. He'd arrived early, stopping to get extra Gatorade packets on the way. "The breeze will push the ball right. You probably want to play for the left side of the fairway, let the wind move the ball back to middle."

I nodded. The bag stood between us, my hand atop the three-metal.

"Well, bossman," he said, "it's your show. Let's run and gun."

I looked at him. "Where the hell did that come from?"

"'Run and gun'?" He shrugged and grinned.

"You've said the exact same thing on the first tee for more than two hundred tournaments."

He nodded. "'Straight and long.'"

"Yeah."

"We haven't won. Time for a change, so now it's 'run and gun.'" He handed me the driver.

Still looking at him, I took the club.

The first hole at Muirfield Village is 451 yards. The tee is elevated, and three traps collect a push or slice. Driver is plenty of club. Three-wood, then a nine-iron approach, is the typical choice. However, the fairway is wide. Hitting driver could replace the nine-iron with a pitching or sand wedge. Run and gun.

After introductions, General hit a three-iron tee shot that left 150 yards to the hole. It was a safe play, but this was a birdie hole, and I was hoping to play in the final pairing Sunday. Truth be told, a fourth-place tie, given my recent outings, would have been excellent. However, fourth place (alone) earned only $240,000. As much money as that was, it wasn't enough to secure my spot in the top 125 at year's end. It would allow me to jump from 188 into the mix, but might not keep me there. As a grinder—a guy who makes cuts, beats balls on the range until his hands blister, putts in hotel hallways till midnight, and grinds over every shot each tournament to keep up with guys born to play this game—I savor the moment each summer when I know I've earned enough to stay in the top 125. Fourth place was good. It wasn't good enough.

A volunteer standing near the gallery raised both hands and held a QUIET sign. I waggled the club back and forth above the ball and exhaled. Then everything disappeared. Only me and the ball.

During the swing, when at my best, I am conscious of nothing; yet, I have watched enough film of my motion to know the kinetics inside and out: The driver moves slowly back. I make a wide arc and full shoulder turn. At the top, just short of parallel, the sun flickers off the steel shaft like the pop of a camera flash. A moment of hesitation. My body catches up to the club. Then the downswing. Eyes never leave the ball until after the strike of the club head. Finally, the finish—full follow-through, belt buckle pointing down the target line.

Then, I re-entered the world. I heard sounds—sneakers slapping the pavement of the cart path, applause, Silver saying, "Nice shot." Then smells—the scent of salt from the perspiration on my upper lip, grass, and the aroma of suntan lotion carried by the breeze.

My drive faded into the heart of the fairway, safe from the bunkers, and came to rest fifty or more yards in front of General's.

"Eat your Wheaties this morning, did you, young man?" General said. "Somebody's trying for a three here."

I winked at him.

. . .

The first green at Muirfield Village is the largest on the course. My approach stopped six feet past the cup. From ninety-seven yards, I would expect to be no farther than six feet. It's why, even if I can reach a par-five in two, I sometimes lay up. From a hundred yards, I know I can put seven of ten within eight feet.

General had nearly the same line, and I watched closely as he rolled his ball four feet past. After General marked his ball, Silver and I went to work.

"Darted hard left about six inches from the cup," Silver said. "It gets very quick two feet from the hole."

I nodded and moved to the side of the green to look at the line. General was a good putter. He had looked over the putt from all the same angles I did. It had rained the day before. He must have thought the green would be slower and, if so, had put a little extra on the stroke to compensate. As I told Kip Capers, the greens weren't as slow as they looked.

Silver knew that, too. "Play it four balls off the right edge and let the break take it."

I agreed and crouched behind the marker, replaced the ball, and pocketed the coin. I brought the putter straight back and through, holding the follow-through, my bottom palm pointing directly down the target line.

I looked up only when the ball was five feet away. The word "Titleist" had become a blurred black line as the ball rolled toward the hole. Rattling against the bottom of the cup, it made a gentle clicking sound.

. . .

I went out in thirty-four and stood on the eleventh tee eight under par. General had played well, tee to green, but had not been rewarded. He was even par on the day.

The eleventh hole is 567 yards, a par-five on which you are confronted twice by the same body of water. It's one of my all-time favorites, a great "arena golf" hole, meaning the fairway forms a valley and hundreds of spectators can line the banks to view the action. Also, it's reachable with two excellent shots. Key-word: "excellent." You drive downhill, but a creek runs through the fairway 320 yards out, then lines the right side and swings left, passing in front of the elevated green. It's a gambler's hole. In years past, I usually laid up, then attempted to knock my wedge within birdie range.

Silver handed me the driver and nodded. "You're swinging real well. An eagle would put you two off the lead."

Leader boards at various locations had told me, through nine holes, Tiger's day was going the same as General's: Woods, too, was even, thus still twelve under. I was four back. A three-metal was safer here, but that selection—save for a hundred-yard miracle hole-out—effectively took eagle out of the picture. I wanted to be in Sunday's final paring.

"Fairway's a little longer on the right-hand side," Silver said. "You've been accurate with the driver all day. Play for the right, and hit the driver." He nodded encouragingly.

I took the club and made a fist with my free hand. He tapped it lightly with his own.

"Run and gun, baby," he said.

General stood behind me with his caddie. He held a three-metal. At 2:45, the sun was an orange blaze in the distance. The breeze fell still. As I stood in the address position, I felt the calm I had found over each shot that day—sounds vanished, mind blank, arms loose. Muscle memory and trust. I made another good swing.

This time, the game bit me.

The ball hit the right side of the fairway, as I'd hoped, but kicked hard left, ran to the short side, and found the bottom of the creek.

"It was a good swing," Silver said.

"Never seen a kick like that on this hole," General said. "Got cheated, buddy."

It had been a good swing. I knew that. I hit the ball where I had wanted. It landed where I envisioned it landing. I'd learned long ago to control only what you can in this game. It was why I never swing *at the ball.* I just swing the club. You can control your swing and vary it, attempting to make the ball do what you want, but that's all. Once the ball leaves the club face, much of the result is beyond your control. The game deals the deck. You play the hand you're dealt.

The creek running through the fairway was a lateral water hazard, which meant I was hitting three and had several choices: I could either replay the shot, go back two club lengths from the point at which the ball entered the creek, or move back as far as I liked and drop, so long as the point at which the ball entered the hazard remained directly between myself and the hole.

I didn't say anything as Silver and I walked to where General was hitting. I had hoped to jump to ten under par. Now I was playing my third shot and still had roughly 250 yards to the green.

A gallery somewhere reacted positively. Maybe someone had carefully navigated a break and sank a long putt. Maybe someone hit an approach shot to tap-in range. My guess was the crowd was not cheering a conservative yet well-struck lay-up. Beside Silver and me, two fans argued whether I should have attempted the aggressive tee shot. In front of me, Dan Ferrin was there, so I knew the tournament was being aired on CBS. Without Lisa, I wasn't aware of which network was hosting the event each week.

"It's a catch twenty-two," Ferrin was saying as Silver and I passed him. "Not many players out here have the length Jack Austin does, so he'd be silly not to utilize it. Just got away from him there."

Silver and I paused to watch General hit his second shot. He had well over 300 yards to the green and held what looked to be a five-iron. He would position the ball probably 120 yards from the hole with the five-iron and play a nine or wedge to the green. I couldn't argue with that strategy. Good common sense. But on this hole, the drive is downhill. My tee shot hadn't worked out as I'd planned; however, I had wanted eagle here.

At the creek, I used my driver for the two club-lengths and dropped.

Silver set the bag down between us. He bent and tossed grass into the air. It fell straight down.

"How do you feel?" he said.

I nodded.

It was all he needed. He pulled the three-metal and raised his brows.

"Yeah," I said. "Two forty-seven from the hazard. Five-wood might get me there, but I don't want to screw around with that water in front of the green."

"No breeze here. Might be a slight cross breeze in front of the green."

I took two slow practice swings, envisioning the ball rising against the sky, leveling off, then descending, and landing softly on the green.

"Think three-wood is too much club?" I said.

"Your three-wood carries two sixty. Five-wood carries two forty. Long is safe."

I nodded again and addressed the ball.

The contact was not crisp this time, and when the ball landed in the front rough but crept onto the green, I was glad I'd taken the extra club. I was still putting for birdie.

.   .   .

At the green, Silver was smirking as he looked at the line the ball would track to the hole. "Do I get a bonus for excellent clubbing?"

"Helping with club selection is in your job description."

"So no bonus?"

"You get an *'atta boy.*"

"But I'm brilliant," he said, crouching to examine the break.

We had eighteen feet. The elevated green meant slope, which meant break.

"Six inches, left to right," he said.

He was an excellent green reader as well, but didn't need me to tell him. I checked the same line, saw the break the same as he had, and walked to the edge of the green. General, with a pitching wedge, had mis-hit and left himself twenty feet for birdie. Silver, Dan Ferrin and I watched as his ball fell into the cup.

"Still some bark in this old dog," General said.

Ferrin relayed the comment to the viewers and smiled.

"We've seen one traditional birdie," he said. "Maybe we can see what would definitely be a nontraditional birdie. Jack Austin has this for a four, from eighteen feet."

I stood over the ball and thought, *Three-second stroke.* I made two long, three-second practice strokes, exhaled, then carefully placed the blade behind the ball, looked up one last time, then drew the putter back, and followed through. The ball tracked and dropped into the heart of the hole. I was nine under par.

.   .   .

An hour and a half later, I was still nine under as I stood near the eighteenth green. The eighteenth is a par four, 444 yards. I had hit driver off the tee, avoiding the right-side bunkers, landing far enough left to be able to play the dogleg with my approach, which I'd done, hitting seven-iron to twelve feet. Now I stood next to Silver at the edge of the green and watched General line up a putt.

"He's frustrated," Silver said, motioning to General.

It was true. After the lone birdie at eleven, General made par after par, putts burning the edges all day, nothing falling. Now he was muttering under his breath. He drew the putter back slowly, made a smooth stroke, and the ball tumbled into the cup.

He threw his arms into the air in self-mockery. Members of the gallery laughed.

Silver and I moved to my ball.

"Okay, bossman," Silver said, "straight back and through."

I nodded. In my mind's eye, I was envisioning the ball rolling, the Titleist label again blurring, the ball tumbling into the cup. Leader boards had told me Tiger was dismantling the back nine—five under on holes ten through fourteen, seventeen under par overall. On this day, the leader board was my ally— my name moved up; other names dropped. Saturday is called "moving day" because many players make moves, up or down. Only two under par on the day, I had leaped several players and now was in third, one behind David Toms, who was six behind Woods.

This putt was important. Woods was renowned as the greatest closer ever to play the game. If he carried the lead into a Sunday, he usually also carried the trophy home. But if I could post a sixty-eight—ten under, overall—I could give myself a chance. I'd shot sixty-five many times over the years, just not consecutively often enough. Yet, if I could drop this putt, effectively making tomorrow an eighteen-hole shootout, anything could happen. Woods could shoot seventy-four Sunday, and I could post sixty-five—and win.

I took several practice strokes and reviewed the line again. When the putt fell, Silver was quickly at my side.

He raised his hand for five, but I gave him a hug instead.

"Is that my bonus, cutie?" he said.

I grinned and shoved him away.

We were both smiling. The sixty-eight had us ten strokes under par and in third place. More importantly, we were back in contention.

"Are you calling to ask how I could possibly shoot sixty-nine two days in a row," I said, "then a sixty-eight?"

I leaned against the bed's headboard, cell phone shrugged to my ear. Back in the hotel room at 7:25 P.M., I had been watching the Red Sox play the Detroit Tigers on ESPN. It was the bottom of the first inning, and I was waiting for room service.

"I'm calling—your daughter and I are calling—to congratulate you," Lisa said. "Third place heading into the final round. You'll be playing with J. P. Hayes, Sunday."

"Sounds good." It made me smile. She'd already looked up final-round pairings on the Internet.

"Did you try to call last night?" she said.

"Last night was crazy."

It took fifteen minutes to tell her the previous day's events, including the Lynne Ashley sighting, dinner with Jim Dempsey, and my after-dinner meeting with Tim Silver. When I finished, she was quiet.

"I'm glad things went well with Tim," she finally said.

"Silver's a good caddie."

"And your good friend. But he has to have faith in your approach. In the past, he's always believed in you."

There was a knock at the door. I kept the cell phone pinched between my shoulder and ear as I let in room service. When I re-assumed my position, propped against the headboard, a plate of tuna and Swiss cheese sandwiches lay on the bed. Two bottles of Heineken stood on the nightstand.

"I watched the round on television and followed your shots on the Internet," she said. "The way you played the eleventh was unique. They showed it several times. It made ESPN's *Sports-Center*'s Top Ten."

"That's a first," I said. "Is that Darcy I hear?"

"It is. She misses you. That was a world-class birdie, Jack. Tell me about it."

"Thought you retired?"

"I'm still working, just writing more."

Retirement was out for her. I knew that. In my mind's eye, I could see a white-haired Lisa, wearing her best Talbots outfit, sitting attentively through a retirement-home twilight league match, pen and pad at the ready, getting results for the "Old Folks Newsletter."

"I made a really good swing. The ball kicked and found the water. I thought, if I could make that same swing again, I could reach the green and still have a birdie putt."

"I don't think Dan Ferrin gave you enough credit," she said.

"I just wanted to give myself a chance, Sunday. Tiger is tough with the lead, as you know." I heard my own voice and thought this indeed sounded like an on-air interview. "But if I can go out a group ahead of him, post a low number, at least I can give him something to think about."

"I like this new aggressive approach," she said. "I understand it."

A television played in the next room. Someone knocked on a door in the hallway.

"You do?" I said.

"Yes."

"Well?"

"It's time for you to win," she said matter-of-factly.

"That's right."

I was a grown man, one who overcame a learning disability to graduate college, a husband, a father, a professional athlete. As I had told Tim Silver, I had not discussed my strategy—or the state of my game—with her. Yet her statement in support of my approach relieved me, as if I needed her endorsement without knowing it. I'd traveled worldwide and had dated other women. However, when I'd begun dating Lisa, it hadn't taken long to realize she was special, different from everyone else. The world saw her on television and knew she was smart and beautiful, but she was much more. She had walked away from her dream job to care for our child and to allow me to continue pursuing the career I'd always dreamed of. She loved Darcy and cherished being her mother, but Lisa had put herself through college, then graduate school, worked her way up the journalistic ladder to the *Washington Post,* then to CBS. In her chosen line of work, she'd been a major champion. And she'd walked away. For Darcy. For me, too.

"How's the article going?" I said.

"Done. E-mailed it to the *Post* this morning. I described Lynne as 'young and sensitive' and didn't mention her departure."

Both beds were made, but there was no doubt I was rooming with Perkins this week. His clothes were strewn throughout. I saw a bullet, like a thick copper tee, protruding from beneath a pair of boxer shorts on the desk.

"Where is Lynne Ashley now?"

"That's the million-dollar question," I said. "Perkins says she never returned to her room last night, so he called Grant at home."

"How is Grant handling the affair?"

"Perkins didn't mention it."

"Grant doesn't know?"

"I don't know," I said. "Grant told Perkins he hadn't seen or heard from Lynne. But Grant told him he's sure Lynne is fine, wherever she is."

"Is she still registered at the hotel?"

"Through Sunday."

"She could've planned on Grant making the cut and paid through the weekend, then left when he didn't make it."

"Possibly, but she obviously didn't leave with Grant. Besides, I don't think she was here to see Grant play golf."

"She was there to see Jim Dempsey?"

"Yeah."

She was quiet, thinking that over.

I took a bite of tuna sandwich. Few foods are better than tuna, be it sandwiches or grilled steaks.

"He really said he's in love?" she said.

"That's what he said."

"You sound like you don't believe him."

"It's not that, exactly," I said. "I'm confused and frustrated."

"You thought you knew Jim Dempsey well. Now you realize maybe you didn't."

I didn't answer. Was that it? Possibly. More than anything, I was mad at Dempsey. He'd thrown away everything—marriage, kids, home—for Lynne. He was working on tossing his career, too. I DATE CLIENTS' WIVES would not make a good slogan on business cards. Maybe I was angrier with Lynne. She was juggling my two friends.

I had muted the television, but the screen told me the Red Sox were already down three. It was the top of the third inning. Uncharacteristically, Pedro Martinez was getting roughed up by the lowly Tigers.

"Playing the PGA Tour takes a partnership," I said. "I don't think Lynne was ever willing to make sacrifices."

"Jack, Jim Dempsey played a role in this. So did Grant. You don't know what kind of husband Grant was. A lot of Tour wives make huge sacrifices."

"I don't know one player who doesn't appreciate what his wife does."

"Maybe Grant didn't," she said. "You never know what goes on in a marriage behind closed doors."

I thought back to my conversation with Grant on the golf course, before he'd reverted back to his all-is-well mode. He was a kid, and I believed he was in love with Lynne. Maybe I wanted to believe that.

"Regardless of Grant as a husband," I said, "nothing justifies an affair."

"I agree."

"They've only been married seven months."

Beyond the darkening window, the final minutes of sunlight waned. Soon the lights of Columbus, Ohio, would illuminate the evening.

"Grant is a kid with a lot of problems right now," I said. "Silver says his caddie is doing drugs. His agent is a mess—divorced, drunk, even cheated with Grant's own wife."

"Jim Dempsey is your agent, too. You should think about that."

"Yeah. Perkins pointed that out."

"And?"

"And I've known him a long time."

"So you're sticking with him?"

I didn't answer.

She sighed.

I could envision her shaking her head as if to say, *Typical.*

"People make their own decisions, Jack. Jim Dempsey and Grant Ashley are grown men, who made poor decisions that spilled over onto each other."

"Dempsey's got two kids."

She waited.

"I've met his wife, had dinner at their home, taught his son how to swing a golf club. It was a nice family."

"There's nothing you can do."

I didn't say anything. The Tigers had men on the corners with one out, but Pedro forced the batter to ground into a double play. People say sport imitates life. I thought of Dempsey and wished it worked the other way around—I wished he could toss up a double-play ball and walk away from all this. More than anything, I hoped he came to his senses.

I heard Darcy cry.

"I'll let you go," Lisa said. Then, with forced enthusiasm: "Taking Darcy to the Children's Museum of Maine tomorrow."

"Sounds fun."

And it did, but Lisa had spoken of sacrifices. She was in Maine—living on the waterfront, listening to waves crash, caring for our beautiful infant daughter, who smelled of powder and spring breezes, and whom Lisa loved more than anything. Still, it all meant Lisa was not in the tower behind the eighteenth green or in the press tent or asking casual questions to players in the hotel lobby. Like a pinch, I felt a twinge of guilt.

"Make sure Darcy hits some range balls, too," I said.

We said our good-byes.

"Play well tomorrow," she said.

"I plan to."

"And, Jack . . ."

"Yeah?"

"Stay aggressive. I have a good feeling about tomorrow."

.   .   .

By the bottom of the fifth inning, the Red Sox were down six runs to a last-place team. I turned off the television and sat at the circular table in the corner of the room. A light hung from the ceiling above the table. The air conditioner was the only sound as I read Philip Levine's poem "I Could Believe." Usually, reading poetry helps pass the time and allows me to relax. This poem, however, didn't offer serenity. It made me think of Jim Dempsey.

> When I can't stand it
> I drive out past the lights . . .
> Except for the dying this
> would be heaven and I,
> 37 years old, would be
> a man I could talk to
> or a body fallen away
> to the dust of Spain,
> a white face becoming
> water, a name no one
> names . . .

Perkins and I had twice dined with Dempsey. The first night, my agent had sounded desperate, lonely, and confused. He'd embarrassed himself by drinking excessively and said his marriage "just didn't work out." He'd said other things that made him sound pathetic. The next evening, he had sounded flighty, lovesick, and above my criticism. He had walked away when I'd called him on his affair, saying he knew I wouldn't understand. He'd been married twelve years.

I had heard of people simply falling out of love. Like everyone, I had friends who were divorced. I knew the statistics—one in two. Divorce was part of society.

So what was bothering me?

The Levine book lay open, pages down, on the circular table, the overhead light reflecting off its glossy cover. For the decade I had known him, Dempsey always seemed contented. That was the change. The drinking came from somewhere. Something was eating at him. Guilt? Sorrow? Failure? All three? Lisa was right. He had made poor decisions, as Grant had, decisions that led to each man's current struggle.

I thought about that as I got a water glass and set it on its side in the middle of the room. My Arnold Palmer blade-style putter had made the trip from the course to the hotel and leaned against the wall. I was entering the stage in my life—husband, father—that Dempsey had thrown away. To me, it was sacred. How could it not be to Dempsey? Surely not everyone was like me, but something was bothering Dempsey. Was there more to what he was saying?

From ten feet, I dropped three balls to the carpet and stroked them at the glass. One hit the back of the cup. The others stopped well short; going from Jack's greens at Muirfield Village to thick hotel carpeting does not offer consistent speed.

If Grant knew of Lynne's affair, it might explain his denial, his everything-is-fine stance.

There was a common blonde denominator Grant and Dempsey shared in this equation. Dempsey said Lynne came to him, asking about an acting career. Seduction? Manipulation? Sure, although I found it tough to believe a grown man could be seduced against his will. But I did believe Lynne was the type to give it a hell of a try.

I retrieved the three Pro V1 balls and made two practice strokes before the second round of attempts. I had putted well this week—twenty-seven putts Thursday, two less Friday, and twenty-five again this day. Now, though, I wasn't concentrating on my stroke. Putting was something to counter nervous energy. The next day, I would play a group ahead of the world's best golfer, Tiger Woods, a man who might well end up the best ever to play. In contention heading into a final round, I was seven back—excited, anxious, and nervous.

I made two of three putts.

There was something else going on with Grant, Dempsey,

and Lynne. Grant Ashley was a kid, not even twenty-five. He had been a friend since joining the Tour. He had agitated the hell out of me in the locker room, interrupting my phone conversation with Lisa. Yet on the golf course, the place where it seems a person's inner weaknesses always surface, he'd told me Lynne had said she loved him. It had been a lie. He must know that now. Nevertheless, at twenty-four years old, Grant Ashley had planned a life with her. He'd married her, bought a house. Was he naive? No more than I had been at twenty-four.

I set the putter aside. Thick carpeting was not going to help my stroke. If anything, it would confuse my judgement of the greens' speed.

I used Cleveland wedges and, as always, had one in my hotel room, a fifty-six–degree sand wedge. I dragged the balls to the foot of my bed, opened my stance, and made an outside-to-in abbreviated swing.

The ball popped into the air and settled in the middle of the bed.

Everything Grant acquired in Lynne—family and home— Jim Dempsey lost at least partly because of her. As a father, I now knew Dempsey had given up much more, in fact. The weight of that knowledge tugged at me.

I had worked hard this week and played well. Moreover, I was focused. For so long I'd been a lone man, going city to city, riding a dream, earning what I made, practicing endlessly. Everything changed during the winter, and I had thought I was ready for the change. However, one thing had been unexpected: sitting before the fire—Lisa across the room reading peacefully—Darcy had lain in the crux of my arm, eyes closed, hair smelling of an autumn breeze. After a decade on Tour, I had a home to go to.

It meant I had a home to leave each time I played golf on the PGA Tour. Jim Dempsey had lost that. Grant Ashley had, too.

.   .   .

By 9:30 P.M., sandwiches eaten, beer drunk, the television was on again, and I was considering the endless struggle of the Red

Sox fan. A non-fan, or, worse, a Yankees fan, should appreciate the full experience: Spring leads to optimism; June and July raise hopes; August crushes you. Annually. Death, taxes, and late-season slumps. It doesn't end there. As a Red Sox fan, from age eight or nine, I knew my duty—follow the entire season, blow by painstaking blow.

It explains why I was torturing myself by watching post-game interviews that told exactly how we had gotten killed by the last-place Detroit Tigers. Philip Levine was from Detroit. At least he was happy. The cell phone beeped. I answered it gladly.

"Congratulations."

The voice was raspy and carried an unmistakable Maine accent. When, to Silver and Schultz, the walls of my game had begun to crumble and panic ensued, my father, living less than two hours north, had not mentioned it.

"Right on Tiger's tail," he said, *Tiger* pronounced *Tig-ah.*

"I'm seven back, but thanks for the call."

"You sound tired."

"I'm watching the Red Sox post-game interviews and analysis."

"That explains it. Me, too. I thought it was safe to watch, since Pedro was pitching."

"Slump is beginning early this year," I said.

"Yours is over. You're back on track. Working out, range balls, putting?"

It made me grin. To Dad, work ethic meant everything. "All of the above, coach."

"It's good to step back every now and then."

"Except we don't have guaranteed contracts or league-minimum salaries," I said. "You eat what you earn in golf."

"That's what makes it great. Sixty-nines and a sixty-eight at Muirfield Village is good scoring."

I didn't say anything. Even over the phone, silences were comfortable with my father.

"We're heading south to see the baby tomorrow," he said. "Your *moth-ah*'s goin' nuts over that girl. I'd just as soon avoid the traffic. Portland's like Boston now."

"Lisa will be happy to see you."

"How's she doing, staying home?"

"Tonight, she questioned me about how the weather affected the course."

He chuckled. "She's a reporter."

"Now she's a mother, too."

The room was getting cold. I went to the air conditioner, adjusted it, and stood looking out the window.

"Jack, I wanted to call, tell you I was proud that you pulled out of the slump."

"I've had rough patches before."

"Not like this. This wasn't mechanical, was it?"

I paused. "No."

The television was muted. We were quiet once more. Beyond the window, I watched cars pull into and out of the parking lot.

"Your gift is your work ethic," he said. "It's hard to work a lot with a new baby."

"You saw the slump coming?"

"Not exactly. But I understand why some golfers take two, three, four months off after having a baby."

"I couldn't afford to do that."

"Now you're back, playing like you can. One big check and you're on safe ground."

"A win would mean a two-year exemption."

"Yeah." He paused.

I knew my father, knew his pauses. He was collecting his thoughts. I waited.

"It took time to adjust to flying home, seeing that baby and your wife, then flying off every week."

"Yes."

"You've got good friends, you know. Silver and Perkins each called me."

"I figured."

"Jack, I've wanted to say something and have waited till now, till you and your game were back on your feet. I knew pride and motivation would bring you around, but there's something I've been biting my tongue about."

I took in some air. A lot of us had been introduced to golf by our fathers. Thus, I'd rather have been face-to-face with the Tour commissioner discussing a policy violation than gazing out the darkened window, phone shrugged to my ear, hearing the edge in my father's voice.

"The way I see it," he said, "you've got the best job in the world. You get paid a hell of a lot of money to play golf. You're too old to get homesick, son. It's your job and it has a downside. But it's your job. You don't like the job, come pound nails with me."

When Dempsey asked if the nights were long in quiet hotel rooms, I'd said mine was the world's best job. But Dad had never been one to hold back.

"That's why I kept playing," I said. "Fighting through it."

"Nice playing this week, son."

"Thanks."

"If your priorities weren't in order you wouldn't struggle with all this."

"I hadn't thought of that."

There was a knock at the door. I told Dad someone was there.

"I'll let you go," he said. "Good luck tomorrow. Lisa said we'll watch on television and follow the TOURcast on the Internet. You have a target score?"

"Sixty-five," I said, moving to the door.

"Tall order."

"Yeah."

I reached the door and pulled it open.

"I love you, son."

Dad's words drew me from my frozen stare.

"Me, too."

The fresh fragrance of wildflowers seemed to dance on the air as she brushed past me into the room.

I closed the door.

"And, Dad . . ."

"Yeah?"

"Point taken," I said.

We hung up, and I stood staring at Lynne Ashley.

16

*L*ynne Ashley was sitting in the wicker chair beside the circular table in my hotel room, which now smelled of her lilac fragrance.

"Can I have a cigarette?" she said, tiredly.

Standing before her, I shook my head. "Sorry."

"That's okay. Guess you wouldn't be a smoker, would you?"

Lynne wore a navy blue suit, a white silk blouse beneath the blazer. The skirt, as her shorts had been the previous afternoon, was very short, and a great deal of her crossed legs showed. She had on navy blue halter-strap leather heels. Her fingernails were painted rose, and the diamond on her left hand took up most of the room.

But something was different. Intensely.

Her short blond hair was worn as it had been in my living room only one week before. Yet the brown fawnlike eyes, which supposedly had squinted against sunlight during her cheerleading career at the University of Georgia, weren't vivid now. This wasn't the woman who had worn the skirt suit and sat erectly in Chandler, Maine, firing insults. In fact, I'd seen her only one day earlier, but only briefly, and although I'd been focused on golf then, I knew her bearing now didn't resemble that of the woman who'd confidently worn can't-miss short-shorts in the rain and stood staring at me even after Dempsey had gone. Her fiery gaze wasn't there now.

"I need . . ."—she took in a long breath and exhaled slowly—"to talk to you."

I nodded. She looked exhausted, her firm and lithe body gone slack. Her jawbone was flexed, and there were dark rings beneath her eyes. She looked like a debutante at the end of an anxiety-filled ball.

"Can I have a drink?" she said.

"Beer is all I have."

She nodded. I went to the bathroom, got a bottle of Heineken from the sink, opened it, and took the paper dust cover off a water glass. Perkins and I drank from the bottle, but guests, even those worn out from home wrecking, got a glass.

As I poured, I tried to put a finger on the change. You play golf for a living long enough, you learn to trust gut instincts.

"Here you go." I handed her the glass, set the open beer on the table in front of her, and sat facing her on the edge of the bed.

Lynne took most of the short water glass in one swoop, which contrasted startlingly with her business outfit. She looked like she'd just stepped off the cover of *People,* yet drank like a beer drinker, like someone who went to bars, watched a game, maybe shot a little pool. Daily. Grant had said he'd partied too much. Probably been trying to keep up.

"Thanks," Lynne said. Her voice had a southern twang any Mainer would notice.

"People are looking for you," I said. "Some concerned people."

She nodded and drank more beer.

"You know that?"

"That the big blond guy is looking for me? Yeah." She leaned her head against the chair, as if the beer had offered more than I was aware of. "That's why I came. I need to talk to you."

"Me?"

She shrugged. "Not the cop following me. *You.*"

"Perkins isn't a cop."

"Doesn't matter. He's like a cop for the Tour. I can't go to him."

I was going to ask why, but she was here for a reason. She'd get to it.

Her hands lay atop the small purse in her lap, her eyes on them. With her right index finger and thumb, she twirled the dime-sized engagement ring, staring at it, thinking.

Maybe I was hung up on her attire, but there was something to the business suits. She drank beer like she'd be comfortable in T-shirts and dungarees. However, she'd worn a suit on a Saturday morning to an informal interview. Now she had one on at nearly eleven on a Saturday night in my hotel room. More than anything, though, what struck me was that the formal attire seemed to go with Lynne's natural persona like a nun at a frat party. Her appearance was calculated.

At my house, she'd wanted to say, *It ain't you.* I'd grown up around contractors and carpenters on building projects. There was nothing wrong with that talk. So why did Lynne seem to force the *It ain't you* away by wearing business suits? Maybe it had to do with the acting career. Were actors expected to appear formal at all times, professional, and, thus, not *It ain't you?* I'd played the AT&T Pebble Beach National Pro-Am—home of Bill Murray—plenty of times. So I knew better. The clothes were part of a front for something involving a couple of my friends, Grant and Dempsey. I wanted to know what was behind the front.

"I want the big blond guy to stop looking for me. I can't go back to my room because he's been sitting outside it."

"Perkins is trying to find you. The Tour commissioner is concerned."

She shook her head. "Grant called *you.* Not the almighty PGA Tour. He called you, *at your house.* It's not the PGA Tour's business."

"Perkins was there when Grant called. He works for the Tour, and it was a player's missing wife. It became the Tour's business. The Tour is a close-knit group."

"Too close-knit."

I didn't respond.

"Jack," she said, her eyes softening, her voice suddenly intimate, "I was out when Grant tried to reach me. He panicked and called you." A smile slowly appeared. "Grant's sweet like that. He worries about me."

The guy was, after all, her husband. It was late, and I had a huge day ahead. But the more she talked, the more I would learn, so I nodded encouragingly.

She nodded back. "I thought you'd understand. You're an understanding man." She leaned closer, tilting her head, smiling.

At once she looked farm fresh and innocent—yet sexy, too. It was a surprising juxtaposition and offered insight into precisely how and why Grant Ashley had taken up partying and married her, and why Jim Dempsey had thrown away everything to be with her. The look also reminded me of my first reaction to her in Maine and made me think her sexuality seemed to appear almost with the ease of her accent, as if she hit a switch when it was needed.

The girl with the curl. Except she knew she had the curl—and how to use it.

"You seemed sensitive when we met at your house," she said. "That's what I told Grant and Jim—that you were reasonable."

I waited.

"Especially compared to Peter Barrett," she said. "I mean, Jesus Christ, he's the Tour commissioner, and he told Grant, if the search went on and police felt Grant 'hindered the investigation,' the police could take legal action—and if they did, Grant would be suspended by the Tour."

She waited for my reply, which didn't come.

"Well, Christ, I mean, who the hell does Barrett think he is? Grant needs golf more than ever right now. You can see that, can't you?"

"You've spoken to Grant?"

"Of course."

"And I saw you with Dempsey."

"We're all in it together."

"In what?"

Like a shade being pulled down, her casual expression turned defensive. She reached for the beer on the table and took a long pull. In the hallway outside the room, people laughed and talked loudly. Someone ran down the corridor. It was Saturday, and there was a party somewhere.

Lynne put the bottle on the table again and blew out a long breath. "This started with you. I need for you to know everything and everyone is fine."

"Okay, I know it."

"And I need you to get your friend off my back. I want the Tour and everyone to let it all go."

"What is 'it all'?"

"What?" Her accent had thickened. *What* took nearly three seconds. She drank some beer.

She wanted to be an actor and was going all out here, but I wasn't buying it. She was no fool; she was avoiding my questions. I got myself a beer, turned the air conditioner down, and sat across from her on the edge of the bed again.

"Will you do that," she said, "for me?"

"What exactly do you want me to do? You were missing; now you're not. Put the Little-Miss-Innocent act on for Barrett. Tell him you were shopping, and Grant confused the dates. And that'll be that."

"There is no act. I can't go to Barrett. I told you."

"Then tell Perkins."

"Have you been listening to me?"

"You can talk to Perkins."

"I ditched him at the mall. *You* tell him everything is fine."

"He followed you?"

She nodded.

"Tough to ditch Perkins."

"I've been followed before," she said.

"Who followed you before Perkins?"

She shook her head. "That was before all of this."

"Tell me about it."

"Just call him off. The Tour has no right."

"To help a player locate his wife? After the player expresses concern? The Tour probably has a legal obligation. A lot of liberty has been taken as it is because Grant requested to wait to call the cops. Soon, the authorities are being brought in."

"I'm fine. Grant's fine. It was just a bad mistake."

"What was a mistake?"

She shook her head, annoyed.

"Be realistic. You think Peter Barrett is going to take my word on this? This is the guy's career. I wouldn't take a secondhand assurance, if I were commissioner."

"The cops aren't involved yet," she said, quietly, staring at the floor. "That's why I came to you—to get this stopped before the Tour goes to them. When they go to the cops, the clock strikes twelve for me, Jack. I'm asking for help."

Desperation was present in her voice. It hadn't been there before. It replaced the attitude I'd heard in Maine, and the manipulative tone she'd used with the southern-belle twang earlier.

For the first time, I heard sincerity and honesty. I sat back on the bed.

"Lynne, why is it so terrible if you tell Barrett or the cops you're fine?"

"Because I know people who've done this before."

"What the hell does that mean?"

She was staring at me, her gaze tight, eyes locked on mine. She wasn't backing down. Any type of authority was out of the equation.

"I'm not a cop, Lynne. I'm a dad and a golfer. And I'm not the Tour commissioner."

"Will you help me?"

"I don't think I can."

"Yes, you can. People trust you. Grant told me what you did for Hutch Gainer and how you tried to help Brian Taylor's little girl. Talk to them. You're my last chance."

"Last chance at what?"

She looked at me for several seconds, deciding how far to go. Then she nodded to herself and said, "Freedom."

"Jesus Christ." I shook my head.

"Jack, I need help."

I exhaled.

"Jack, please."

"If he'll see me, I'll talk to Barrett. It probably will do no good."

For all I had learned, I could've said it twenty minutes earlier and saved myself the headache of her repeatedly vague answers.

"But I do want to know one thing," I said.

"What?"

"Why'd you pick Jim Dempsey to use? Why ruin his marriage?"

"What do you mean?"

"Dempsey is a sports agent. He's got a wife and kids. There must be a million agents who could help you try to break in to acting. Why Dempsey? Why ruin *his* marriage?"

"I don't know what you're talking about."

"Cut the crap, Lynne. Give one straight answer tonight."

She sat up and leaned forward. Her blue eyes narrowed. Her face turned hard. "You self-righteous ass. You don't know a fucking thing about me. You've got a pretty and smart wife, a baby, money, a house on the ocean. How dare you judge me. You know nothing about me."

"I know you married a kid I like and are dumping him to latch on to his—and my—agent. I know you're ruining my agent's marriage and his life with his kids."

"Is that what you think—that all this is about me? Jim never said I used him."

"Oh, no. He's in puppy love."

Her head shook slowly. "I've been telling you everything, and you don't understand a thing."

"Then tell me what's going on between you, Grant, and Dempsey."

"I did: I thought I loved Grant. I love Jim."

"Where did you go when you left my house?"

"It's not important."

"Grant says some nights you need to talk. What's that mean?"

"It's between him and me."

"Then I'm out of this," I said.

I set down my beer, three-quarters full, and slid it to the center of the table. It was late. I had the most important golf round of my life the next afternoon, and this was making me tired.

"You push and push, don't you?" she said.

"You're asking me to trust you."

We sat looking at each other. The air conditioner cycled on. I heard a television playing in an adjacent room.

"All right," she said. "I made a mistake with Grant. I thought I loved him. We both thought we were in love."

"What if he still is?"

"I don't like to think about that."

"Maybe you have to."

"Maybe I can't."

I exhaled and shook my head.

"Don't judge me. It had been so long since anything meant anything. I just didn't know."

I waited.

"Now I do know," she said. "I'm in love this time. I never knew it could happen. I've done a lot I'm ashamed of, things I never want anyone to know."

"That's why no cops."

She didn't answer.

"I'm not hiding a fugitive or covering up a crime, Lynne."

"Nothing like that. I just need help. Will you call everyone off?"

I looked at her carefully. Her eyes pleaded.

"I need you to trust me," she said.

"That's asking a lot. I know nothing about you or what's going on."

"I know. I have no one else."

"Christ," I said. "I'll try."

She slouched forward as if the air had left her body. Then she smiled, relieved.

"Did you go to the University of Georgia?" I said.

"Of course I went there."

"When?"

She stood. "I'm tired, Jack. Thank you so very much."

I sat in her lilac wake, watched the door close behind her, and shook my head at all she wasn't saying.

This room did not smell of lilacs.

Sunday at 7:45 A.M., Perkins and I sat with PGA Tour Commissioner Peter Barrett in the dining room at Muirfield Village. The aroma of strong coffee mixed with Barrett's Polo cologne, which always reminded me of the scent of Maine pines. Barrett sat looking at me, waiting to find out why Perkins scheduled the meeting, said I had to be there, and called the whole thing "crucial." I felt as comfortable as a sixth grader who'd asked to speak to the principal.

I had awakened before 6:00, and, thankfully, the day's first thoughts had been not of Lynne Ashley, Grant, and Jim Dempsey. In fact, my predawn musings had been positive, contemplating the knowledge that all around Muirfield Village, leader boards listed mine among surnames at the top: T. WOODS, −17; D. TOMS, −11; J. AUSTIN, −10; and J. P. HAYES, −9.

But today's final round would not be easy. The weather wasn't cooperating—it was sunny with little or no wind. Woods was six shots clear of his closest competitor. Good scoring conditions, coupled with that size lead, would allow him to put the pedal to the metal and go at the pins all day.

"It's not even eight A.M.," Barrett said, after sipping some coffee. "I have an interview at eight-thirty and a meeting with our director of competitions at nine-fifteen."

"Commissioner," Perkins said, "I think you'll really want to hear what Jack has to say. It's about Lynne and Grant Ashley and Jim Dempsey."

"Dempsey? Jack's agent?"

Perkins nodded. "And Grant's."

I hadn't heard Perkins come in last night, but he'd slept in his clothes. When he'd awoken, I had told him of Lynne's visit. It had been like offering a starving pit bull a Wheat Thin cracker— he'd pummeled me with questions I couldn't answer.

"What's going on, Jack?" Barrett said.

Barrett was a smallish man who looked like he should be wearing a three-piece suit, toting a briefcase, cutting a deal. His actions were quick and concise. He had seen the Tiger era as a chance to grow the Tour, and he had done so, landing huge television contracts, which, much to my liking, generated staggering weekly purses. Barrett wore a white polo shirt with the PGA Tour emblem on the breast and black trousers. His cordovan loafers had tassels. He reached forward and snared a warm roll from the bread basket in the center of the table.

"Lynne Ashley came to my hotel room last night," I said, spooning sugar into my coffee. "She asked that I speak with you, sir."

Barrett looked at Perkins. "You took her to see Jack?"

"No, commissioner," Perkins said. "Embarrassingly, I was looking for her when she went to Jack's room."

"I thought you found her?"

It was tough to watch Perkins squirm, but he took it on the chin.

"I had Lynne Ashley under surveillance," he said. "She went into Victoria's Secret in the mall, went to a changing room. I never saw her come out. I told the lady at the counter *my wife* had been in there awhile. When they couldn't find Lynne, they were ready to call the cops. Took me a half hour to get out of there without a call to police. I apologize."

"She told me she'd been followed previously," I said.

"By Perkins?"

I shook my head. "I think her life was very different before Grant."

Barrett thought about that as he chewed the last of his roll.

"She said she thought she was in love last fall when she married Grant. Last night, she said, 'It had been so long since anything meant anything' that she now knows she made a mistake."

"'So long since anything meant anything'?" Barrett said. "What does she mean? Relationships?"

"I don't know. She asked me to tell you that she and Grant are fine."

Barrett looked at Perkins, then back to me. He spread his hands. "Let me say it again, gentlemen: It is not even eight in the morning. What are we talking about here? This is what I hired you for, Mr. Perkins. Tell me what is going on."

"I haven't spoken to Lynne. But she wants nothing to do with authorities. I don't know why. She and Grant are on the verge of divorcing."

Perkins told him about Dempsey. I sipped coffee and listened.

"Why not come and tell me herself?" Barrett said, as the waitress reappeared with our meals: Wheaties and orange juice for me; juice for Barrett; and for Perkins—steak and eggs, whole-wheat toast, orange juice, a side of hash browns, and extra sausage.

Barrett shook his head and grinned. "Take it easy on the expense account."

Perkins smiled. Although formal, their relationship, despite the glaring personality differences, seemed amiable.

"Commissioner, what's the Tour's stake in this?" I said.

"What do you mean?" Barrett said.

"Something's very wrong with Lynne Ashley and her scenario with Grant and Jim Dempsey. But Lynne was missing and now is not. Does the Tour's interest end there?"

Barrett drank some juice and looked around the room like a ruler surveying his land. "I'm commissioner of the greatest professional sport in the world. It's my duty to watch over, grow, and nurture the Tour. Anything that may go against those goals is my business." He looked at me, then Perkins. "Could whatever is 'very wrong' damage the reputation of the game?"

"I don't know," I said.

"What Jack is getting at," Perkins said, "is that it's not the PGA Tour's job to prevent players and agents from screwing up their lives. It was different when this was a missing-person case."

Holding his juice glass in both hands, Barrett leaned back, sipped, then looked at me for several moments. "I see your point. Jack, are you suggesting I let this go?"

I thought about that. "I guess what I'm saying is I'm concerned for a couple of friends here—Jim and Grant. Dempsey's my agent, a guy I've known ten years. Grant is a kid I took under my wing when he was a rookie."

"There's a lot that doesn't fit," Perkins said. "We've got a blonde bombshell who we think married a Tour player for his money, but, if that's true, is trading down to be with his agent. And why wouldn't she just stop me in the mall and tell me everything's okay? And why did Grant go to Jack in the locker room? Why not see me? Again, why no officials? There's a reason for that."

"Your personality?" I said.

Barrett shot me a look.

"I'm like a cop, and cops make them uncomfortable."

I had spent maybe an hour, total, with Lynne Ashley. She was self-serving but tough, too, and streetwise. She'd been able to give Perkins the slip, so she could talk to me. And when I asked questions she didn't like—did she attend college with Grant?—she simply left. Everything was on her terms.

"Lynne Ashley is running this show," I said. "She chose Grant. Now she chooses Dempsey. She decides who to speak to and when."

"Blondes always run the show," Perkins said.

Barrett smiled.

"The thing is," I said, "I think Grant really loves her."

"But Lynne said she thought she loved Grant but was mistaken and now loves Jim Dempsey," Barrett said and looked at his gold watch. "This is making me tired. Perkins, do you see this turning into a P.R. nightmare? Yes or no, please. I want to prepare my staff."

"Commissioner," Perkins said, "I don't deal with yes-or-no scenarios. This is potentially bad for your tour. This woman has a past we can't figure out, but one that she doesn't want us to find out about. She said she met Grant at UGA. UGA Registrar's Office never head of her—as Lynne Ashley or Lynne Meredith, her alleged maiden name. When they got engaged, Atlanta papers offered noticeably little on her. I can find no parents, and the sibling I can locate died tragically on nine-eleven."

"I'm glad to know you're digging," Barrett said. "I want to know who she is. At the same time, I don't want a harassment suit on my hands."

"I understand," Perkins said.

"UGA Registrar?" I said. "You're not a bad detective."

Perkins grinned. "When I'm not making myself look like a peeper at Victoria's Secret."

Barrett smiled again. Maybe that was how two such different people coexisted. Perkins had finally found someone who thought he was funny.

The smile on Barrett's face didn't last long. He was a guy used to getting answers that he liked and getting ones he could organize and stack neatly before moving on to his next project.

Lynne Ashley wasn't going to be neat or easily organized. That was becoming clearer to all of us.

"Your wife usually has her finger on anything and everything," Barrett said to me. "And she's writing about Tour wives. She know anything about Lynne?"

I shook my head. He'd made a good point, though. Lisa could find information better than just about anyone. Contemplating that, Perkins ran a hand over his face, his thumb and forefinger meeting at the tip of his chin. I knew Lisa might get a call.

"So what do we have here?" Barrett said. "Lynne Ashley, who supposedly met Grant at UGeorgia, apparently did not. After eight months, she is divorcing Grant for his and Jack's agent, Jim Dempsey. She has no family. Lastly, she won't speak to any authority figures. I have a teenaged daughter who thinks like that."

"Not like that," I said. "Commissioner, Lynne was really terrified at the prospect of cops being brought in to look for her."

"What happens if cops look for her?" Barrett said to Perkins.

"They comb her past to see if there's anything that might account for her disappearance."

"Much like you are doing."

"Yeah."

"Stay at it," Barrett said, then to me: "Jack, how much of this does your wife know? I plan to call her. She'd be an asset, I think."

"I talk to her twice a day."

He nodded, understanding.

A young Hispanic man, with longish raven-colored hair, eyes like coal, and a small jagged scar on one cheekbone, approached our table. His name was Emilio. I had met him a year earlier when he'd been a CPA with the PGA Tour Charities Office. He had been a quick study then, and I had heard his work tracking greenbacks in Nikoli Silcandrov's money-laundering scheme now made him Barrett's right-hand man. He didn't look to be enjoying his job on this morning.

"Jack. Mr. Perkins." He looked at Barrett. "Commissioner, there's a situation I need to make you aware of." Emilio handed Barrett a neatly folded piece of paper.

Barrett shook his head. "I won't like this, will I?" He read the note. "Emilio, schedule a press conference for late this afternoon."

"Sir, it's Sunday."

"Right. Of course." Staring down at the table, thinking, Barrett ran a forefinger across his forehead.

I glanced at Perkins, who was looking at Barrett. We both knew it took a lot to shake Barrett.

"Save the late press conference for the tournament winner. Schedule mine for ten a.m."

Emilio nodded and dutifully walked away.

Then Barrett looked up at Perkins. He took in a lot of air and blew out slowly. Something caught in his throat and made a tiny whistling sound.

"A caddie was murdered last night between one and three a.m.," Barrett said.

"You okay, commissioner?" Perkins said.

"No, I'm not, especially given what you've both said here."

My stomach seemed to fall as I waited to hear the victim's name.

I can't speak to his state of mind or physical form, but to me—on the heels of Peter Barrett's telling Perkins and me who the dead caddie was—Tim Silver looked particularly vivacious when we met Sunday afternoon on the range.

Conversely, there would be no more stoned caddies walking PGA Tour fairways. No yardage guesses. Grant Ashley's caddie of a mere month was dead. Mike Easley had been stabbed four times in the back, according to Perkins, who, after Barrett excused me, had gone with the commissioner to congregate with local cops at the murder site, a parking lot at Ohio State University in Columbus.

Silver knew my routine and pulled the wedge from the bag. To both sides of us, players took frequent breaks from hitting balls to huddle in twos and threes and, I guessed, speculate. You couldn't help yourself: What had happened? What was Easley doing at Ohio State? To my knowledge, only a handful of people—Perkins, Silver, Dempsey, Grant, and I—knew Easley had been a stoner. Was he at OSU making a buy? The school year was over. Why was he there at 2 A.M.? I had last spoken to Perkins shortly after noon, and he'd told me, as of then, there were no witnesses, although cops planned to continue combing the area, questioning everyone. Also, Grant was flying back from Atlanta to meet with investigators. Likewise, Jim Dempsey and, ironically, Lynne Ashley had met with cops earlier that morning, Perkins had said, each claiming never to have spoken to Easley.

"Quiet out here today," I said to Silver and hit an easy wedge, the ball dancing around the hundred-yard marker.

The temperature was a perfect eighty-three; the humidity, at 87 percent, was less comfortable to a Mainer than to a guy from Houston, but tolerable nonetheless.

"Somber in the bag room, too," Silver said. "Even Stump Jones, who hated the kid, is upset."

I began every warm-up the same way—pitching wedge at about 50 percent. I flew another ball that bounced three times near the hundred-yard marker.

Silver nodded approvingly.

I held the follow-through. "Did Easley ask Stump for help?"

"Christ, no." He laughed. "Easley was no Nash Henley."

Nash and I had played practice rounds with Stump and two-time U.S. Open Champion Pete Taylor, and Stump had talked to Nash often about duties that accompanied the job and offered insight, which Nash had eaten up to the point of quoting from the U.S.G.A. publication *Official Rules of Golf*.

I hit ten wedge shots, all of which felt crisp. Next, I moved to my seven-iron. Full throttle, I could hit the seven 165 yards. I was, however, swinging about 85 percent and easing the ball at the 150-yard marker.

More spectators quickly crowded behind us. Tiger Woods and caddie Steve Williams appeared. They went to a spot next to David Toms, but Tiger wasn't chatting. He took a wood from the big Nike staff bag, set the club across his shoulders, and rotated his torso.

"Ever watch Mike Tyson fight early in his career?" Silver said. I nodded.

"Woods reminds me of that—that stare Tyson had. He'd enter the ring, meet the other guy in the center to touch gloves, and scare the bejesus out of the opponent. It was over before it began."

"Not today," I said and jumped on a four-iron. The Titleist rose slowly against the pale blue sky, leveled off, and finally descended, landing, and gently bounding beyond the 200-yard marker.

"Every Tyson has a Buster Douglas," Silver said, watching the ball. He held out his fist.

I tapped it lightly with mine.

"Run and gun, baby," he said.

.   .   .

Some days you know you're on from the first swing. This day was one of those, and the timing couldn't have been better. My drive on the 451-yard par-four first hole carried the bunkers on the right and stopped 141 yards from the pin.

Final rounds at the Memorial Tournament were just short of major championship status and people turned out to see them. This day was no different. My season's sudden rags-to-present-week-riches story had been featured in papers nationwide, and, as a leader, I'd been asked to the interview room after the third round. Although the crowd at each green seemed larger because many spectators arrive early and stake out a green-side claim for the day, no more than fifty, including my playing partner J. P. Hayes's wife, Laura, and two-year-old Hank, moved tee to green with us. This had long been Tiger's event. He'd won three times, and it was my sense that most fans had come to see Tiger win it again.

If I were being objective—which, as I walked the fairway, I certainly was not—I might have said Woods was a good bet. The sun was bright overhead at 1:27 P.M. with no rain in sight, meaning Tiger had six shots to gamble with, like a poker player with excess chips. But as I moved in step with Silver down the first fairway, I had only one thing on my mind: birdies. The course record was Kenny Perry's sixty-three. My target score of sixty-five would be close.

After breakfast, I had gone to the fitness van, rode the stationary bike, and read from Philip Levine's *New Selected Poems.* My goal had been to place myself amid the hubbub of the golf course, chat, do an interview if asked, putt, hit balls, work out— do whatever to keep my mind off Lynne, Grant, Jim Dempsey, and my gut instinct that Easley's death was in some way related to the other three. I wanted to focus on the task at hand. However, Levine's poem "Milkweed" read:

> Remember how unimportant
> they seemed . . .
> The windows
> went dark first with rain
> and then snow, and then the days,
> then the years ran together and not
> one mattered more than
> another, and not one mattered.

In my work environment, pedaling away, I had opened the Levine book, hoping for a reprieve. However, there was Lynne Ashley—the blonde with the cryptic past that I didn't understand yet knew to be in some way prevalent to Grant's failing marriage, Dempsey's downward spiral, and her own effort to remain under the authority's radar.

The days, then the years ran together and not one mattered.
"It had been so long since anything meant anything."

What the hell was "anything"? I had wondered, seated on the stationary bike for thirty minutes.

"One forty-one to the pin," Silver was saying. "Only a hint of breeze at our backs."

His voice was machinelike. Everything about him spoke of organization. He seemed to be able to gauge all that was going on, on the course—at all times—and relay the facts to me.

"The hole is cut back-left," he said.

I knew what he was telling me: The green was shaped nearly like an upside down L, a bunker guarding the left-side back portion. To go at the pin meant carrying the bunker and sticking the ball tight.

"How much are we gambling today?" Silver said.

"All the chips."

He looked at me, his tongue running over his upper lip, then finally: "I was afraid you'd say that."

Hayes had positioned a three-wood off the tee, and Silver and I stopped near his ball to watch his approach. He was a Wisconsin native, a successful veteran, winner of two events. The shot illustrated his knowledge of the course. He did the smart thing, playing to the center of the green. I knew Silver was fully aware of Hayes's decision. But Hayes was also in the top ten on this season's money list. With the exception of the final two pairings, the entire field was on the course and the scoring conditions had the leader board in flux. Chris DiMarco had moved up, tying Hayes at nine under; three players, including Ernie Els, who still had fourteen holes to play, were now at minus eight. It was going to be a shootout. Hayes was being patient.

"Little eight-iron?" I said. "Or a big nine?"

"I don't think the wind is going to help the ball much," Silver said, as we walked. He passed me a water bottle, knowing I often drink one every couple holes.

When we reached my ball, however, the club selection was made for me—the ball had come to rest in a divot, a five-inch-by-two-inch crater. Worse, my ball rested against the front lip. I had no choice but to play for the center of the green now and hope I could make a long birdie putt. Par, though, would be a good score from the center of one of the largest greens on the course.

"Bad break," Silver said. "Get it on the dance floor. Maybe we can steal a bird."

I pulled the eight-iron, choked down on the club, and took two practice swings. I selected a target—the right edge of the back bunker—then addressed the ball, positioning it back in my stance. This ball position would make the ball fly low and run and allow me to make an abbreviated swing, the motion used to hit knock-down shots in gusts.

"Just like we drew it up on the chalkboard," Silver said, when the ball landed between the two front sand traps and ran to the middle of the green.

"I was hoping it would draw and run toward the flagstick."

"We're putting for birdie either way. Just a little longer from there."

At the green, Hayes and I had virtually identical putts. The bad news was that I would go first and thus couldn't learn from watching his putt. But as Kip Capers had said, I'd played here many times. To my eye, the thirty-five–footer would move four inches right to left. Silver, though, called for a six-inch break. Two inches is nearly half a cup's width. One of us was wrong.

"Saw this putt on television yesterday afternoon," Silver said. "Breaks more than it looks."

When we had spoken in the restaurant, Silver had believed in me.

"We'll go with your read," I said.

I crouched behind the ball and selected a spot four inches in front of the ball over which to roll it. I made practice strokes, looking at the cup, trying to gauge the speed. Finally, I set the putter behind the ball, squared my body to the line, and gripped the club.

The gallery was silent. Mind blank, putter loose in my hands, I pulled the trigger.

The ball took a full three seconds to get to the hole. It broke all of Silver's six inches, catching the left edge, rolling 180 degrees around the perimeter before dropping.

I try to remain in the moment at all times but was unable to help myself. I made an all-out fist pump. The gallery erupted. We had begun with a birdie.

. . .

After nine holes, the leader board was very different. My thirty-two (minus fourteen overall) had me not only on pace to better the sixty-five I sought, but allowed me to leapfrog Toms, who had slumped with a thirty-seven (minus ten). Hayes had kept pace, going out in thirty-three (twelve under). Woods, however, was still the principal player, making the turn with a conservative thirty-five (minus eighteen), yet still four shots better than me.

I stood with Silver on the tee of the course's most picturesque hole, the 166-yard par-three twelfth. Nicklaus was not only a great player, his course design is noteworthy, too, and connoisseurs often claim Muirfield Village to have a little Augusta National in it. Like the famed par-three sixteenth at the home of the Masters, Nicklaus's twelfth plays entirely across water. The green, guarded front and back by bunkers, is two-tiered.

Yet the tangible elements of the hole had never been what I found most difficult. In my years playing the Memorial, I'd left plenty of strokes on No. 12. The diagonal positioning of the green always gave my mind's eye fits—you're not hitting to a straight-on target; rather, you feel as if you must carve the ball into a landing area that, to your instincts, runs nearly sideways. Rationally, I knew the tee shot required only that I hit the ball with precise distance control. Yet, typically, one attempts to hit into a narrow visual tunnel, be it on the practice range or driving into a fairway—always, you visualize a pathway for the ball to follow. A diagonal target skews that vision.

"You know the club," Silver said. "Stop analyzing. Six-iron worked all week. There's no wind. Swing the club—no ball, no green—just an easy practice swing, Jack."

I nodded, took the six-iron, and teed my ball. I stepped behind the ball and went through my pre-shot routine—two practice swings, aligned the ball from behind, selected a distant tree-top to aim at, and addressed the ball.

Then I made a third practice swing—no ball, no green, just a smooth swing.

It wasn't a carved shot; it wasn't a push or a slice. I knew that even before my follow-through.

"Beautiful fade," Silver said. "Within six feet of the pin. This is an easy game."

As we made our way to the green, a roar erupted behind us. Woods was playing the tenth, and the sound appeared to have come from there. Hayes stopped beside me, and we both looked back. He looked at me, and I shrugged.

"Woods holed out for eagle," Dan Ferrin, CBS on-course commentator, said.

Without attempting my birdie, I'd just dropped two shots. I forced that thought away. Only my target score was within my control.

The pin had been cut in the back and my ball had flown to the second tier, bounced once, and sat. The sun felt warm on my back as I bent to fix my ball mark. I placed my coin behind the ball and tossed the ball to Silver, who wiped it, and tossed it back.

Hayes was facing a thirty-footer, up the ridge, to the second tier. He was a quiet guy, unassuming and modest despite two Tour wins. And the guy could putt, consistently ranked in the top fifty on Tour. On this day he had yet to fully get the flat stick going, but had a stroke that could make up ground quickly. I was watching his putt particularly closely—the final six feet would show me the line.

His ball broke very little and was paced perfectly, dying into the cup. A healthy putter can overcome a lot. I had hit a far better shot to the green, yet, had this been match play, I'd need this six-foot birdie putt to halve the hole. With his thirty-foot laser, Hayes had just moved to thirteen under, one shot behind me, and, due to Woods's eagle, now seven behind the leader.

Our gallery had dwindled. Maybe thirty people were around the green now. Woods had shifted to fifth gear, and people had gone to watch. But I wasn't done. A birdie would get me to fifteen under with six holes to play, including a par five and a par three.

Laura Hayes, holding son Hank, stood near the green and

waved to J.P. For a moment, I missed home and thought of my own family, looking forward to the time, several months away, when Lisa and Darcy would be traveling. I thrust those thoughts away and committed to my pre-shot routine.

I leaned over the putt and slowed everything down. I took in a gulp of air and exhaled through my nose. Then I squeezed the putter as tightly as I could, releasing the death grip, and settling my hands lightly. Finally, I thought, *Three-second stroke* and brought the putter back slowly and through, holding the finish, my head still, not looking up until I heard the clicking of the ball tapping the bottom of the plastic cup. That sound quickly blended with the ovation.

"Boo-yah," Silver said, giving me five.

"Boo-yah?" I said.

"Stuart Scott," he said. "The ESPN hotty." He looked around to see that Hayes and his caddie were out of earshot.

I knew what would follow.

"Guy is gorgeous," Silver said. "If he's not doing *Sports-Center,* I won't even watch."

"Even if I'm in the highlights?"

We were fifteen under par, five shots back. However, the holes ahead offered scoring chances. And, as my original game plan dictated, there was always the chance Woods might come back to the field. Boo-yah.

.   .   .

The fifteenth at Muirfield Village is a par five, 503 yards. That yardage alone, given that most Tour players can crank the volume past 300 yards when needed, suggested the tournament could swing on this hole. Birdies were sought there—some made; for others, though, the risk of going for the green in two was not rewarded. A creek cuts the fairway, short of the green. The fairway dips in front of the green, providing a challenging uphill chip for those who play the hole in three shots. The slope also means anyone going for the green in two must have plenty of carry to get the ball on the dance floor.

I had the honor, as Hayes was coming off a bogie. At nearly 5 P.M., the nearby leader board read: T. WOODS, −20; J. AUSTIN, −15; and J. P. HAYES, −12. This had become a two-horse race.

"Woods had his big hole," Silver said, "that eagle. Par golf since."

"Conservative."

"He's waiting to see if you push him." There was an edge to Silver's voice, a challenge.

He held out the driver. The fairway was tree-lined but three-wood was out of the question. We weren't going for birdie. We were trying to throw a three at the leader board—an eagle—and let Tiger see the minus seventeen, give him something to think about.

The gallery surrounding the tee box sensed the drama. I heard my name shouted encouragingly. The late-afternoon temperature was now eighty, the sky still clear. In Chandler, Maine, my parents, wife, and seven-week-old daughter were viewing on television. I was playing on the most competitive golf circuit in the world, had faced the best competition the sport offered this week—and had put myself in position for a showdown with the world's top player. The success had come on the heels of a two-month slump that challenged my game, my confidence, my desire, even led those around me to question my fortitude.

I took the driver from Silver, bent to tee my ball, went through my practice swings, then took a wider stance than usual for additional balance—this swing would be my fifth gear.

My drive carried 330 yards.

As Hayes, his caddie, Silver, and I descended the fairway, we heard another roar from behind. This time, however, the sound failed to covey that sense of grand excitement that accompanies an outstanding shot; rather, it was long sigh. Hayes looked at me with raised brows. We slowed to watch the score change on the leader board.

"Boo-yah," Silver said.

And it was a boo-yah change, indeed–T. WOODS, −18; J. AUSTIN, −15. Woods had made double bogie behind us, coughing up two strokes. It made my 330-yard drive look even closer to the green. An eagle would pull me to within a shot.

Hayes was first to play. I watched him pull a three-iron. The ball hit the slope in front of the green and died, stopping several yards short of the putting surface. I knew he could normally hit a three-iron over 200 yards. Had he mis-hit? Was there wind above the trees lining the fairway? Had Hayes attempted to land the ball short and run it onto the green? The course had taken a great deal of water this week, consequently diminishing the roll, but he would know that.

"Six-iron," I said to Silver, when we reached my ball.

"Those two bunkers in front worry me," Silver said. "Hayes played what I thought was a perfect shot—carried the first bunker, rolled it just left of the second one." He shook his head. "The fairway in front of the green is wet and soft. Let's fly the ball up there. Hit five-iron."

I thought about that. We had 173 yards to the center of the small green. My typical five-iron carries 185 yards. If I played the ball forward in my stance, I could hit it higher and shorter, thus landing the ball softly. I nodded and took Silver's advice.

But I never fully committed to the shot. This is a game of blind trust. Once you select a club and choose a shot to play, you must commit fully, never knowing until later what the result will be. That gamble is probably what hooks so many golfers. It didn't hook me—not with the opportunity to force a four-shot swing here, if I could make eagle, coupled with Woods's double bogie.

Five-iron might be too much club. I don't want to be long. It was a poor mindset, the result predictable.

I hit the ball fat, landing on the slope in front of the green next to Hayes's ball.

I took a deep breath and shut my eyes tight. Heat seemed to rise from within. A smooth swing was not asking too much of myself. I had practiced the shot thousands of times. All that was required for an eagle putt was a solid swing. Worse, I prided myself on rising to the moment.

I slammed the five-iron back into the bag. It bounced up, the club face leaping, nearly clipping Silver. He said nothing. We'd been together a long time. He knew I wanted to win more than nearly anything.

"Don't be too hard on yourself. I called the club, Jack."

"No," I said. "I made the swing."

.   .   .

At our green-side balls, Hayes chipped to within tap-in birdie range. I was next to play.

But Silver slowed things down. We had practiced this chip shot during the week. He had dropped several balls and paced the distance to various spots on the green including the back right corner, where the hole was cut this day. However, he paced it off again—keeping the bag on his shoulder, preventing me from selecting a club.

I took some deep breaths. Everyone on Tour prides himself on his mental fortitude. If you don't truly believe you have what it takes, then you don't. Consequently, Jack Austin is a guy who gets the most out of his talent, a guy who has squeezed every ounce of juice from his natural ability. Moreover, the Jack Austin I know is a guy who can hit the required shot when an opportunity presents itself.

Silver handed me the sand wedge. "Thirty paces," he said. "Hit it well and she should skip a couple times and stop on a dime."

I nodded. I had blown one shot. All I could do now was prove to everyone I could claw back.

The fifty-six–degree loft was a lot, considering I was chipping uphill, as the hill would add loft. I wasn't, however, playing a bump-and-run. I wanted to hit an aggressive shot—fly it to the pin and stick it close, like throwing a dart.

Silver and I were out of earshot. I felt my jaw flex. "I'm making eagle here. One goddamned way or another."

I stood staring at the flagstick for several moments, visualizing the ball landing ten feet short and rolling to it. At address, I could feel my heart pounding. I hit the ball too hard, clipping it like a flop shot, sending it high, and landing it too close to the pin.

"Slow down," Silver yelled.

It didn't slow. It hit the flagstick on one bounce and dropped straight down—into the cup. Later, I was glad for television. There are times in life when we wish we possessed rewind, a way to go back, watch things again, see ourselves as we had been. In the heat of the moment, I never realized how big that shot was, only that I had made the eagle I desperately wanted. And that—hollering, pumping my fist—I was seventeen under par.

. . .

The eighteenth is a par four, 444 yards. As I stood on the tee, I knew Woods hadn't brought what he'd deem his "A game." I was one shot back and on pace for a sixty-five. A birdie would allow me to tie Woods.

However, if you make a three on eighteen, you earn it. You drive to a fairway that doglegs right. Bunkers and trees guard the right side and take away the option of cutting the corner, while a stream runs just left of the fairway. Precision or perish.

In years past, upwards of 20,000 spectators lined the fairways and greenside bleachers on the eighteenth. Near the crowds, I could see the leader board. Woods had three holes to play. That meant three more birdie chances. I wouldn't worry about him. I couldn't control what he did.

As I reached into the bag, my hand on the driver, I felt Silver's gaze heavy on my hand.

"Second place, alone, is worth five hundred forty thousand," he said, palming the three-wood. "We're two shots clear of Hayes."

"And one back of Woods."

"Yeah," he said, his tongue moving deliberately over his lips. "One back."

I pulled the driver out of the bag and tossed the head cover to Silver. I knew what he was saying—$540,000 would guarantee my card the following year. The safe play was three-wood, four-iron, and a two-putt for par and my sixty-five. But my gut said, Driver. I had failed to trust myself once already on this day.

I hit driver to the heart of the fairway.

Hayes hit a monster drive that bounded beyond my ball. I had 138 yards to the center of the green, which, like the twelfth, sat diagonal to the approach area. *Trust your swing.* I positioned the ball off my front instep, took the club back slowly and smooth, and held the follow-through. The ball stuck close to the pin. The gallery sensed my charge and reacted with a long ovation and shouts of encouragement.

Hayes was first to putt and rolled his eight-footer two feet past, then finished for a sixty-six, fifteen under par.

I had six feet, straight. Silver and I read the putt from all sides. I glanced once at the TV tower behind the green, where Lisa had once sat, and wondered what she'd be saying if she were up there. Subtle sounds emerged from the huge gallery around the eighteenth green.

I addressed the ball and brought the putter back slowly, then through, never looking up. I did not hear the ball rattle the bottom of the cup. Instead I heard the gallery sigh. The ball sat on the right edge.

"A hundred eighty degrees and lipped out," Silver said.

I was still in second place at seventeen under. Yet I had shot my sixty-five.

· · ·

The scorer's tent is, in fact, a trailer. The PGA Tour travels circus-like, city to city, in a succession of trailers each week. Perhaps the last thing television viewers saw that Sunday was Hayes, his caddie, Silver, and me shaking hands all around, but that wasn't the end of the tournament for us. Now came the wait.

Hayes and I sat side by side in the scorer's tent, totaling scores, in preparation for signing our cards and attesting each other's. I tilted my hat back, slumped in the folding chair, and sipped bottled water.

We had never played a final round together, and Hayes looked at me when I set a small solar-powered calculator down next to the water. He wasn't the first playing partner to offer a surprised reaction.

"Dyslexia," I said. "I can do the math without it, but I always use the thing, just in case. Sign an inaccurate card and get myself D.Q.ed—that would be a tough pill to swallow."

"Tough to make mortgage payments doing that." He smiled. "Bunch of you guys from Wisconsin out here now, huh?"

"A handful."

"Good to have some more cold-weather guys around," I said.

"If we can add an Alaska Open to the schedule, you, me, and Jerry Kelly will be the favorites."

I grinned.

I punched numbers into my calculator. It totaled sixty-five. I double-checked the score. I leaned back again, crossed my legs, and stared at the card for a moment with mixed emotions—I had done what I'd wanted but would have to see if I accomplished enough. Then I slid the card to Hayes to attest and sign. I did the same for him. We gave the cards to the scorer.

"It turned into a golf tournament, huh?" the scorer said. "Woods came back to the field."

I shrugged. "Rather have it the other way around."

"Well, you had a lot of ground to make up. Anyway, you boys better stick around."

The trailer had only one window, and the old guy was dressed in slacks and a long-sleeved button-down shirt. His face was lined with the tiny red veins of an Irish drinker; his thick pate was damp with perspiration.

Indeed, I planned to stick around. Contrary to Woods's remarkable record as a closer—when leading or co-leading after fifty-four holes, he had won an astounding twenty-nine of thirty-one events—this day Woods was limping to the finish line. He'd begun the final round eighteen under par and, with only two holes to play, remained minus eighteen.

"I'm sticking around," Hayes said, "even though I'm two back. But I don't see Tiger making bogey on the final two. You, on the other hand, might be in a playoff."

I nodded.

"If you get into a playoff," Hayes said to me at the door, "win one for the northern guys."

. . .

"Goddamned target score doesn't look low enough," I said to Silver on the range, where I'd gone to stay loose.

He held the pitching wedge out to me, then pulled the five-iron and scrubbed the grip with the towel he wore flung over his shoulder. A tournament official stood nearby, overseeing the practice session.

"Sixty-five is still good, Jack. This is a tough course."

"I know."

"Talk to Lisa?"

I shook my head. "I want to finish this first."

I hit an easy wedge that carried 105 yards; I was plenty loose.

"Almost surreal having the whole range to ourselves," Silver said.

"The way you talk, you could write a book."

"Funny."

I had just hit an eight-iron and turned to see Jim Dempsey standing behind the ropes. I walked over. Dempsey wore his usual—blue jeans, a button-down denim shirt, low-heeled Roper boots, and Oakley shades.

"Just wanted to stop by to wish you luck. Tiger parred the seventeenth."

I nodded. "Tell Lynne I did what she asked of me."

He took the sunglasses off and tucked them into his breast pocket. "What did she ask?"

"She wanted me to tell Barrett that she, you, and Grant are fine, that the Tour doesn't need to worry."

"That's true." His eyes ran past me to Silver, who was out of earshot. "Not that it matters a hell of a lot now."

I was loose and didn't need warm-ups. I did, though, want to putt. But my curiosity got the best of me. His last comment opened a door, and I walked through it.

"Yeah," I said, "I heard you were all questioned."

"That's right. I never met the guy. I told the cops what you had said about the kid being high, though."

"Thanks for the heads-up. How did Lynne's interview go?"

"Same as mine"

"She must've been terrified." I didn't know of what or why she was terrified, but I was hitting a blind tee shot.

Dempsey, his eyes narrowing, knocked that ball into a bunker. "She's a private person."

"Bullshit," I said. "I'm going to putt. Tim, you ready to go?" Silver grabbed the bag and approached.

"Jack," Dempsey said, "I also wanted to say thanks for everything over the years." He held out his hand.

I took it.

"You were my first client and stuck with me through thick and thin. Thanks for that."

Something in his face had changed. He wasn't there to wish me luck. His eyes were pooling. When the first tear fell, he put the Oakley glasses on again.

"You sound like you're saying good-bye," I said.

"I'm going with my tail between my legs."

"Why?"

"Because I'm a fool. She's not who I thought she was. Thanks again." He turned and walked away.

Before Silver and I reached the practice green, the tournament official's walkie-talkie sounded. Woods had parred in and won. I'd finished second. In the distance, Dempsey got into a black Lincoln and drove slowly away.

The next morning, I was doing it all over again. Same golf course, same pressure. This time, though, I was trying to qualify for the U.S. Open. A 156 PGA Tour players—all, like me, with non-exempt Open status—vying for roughly thirty spots into the major. The rain was back, but this was a one-day qualifier. We would finish the thirty-six holes, unless lightening halted play. Even then, eventually, the Sectional Qualifier would, no doubt, be completed.

"Well," Silver said, "you didn't say much on the range. How'd you sleep?"

"So-so." We were on the first tee. I was tired. The previous week, the previous day, had taken a lot out of me.

"You up for this?"

"Yeah," I said. "I'm ready."

Ready, but not all that willing. I didn't want to be there. This was a chance to gain entry to a tournament I dreamed of winning. Yet, fourteen hours earlier, I'd been on a competitive high—battling Tiger Woods, the world No. 1, for the Memorial title. Now, I was back having reassumed my place among the Tour's "bubble men," those players who seem to walk the cut line weekly, annually on the bubble of the PGA Tour Money List's top 125. It was tough to return.

"Let's build on yesterday," Silver said.

"That's what I plan to do. I'm sick of qualifying."

"Top fifteen, Jack."

I knew what he was saying: A top-fifteen finish in the U.S. Open makes you exempt the following year. In golf, though, you can't think that far ahead. I had thirty-six holes, to get to the Open. One shot at a time.

"We've locked up our card for next year," he said.

I just nodded, again not wanting to look past this first tee shot. But he was right. My second-place finish had been worth enough money to guarantee my place among the top 125 at year's end. Typically, I live for the day each summer when I know I've secured my Tour card. That knowledge frees me. Tournaments become more fun, as if I'm gambling with "house" money. It's usually a time for celebration—a steak on the grill, a beer, or dinner out with Lisa. The year before, I had finished second at the Buick Classic. Not only had the strong finish preserved my Tour card, but, as with the previous day's final round, the Sunday-afternoon duel had offered hope that my breakthrough to the winner's circle was near. Thus, the U.S. Open Sectional Qualifier, on this day, represented something beyond a wonderful opportunity. It reminded me of what I did not want to be. No one remembers the runner-up. Qualifying was reminiscent of what I'd come so close to only hours before—a Tour win.

I hit my tee shot on the first hole into a bunker protecting the right rough, something I had not done once the previous week.

"That swing looked like you're tired," Silver said. "No real drive in your legs. Hung it out to the right. Legs tired, Jack?"

I shook my head no, squinting through the drizzle to see my ball.

"You'd say that anyway," he said.

The trap was over 250 yards away. I didn't see my ball against the lip. So, unless my vision failed me, I'd be hitting from the center of the trap. I'd have a play to the green, which meant I still had a chance at birdie. Birdies were paramount this day.

"Six and seven," Silver said. "Put those two numbers in whatever order you want, but it might as well be one or the other—sixty-sevens and we play; seventy-sixes and we go home."

"You saying you want me to take more risks?" I said.

"Just stating the *facts, Jack.* Everyone's trying to go low. That means birdies and bogeys."

He was right. I'd been in this spot previously. I'd qualified for the U.S. Open twice, doing so by shooting sixty-seven, sixty-six (133) both times. My highest eighteen-hole score in attempting to qualify was, in fact, seventy-six. Positioned in a fairway bunker on the first hole, I was not off to a good start.

.   .   .

We fought back to play the front in thirty-five, one under par. I had looked at the leader boards and knew, to qualify, I had to throw down a full house on the back nine. A pair of deuces, like an even-par thirty-six, wouldn't do it.

I was thinking strategy as Silver and I walked to the eleventh tee and found a logjam of golfers in Gore-Tex rainsuits. Silver had been right, of course. I was spent and running on fumes, but talking about it did no good. In fact, to speak it was to admit it, and admitting it would've been fatal.

The leader was Jonathan Kaye, in the clubhouse with a sixty-five, seven under par. Several players still on the course were on pace to better that. Opening with a seventy-one wouldn't go far.

The group ahead of us sat waiting. I had been on the putting green when the group had gone off the first tee and had not noticed who was among them. Now I did.

"Hi, Grant," I said.

Grant Ashley's "back injury" had apparently healed following his sudden withdrawl earlier in the week. He was seated on a bench near the tee. Corey Guilford, the rookie with whom I was paired, told Grant he was terribly sorry to hear what had happened to his caddie. Grant thanked him, then turned slowly to look at me.

"Hey, Jack."

Grant's expression was one of sorrow, even pain. The look surprised me. Certainly, I didn't doubt that Grant, like anyone, would feel sympathy for someone stabbed to death. Yet my interaction with Grant and Mike Easley—on the golf course—had not indicated any bond between them. The antithesis, actually, of what I'd witnessed playing with Tom Watson and Bruce Edwards. Watson had been devastated when longtime caddie Edwards was diagnosed with amyotrophic lateral sclerosis, ALS or Lou Gehrig's disease. However, Watson's reaction to his friend and caddie's illness was to be expected. By contrast, Grant and Easley were no more friends than Madonna and myself. Moreover, Easley had performed poorly, even been high during a PGA Tour event—an act so heinous Grant himself could have been punished by the Tour. I didn't think Grant's woeful expression had much to do with Mike Easley.

"I'm sorry," I said.

"Thank you."

I'd heard Lynne's version of their marriage, of what had taken place, of why she'd left. I'd not heard Grant's account, but this was neither the time nor the place.

"Good playing yesterday," he said. "I thought you had Tiger beat."

"Thanks." I shook my head. "I wanted that one badly."

"See you around." The fairway cleared and Grant started toward the empty tee.

"Hey," I said, remembering something. "You seen Dempsey?"

Grant turned back to me. His expression was not sorrowful now. He moved back and stood closer than he'd been, leaning toward me, speaking into my ear. "Jim Dempsey is a fuck who'll steal the fucking shirt off your back." He straightened, his tone back to conversational. "Stay away from him, Jack. Free advice. Stay clear of that son of a bitch."

There were six others on the tee. I said casually, "Sure."

"There's nothing worse," Grant said, his voice cracking, "than a five-bedroom house with no one in it."

. . .

That day, the rain never fell hard, but like a dull, constant headache, never let up either. Thirty-five holes had been played. I was even par, not good enough on a day when so many players were taking gambles.

Moreover, we had been playing "pick, clean, and place" all day, which referred to the handling of the ball on wet fairways. A player may always clean mud or dirt off his ball once it's on the green. But "pick, clean, and place" allows players to do the same thing in the fairway—clean the ball and place it on the fairway, preventing golfers from having to hit from a "plugged" lie. Anytime you give PGA Tour players soft greens, they will tear up the course. Even par was like shooting seventy-five. The cut was six under for thirty-six holes.

"We've been out here six hours," Silver said, setting the bag on the eighteenth tee. He held an umbrella over the golf bag, protecting the clubs from the rain. The fifty-five–pound bag, the rain, the more than eight miles he'd hiked on this day all seemed to catch up to him now. Then he blew out a long breath and leaned on the bag. "You know what I'm going to have tonight?"

I shrugged.

"A latte. Sit in a hot tub and drink a latte. No, no. An espresso." His eyes livened. "That's it. I'll find a quiet coffee bar somewhere, have a nice espresso. Then go back to the hotel and sit in the hot tub. Start spending my ten percent."

I nodded and took the driver from the bag. Typically, PGA

Tour caddies get 10 percent of winning checks. I gave Silver 10 percent of top-three paychecks, so he was cashing in on his share of my Memorial check for $540,000.

"You haven't spoken since the sixteenth hole," he said, checking the umbrella to be sure the clubs were dry.

"What's to say?"

"Jack, you gave it your all. You're spent, man. And the rain makes it even more tiring. Had a hell of a week. Played better than a hundred and fifty-four of a hundred and fifty-six guys."

Silver understood my silences. I'd come here to qualify. He let it go.

I took the driver and hit a downhill drive over the traps guarding the right-side rough, leaving less than 150 yards to the green.

"Let's finish with a birdie," I said, finally.

.   .   .

On the green I had five feet for birdie. I had positioned the ball on the second tier, where the pin had been cut. Few putts are straight on this green, and this one was not. However, the green was wet, which would deaden much of the break.

Corey Guilford was working on a score worse than mine—he had a twenty-footer for seventy-nine. I was crouched behind my ball, reading the contour of the green, as he lined up his putt.

Guilford stood behind the ball for all of two seconds, addressed it, and quickly slapped it at the hole. It ran past my ball marker. He didn't bother to mark the ball and clean it.

I walked across the green to view my line from behind the hole. As I crouched, Silver stood behind me. "Four inches," he said, "right to left."

"Let's finish this with a birdie," I said again.

I walked back across the green to my ball.

Guilford watched me and glanced at his watch.

I took two practice strokes, addressed the ball, carefully setting the putter face behind it, then pulled the trigger. It caught the right edge, did a three-sixty, and spun out. I dropped the putter, pressed my palms to my eyes, and sighed. "Damn it."

Guilford stood waiting.

My ball had stopped two inches from the hole, directly in his line. Common practice dictates that I would "finish," not mark, tapping in to get out of Guilford's line.

Except Guilford apparently didn't want to wait. He hit his second putt—missing—nearly before my ball was in the cup. I had to jump out of the way of his ball.

"Hey," Silver said, "what's the rush?"

Guilford was walking toward his ball to tap in. He stopped and turned to Silver.

"Why don't you slow down, take a little damned pride—"

"Tim," I said.

Silver looked at me. I shook my head.

"It's goddamned rude, too," Silver said.

Guilford continued to his ball and tapped it in.

The concluding handshakes were skipped. Guilford was off, headed to the clubhouse and out of the rain.

"That kid might as well have left the course three hours ago," Silver said.

"I know."

"It's these endorsement contracts," Silver said.

"I don't believe that," I said. "Money's got nothing to do with playing hard, start to finish."

Galleries were thin on this day. Everyone had come to see the final round the day before. Those who had come this day were probably following Kaye and Stewart Cink, the leaders. I was glad. No one had been there to see Guilford's antics. I handed Silver my putter. He wiped it and slid the leather head cover on it. Head down, moving briskly toward the dry clubhouse and a hot shower, I heard my name called and turned.

Despite the tiny galleries, one person stood greenside, waiting for me.

20

The house in Chandler, Maine, was dark when I got home, shortly after midnight. Although the home was new, the routine was not: I set my suitcase near the door, slipped out of my loafers, and went to the fridge, where I found leftover pasta primavera. I grabbed the Tupperware container and took a fork from the drawer. Then I sat at the kitchen table to eat the cold pasta. Chewing, I saw—amid the coffee maker, blender, knife rack, food processor, and a variety of other items lining the kitchen counter—a bottle of beer in an ice bucket with a note. I got up and retrieved it.

> *Your dad says this one's on him. He says to tell you you're not slumping like the Red Sox any more (and that you'll know what that means). Darcy and I are very proud. You hung tough Sunday. See you in the morning. (I'll get up with the baby tonight, if she wakes.)*
> *Love,*
> *Lisa*

A window was open, and I smelled the salt that rode the cool evening breeze. In the distance, the low rumble of a foghorn sounded. Through the sliding-glass door that led to a deck, I saw a boat's light in the distance. The light wasn't bobbing, so the sea was calm.

I finished the beer and went upstairs. Darcy lay asleep in the crib at the foot of our bed. I slid in beside Lisa, who slept like the dead, and listened to Darcy's breathing for another hour.

. . .

Tuesday morning, I woke at 7 A.M. and crept downstairs. Lisa was asleep on the couch and the television was on, playing The Golf Channel. Darcy must have awoken during the night, and Lisa had apparently gotten up with her, then been unable to fall back to sleep. I'd slept through the entire sequence.

I took the baby monitor from Lisa's side. In the kitchen, I took a Gatorade bottle from the fridge and went to the basement to work out while the ladies slept. I clicked on the television in the corner of the basement, and leaned back on the bench press. As I went through my chest workout, walking to the makeshift putting green to hit six-footers between sets, The Golf Channel played its version of the daily news, a show called *Golf Central*, and offered updates and predictions from the U.S. Open. I hadn't checked the listing on the Internet or the sports pages to see my exact position on the money list, but my finish at the Memorial Tournament would have moved me well inside the top hundred.

The sun had just risen, and the ocean breeze blew in the rectangular cellar windows. I heard Lisa's footsteps on the stairs.

"You must have only gotten four hours' sleep," she said, descending the stairs, holding a coffee mug. She looked around until she saw the baby monitor.

I stood, and she gave me a hug and a long kiss.

"Congratulations."

"Thanks," I said. "I had hoped to hand you the trophy."

"You did great. Outplayed the world's top-ranked golfer, Jack. Be proud."

"I am."

"Should've seen your father." She smiled, recalling. "'He's lapping Tiger Woods,' he kept saying. I got him on video holding Darcy, telling her, 'That's your dad on television.' It was a magical afternoon." She looked at her watch, then sipped from her mug, considering. "Second place has you encouraged?"

"Hungry."

"Good to see."

I sat on the bench, leaned back, and did a set of twelve with 225 pounds. She got the baby monitor and sat on the military press and looked up at the television.

"Lisa," I said, exhaling as I pushed a repetition up, "do you miss it?" From the corner of my eye, her expression did not appear to change.

"Golf journalism, full time? Sure, I do. It was my life. Now I know there's more to life, though. I think you went through something similar this year."

Finished, I sat up and looked at her. "Yeah, I did. You never really said much about my play the past two months."

"I know. And, at times, it was hard not to."

"Why didn't you?"

She shrugged and sipped from her mug. "I didn't have to, Jack. I knew you had a lot on your mind—me, Darcy, a new house. I just knew." She spread her hands.

"Knew what?"

She turned up the volume on the cordless monitor and set it near her feet. "I've interviewed Phil Mickelson and his wife, Amy. I know what golf means to him—what winning the 2004 Masters meant—and I respect him. He said, at the 1999 U.S. Open, that if Amy went into labor, no matter where he was on the leader board, he'd withdraw to be with her. "

I nodded, remembering.

"And Mickelson took off part of one season, a few years back, after the birth of his son," she said. "He took a lot of heat from some members of the media for taking the break. Some people said he needed to play more, to be hungrier."

"I remember."

"Well, I wasn't one of them. And he came out and won the Bob Hope Chrysler Classic, as soon as he came back."

I nodded. "Hit that shot over water to about two feet to clinch it."

"That's right." She leaned forward and looked at me, her eyes directly on mine. She still had on her flannel pajamas and thick white slippers. She had an ability to focus when talking to people that I'd never seen in anyone else. When you spoke to her, you felt like your words were of utmost importance. And you knew her interest to be sincere—something that separated her from many journalists.

She considered her words, then said, "You couldn't take time off, Jack, and I knew it was killing you."

"So you never mentioned it?"

"I know you, Jack. I know you don't play golf for the pension plan. I know what drives you." She got up and kissed me on the cheek. "I love you. Finish your workout. We'll talk after you shower. I'm going to check on Darcy."

"Before you make plans for the day," I said, "we're having a visitor."

"Visitor?"

I nodded. I told her who had been waiting for me at the eighteenth green Monday afternoon.

She shook her head. "Finish your workout."

The workout lasted an hour and a half. In total, I did five sets each of bench presses, dumbbell flies, dead lifts, and tricep extensions. I was finishing a hundred crunches, watching the highlights of the European Tour's Celtic Manor Resort Wales Open, which Lee Westwood had won, when I heard tires on the driveway. Through a basement window, I saw blue jeans and tennis shoes move briskly past, toward the front door.

Above me, I heard the muffled voices, then Lisa padding across the kitchen floor. Finally, the basement door opened, and they descended. Lisa came into view first.

Grant Ashley was behind her.

I set a glass of orange juice on the kitchen table in front of Grant.

"Thanks," he said, quietly, his eyes fixed on the glass.

Grant didn't drink. He sat staring at the glass. He didn't look like a world-class athlete and multiple winner on Tour now. Nor did he resemble my carefree friend of three years, the guy with whom I'd often had drinks.

I went back to the stove. A shaft of morning sunlight entered the kitchen through the window over the sink. Seated across the kitchen table from Lisa, Grant didn't look like the guy who'd cursed Jim Dempsey on the eleventh tee the day before, either. The anger had been replaced. With what, I wasn't sure. He appeared overwhelmed by it all—Lynne's departure, Easley's murder, Dempsey's betrayal. This was his life—his golf career, his marriage. Now a murder had been thrown in the mix.

He wore a gray UGeorgia Athletics T-shirt. The tips of his brown hair were sun-bleached, and, coupled with his attire and his small lean frame, he resembled a college kid on break.

"Good playing Sunday," he said, looking up from the orange juice. "That qualifier Monday was a bitch. I hate doing that."

I nodded in agreement. I didn't know what else to do. Monday, he'd asked if he could come to the house to talk—had stood beside the eighteenth green in the rain to do so. I waited. He hadn't come to say that.

"I'm making breakfast," I said. "You eat yet?"

He shook his head.

"Want eggs?"

"No, I'm fine."

"Grant, you're staying in Maine. Grits aren't available, so you could starve to death. Better have eggs with me."

A smile spread across his face. It didn't last long, but I knew I'd broken the ice.

Darcy made gurgling sounds, and Lisa took her to the other room to feed her. The door near the kitchen table was open, and sounds from outside entered—the ocean washing softly onto the rocky shoreline, a distant foghorn, a far-off fisherman's voice barking orders.

I took a frying pan from an overhead rack, got Pam out of the cupboard, and pulled a loaf of bread from a basket on the counter. I took the eggs out of the fridge. The scent of eggs and ham frying soon mixed with the salty odor of the ocean. Grant was still seated at the table reading the sports section of the *Portland Press Herald.* I saw a photo of Tiger shaking hands with Jack Nicklaus while accepting the crystal trophy. The headline stated the obvious: Woods was the favorite at this week's U.S. Open. Next to the article, a sidebar ran with the headline CADDIE MURDERED NEAR TOURNEY SITE. I sat down across from Grant with two ham-egg-and-cheese sandwiches and pushed one plate toward him.

"You get plenty of press," Grant said, pointing to an article titled MAINER AUSTIN BREAKS FROM SLUMP AT MEMORIAL.

I took a bite. I had put Tobasco on my sandwich, and my nose started to run. Chewing, I shrugged. "I'm the only Tour player from Maine."

"Big fish, small pond," Grant said and grinned.

I smiled. We'd returned to how things had once been. Grant had never been my closest friend on Tour. That title belonged to Padre, but we'd been good friends, nonetheless. Now I sensed Grant could once again talk to me. I waited.

"I want to apologize for going nuts on the eleventh tee." He chewed the sandwich. "You heard from Dempsey, Jack?"

"He wished me luck Sunday."

"The guy is a back-stabber, you know? What a fool I was, trusting him. He told me he'd make me rich, he'd—get this—'look out' for me." He dropped his eyes. "What a fuck."

I took a bite of my breakfast sandwich and sat chewing, elbows on the table, sandwich poised for another bite.

"Sorry," he said, drifting back from the past. "I know you just got home and that you have a classy wife and a baby. And here I am showing up, talking like that."

"It's okay, Grant. I'd probably be saying the same things."

He took a bite of his sandwich. Then he shook his head. "No, you wouldn't."

"What do you mean?"

He swallowed. "You wouldn't talk, Jack. You'd kick Dempsey's ass."

"I don't know how I'd react, Grant."

We ate quietly for a while, each of us finishing our sandwiches. I got up, poured myself coffee, and spooned in sugar.

Grant motioned for a cup. "Black," he said.

I sat across from him again and set the coffee down next to his orange juice.

"Second place alone will move you from number one eighty-eight on the money list to . . ."—he glanced at the paper—"about sixty-seventh. Pretty good week's work."

"I'm pleased with the timing," I said. "I don't have to sweat out the summer."

"Got your card. Now you can work on your game."

"That's right."

He took his coffee and went to the sliding door and stood before the screen. "Some view, Jack. What's this house, four, five bedrooms?"

"Five. Two are offices now."

"Nothing worse," he said, "than a five-bedroom house with no one in it."

He'd said that before. I knew he was hurting.

"View must've cost a fortune."

"I'm lucky, and Lisa and I both work hard."

He nodded once, his back still to me. "This is what I always wanted, you know? Nice house, wife, kids. It's how it was with my folks. Maybe not the money, but happy. It was a family, you know?"

He didn't turn around to see my response. It seemed he was

saying what he needed to say, to someone—and I was there. The fragrance of Lisa's deadline-strength coffee rose and mixed with the scent of the salt water.

Grant took a deep breath of ocean air. His shoulders slumped, and he stared down at the hardwood floor.

"I was lucky I got Lisa," I said. "Or, actually, that she chose me. She could've had about anyone."

"You waited, too. I think that's the key." He stared out as a lobster boat rumbled slowly past the dock. "How deep's that water at the end of your pier?"

"Deep enough to make me worry about Darcy walking. No beach. It's rocky shoreline."

"Water cold?"

"Right around fifty-eight degrees. Too cold for your southern butt."

He chuckled and turned to me. "You swim in there?"

"Sure. I get done lifting weights, I jump in."

"You're a hard-ass, aren't you?"

"The hardest." I grinned.

His smile faded quickly, and he turned back to face the ocean. "How old were you when you got married?"

"Thirty-five."

"Yeah. That's what I thought," he said. "The thing is, my parents have been married thirty-two years. Never fight. Always loyal. Would never do anything like this to each other."

"You mean the Lynne-and-Dempsey thing?"

He nodded. "Dempsey's gone now. He's a bigger fool than I am. But, yeah, that. And the stuff I'm just finding out about."

"Like what?" I said.

He shook his head.

"Grant, you flew up here for a reason. Tell me what's going on."

He came back to the table and sat across from me. "I met with the cops Sunday morning. You know someone stabbed Mike Easley."

I nodded.

He shook his head. "Unbelievable, huh?"

"Sort of. Guy was into some bad stuff."

The color drained in his face. He straightened in his chair. "How do you know about that?"

"I played with you. The kid was stoned. Silver told me."

"Oh, drugs. Yeah, well . . ." He leaned back in his seat again. "No one gets killed for smoking dope."

"They might get killed buying it."

Lisa walked into the room with Darcy. Holding the baby on her hip, she expertly poured a cup from the decaf carafe, and took it, black, to the living room. Grant waited until she was gone.

"He probably did other drugs, too," he said. "He's that type."

"What was he doing caddying for you? How'd you meet him?"

He shut his eyes tight as if fighting back tears. I didn't know if that was what he was doing, but I had no desire to watch a grown man cry.

"Lynne," he said.

Caddies come in a variety of packages. Yet this answer was completely unexpected. What did Lynne know about caddies? And I'd seen Easley work. He was no more a caddie than I was an astronaut. "She set you up with your caddie?"

"Yeah," he said. "It was her idea—a long story."

I looked at him, thinking.

He shifted in his chair. "Why are you looking at me like that?"

"Lynne told the cops she never met Mike Easley," I said.

Grant sighed and leaned back in his seat. His eyes narrowed; his face tightened again. This time he looked as if he were preparing to fight. He had come to see me for something, apparently not to tell me of Lynne's relationship with Mike Easley.

"Well, she knew him. That's all."

"How did they meet?" I said.

"She partied with him once in a while. Anything wrong with that?"

I finished my coffee and went to the counter to refill. "Tell me why you flew to Maine, Grant. You didn't come here to ask how old I was when I got married." I leaned against the counter.

"My wife left me for my agent," he said. "Now she's gone and so is my agent. Have a little sympathy."

"You tell the cops Lynne knew Easley?"

He shook his head.

I was getting tired of Lynne, Grant, and Dempsey. I had worked my butt off and secured my card for the following season. More than that, I had turned my game around and was planning to go to the course to work on the high, soft five-iron shot that had failed me Sunday.

Grant saw something in my face. "Look, Jack, I came here because I feel like I'm fucked." He looked around to be sure Lisa was out of earshot. "Sorry."

"Go on."

"They've left me holding the bag."

. . .

Grant and I stood on the dock. He leaned against one of the metal poles that serve as legs for the structure and rise four feet above the dock so a boat can be tied to them. The sun was bright in the distance, and the ocean seemed to run to the end of the earth.

"So Lynne and Jim Dempsey split up and now Lynne is gone?" I said.

"Yeah. I don't know where. She said the divorce papers will be in the mail."

"Thoughtful. Does Dempsey know where she went?"

He shook his head. "I doubt it. She wouldn't tell him."

I thought about that—and about Grant's left-holding-the-bag reaction. "Why was Mike Easley caddying for you? He was the single worst caddie I've ever seen. I want to know why you let him loop."

"He needed money, and Lynne owed him a favor."

"Must've been a big goddamned favor. Easley couldn't even give yardage. He was stoned. The guy was a disgrace."

"I know that. I don't feel good about it, Jack."

"Then why the hell was he working for you? What could Lynne have owed him?"

"Absolutely nothing. Guy was heartless." His eyes got very bright under the mid-morning sky. "The guy is where he fucking belongs."

I watched a man in a kayak paddle past us. I turned to Grant. He didn't look like a deer caught in headlights now. "Did you kill him?"

The look left his eyes. His face reddened. "Jesus, is that what you think?"

"I think you know something about it. And I know you're pissed. What did you mean by 'left holding the bag'?"

He didn't say anything.

"If you came here to ask me how to get out of answering tough questions about the murder of your caddie, you came to the wrong place. I didn't like Easley, but I don't think he should be dead."

"I came to see how you did it."

"Did what?"

"Made it work—golf, marriage, baby. How you got a real home."

He sounded sincere. He was twenty-four; life was coming at him awfully fast, and I felt for him. But he knew something about the murder.

I shook my head. "Grant, I can't help you until you tell me what's going on. Do you know who killed Mike Easley?"

"No, I don't."

"How did Lynne know Easley?"

He turned away from me and looked out at the water. The guy in the kayak was almost out of view. A sailboat was passing the dock. The man and woman aboard were dressed in shorts and T-shirts, the guy steering, the woman leaning back. Both waved. We waved back.

Grant watched the boat drift by and stared out as if it had not been there, his gaze settling on the horizon. "Lynne knew Easley before she knew me. She was never like that with me. I had no idea." He turned and looked directly at me. "I fell in love with her."

I waited. Pushing hadn't gotten me far. I'd give him space.

"Jack, she tried, you know? Really tried."

I nodded, encouragingly.

"She had a problem once and got help," he said. "Did that on her own. A lot of people wouldn't. Says something about her."

"Sure."

"But then it was all for naught, in the end."

"Problem with what, Grant? Why was it 'for naught'?"

In deep thought, he rubbed his cheek, then went on as if I'd not spoken.

"Sweet." He shook his head. "That was how I described her to my mother. I met her outside my condo in Atlanta. She had a flat and needed help. I was walking out to go to the course to practice. And there she was, this beautiful blonde who needed help. I changed the tire and asked if I could take her to dinner. I called my parents and said I'd met someone, someone sweet."

I had spoken to Lynne twice. "Sweet" would not be my description of her. The first time, I'd have called her abrasive, self-centered, yet sexy. Following the meeting in my hotel room, I'd have described her as frightened, even confused. Not sweet. To me, "sweet" denotes innocence. Lynne Ashley was a lot of things, but innocent wasn't one of them. Then again, I was older than Grant. Maybe, at thirty-six, I was becoming cynical.

"She was so damned good-looking," Grant said. "Of course, that's what I first saw in her. And it's what got her in so much trouble, but she really thinks that's all she has—the looks. She wants to be more. She wants to act. I don't even know if she believes she can do it. But she wants to try it at all cost."

Again, I was silent. Grant looked out at the ocean.

"Sad thing is," he said, "is that it isn't true, you know? She's much more than her looks. She really is sweet, when she wants to be. And she's smart. And she's tough, too. Tough enough to try."

The more he talked, the less I knew. I shook my head. "How did she know Easley?"

He turned back to the sea and stood staring out as if he'd not heard me. Then he dropped his eyes. "You got Internet access?" he said.

22

I never made it to the Woodlands Club. Perkins was home in New Hampshire catching up with wife, Linda, and my godson, Jackie, when I called at 1:15 P.M. Now it was 3:45, and Grant had gone back to the hotel but left behind a Web site and one hell of a story.

Perkins sat at Lisa's desk, narrow reading glasses on, looking at the Web site. His head was shaking side to side slowly. The office door was closed and locked. I didn't want Lisa seeing this.

"So now we know," Perkins said. "This is why Lynne Ashley wanted no cops, no PGA Tour brass."

I was standing behind him. "She didn't want anyone looking into her past."

The site was called "Wild Meredith Hardcore." And Lynne was there, in several action photos. In some, she looked a little younger, her hairstyle differed from picture to picture. So did her outfits, what little clothing she wore. The people she was with changed, too—in some, men; in others, women; in others, still, there was more than one partner. And, in most of them, she was with Mike Easley.

One corner of the screen read, "Join Now to See Videos. Only $24.95/Mo." Perkins clicked the exit icon, and "Wild Meredith Hardcore" vanished. The two of us sat staring in silence at the blue Windows desktop. I blew out a deep breath. Perkins took off his glasses, folded them, and set them on the desk with great care, as if perfectly centering them. Outside, on the deck below, I heard Lisa talking quietly to Darcy, her voice a soothing motherly tone that seemed juxtaposed against what we'd just viewed.

"Remember your bachelor party?" Perkins said.

"Sure."

"The strip club I took you and Padre to?"

"Yeah."

"I don't remember feeling like this after watching that."

"Me, either."

For my bachelor party, Perkins had deemed himself the designated driver, loading Padre Tarbuck and me into my Suburban and driving us to Boston. We watched a Bruins game, then hit one too many bars, ending up at a strip club. I'd been to only three such venues—the other two while in college—and I was no sociologist, but I remember feeling a mixture of guilt, sympathy, and lust. Also, on some level that I didn't fully understand, I felt as if the women on stage were mocking us. This Web site, however, was different—no playful striptease, no erotic dance. This was, as the name indicated, hardcore pornography featuring a woman I had met, a woman I knew was fearful that her current social stratosphere would gain knowledge of her past and of this Web site.

"The bottom of the site reads 'Easy Mike Productions,'" Perkins said.

"What's that mean?"

"That's the owner, I assume. And, if it's 'Easy Mike,' like the former Lynne Meredith, now Lynne Ashley, is 'Wild Meredith,' it means we have a murder suspect."

"Lynne," I said.

"For starters. And Dempsey. And you told me Grant was pissed, too."

"I don't see Grant stabbing anyone four times in the back. That's a particularly vicious act. Shooting someone is different— point and squeeze the trigger. To stab someone, you have to walk up to him, put the knife in his back. To do it four times, you'd have to pull the knife out, do it over and over."

"Jack, that was the guy's wife screwing his caddie—and others—for the whole world to see. And, if 'Easy Mike' is Mike Easley, doing it so Easley can make a buck."

I turned away. Outside, a different world existed, one of clarity, cleanliness, and precision. It was a place where hard work paid off, where a woman I loved spoke softly to a baby brought into this world by an act based on caring and commitment. It was my world, and everything fit neatly. Lynne Ashley, young Grant Ashley, Jim Dempsey, and the dead caddie, Mike Easley, fit their surroundings like triangles into squares.

Absently, my hand ran through my hair. Grant had always been a quiet kid. Monday on the eleventh tee and today, he'd displayed many emotions—anger, disgust, shame, and, I believed, love. He thought Lynne beautiful, as anyone would, but "sweet" and "smart," too. I believed he loved her. Surely, he loved what she and their marriage represented—he wanted the white picket fence, the tricycle in the yard, the rope swing. Those were the images of his youth.

Dyslexics often see things in black-and-white. I'd been guilty of this for years. Now I wanted Grant's world to fit as neatly as the one I viewed as I stood looking down at the deck below, where Lisa sat a stone's throw from the ocean, holding Darcy.

"'So long since anything meant anything,'" I said.

Perkins sighed and leaned back in his chair. He ran a hand across his forehead. "We're dealing with some messed-up shit. This isn't money laundering like the scam that landed me this consulting job. These are people's lives. Christ, how old is Lynne? Twenty-three, twenty-five?"

I shrugged, then nodded. "Grant's about the same."

Perkins clasped his hands behind his neck and pursed his lips.

"Grant said they were married three months before she finally came clean," I said. "The UGA story just stopped making sense, so she finally told him what happened."

"This must be where the Easley favor comes in."

"Yeah. Grant said Lynne's childhood was a mess. She's from a small town in Georgia. Poor. Parents split up when she was little."

"Don't tell me she went to Hollywood to make it big but ended up in the porn industry."

"No. She went to Athens, Georgia, to wait tables and take classes. Somehow she never made it to UGA. She got mixed up with Easley before she had the chance. Started partying, things got out of hand, and she started doing this"—I pointed to the blank computer screen—"for money, then, according to Grant, for cocaine."

Perkins was very still as he listened, his eyes locked on mine.

"Grant said she got help, checked herself into a rehab program," I said. "Then he called the whole thing 'for naught.'"

"Because it didn't work out in the end?"

I shrugged. "I guess."

"She wasn't a cheerleader at UGA?"

"Grant says she never took classes, had nothing to do with UGA. Said he didn't meet her until he left UGA and that she modeled a little bit, enough to put together a small portfolio for Dempsey to show the acting world."

"Then how, exactly, did Grant meet Lynne?" Perkins said.

I told him what Grant had said about changing the tire.

"Why did Lynne move from Athens to Atlanta?" he said. "What was in Atlanta?"

I shook my head. I didn't know.

"What was the favor Lynne owed Easley?" he said.

"Grant said Easley needed money."

"Maybe Easley shows up, says he'll blab if Grant doesn't let him caddie."

"Why not just hit Grant up for money?" I said.

We were quiet again, both listening to the sounds from outside and looking at the blank computer screen. The woman who had just been there was Grant's wife. Grant played a solitary sport. No teammates to rely on when times got tough. He had an agent, but there'd be no consolation or assistance from that source.

Twenty-four years old. What had I been like at twenty-four? A rookie, trying to keep my card, trying to take slightly above-average ability and form a golf game that would allow me to compete with the best of the best. I'd been young, working hard, having fun living on the road, and getting paid to play a game I'd have paid to play. Grant wasn't prepared for this. At twenty-four, I wouldn't have been, either.

"Where does Dempsey stand now?" Perkins said.

"I don't know, exactly." I told him what I did know, about the scene on the range Sunday, and what Grant had said about Lynne going solo.

"You think Dempsey went home?" Perkins said. "You think Lynne dumped him?"

"I don't know."

"I hate those three words."

"I do know this: Grant's a kid. He shouldn't suffer because he fell in love with a woman with a past."

"He should if he murdered someone, Jack."

"You think Grant killed Easley?"

"He's a suspect."

"I'm talking about the media. The kid doesn't deserve to be a tabloid headline."

"Don't ask me to cover this up, Jack. I took a job with the PGA Tour, and I'm damn well going to do it."

"I'm not asking you to cover anything up. I know he's a suspect. But this situation sucks. I think he really loves her."

"I'm not Dr. Phil," Perkins said. "I'm an investigator. Let me have your phone. I've got to contact some people."

We had taken I-95 south to U.S. Route 1. Now Perkins and I were on Columbia Road, heading to One Center Plaza, suite 600, the FBI's Boston field office. The bad news was commuter traffic was a nightmare. The good news was, although he'd yelled obscenities at between ten and fifteen other drivers, Perkins had yet to shoot anyone.

I'd woken at 5 A.M., hit Dunkin' Donuts for a large coffee with cream and sugar, and driven to Perkins's New Hampshire home. Now, Wednesday at 8:15, he was driving us to Boston in Linda's Chevy Malibu. The sun was bright, and Perkins wore wrap-around shades as he drove. With blue jeans, he had on a white XL golf shirt I'd given him with MAXFLI on the breast. XL, however, didn't fit. Length and width were fine, but his arms stretched the sleeves so badly I thought either the fabric would tear or he'd lose circulation in his hands and we'd go off the road.

"What are we listening to?" I said.

"Limp Bizkit."

"What happened to Springsteen, even Everclear or Pearl Jam?"

"Where I lift, kids at the gym blast this stuff. Starting to grow on me."

"What are you weighing?"

"Two seventy-eight."

To say he carried it well was like saying Jack Nicklaus had a decent career. His legs were the size of my thirty-six–inch waist. His body-fat percentage, last I heard, was 6 percent. I imagined the kids at the gym would be more than willing to pop in the occasional Pearl Jam CD for Perkins, should he ask.

"Still lifting every day?" I said.

"Five to seven a.m., six days a week."

"Doesn't show," I said. "In fact you look like you quit working out altogether."

"My ass." He smirked, still focused on the road. "I read Lisa's *Washington Post* article on the Tour wives. Not much mention of Lynne."

"It was a slice-of-life piece. And Lynne didn't say much to contribute to that."

"Lisa going to write another one, on Lynne?"

"I doubt it," I said. "She's a freelancer now. That's breaking-news stuff. The paper has staff writers who'll want to follow the story."

A year earlier, I'd driven farther south, on Massachusetts Avenue, looking for Nash Henley. Silver had gone with me then. This ride, though, was more fun because Perkins's six-feet-five frame was so obviously uncomfortable in the cramped car.

"You drive this thing often?" I said.

"What do you think?" He shook his head. "Only when I need to be inconspicuous. But it's easy to park."

"A two-hundred-seventy-eight–pound guy crammed into a compact car is hardly inconspicuous."

"Why don't you stop talking and buy more coffee and donuts?"

"Don't you have an expense account?"

"If I run it up, the purses you play for might get smaller."

I grinned.

"Seriously, Jack, are you ready? This is a formal statement to the FBI."

"I went over things last night. I'll tell them what I know."

"You met Lynne Ashley. And you've known Grant three years and Jim Dempsey for more than ten. You played with Grant and Easley. They'll be looking for background and insights."

I nodded.

As the faces and buildings danced by, I thought nothing much changed in the year since I'd last been to the area. The year before, I'd been amazed that you could start at one end of Mass. Ave. and drive to a different world.

"Thinking about Nash Henley?" Perkins said.

"Yeah."

"What's he doing this summer?"

"Working football camps, staying at Curry College for the summer."

Perkins looked at the scenery and nodded to himself slowly.

. . .

When I walked into the conference room, I felt underdressed in khaki pants and a golf shirt. Everyone there wore a suit, save for two uniformed cops. Even Perkins had put a navy blue blazer over his golf shirt. He looked at me as if just realizing I was dressed for a hotdog stand and he'd taken me to a five-star restaurant.

"You wear more khaki than the fucking Crocodile Hunter," he said, shaking his head.

"Hey, these guys called me. I ought to be practicing."

No one was listening to us. In fact, the room was hopping. It smelled of burned coffee and strong cologne. There was no coffeepot in view, but everyone had a paper cup. There were four tables with five or six folding chairs at each. The two uniformed cops sat with three guys in suits—two in navy blue, one wore gray—looking over typed papers. At the middle table, a skinny kid in a crisp white shirt and red silk tie sat behind two laptop computers, his head swiveling from one to the other. He turned to look at me and Perkins, didn't find us interesting, and turned back to whatever he'd been doing. The computer kid's shirt collar was far too big and made his neck look birdlike.

From my vantagepoint, the computer screens blinked rapidly the way they always do when you stand back. But I wasn't focused on their blinking. One screen displayed a Web site with which I was familiar. Perkins was familiar with the site, too. So were Grant and Dempsey. On the opposite computer, the screen was white with black text, some sort of code.

The FBI agent in charge was a guy named MacDonald, who approached with a smirk—an expression rarely seen on a Bureau member's face. MacDonald shook his head as if he were the principal, I the recalcitrant student, and we were meeting once again.

"You missed me?" I said.

"No. I'm thinking of the odds of my seeing the same golfer two years in a row."

"Think how lucky you are," I said.

"Yeah, I'll run out and buy a lotto ticket."

MacDonald shook hands with Perkins and me. The year before, he'd been called in to investigate a high-profile murder, the wife of U.S. Open champion Pete Taylor. I hadn't learned MacDonald's first name then and didn't think I'd learn it now. He was about my height but thinner and, as if in uniform, wore a navy blue suit. He still had neatly trimmed brown hair but must've been a rebel because with his blue suit, he wore a diamond stud in his left ear.

The conference room was nearly the size of half a basketball court. MacDonald put me alone at a table in a distant corner with two Bic pens and a yellow legal pad. I began at the beginning, explaining how long and in what capacity I'd known Grant, then I outlined Lynne's visit to Maine, my practice round and shortened tournament round with Grant, dinner with Dempsey, my hotel-room meeting with Lynne, and, finally, detailed Grant's eleventh-tee outburst and his recent trip to my home.

As I wrote for an hour and a half, I realized I knew very little of the context within which everything had occurred. Who were Lynne's parents? Where were they? What were the specifics of her childhood? Perkins hadn't been able to find Lynne's parents, although, to date, they weren't atop his priority list; discovering who killed Mike Easley was. Likewise, I knew few facts. For instance, which rehab facility had Lynne attended? How long had the pictures been on the Internet?

I wondered if Lynne's parents knew of the Web site. I decided they probably did not. I don't know why I made that conclusion. Maybe I didn't want them to have seen the pictures. (I had a daughter now, too.) Or maybe I didn't believe they cared enough to have remained in contact with her, or were savvy enough to search the Internet, or, based on what Grant had said, cared enough to look.

The picture Grant painted had not been one of Lynne going off to college in a packed Volvo with Mom, Dad, and the family dog. According to him, Lynne had gone to Athens, Georgia, to work her way through school by waiting tables and doing whatever. "Whatever" had cost her dearly, and all parties— Grant, Dempsey, Lynne, even Perkins and even I—knew that. And, at some level, we all knew Lynne herself had been partially responsible for "whatever" occurring. Even Grant surely realized that. Even Dempsey, the middle-aged man who'd acted like a love-stricken teen, must have realized it, too. Surely I did. We are responsible for the decisions we make.

However, what Lynne had done for cocaine had been more than payment. Easley had gotten hold of the addiction, twisted it around her throat, and led her around by it. Yet, somehow, Lynne broke free. Regardless of the attitude at my house or her involvement in the ruin of Dempsey's marriage, I respected her for realizing she needed help and seeking it.

The completed statement was six pages. In the act of writing and realizing how much I didn't know, I learned something: I realized I felt Lynne had been through so much that I was pulling for her.

.   .   .

I waved over MacDonald and Perkins after completing the statement, and they approached, toting coffee. MacDonald set a paper coffee cup in front of me and pushed a paper sack to me. Inside, were blueberry muffins sprinkled with sugar. I wasn't about to make my "What, no donuts?" crack. Fact was, MacDonald scared the hell out of everyone who saw him. Even Perkins, if not frightened, at least looked at him with approval.

Despite the coffee tasting like it smelled—burned—I thanked MacDonald. The muffins, in fact, were nearly as good as those you'd find in coastal Maine, where blueberries grow in abundance.

MacDonald read my statement, nodding to himself. Then he formally reviewed it with me and swore me to it. "Just so we're clear," he said, "you understand this could be brought in as evidence or, should you testify, used to impeach any testimony you offer that doesn't jibe with this."

I told him I realized that.

"We'll have this typed up, Jack. Then you can read it over and sign it. If you want to make changes to the text, you'll have to initial them." He motioned to one of the other agents, who quickly took the cue. MacDonald handed the statement to him, and the agent left, apparently knowing what to do.

"This is, as you know, an ongoing murder investigation," MacDonald said. "Please keep that in mind when dealing with the media."

"I understand."

MacDonald nodded again, then drank from his coffee cup. "Investigating," he said, "oftentimes means gathering material until two seemingly unrelated pieces fit together. For that reason—and because last year you did what you said you would and kept your mouth shut—I'd like to talk candidly."

Perkins was leaning back in his chair, hands clasped before him.

"Sure," I said.

MacDonald's bearing eased slightly, as if the formality was over. "See that kid, Riley, over there," he said, pointing to the bird-necked guy with two laptops. "Kid can barely load a pistol, let alone shoot one. But he knows all about computers and the Internet, so he's an FBI agent. He tells me almost six hundred million people worldwide used the Internet in 2003. A hundred and sixty-six million were in the United States."

I sipped some coffee and worked on my second muffin. Perkins reached over and took the bag, pulled three muffins out, carefully examined each, then returned the two that didn't meet his standards.

"In 2002," MacDonald said, "retail Internet sales totaled seventy-six billion dollars. Michael Easley left the University of Georgia in 2001 at the age of twenty-three. I say 'left' not 'graduated.' He left after four years with the credits equivalent to a sophomore. But with the bank account of a surgeon."

I looked at Perkins. He sat expressionless.

"In 2001, the on-line porn industry took off. It made two hundred thirty million dollars."

"Timing is everything," Perkins said. "I knew I was in the wrong business."

MacDonald considered smiling but probably remembered he never smiled and kept going. "Easley, according to the Internet stats Riley has, set up one of the most visited—meaning one of the most potentially lucrative—porn sites. I guess Easley can thank Lynne for that. In Easley's best month, he took in three hundred thousand dollars."

"Grant told me Easley needed money," I said. "He was caddying."

MacDonald nodded. "I noticed that in your statement. Easley spent millions, Jack."

"Spent so much he needed to caddie?" Perkins said.

"We're going through Easley's financial records. His Web site was a subscription service. He got in when the industry was at its all-time high."

"Meaning the industry took a downturn?" I said.

"Yes."

"And Easley stayed in through its downturn," I said.

"Yeah," MacDonald said. "And continued spending. The parties the kid threw—renting clubs, running tabs—and he went through vehicles like Evil Knievel. As a college student, the kid had a nine-hundred-thousand–dollar home."

"Unbelievable," Perkins said.

"Yeah. A Hummer, a Porsche, and a Volvo Cross Country for the days he wanted to play grown-up. Also, we're learning Easley spent a great deal on drugs."

"Was he broke?" Perkins said.

"We're still going through things," MacDonald said. "Our estimates figure Easley made between three and five million from 2001 to 2004. There's a lot of money we can't account for—cash withdrawals all the time. Kid had restaurant and monthly bar tabs in Athens, Georgia, that are simply staggering. I think, when all is said and done, we'll discover he simply ran out—cars, the house, the parties, and drugs. It couldn't last forever."

"Sex and booze and cars," Perkins shook his head. "Probably the most popular kid on campus."

"Popular, but not much of a businessman." MacDonald paused to sip his coffee. "The bottom didn't exactly fall out, but the on-line porn industry is not what it once was. There's too much for free now. The research we have says, by 2006, porn will only be the Internet's fourth biggest industry, behind gaming, music, and movies."

"So, if Easley's spending didn't slow to reflect that," Perkins said, "he took a serious financial hit."

"How did Easley start the business?" I said.

"Riley"—MacDonald called to the laptop kid—"come over here, please."

Riley moved quickly. "Yes, sir."

"Please explain how a Mike Easley–type can set up a porn site."

"Sir, there're two ways to establish a Web site. You can either get an ISP account or set up your own server."

"English, Riley," MacDonald said.

"ISP, Internet service provider—sort of a central host that lets you onto the host's area of the Web. Or you can buy the software and hardware and set up your own server. Costs roughly a thousand dollars, sir. But it's much more confidential. You also need to really know what you're doing."

"So Easley got an ISP account," MacDonald said, steering Riley.

Riley nodded. "Yes. And he registered the domain name wildmeredith.com. The whole thing totaled about two hundred and fifty dollars with a credit card. Also, we have his merchant credit card processing account, so we have a paper trail."

"Thanks, Riley," MacDonald said, and the kid left.

"Grant said Lynne told him Easley needed money," I said, "and that she owed Easley a favor, so he let him caddie."

"What do you think of that," MacDonald said, "as a golfer?"

"I think it's crazy. I've used inexperienced guys before. But Easley was awful—didn't do the basics, didn't try. For Christ's sake, the guy was high while he was working."

Perkins nodded. "Enough said."

"What the hell kind of favor could Lynne have owed Easley?" I said. "You think it was blackmail?"

MacDonald's face showed no expression. "You mean Easley threatened to go public with Lynne's past?"

"Yeah," I said.

"Could be," MacDonald said. "But in 2001, Lynne was only seventeen."

"What's that mean?" I said.

Perkins tilted his head and looked at MacDonald. "Lynne is only twenty now?"

"Just turned twenty-one," MacDonald said.

"I thought Lynne was twenty-three or twenty-five," I said.

"No."

"I'll be damned." Perkins shook his head. "That changes everything, doesn't it?"

"It does," MacDonald said.

I didn't know exactly what or how things had changed. I sat, waiting.

"So she had Easley for child porn," Perkins said.

MacDonald nodded. "Or statutory rape. She could've blackmailed Easley. She had been underage when it began."

"He probably never asked her age," Perkins said. "Probably didn't give a shit. She could make him money and he knew it."

"And she did," MacDonald said. "Lots of it."

"So they could've blackmailed each other?" I said.

"Except one of them is now dead," Perkins said. "Easley isn't going to blackmail anyone now."

MacDonald nodded slowly.

"I know that crime scene bothers you," Perkins said.

"No fend-off wounds," MacDonald said. "That bothers me. The guy was stabbed four times in the back. Never turned around. His blood-alcohol level was point one five, so he was drunk, but no fend-off cuts on his forearms? Not even a bruise on either arm? No cuts on his hands, either. What did he do, lie down so the killer could stab him?" He sipped some coffee, shaking his head.

"Makes no sense," Perkins said.

"Dempsey is a big guy," MacDonald said. "He told us he played college football."

"You think he manhandled Easley?" Perkins said.

MacDonald shrugged. "Regardless, it's very rare that a guy is stabbed to death and gets no defensive cuts. Something is not right."

"Any wounds postmortem?" Perkins said.

"That's the kicker. His heart was pumping blood the whole time."

I leaned back in my chair, struggling to follow them.

Perkins looked at me. "If there were scratches or cuts with no blood in them, you'd know the heart had stopped pumping before those cuts were made. You'd know they occurred after death."

I nodded. "So you know the stab wounds were what killed him."

"Yeah," MacDonald said.

The three of us sat listening to the cacophony of keyboards, shuffled papers, and faint voices. The coffee was finished, the muffins gone.

I had a headache.

24

$\mathbf{I}$t was Friday. The weather was to die for, and my foursome was, too. I'd gotten up at 7:30, spent an hour downstairs lifting weights, showered, then from 9:30 to 11 A.M. worked with Schultz on the driving range at the Woodlands. Now it was playtime. While my mother watched Darcy, Schultz, my father, Lisa, and I were playing eighteen holes at the Woodlands Club—Lisa and I versus Schultz and Dad.

I had a secret weapon. Lisa had gone into golf journalism after she'd gone into golf. In fact, having grown up in Maryland, she'd headed south to play for the College of Boca Raton—now Lynn University—in Boca Raton, Florida, a Division II school with three NCAA women's golf championships. She'd earned both academic and athletic All-America status while majoring in journalism. Now, she didn't golf very often but still played to a nine or ten handicap. Our opponents, however, didn't need to know that—we'd listed her as a fifteen.

"How is Lisa a fifteen if she's even par after two holes?" Dad said. "I'm a fifteen and I'm two over."

Dad was moving briskly from the golf cart he and Schultz shared to the third tee. He walked like he did everything—high octane. No practice swings. Throw the ball down and take a slash. He loved to compete, not think about it. He had a gray beard, a belly, and the vivid eyes of one with a joke at the ready.

"It's only two holes," Lisa said.

"You see what's going on here, Peter?" Dad said.

"Sure," Schultz said. "We're getting hustled. Jack played bad all summer to set this up."

We all laughed. I was shaking my head.

Lisa and I sat in our cart, parked behind the cart Dad and Schultz drove, near the white tees. I'd already hit, and we were waiting to move to Lisa's red tees. The par-five third hole at the Woodlands plays 568 yards from the black tees, where I hit from, 511 from the whites, and 468 from Lisa's red tees. The fairway narrows and the green is guarded on both sides by sand traps and water, but I had jumped on my tee shot and had about 250 yards to the hole.

"How many strokes am I getting?" Dad said, from the tee.

"One a hole," I said.

He shook his head. "If you reach this goddamned par five in two, I get two strokes on the par fives." He teed his ball, shot me a menacing look, then slashed the ball into the heart of the fairway. "Short but straight. Tortoise and the hare, Peter. We'll catch the kids."

"That we will," Schultz said.

Schultz had spit at my offer to play from the red tees. His swing was everything Dad's was not—slow, smooth, a symphony of motion. The ball seemed propelled by all of his 140 pounds and landed in the heart of the fairway, still well over 300 yards from the green.

"Peter, I could watch you swing that club all day long," Dad said. "Goliath, there"—he pointed at me—"would do well to copy it."

"My father gave me a hickory-shafted club when I was a kid," Schultz said. "You grow up swinging that, you learn tempo."

We drove to Lisa's tee. She took several practice swings, then hit her drive past Dad's and Schultz's. I leaned back and smiled. And waited. It didn't take long.

"A fifteen handicap," Dad said. "Look at that drive. . . ."

Lisa got in and we sped down the fairway.

.   .   .

"Does the FBI think Lynne Ashley killed Mike Easley?" Lisa said. We were still on the third hole and watched Dad hit his second shot. His ball sliced into the trees, right of the fairway.

"I don't know," I said. "MacDonald shared a hell of a lot more than I expected, but not everything."

"He trusts you."

"I took his openness to mean they're at a loss. He probably thought that if he said something that clicked for me—something that went with something I knew—maybe he'd get somewhere."

"I think he just trusts you," she said and leaned over to kiss my cheek. "You did help him out a lot last year. Damned near got shot in the process."

"True."

Schultz hit his second shot 150 yards up the fairway. I drove the cart to Lisa's ball. She got out and walked to the back of the cart.

"What are you going to hit?" I said.

"Five-iron. I'm rusty."

"Smart play, partner."

She took the iron from her bag and made several practice swings.

The sun was bright overhead, and I was thoroughly enjoying myself. I was playing in my ideal foursome. Someday, I'd bring Darcy to this course, as my father had taken me to play. Maybe she, too, would wake at five and pace, anxious and eager to golf.

I heard Schultz laughing across the fairway. He was looking at Dad, who smiled and shrugged, innocently. I could smell Lisa's berry-scented perfume. She was wearing a pale-blue Ashworth shirt with a Golf Channel logo, khaki shorts, and sunglasses. The shorts fit her very well and she had the tan of one no longer spending time in a television studio or on a TV tower.

"If it were appropriate golf etiquette," I said, "I'd tell you you've got great wheels."

"You can tell me," she said.

So I did.

"We're waiting for Annika to hit," Schultz said.

"All right." Lisa addressed the ball and made a long slow swing. Her motion reminded me of Dad's remark—that he learned more by watching the LPGA than the PGA Tour, because professional women swing with such rhythm and control that he could "see more of the swing," as opposed to viewing the 120-miles-per-hour club head speed of some PGA Tour players.

Lisa's second shot strategically positioned the ball farther up the fairway. She returned to the cart. "I feel for Lynne Ashley," she said.

"Me, too."

"I know you do, Jack. I know situations like the one she's in bother you. But I mean from a female perspective, I feel for her. At the *Post* I covered a story about a woman who made adult films then wrote a book about her life."

The *Washington Post* had been Lisa's job prior to CBS, and was before we'd met. Lisa had been coaxed from hard-news journalism to golf by CBS after she'd interviewed Annika Sörenstam, the world's top female player. The interview had been conducted during an eighteen-hole outing. CBS had been impressed not only by Lisa's probing questions—which went beyond the generic, to topics the likes of *Is there any rivalry between Annika and sister, LPGA player Charlotta?*—as well as her obvious knowledge of the game's current state and past, and her understanding of the golf swing. That, coupled with what TV execs called an "outstanding on-camera persona," led CBS to make an offer she couldn't refuse.

"It was a tragic story," she said. "Sexually abused as a child, the woman was told she was pretty and could model in California. The modeling included nude shots. It also included cocaine."

"And from there," I said, "the rest is . . ."

"Yes. I felt for the woman. And I feel for Lynne Ashley."

We were playing four ball, meaning each of us played his or her own ball and the team recorded the best score of the pair, using handicaps. Lisa was getting a stroke on this hole. I knew she'd make par, so I was going for an eagle. My ball had come to rest 255 yards from the center of the green. A three-wood would be plenty of club. I took my customary two practice swings, briefly envisioned the shot, then addressed the ball.

The take-away was smooth, the follow-through well balanced. The ball bounced on the front edge of the green and rolled, stopping twenty feet right of the pin.

"You hit that like a PGA Tour star," Lisa said.

"Got to win to be a star."

"Jack, you have two runner-up finishes in less than twelve months. Don't be so hard on yourself."

We moved up the fairway and waited for Dad and Schultz to hit.

"It's like age has no affect on Peter's swing," Lisa said.

"Like watching old footage of Sam Snead. I'd kill for that tempo."

Schultz's game now consisted of 150-yard shots—each one as straight as a power line—over and over. He played a fifteen-degree three-wood from about any lie and used the club for nearly three-quarters of his shots.

"Have you heard from Jim Dempsey?" Lisa said.

I shook my head. I had spent Thursday at home. I had relieved Lisa of household duties—vacuumed, dusted, did laundry, cleaned the bathroom—and had her leave two bottles and go to the Maine Mall, where she'd met Perkins's wife, Linda, for shopping and lunch. That evening, I practiced. I hadn't tried to contact Dempsey. MacDonald was doing that. But where Dempsey was now and what he was doing were good questions.

"Dempsey just said he was going away," I said. "Grant said Dempsey was a fool."

"Meaning what? Lynne used Dempsey to make some acting contacts, then dumped him?"

"I don't know. I don't think that's accurate. I think Lynne really felt for Jim Dempsey. Maybe when he found out about her past, he called it off."

"A lot of his business," Lisa said, "is credibility."

"Yeah. Dumping your wife and kids for a porn queen doesn't help that."

Lisa looked at me, her eyes narrowing. As when Lynne had offended her in our living room, Lisa ran her tongue along her upper lip. She only did that when she was angry. I knew my phrasing had been poor.

"I feel for Lynne Ashley," she said again, "because *that* is precisely what people will see when they look at her. I thought you'd be a little more sympathetic."

"Lisa," I said, "I am sympathetic. But Grant came to me to see how I made my marriage work. He's left all alone. Another guy is dead. That guy was a dirtball, but no one has the right to stab someone to death. It's a particularly gruesome way to murder someone. And my agent—also a longtime friend—is now divorced. Lynne is at the root of all this."

"Jack, she is a female, manipulated by a man to the point where she sought refuge in Grant Ashley and married him for the wrong reasons."

I kept quiet this time. Lynne had been a seventeen-year–old girl, six years younger than Easley.

"Look," Lisa said, "all I'm saying is this: When I wrote that article for the *Post*, I did a lot of legwork—interviewed a lot of secondary sources, experts in human behavior. One feminist scholar said the woman who lived that life, then wrote her book, 'used men to profit,' said that woman knew full well she had what men wanted and used it to manipulate them and get what she wanted."

"Which was?"

"Money. Power." She shrugged. "Fame."

I was quiet. I thought of how I'd felt when Perkins had taken Padre and me to the Boston strip club—as if the women there were partially mocking us. I also thought of how that contradicted my initial reaction to seeing Lynne on the Web site.

"To me," Lisa said, "neither Lynne nor the lady who wrote that book fit that mold. They were young. They were manipulated. They were used so others could profit. She was seventeen, for God's sake."

"I agree," I said. "I know Easley used Lynne. I'm torn because I think she, in turn, used Grant to get away. He was sort of a safety house until she got it together. Except he didn't know that and fell in love, planned a future."

She looked down at the black rubber floor of the cart. "Poor Grant. He is so young."

"Regardless of all that, though, if Easley tried to blackmail Lynne, she had motive."

"And now Mike Easley is dead," she said and sat staring at me.

We had reached her ball. Slowly, she got out to hit again, this time from seventy-five yards. Her mind was no longer on golf. Her practice swings were stiff, mechanical.

Schultz, however, whose ball lay just inside Lisa's, called from across the fairway, "Lisa, closest to the pin for a buck?"

She came back to our golf outing. "You're on, Peter."

She played the ball nearly off her back foot and choked down on a wedge. The ball bounced twice, skidding to a stop on the green, eight feet from the pin.

"Just like you had that ball on a string," I said. "For someone rusty, this is some playing."

She winked, got back in the cart, and kissed me on the mouth. "You're a good man, Jack Austin."

"What's that for?" I said. "I mean, I know it's true. I just want to know how you know it."

She smiled momentarily, then was serious. "The way you see this Lynne Ashley situation. You have great loyalty to your friends. But you always feel for the underdog—it's just your nature, to help the people who need it. This time those two instincts are in conflict. And you're doing the best you can."

"I just want to win golf tournaments."

"But you can't walk away. That's not who you are."

e called yesterday," I heard Joan Dempsey say from Houston, Texas. "He said he had to stay away for a while. But that he wanted to talk. We've been divorced since winter."

"I know. I'm sorry."

It was 11:15 A.M. Saturday. I had called looking for Jim Dempsey. I knew he was divorced and living elsewhere. I'd tried his office and cell phone and left messages. I'd sent an e-mail. No response. Dempsey had indicated he planned to go away for a while. I didn't know if that meant leaving the Tour for an unknown destination or heading back to Houston to see his ex and kids. I hoped the latter and had been glad to hear Joan say he had indicated a desire to talk with her.

"This has been a tough time, Jack," Joan said, *time* sounding nearly like *tame*. "He left me—left us—for another woman."

"I'm sorry." It was all I could say.

"Jack . . ." she said and took in a long breath, "do you know her?"

When considering this call, I hadn't thought that question a possibility. It was, though, the single last thing I wanted to answer. "Yes."

Joan was crying now. Full out. "It's hard, you know? I'm just trying to understand how, why. What does she have . . . ?"

I heard the sobs and sat staring at the floor.

"Is she very young? Pretty?"

I looked out the window. To the east, I saw the ocean. It seemed to go on forever.

"I don't know," I said.

"But you've met her, Jack. Please tell me."

There was a desperation in her voice I had not expected. I had lied and told her I didn't know that Lynne was young and pretty. But Joan needed to know. I hadn't expected that need and didn't fully understand it. I had half expected her to hang up at the mention of her ex-husband's name. I had anticipated anger, not desperation. Now I wished she'd slammed the phone down.

"Did he ever say why, Jack?" She blew her nose. "I mean, did he ever say what I didn't give . . . ?"

She couldn't finish.

"No, Joan, we never talked about that."

"I just thought . . ."

I waited.

"You and he were close. Maybe he said something."

"No."

"When he told me he was leaving, I asked what I had done."

"Nothing," I said. "You didn't do anything. Joan, don't blame yourself."

She didn't reply. Then I heard her sobs. They were long and loud.

The line went dead.

I set the phone back on the receiver and looked at the ocean. Forever. A big word. The ocean had seen forever and would continue on long after us all. A woman in Texas was trying to understand why her husband left her and was desperate enough to ask me, a friend of her husband, but a man thousands of miles away, one whom she'd met only a handful of times. Grant Ashley was alone. Lynne Ashley had been exploited and very likely had, in turn, exploited Jim Dempsey. Mike Easley had been stabbed in the back. But it was Joan Dempsey's question that made me sick to my stomach.

I left the house and sat on the rocky shore alone for an hour.

. . .

At 5:30 p.m. Sunday, Peter Schultz and I were driving back to Chandler from Falmouth. I'd spent the afternoon with Schultz at the Woodlands Club, hitting balls under the mid-June sun. It had been a perfect afternoon for golf—temperature, low-eighties; very little breeze. I'd received no word on the Mike Easley murder investigation, which was now nearly ten days old. Perkins had once said the longer a murder remains unsolved, the more difficult the case becomes to close.

Pounding my driver for forty minutes had relieved tension in my shoulders and back that had been there since the talk with Joan Dempsey. I'd finished the forty-minute driver session swinging at my ideal tempo, 80 percent of full throttle. But I had begun—despite Schultz's presence—imitating John Daly's "grip it and rip it" mentality.

After the driver, I hit high soft five-irons for half an hour. The five-iron rehearsals were more self-punishment than practice:

The mistake I had made at the Memorial Tournament, the mis-hit five-iron one week earlier, had not been a mechanical error. Rather, it had been a mental blunder. After the five-iron, I had spent a long time in a practice bunker. Then I had putted. All the work had been under the watchful and knowledgeable gaze of Schultz.

Now I felt confident. I'd spent a lot of time with my coach, had hit the weight room hard during the past week, and had spent quality time on the range. Practice always made me feel good. Preparation does that. I knew that very few players had spent more time than I this week readying for next. That knowledge bred confidence. The next morning, I was to fly to New York for the Buick Classic, where, as Lisa mentioned during our rout of Dad and Schultz, I had finished second to Phil Mickelson the year before.

The old Suburban was still spinning like a top, and I had an Everclear CD, *So Much for the Afterglow,* in the player. "Amphetamine" played.

"Holy Jesus," Schultz said. "It takes me ten minutes to climb into this vehicle, and now you make me listen to this screaming."

I replaced Everclear with the classical radio station.

"Hitting the ball well, Jack."

"Thanks for all your help."

"You know I enjoy it. I enjoy coming here."

"To Maine?"

We were on I-295. The late-Sunday traffic was mild. Schultz looked small in the huge vehicle and seemed to sit low in the seat, wearing his wrap-around shades.

"It's not about seeing Maine, although the state is lovely," he said. "It's not even about golf."

I looked at him. I knew we were treading in new waters.

"It's Darcy," he said.

"Darcy?"

We passed the B&M Baked Beans factory on the left and began weaving through the Portland exits, near the University of Southern Maine and Hadlock Field, where the Double-A affiliate of the Red Sox, the Portland Sea Dogs, plays. Lisa and I had gone to several Sea Dog games. Baxter Boulevard, a four-mile path, was on the right, lined with joggers and walkers.

"Darcy reminds me of my daughter, June. She passed away when she was sixteen." He was facing the window, looking at the USM library.

He'd never mentioned June before. I knew he'd been married and that his wife of forty-plus years had passed away. He'd never mentioned children. I knew he'd been a Hall of Fame PGA Tour player, despite losing years to WWII, and had assumed he'd not had children.

"A lot of what I did, that eight-and-one playoff record, was for June. I accomplished that and the Masters before . . ."—his voice got quiet—"she passed away."

I didn't say anything. I drove and waited. I'd let him direct the conversation.

"When we got June home from the hospital, all I wanted to do was rock that baby—like you do, Jack."

I nodded.

"Then I got hungry."

I glanced from the road to him. We were nearing the junction of I-95.

"I wanted to leave a legacy," Schultz said. "Even if the legacy went no further than my own family. I wanted to leave something June could look at proudly when I was gone."

I nodded. I understood.

"You always assume your kids will outlive you," he said. He studied the floor mat. "It should be that way. I wanted to leave some record behind for June."

"The Masters win."

"Yes. And the Hall of Fame."

We were quiet as we headed south.

Schultz had his glasses off when he turned back to me. "Unfortunately, June only saw one on those. She was there when I won the Masters. Emily and June were both gone when I was inducted to the Hall."

His eyes were wet and he turned back to the window.

. . .

Two suitcases lay open on the bed. Schultz was downstairs, rocking Darcy. Dinner had been eaten. Afterward, coffee had been drunk on the deck overlooking the ocean. Now, Lisa and I were in the master bedroom at 7:30 P.M.

"Thanks for packing for me," I said, "but you think I need two suitcases?"

She had been facing the closet and turned to me, hands on hips. She shook her head sadly. "Vanity, vanity, vanity." She turned back to her closet, took some things out, and delicately folded them before dropping them into a suitcase. "I'm packing for Darcy and myself, Jack."

"Does this mean what I think it means?"

"That you're self-absorbed?"

"Lisa, I'm being serious."

"Or that you now have to pack for yourself?" A broad smile spread across her face. "Yes—on both counts." She turned back to the closet, giggling.

I smiled and stood watching her.

When she realized I hadn't moved, she turned around. She was wearing blue-jean shorts and a white cotton top.

"The way those jeans fit you proves we're not aging at the same rate," I said. "You look about twenty-two."

"Thank you, but I still won't pack for you."

"You're going to Westchester?"

"Darcy is two months old now, Jack."

"Should I call and change the reservation?"

"Done."

"You had this planned?"

"I had Westchester and this date circled on my calendar. The doctor said Darcy could fly at two months."

My smile widened. I heard Lisa's new Springsteen CD, *The Rising,* playing softly downstairs. Schultz never complained about her music. In fact, he never complained about anything having to do with Lisa. It made me think of what I'd learned about his late daughter, June. I was starting to realize why he'd always enjoyed spending time with Lisa.

"So you're coming to see me play." I grinned. "Missed seeing my towering drives, huh?"

"Oh, please." She laughed and went to my dresser, opened a drawer, and took out a stack of boxers. She took one step toward the suitcase—and threw the boxers at me.

They hit me in the chest and fell to the floor.

She laughed and stepped closer, still giggling. "I'm going to Westchester to show off my daughter, Jack. Not so I can see you play golf."

"Excuse me?"

"So vain." She shook her head again. "I sent all the wives photos of Darcy. And they all called. Don't you know how these things work?"

I spread my hands.

"Now she's old enough to travel. So it's time to take her and show her off." She patted my cheek lightly. "Pack yourself, Mr. Longball." She turned and walked to the bathroom with an accessory bag.

I looked at the two suitcases and stood smiling.

A 6:40 A.M. flight from Portland put us in White Plains, New York, at 1 P.M. I was amazed the plane had gotten off the ground. Aside from my standard travel gear—a hard-shelled protective case with wheels for my clubs and a single suitcase—there were the two additional suitcases, a porta-crib, a diaper bag Lisa used as a purse, a toy bag, and a duffel in which were bottles, teething rings, pacifiers, bibs, and the tiny pink blanket Darcy slept with. After taking the Buick courtesy car to the hotel, I helped Lisa unpack (a thirty-minute process) and went directly to the golf course.

Westchester Country Club offered good vibes. A year earlier, I'd played well there, finishing second. Despite my belief that only the winner is truly remembered, when I entered the locker room Monday afternoon, an attendant slapped my back. He was in his seventies and looked Irish with watery pale-blue eyes, a wide red nose, and a thick head of white hair.

"Good playing last year," he said. "Name's Marty O'Reilly. Mickelson's won enough. I was pulling for you last year, Jack."

"Thanks," I said. The mandatory locker room fee is $50. I was already planning to tip Marty O'Reilly more.

Some of the regulars were already there. Two past Buick Classic winners, Sergio Garcia and Chris Smith, were tying their spikes. Padre Tarbuck sat across the room. Near him, was Grant Ashley. Some players had already gotten in practice rounds or workouts in the HealthSouth fitness van and were headed to or coming from the showers. Others were dressing to play a round or hit range balls, pulling on shirts bearing sponsors' logos, bending hat visors, or rifling through lockers for new gloves and balls. Some contestants were still unpacking.

Padre saw me and walked over. "Just getting here?"

"Yeah." I hung several Maxfli shirts in my locker. I tossed a T-shirt and workout shorts on the top shelf.

"Grant Ashley and I are going off in about ten minutes," Padre said. "Want to play?"

I thought about that. I hadn't seen Grant since he'd come to my house. "Sure."

"Fifty bucks for the front nine. Fifty for the back. Fifty for total score," Padre said. "Bring your wallet. When I get done with you, Lisa will have to go back to CBS so you can pay me."

"Or maybe I'll see to it that you remember your oath of poverty, Father Tarbuck," I said.

He grinned and went back to his locker.

. . .

Westchester Country Club plays to 6,722 yards from the championship tees. Par for the PGA Tour event is seventy-one. Water isn't feared; there's only one water hazard. But there are fifty-five sand traps. Likewise, the track is hilly, and the fairways are tree-lined and tight.

Grant and I were on the first tee. Silver was to the side of the tee, chatting with Grant's new caddie, a gray-haired guy named Fur Lomax. Fur was aptly nicknamed, as a patch of black chest hair protruded from his shirt collar. He was a veteran caddie. I first heard of Grant's new hire on The Golf Channel and whole-heartedly agreed with the decision. A veteran looper like Fur might add stability for the young and troubled Grant.

We stood silently waiting for Padre, who was signing auto-graphs for a collection of female golf (read: Padre) fans near the locker room.

"FBI agent named MacDonald showed up at my hotel room," Grant said. "He told me he met with you."

I nodded.

"The guy asked me some pretty serious questions, Jack."

"I'm sure he did."

"What the hell does that mean?"

I was swinging my driver back and forth to stay loose, the club head brushing the turf on the first tee. "Means I've met MacDonald. I know what he's like."

"What exactly did you tell him, Jack?"

"Everything I know."

"That's fucking great. Nice to have friends you can count on."

I stopped the practice swings. "He called me to the FBI's Boston office. With Perkins."

He shook his head and looked at the ground. "You sold me out, too."

"Grant, MacDonald wanted me to make a formal statement. I did that. And told the truth. You familiar with perjury?"

"I flew to your house to talk in private, Jack."

"You showed me the damned Web site. MacDonald asked me what I knew." I spread my hands. "It's a criminal investigation."

"The guy thinks I did it, Jack."

There wasn't much to say to that.

"I'm a PGA Tour player, for Christ's sake. I couldn't murder anyone."

I stood looking at him. I hoped that hadn't been the alibi he'd offered MacDonald.

"He hammered me about getting upset on the eleventh tee, being pissed that Lynne was gone. You told him about that."

"Grant, a guy is dead." I shook my head. "I told the truth."

"That wasn't the worst of it," Grant said. "I told you and some other people that Easley got what he deserved. Mac-Donald interviewed everyone I said that to."

MacDonald was thorough. That didn't surprise me. What Grant said next did.

"That was my mistake," he said.

"What was your mistake?"

He looked at me as if he'd not intended to speak aloud. "Nothing." Then he turned to the caddies. "Come on, Fur. Let's hit range balls." He started walking away.

Fur rushed to keep up.

I watched them go, wondering if Grant and I would ever finish a round of golf together. And wondering what his mistake had been.

"He get another back injury?" Silver said. "Or he just finally figure out you're an asshole?"

"The latter," I said.

. . .

The ninth hole at Westchester CC is a par-five, 505 yards. The yardage doesn't sound intimidating, but your tee shot must carry 250 yards just to reach the fairway. I had nailed my drive and stood with a three-iron in hand in the center of the fairway. The sun was hot on my back. It was approaching ninety and humid. Being Monday, only a handful of spectators were on the course, one of whom was six feet five and close to three hundred pounds.

"Got to love having our own security guard," Silver said, motioning to Perkins, who stood at the edge of the fairway.

I looked at Padre. "We're even to here, right?"

He nodded. "Tied." He'd hit his second shot already. I hadn't seen the ball land but knew the shot had wandered right of the green.

"What's my cut of fifty bucks?" Silver said.

"You're salaried."

"Damn."

I took two practice swings.

Silver got serious. "One ninety-one to the green. Two oh three to the pin. Hole is on the first tier. It'll take a high shot to stop the ball close."

I nodded and put away the three-iron. I pulled the four-iron from the bag. I hit the four-iron much higher than I did my three. Standing thirty yards away, Perkins looked bored. Oddly, his expression didn't change—even after my four-iron flew high and landed softly. From where I stood, the ball looked to be within ten feet of the pin.

Silver and I moved to Perkins.

"Anyone ever tell you you've got biceps to die for?" Silver said.

"Jesus Christ, Silver." Perkins stood away from the other fans and wore a white golf shirt with the blue PGA Tour emblem on the breast and navy blue slacks. "Jack, MacDonald is here."

"Grant told me he went to see him."

He nodded. "MacDonald may want to talk to you again."

There was something in the way he said it. Not a warning exactly, but he wanted me to be aware of something. "What's going on?"

"They're getting search warrants signed to go through Grant's house. I think there's going to be an arrest forthcoming."

"'Forthcoming,'" Silver said. "More than just a pretty arm."

Perkins ignored him.

"Grant?" I said.

Perkins nodded. "Looks that way. I'd stay clear of Grant. Just let things run their course."

"You think he did it?"

Perkins shrugged. "We'll see. I think MacDonald will get to the bottom of this."

.   .   .

I was up a hundred bucks when we got to the green at the par-five, 526-yard eighteenth at 5:30 P.M. I'd won the front and was ahead on total strokes by a landslide. Despite the day's profits, it was hard not to think of Grant, of what he'd said to me—both at my home and on the first tee. And it was difficult to get Perkins's remarks out of my mind. On the eleventh tee at the U.S. Open qualifying round, I'd seen people tell Grant they were sorry for his loss. Could Grant have stabbed Easley? What had been his mistake? Losing his cool and saying Easley got what he deserved? Grant had a lot to regret: his marriage and choice of agents. The words had seemed to rise from somewhere far below the surface.

Padre stood next to me on the green. Our balls rested side by side. We had nearly identical putts. He shook his head and slapped my back. "And I offered you a lesson at the Memorial. What was I thinking? Peter Schultz still working with you?"

"He stayed with us part of last week."

"That's unbelievable." Padre shook his head. "He gets five hundred bucks an hour, but works with you for free."

"Who could pass up the chance to work with this finely tuned swing?"

"Finely tuned like a rusted bike chain." Padre grinned.

"Schultz enjoys being with the baby," I said. "Having him take me under his wing has been like winning the lottery. Guy has forgotten more about the game and the golf swing than I'll ever know."

Padre nodded and crouched to examine the line from his ball to the hole. "Schultz or not, you still have to make this putt, Mr. Austin."

He was right. I had twenty-five feet for eagle. But Padre was putting for birdie. Advantage: Mr. Austin.

"I think a two-putt wins the match," I said.

"You saying I can't make this birdie?" Padre said.

"*Si.*"

Tournament officials routinely select No. 18 as the first play-off hole. And not by accident. The eighteenth green is a test. Twenty-five feet—from seemingly anywhere on the putting surface—offers a lot of break.

"You're putting into the grain," Silver said. "Play it a foot, left to right."

I leaned over the ball, brought the putter back slowly, and made my "three-second" stroke. The ball fell, dead center.

Padre gave me high-five and handed me $150.

"No commission?" Silver said. "I read the break perfectly."

I handed him the hundred-dollar bill.

"Excellent," Silver said. "I was going to take you and Lisa to dinner to congratulate you on having Darcy. Now I can do it, and it won't cost me a dime."

He amused himself greatly and laughed all the way to the clubhouse.

As I moved to the locker room, I was not thinking of the fifty bucks I'd managed to keep. My mind was still on Grant, the kid who'd come to my house to ask questions about life. The same kid, who, according to Perkins, was on the verge of being charged with murder.

"Well," Lisa said, "let's hear a progress report."

It was Wednesday evening. We were in the restaurant at the Courtyard. Silver had beaten me to the seat next to Lisa, but at least he was making good on his promised dinner. We'd put in a long day of practice Tuesday and had been on the range at 7 A.M. this day. Now Silver sat slumped in the booth. I was across from Lisa and him, with Darcy asleep in her car seat beside me.

"We've been here two days," Lisa said and sipped some iced tea. "Darcy and I have seen the sites and gone to the daycare facility with Angela Davis. We've seen you only at dinner. Are you ready to play?"

"Oh, yeah," I said.

"We've sure practiced enough." Silver sunk lower in the booth.

"You look exhausted, Tim," Lisa said.

"Don't baby him," I said.

"Baby me, Lisa," Silver said.

As she told Silver how bad she felt for him, I shook my head and looked around the restaurant. Frequent travelers always seem to go back to the same hotels. We were staying at the Courtyard in Rye, New York, again this year. The hotel was five minutes from the course. Dempsey hadn't gotten me the Marriott contract. Grant had landed that deal. But I liked Courtyard hotels, and the restaurant was spacious and quiet. At thirty-six and a father, I was no longer interested in the bar scene. Rather, at day's end, I wanted solitude, good food, and a Heineken. This evening I had those, and the company was excellent, too. At least two-thirds of it: Darcy and Lisa were traveling with me now. However, Silver was there, too, and I knew what to expect anytime he and Lisa got together—talk of clothing, shoes, and Silver's lust object, Montel Williams. I would be on the outside— by choice—of most conversations.

"Poor thing," Lisa was saying, rubbing Silver's back.

"He had me on the range at seven this morning, Lisa. Then thirty-six holes. Same thing yesterday."

Lisa looked at me and grinned. "Meany."

"This is S.O.P.," Silver said. "Every week. Maybe not thirty-six holes a day, but Jack is back to his old self. I ought to work for someone with a bad back who can't practice as much."

"I never said he had to go to the range with me," I said.

"He needs me there."

I rolled my eyes and sipped my Heineken.

"So, you're ready to play," Lisa said.

"I love that outfit," Silver said to Lisa.

She wore an apple-green cotton sundress and white sandals.

"Is that Talbots?" he said.

"Just got it." She nodded. "So you like it?"

"I adore it," Silver said.

"For Christ's sake." I drank some beer.

"Tim, don't listen to Jack," Lisa said. "You appreciate fashion. I value that."

"I love that color," Silver said. "Apple green."

I drank more beer. Several golfers were eating. Some alone, others with families. I saw Padre Tarbuck across the room with a brunette.

"Tim," Lisa said, "thank you so much for treating us to dinner. It's really very sweet."

"It's the least I can do. I wanted you to know how happy I was for you. And I hope Darcy knows how much Uncle Tim loves her."

"Oh, boy," I said.

"*Tsss,*" Lisa said and leaned toward Silver. "That's very sweet."

They kissed each other's cheek. As they did, Silver looked at me and winked. With his hand behind Lisa's back, he flashed the $100 bill I'd given him Monday.

I shook my head.

When dinner arrived—chicken parmesan for me, some sort of chicken salad for Lisa, and Silver had the T-bone—Silver brought up Grant's departure from the first-tee Monday afternoon and what Perkins had said aside the ninth fairway. I had seen neither Grant nor Perkins since and had yet to mention Monday's events to Lisa. Our evenings had found a routine: After golf, I'd taken Darcy on walks; Lisa had jogged or used the hotel's workout room. I thought Lisa, only two months removed from having the baby, looked as she had prior to childbirth. I was, however, smart enough not to ask her weight.

She sipped iced tea. "Perkins thinks Grant will be arrested?" She said it the way she asked serious questions when she'd been in journalism full time—casually. *No rush. Think about it, and take your time. But give me an answer and make it honest.*

"That's what he told us," Silver said.

I sat looking at Darcy.

"Asshole or not," Silver said, "poor bastard, Easley got stabbed in the back. And Grant told some people the guy got what he had coming."

Silver ate a bite of steak and sipped his rum and Coke. Judging from the color of the glass, they wouldn't run out of Coke on Silver's account. The chicken parmesan was good. Not like they made it at DiMillo's Floating Restaurant in Portland, Maine, but it was good. Besides, it's tough to make a bad pasta dish.

"Did MacDonald think Grant killed Easley?" Lisa said to me. "You never indicated that."

I shrugged.

"What is it, Jack?" she said.

I was quiet a moment, then took a long pull from my beer. Finally, I told them what Grant said to me before departing from the first tee Monday.

"The guy's 'mistake,'" Silver said, "was getting mixed up with Lynne. That's obvious."

"I feel for Lynne," Lisa said; however, she nodded in agreement. "But she is having difficulty pulling her life together, Jack. Grant did make a mistake in his marriage to her."

"Sure." I stroked Darcy's hair.

"What is it?" Lisa said.

"The way he said it. It was like he'd meant for no one to hear it. Like the statement slipped out."

"I say things all the time I wish I hadn't said." Silver shrugged.

"That's very true, I'm sure." I smiled.

He drank and swallowed, then looked at the glass. "No big deal."

"You're not in the middle of a scandal," I said. "You can afford a slip."

After dinner, we sat drinking coffee. Lisa and I watched Silver polish off something called the "Mud Top," a brownie with ice cream, whipped cream, and chocolate.

"How can you eat that," Lisa said, "and never gain a pound?"

"Genes. My father weighed one fifty-five from the time he was twenty until he died at seventy-five."

"And, you walk five miles a day," she said.

Darcy woke and began to gurgle, then started to cry. I picked her up and held her against my shoulder, patting her back lightly. It didn't work. She cried louder.

"Should we go?" Silver said, looking longingly at his sundae.

"No. Finish your dessert." I stood and rocked Darcy, shifting my weight from foot to foot.

I stopped short. "I'm not so sure Grant regrets his marriage," I said over Darcy's wail.

Silver and Lisa looked at me. With my chin, I motioned to a booth across the room, where Grant sat with his wife, Lynne Ashley.

I sat down again. No one spoke, excluding Darcy. Across the room, Grant saw me, looked down at the tabletop, and shook his head. Lynne said something. Grant replied. Then Lynne looked over. I saw tears on her cheeks. She glared at me and held that pose as Silver paid and the three of us, with Darcy, left the dining room. As we moved past their booth, no one spoke; yet, I saw that Grant was crying, too.

"I'll say one thing," Silver said. "It's never boring working for you, Jack."

. . .

That night wasn't boring either. Nor was it restful. We had a double-occupancy room. Darcy slept in the porta-crib at the foot of the bed, and I'd fallen asleep to the soothing lullaby her musical mobile offered. I was tired from all the golf and dinner, which provided the week's second run-in with Grant Ashley and the inexplicable Lynne Ashley sighting. Apparently, though, Lisa was even more tired. I had spent the day engrossed in what many consider a recreational activity. My practice had been taxing; yet, Lisa had contended with a far more serious matter—child rearing. She was quickly sound asleep. This night, when Darcy woke and cried, Lisa put a hand on my shoulder and pushed once, prodding me to get up with the baby.

I did, and at 11:35 P.M. stood behind the stroller in the hotel lobby. I wore running shoes, shorts, and a T-shirt. My hair was out of sorts, so I'd put on a Maxfli hat. The cell phone was shrugged to my ear.

"Whaaat?" Perkins answered on the first ring.

"What if Linda were calling? Or your boss, the Tour commissioner?"

"You're neither. And that was me being polite. It's almost midnight. What do you want?"

"You weren't asleep."

"So what? I'm doing push-ups and sit-ups."

He didn't sound winded. "Where have you been all week?" I said.

"Working—here and Atlanta."

"How did the search in Atlanta go?"

"You on a cell phone?"

"Yeah."

"Can't say."

"The baby's crying. I'm taking her for a walk. Want to go?"

"My kid's almost five, Jack. I paid those dues already. Have fun."

"I saw Grant and Lynne Ashley eating dinner together tonight. Know anything about that?"

"The hell you did."

"Like I said, I'm taking Darcy for a walk. Care to join me?"

. . .

"So that's all?" Perkins said. "Neither of them spoke to you?"

I shook my head. "We left."

We were outside the hotel entrance. Perkins had on khaki shorts and a white National Rifle Association T-shirt. His white hair was jelled and glistened yellow beneath the street lamps that lit the parking lot.

"I thought you didn't like khaki?" I said.

"I don't like it enough to wear it every goddamned day like you do. Christ, your boxers are probably khaki."

I chuckled.

"Give me that." He nudged me out of the way and got behind the stroller. Then he leaned over it. Darcy's car-seat snapped to the top, and she lay facing him. "Couldn't sleep, sweetheart? Don't you worry, Darcy. Uncle P. is here."

He turned and looked at me. "What?"

I shook my head. It was a side I didn't see often and reminded me that contrary to his size and typical expression,

195

Perkins, former professional football player and current professional tough guy, was much more.

Cars were scattered throughout the lot. Perkins pushed the stroller, and we moved in a large circle, walking the perimeter of the parking lot.

"Place looks like a Buick dealership," he said.

"Courtesy cars."

"I know. Even I get one."

"I shook my head. Job gets cushier and cushier. What happened in Atlanta?"

"Grant told you he made a mistake, right?"

"Yeah. He said it like it slipped out. We'd been talking about what MacDonald had asked him, about how MacDonald knew Grant told people Easley got what he deserved."

"Saying Easley got what he deserved wasn't Grant's mistake," Perkins said. "In fact, that was probably just the truth."

As we walked, Perkins pushed the stroller with one hand and pulled the pink blanket to Darcy's shoulders with the other. He patted the blanket lightly, making sure she was completely covered. She was still crying, a softer variation of the sound that had forced me from the hotel room.

"Got a bottle?" he said.

"Tried that."

"Diaper?"

"That, too."

Perkins shrugged. "Grant's mistake was leaving a sneaker in his house that had Easley's blood on it."

I froze.

He stopped next to me. "Don't shake your head. He doesn't know they found it yet. MacDonald's getting everything together. Grant will be charged Thursday or Friday."

"Grant wasn't there when you searched?"

"No. You get the warrant, knock, if no one answers, you go in. You leave the warrant on the door and list of anything you confiscate. He knows we were there, and he's probably seen the list of items. He doesn't know there's a DNA match."

"I don't believe it."

"A tiny drop, but it's a DNA match, Jack. Believe it."

"This is Grant Ashley we're taking about."

"I'm sorry," he said. "You're his friend. Makes it more difficult for you to see. I'm looking at what he has said and what the evidence tells me: The guy was caddying for him, the result of blackmail—Grant admitted that to MacDonald. And you know Easley was hurting Grant's game. You witnessed that yourself. There's a lot of motive in all that."

"What did Grant admit about the blackmail?" I said. "What are the details?"

"Easley was broke, according to Grant. So he gave him a job."

"Or what?"

"Or Easley went public with Lynne's being Wild Meredith."

"Back up," I said. "Why not just hit Grant up for money?"

"Grant says Easley wanted to caddie. Says he gave Easley cash and the job. Maybe Easley got off being on Tour."

"And it let him keep tabs on Lynne."

He shrugged.

I shook my head. "This is the part I don't get. Grant wanted the All-American family. When Lynne dumps him for Dempsey, instead of being mad at Lynne, Grant is pissed at Dempsey."

"So?"

"So, he still loves her," I said.

"Which, again, gives him motive to kill Easley." Perkins stopped walking so he could readjust Darcy's blanket. "Easley slept with Grant's wife. He made goddamed movies of it, Jack. Put it on the Internet and made a fortune—at the expense of a seventeen year old, who Grant later married."

"And he still loves her," I said, nodding. We were walking again. It had been a hot week, and even at midnight the temperature was still in the seventies, the air still humid. "I know what you're saying. I just can't see him doing it."

"I think you don't want to see him doing it."

"True," I said, "but one thing that still bothers me is how much Lynne gained by getting together with Jim Dempsey—a shot at an acting career."

"Makes you doubt her Dempsey-is-my-true-love story?"

Two rookies, single guys, got out of a Buick and moved past us. They were dressed up, and I smelled strong cologne.

"Probably back from the city," Perkins said. "And they'll get to bed before us."

"Darcy has an iron will," I said. "When you think about all this, everyone loses but Lynne—Grant is alone and probably gets charged with murder; Dempsey has lost his wife and kids; and Easley gets to be dead. Lynne, on the other hand, after telling me any media attention would ruin her, now is back to dining with Grant. To date, the investigation has been quiet and confidential."

"FBI knows what it's doing. MacDonald's not some state trooper who wants to be on *Geraldo Rivera Live*."

"But it's been quiet. You think that's why Lynne came back to see Grant?"

Perkins bit his lower lip, considering. "How badly you think she wanted that acting career?"

I shook my head. "She only wanted a way out. Why?"

"It's a loose end. She'd know fame comes with a heavy price."

That made me pause. "Yeah, of all people, she would know that. And life with Dempsey, especially if the desired acting career is bogus, would be much further from the spotlight than life with Grant."

"Maybe the acting career was a way to meet Dempsey."

I thought about Grant's story of walking to his car and seeing Lynne stranded. She came from nothing and, I believed, had been exploited. I'd been pulling for her since this had begun. When I'd originally asked her why she'd selected Dempsey, she'd said she loved him. Now, I wanted to know if she had sent Dempsey packing or if it had been the other way around.

I sighed. "When Lynne was at our home, the plumber walked out from the kitchen, took one look at her, and nearly fainted. Now I know why. One of the other wives said the guy probably thought Lynne was attractive. Lynne said he was a disgusting slob. When she said it, I thought it was cruel. Now I get it. She realized how he knew her."

"People probably recognized her every so often."

"And people probably did worse than just stare," I said. "Comments, gestures. Might be humiliating."

He nodded.

I blew out a long breath. "And maybe Grant witnessed some of that."

"Which brings us back to where we began—Grant's motive."

"Shit."

"Sorry, Jack." Perkins looked at Darcy. "She ever going to fall asleep?" Darcy lay, eyes wide open, smiling up at him. "She's smirking. She knows she's keeping us both awake."

The humidity had pushed 95 percent all week and finally, Thursday morning, had won the fight. Tee times had been delayed due to thundershowers. My 8:36 A.M. starting time had been pushed two hours, though I didn't mind. Rain had softened the greens, and I'd taken advantage. At six strokes under par, Silver and I stood on the eighth tee, waiting for a group to clear the fairway. I'd made eagle at the par-five fifth hole and four birdies.

"Looks nice there, doesn't it?" Silver said, motioning to a leader board.

My name was atop it. I'd gone six under through seven holes once before, but that had been on an easy track in Maine. Minus six through seven holes was my best professional start. So when Silver brought up the leader board, I didn't answer.

"Won't answer me?" he said.

"Nope." Some guys won't even look at leader boards. I'm not that superstitious, but I don't believing in tempting the golf gods, either.

"Like telling a pitcher he's hurling a no-hitter?"

I didn't respond.

"We've led tournaments before," Silver said.

"And talked about it, too."

He smiled. "And finished second." He nodded and pulled the five-wood from the bag. "I see."

Five-wood was my only option for club selection at the eighth tee. The double-dogleg eighth hole at Westchester CC does not care where you stand on the leader board. The hole can—and if you're not precise, will—eat you up. Annually, it seems, No. 8 ranks as one of the most difficult holes played on Tour. The first dogleg requires a tee shot to carry 235 yards to reach the corner. Yet your drive must stop short of the water hazard, 265 yards away. However, even a well-positioned drive still leaves a three-, four-, or five-iron approach, over the water, to the green.

I had on rain gear—Gore-Tex jacket and pants over my Maxfli shirt and khakis—and heard the dim tapping of rain against my shoulders. I had burst out of the gate at the Buick Classic last year, too. I knew the best thirty-six–hole score had been shot by Bob Gilder—127, fifteen under par. The year before, I had equaled that. I also knew sixty-two was the record eighteen-hole score, having recently been shot by Peter Jacobsen. Rain made the course play longer, but that was fine with me. The Tour's launchers enjoyed the long courses because they offered us an advantage. I was sure Tiger, Phil Mickelson, and Hank Kuehne were sitting in the locker room rubbing their respective palms together, thinking about hitting eight-irons to greens when others were knocking fives onto the putting surface.

My threesome included Tom Crispey, a college-aged rookie up from the Nationwide Tour, who apparently did not want to talk, and Kip Capers. Capers wore a turtleneck beneath his rainsuit today, a cross dangling from his ear, and a hat with the Nike swoosh. His game was much better than I remembered. This day, he was two under par. Equipment never makes the player, but I noticed Caper's bag had changed. The Nike deal that had upset Silver was now obvious. NIKE GOLF was on one side of the bag; JESUS SAVES was on the other. Capers now played Nike irons. He still hovered near 180 on the money list, though. He was a good kid, and we'd chatted easily through the first seven holes. He still paused mid-hole to speak to fans, but much less frequently than before. Regarding his career, I viewed that as a positive sign.

I had the honor and hit my five-wood about 245 yards. It was safe but would leave over 200 yards to the green, a three-iron approach. On this hole, however, I wasn't thinking birdie. Par would be fine.

Capers hit a drive near mine and looked relieved. By contrast, Crispey found no relief. He'd been four over before the swing. His drive found the hazard. He reloaded and put his third shot in play.

"Finished second last time out, huh?" Capers said.

"Yeah. Memorial was a good week."

"Just good? Not great?"

"I lost."

"Second place keeps your card, though."

I nodded.

"I've got a long way to go to keep mine," he said.

"You can jump a bunch of spots quickly with purses this big. This week's winner takes home nine hundred forty-five thousand."

Capers nodded. But he did so as if trying to convince me that he believed he could do it.

I had to focus on my next shot. Capers would hit first. Sand traps guarded the front right and left sides of the green. Often the hole averaged 4.3 strokes or higher. Capers hit a high shot that moved right to left and landed softly on the oval-shaped putting surface, rolling close to the pin.

"Nice shot," I said.

"I've been working day and night on a draw."

"Paying off."

We watched Crispey hit his fourth to the green. The ball stopped about thirty feet from the pin.

At my ball, I bent, pulled some fairway grass, and tossed it into the air. It fell straight down. No breeze, just drizzle. I glanced at the water hazard. Thousands of tiny ripples pocked the surface.

"Don't think too much," Silver said. "Take the three-iron and swing. Keep the momentum going."

I took the club and nodded. Standing behind the ball, I adjusted the Velcro strap on my glove, shrugged the sweat-soaked shirt away from my shoulders, and envisioned the ball forging straight, rising against the gray sky, and landing on the wet green, bouncing once, twice, and stopping near the cup. I moved to the ball, carefully positioned the club face behind it, exhaled, and swung.

I never felt the club face strike the ball.

"In the zone," Silver said.

I handed him the club. The ball sat within ten feet of the pin.

At the green, Crispey two-putted for his six, a good effort from where his ball had come to rest. Capers, crouched at the fringe, trying to judge if his three-foot birdie putt would break, was waiting for me to putt.

I had seven feet, into the grain. Occasionally, over the years, I'd birdied this hole in practice rounds. I couldn't remember birdying the hole in tournament play. I moved to the green's edge, near the spot where Capers crouched. I stood examining the line.

"Give me a good vibe," Capers said.

I nodded and went to my ball.

"I read it two balls outside the left edge," Silver said.

Again, I only nodded. I listened but didn't really hear him. His words floated past me, uncollected. Unneeded, too. I saw the line over which I not only wanted to roll the ball, but knew the ball *would* roll over and follow to the cup. The line couldn't have been more obvious if painted bright yellow.

I set the blade of the putter carefully behind the ball and made my stroke. The Titleist fell, center cut. I parred the ninth and went out in twenty-nine, the lowest nine-hole tournament score I'd ever shot.

. . .

"Now this is what I'm talking about," Silver said, looking around, smiling broadly. "TV cameras, hordes of fans. This is the attention I deserve."

It was 3:45 P.M. The drizzle had continued on and off, the sky was still the color of cast iron, and beneath my rainsuit, my shirt was matted against my chest. Silver, too, felt the humidity, but the heavy media presence seemed to alleviate much of his discomfort. He wiped his face and shaved head with the towel he uniformly wore draped over his shoulder. It was drenched.

"Why didn't you put the towel inside the bag?" I said. "Or better yet, get a dry one?"

"Not changing a thing," he said. "We're minus twelve, on pace for—"

I held up my hand. I didn't want to hear the number I knew twelve strokes under Westchester's par of seventy-one totaled.

Silver nodded. He understood.

We were on the seventeenth tee. I saw Perkins standing nearby. He shook his head once as if to say, *Not here on business. Just watching.* Thursday crowds are rarely exceptionally large and rain certainly wouldn't help the draw, although our gallery had swelled to maybe four hundred people. After the front nine, the USA network had stationed on-course commentator Peter Kostis with our threesome. Kostis, a Maine native, had a membership at a club near the Woodlands. We'd spoken once at a charity event in Portland; however, I wasn't used to receiving his attention away from the Pine Tree State, let alone being his focal point.

I knew what was going on, and something tightened in my stomach. Not nerves. I'd once made a putt in fading Friday-evening light to make a late-season cut, thus retaining my Tour card. I knew what nerves were and how they felt. The sensation in my gut now wasn't due to pressure. It was high-octane excitement. On the heels of battling Tiger Woods for the Memorial title, the U.S. Open Qualifier had been a comedown of crushing proportion. This day, I was not only contending, I was leading. My round was now the day's major story. I felt like a kid just told to pinch-hit with the winning run on third. Tiger Woods is the center of the golf universe most days. I was getting a turn—and loving every second of it.

Lisa wouldn't be able to come to the course; she wouldn't bring Darcy out in the rain. I knew she was watching, though, either on television or following on the Internet. Maybe both.

"Peter Kostis just asked what club you hit on sixteen," Silver said. "I told him *I suggested* the four-iron."

I grinned.

"This is better than Sunday at the Memorial."

"It's exciting," I said, "but not like facing down Tiger."

"You're facing down history, Jack. I won't jinx you, but go for the number, my man."

I was quiet. At twelve under par, I was seven shots clear of Sergio Garcia, who was in second place after eleven holes. Woods was in the clubhouse at minus four. I knew sixty had been bettered by one only three times in PGA Tour history. Al Geiberger (1977), Chip Beck (1991), and David Duval (1999) had all shot the magic number. But I was also fully aware that the seventeenth hole at Westchester CC had dashed my hopes on a semi-annual basis. Once, when Lisa was still with CBS, she'd had the network's statistician crunch the figures. The numbers told me I'd dropped more strokes on No. 17 at Westchester than on any other single hole played on Tour. That knowledge had not been requested; nor did it benefit me as I pulled the three-wood from my bag.

The seventeenth is only 374 yards, a par four, but it plays uphill and has a bunker in front of the green deep enough to remind many of the "pot" bunkers seen across the Atlantic at an Open Championship. The front sand trap is fifteen feet deep; moreover, an eighteen-foot drop-off awaits anyone whose approach shot flies the green. From the tee, where I now stood, fairway bunkers catch pushed or pulled tee shots. Those bunkers, coupled with the ensuing approach shot, make it paramount to find the fairway off the tee.

I made two nice practice swings with my three-wood—slow, rhythmic, and controlled. *Steady* was the only way I could describe how I felt this day. All systems—driver, fairway metals, long- and short-irons, my short game and putter—seemed *easy*, a word not often associated with golf, even by those who play at the highest level. Yet this day, those clubs, and the most important club in my bag, the one between my ears, operated at peak capability. In fact, the day was like no other. I recall very little chatter between Silver and myself or Capers and me. Maybe Capers had stopped talking to me, not wanting, as Silver had said, to "jinx" me. Regardless, I felt like a bystander, a conduit through which my ability and the game of golf worked. I like to think hard work pays off and results in low scores. On this day, however, hard work had little to do with my play.

I'd often heard of "the zone." I'd entered that state occasionally and, like anyone who'd ever visited it, wished I lived there. No one can have permanent residence, but some athletes have a timeshare and seem able to visit almost at will, as if, when things get tough, they hop a mental flight, land in "the zone" in a matter of minutes, and stay as long as it takes to win. Tiger can do it. Before him, Jack could as well. There have been occasions on various golf courses, at various times in my life, when I'd entered the hallowed ground. This day, though, was different. I'd never before entered "the zone" with my first swing.

I made a third practice swing on the seventeenth tee. The gallery continued to swell and voices expounded on the moment, sneakers squawked on wet grass and slapped pavement; Peter Kostis was nearby bearing his microphone, the cameraman beside him. I moved to my ball. With the authority of a finger snap, everything vanished and I stood in a tunnel of clarity. I glanced down at the ball, then out at the fairway, selecting a spot in the center to which I would hit the ball. And I did. No "three-second-stroke" on this day, no swing triggers, or ball-position thoughts. Just pick a target and swing. The tee shot stopped just over a hundred yards from the green.

On the green, I had ten feet for birdie and would putt last. Silver stood next to me but didn't speak. The drizzle continued. I moved around the putting surface, lining up my putt from various angles. The wet turf would not break much.

When my turn came, I crouched behind the ball, getting a final read, then slowly placed the putter's face behind the Titleist. I looked up once more, getting a last feel for the speed, then stroked the ball. It tracked the whole way but the wet green killed it; the ball stopped two rolls short. I tapped in for par.

.   .   .

Westchester CC's eighteenth plays 526 yards, a par five. From the tee, the fairway doglegs left. The yardage and layout can be misleading. The hole routinely plays the easiest on the course. I knew what par would mean: history, plain and simple. Which explains why I hit three-wood off the tee. My plan was to play the hole in three shots, try to stick my third close, and one-putt for birdie or two-putt for par. I'd kept the pedal to the floor all day, and hitting three-wood instead of driver meant I was letting off the gas.

Silver nodded once when I asked for the fairway metal instead of driver, his tongue moving slowly over his lower lip. "Your call," was all he said as he handed me the three-wood. He nodded again, this time to himself, and moved away.

I pushed my drive into the right rough.

Capers, working on a sixty-nine, launched his driver and drew the ball around the corner of the dogleg. Aggressive and ideal. Crispey, staring eighty in the face, had little to lose. He hit driver through the fairway into a cluster of trees.

As we moved down the fairway, Silver and I walked apart from the others. Fans hollered.

"The clock hasn't struck twelve yet, boss," Silver said. "Even if we can only move the ball a hundred yards, we can still reach the green in three shots."

I saw the TV tower behind the eighteenth green and momentarily thought of Lisa. I wondered what she would say if she were up there. At my ball, neither Silver nor I spoke for several long moments.

"Must be sitting down there pretty good," Silver said.

It was an understatement of massive proportion. In fact, without the volunteer flagging the ball down for us, we probably would've walked past it. A skinny teen had placed a tiny flag next to the ball, which had come to rest twenty feet from the fairway.

Silver bent very close to the flag. "There's no ball there," he said to the kid.

"I saw it land. It's in there."

The rough had begun the day treacherous enough—four-plus inches of fescue, bluegrass, and ryegrass. Since 6 A.M., it had received drizzle, off and on. It was high, thick, and heavy with rain. There was no way even a five-iron would move through it. The grass would wrap around the club, twisting and pulling the club face closed, the ball—if moving at all—would go weakly left. The best I could hope for was to chop a pitching wedge back to the fairway.

"I see it now," Silver said. "Top of the grass is laying over the ball."

"And it's wet and heavy."

He nodded. "What do you think?"

I looked down the fairway. I had all of 250 yards to the green. I had wanted to leave myself a hundred-yard third shot. I could stick the ball close from a hundred yards.

I stared down to see a spot of white through the grass. I shrugged. "Give me the pitching wedge."

Silver hesitated.

"It's the only play we have, Tim. I'll hack it out, then hit a long-iron or even five-wood to the green."

I addressed the ball in the calf-high rough. I heard someone say, "Tiger's strong enough to muscle it out of that."

Tiger is smart enough not to attempt it, too, I thought. Silver and I had discussed risk taking earlier in the season. There are risks, and then there are situations in which you know your limitations. I knew what was at stake on this hole, what a bogey would mean. But I was here to win the tournament. The year before, I'd come close. I wasn't going to throw away two or three strokes attempting a miracle shot.

Westchester CC is generally considered a tree-lined venue. Yet there was no obstruction between me and the fairway, so I could advance the ball. I squeezed the grip once, as tightly as I could to release tension, then I brought the club back slowly, stopping just short of parallel at the top. The downswing was 100 percent of full throttle—everything I had, while keeping my head still. The contact was not crisp, but I knew I'd struck the ball as I came up and out of the shot, the result of such a violent hack.

"Shit," Silver said. "Nice try, Jack."

If Silver's remark hadn't told the story, the gallery's long, soft

Ooohhh surly would have. A smattering of applause followed. My ball sat ten feet from where it had begun, still in the rough.

"At least it's sitting up now," Silver said. "No problem this time."

"Come on, Jack," a voice sounded above the others.

I recognized it and turned. Jim Dempsey stood clapping twenty feet away, an umbrella leaning against his blue jeans. He wore a short-sleeved denim shirt and his standard black cowboy boots. We made eye contact. His gaze was not distant now, as it had been the last time I'd seen him. He gave me a quick thumbs-up. I nodded once and moved toward Silver, who was surveying our third shot.

"Got a clear pitch to the fairway," he said. "Or, think you can hit a high fade? Probably only two thirty from here. What are you looking at?"

I shook my head.

"Someone say something, trying to distract you?"

"No. What do we have for yardage?"

He told me again.

"Give me the five-wood."

I opened my front foot, positioning my feet to hit the ball left, but squared my torso, the set-up for a fade. I didn't hack this time. The swing was solid, but the five-wood slid under the ball just a hair. It carried only to the front bunker. I'd have a sand blast of more than thirty feet to get up and down for par.

"Traps are wet," Silver said. "It'll be like hitting out of quicksand."

.   .   .

The resulting bunker shot had left me twenty feet for par. The eighteenth green has three tiers, and my ball had squirted from the mud and stopped on the first plateau. The pin was positioned on the middle level.

"Twenty-three feet," Silver said, rubbing his cheek.

I nodded. I had one putt for par and a twelve-under total. The leader board behind the green told me things were happening. Sergio Garcia had made another birdie and now stood at six under par, six strokes behind me with seven holes to play. Grant Ashley was in the field and had one of the day's first tee times. He, like Woods, was in the clubhouse at four under par, shooting sixty-seven.

Reviewing the line from ball to hole illustrated a two-foot break. But the green was wet. The ball wouldn't break the way it might if the surface had baked in the sun all day.

"Run and gun," Silver said and clapped my back. "Give it hell, Jack."

I addressed the ball, carefully placing the putter blade behind it. I brought the putter back slowly, counting off my three-second stroke, and followed through at the hole. The ball tracked all the way to the cup, never wavering, then darted left and ran three inches by. Momentarily, I hunched as if hit in the gut. Then I stood and shrugged. It had been all I could do. I'd dropped a stroke but hadn't tossed away my lead.

"Tough to judge speed on wet greens," Capers said.

"Sixty is a pretty good day, Jack," Silver said.

I nodded. He was right.

"Fifty-nine would've been nice, though," Silver said. "A place in history."

I thought of my ride from the Woodlands with Schultz, of his comment about leaving a legacy for his daughter.

"I'd rather have the trophy than the fifty-nine," I said, "and we're in the lead."

*M*y sixty was the new course record, so a woman from the Tour's Media Relations Department led me to the press tent for post-round interviews. She couldn't have been more than twenty-three, wore a navy blue skirt and white golf shirt with the Tour logo on the front, and carried a clipboard.

It was 4:45 P.M., and the day had been long. I'd fought rain and history, but was not tired when I got to the high-backed leather chair on the stage, a microphone and bottle of water before me, the white and blue PGA Tour script providing the backdrop, hanging behind the chair. More than a hundred reporters and several television cameras were there. Lights made the stage hot, but it felt good because I was still in wet clothing. In fact, everything felt good, and, taking my place, I swallowed an ear-to-ear smile. I was still playing Tiger Woods for the day.

The young lady introduced me. The questions ranged from the golf-specific (how did the weather conditions affect me? Did I like the course set-up?) to the simple and bland (how did it feel to hold the record? Was I disappointed not to shoot fifty-nine?). Standard post-round inquisition, my answers likewise standard.

It was a staffer from *Golf World* who asked the question that made me think.

"Jack, do you feel the birth of your child led to the sudden resurgence of your game?"

You learn interview tips during the Tour's media-relations training sessions. One way to buy time, after being asked a tough question, is to repeat it.

"Has the birth my daughter led to the resurgence of my game?" I said. "Interesting question."

I leaned forward, grabbed the bottle of water, and opened it. I pushed my hat back on my head. During the preceding two months of on-course struggle, I'd refused to discuss my feelings regarding parenthood and my desire to be with Darcy. It had been my father, calling Ohio from Maine, who'd broken that silence. Later, Lisa told me she'd known all along what the trouble had been; she'd seen it before. Finally, Schultz had put the whole thing into context, getting me to think in terms of legacy. It had been a long struggle, and I was clear on it all now. I also felt like I could talk about it now, at least some of it.

I drank the water, set the bottle down again, and looked up. "Sure. There's a little extra motivation."

"Is it pressure?"

"Motivation," I said, shaking my head. "You want to do well. Now you have an additional reason for doing so. I don't know anyone with kids who wouldn't say that."

"Is that how you explain the turnaround? Putting in more practice in an effort to do well for your daughter?"

Leave it to the media to oversimplify. I'd battled with it through two months of missed cuts. I shook my head politely.

"I've been driven to play this game well since I was nine years old," I said, smiling. "She might provide additional motivation, but I've always been motivated."

"Did you find a swing flaw and correct it?" a guy with close-cropped jet-black hair and a goatee said. I recognized him from *USA Today*.

"For one thing," I said, "I owe Peter Schultz a great debt of gratitude. The last week, he stayed with us in Maine and worked with me. As I'm sure you know, Peter's not only a former Masters champion but a world-class instructor, too." That sounded pretty good, I thought. Paid to be married to a reporter.

"What type of swing help has he given you? Any specifics you can mention?"

At the back of the press tent, a murmur resonated and moved forward rapidly like a wave rising higher and gaining momentum. One by one, members of the media stood and left.

"Take away," I was saying. "Schultz is trying to get me to bring the club back . . ." I didn't complete the sentence, and I don't believe anyone cared. Only five or six reporters remained.

The guy from *USA Today* said, "Jack, today, following his round, Grant Ashley was arrested for the murder of his caddie. Grant is a friend of yours, correct?"

The muscles at the base of my neck and shoulders tightened. "Yes," I said. The lights no longer felt warm; they were hot now.

"How long have you known Grant?"

"Three years."

"How would you describe him?"

"Talented."

The *USA Today* guy was young. He looked frustrated as if he thought I'd say something to incriminate Grant. He was disappointed. Yet I couldn't no-comment. That would fuel the fire. But I'd spent several years with one of golf's most serious journalists. I knew what to expect, which gave me time to pull several well-honed sports clichés and hold them at the ready.

"Can you describe Grant's working relationship with Michael Easley?"

"The Tour is a close-knit family."

"Was it what you would deem a typical player-caddie relationship?"

"Like any good team, its members are just happy to contribute."

The *USA Today* kid looked at me. He nodded to himself, sighed, and said, "Do you think Grant Ashley is capable of murder?"

"I'm just happy to be here," I said, "thankful for the opportunity."

"You could've just declined to comment."

"How about, *It ain't over, till it's over?*"

"Cute," he said and stood and walked out.

So did I. No one wanted to hear about my sixty now.

.   .   .

"How it went down," Perkins was saying, at 5:45 P.M., upon meeting the Austin clan at the hotel restaurant, "is MacDonald and his guys waited for Grant to finish the round, followed him back to the hotel, and collared him there. No scene at the golf course. Nothing like that. The media didn't find out until maybe an hour after he was arrested."

In the booth, Lisa sat next to me. Darcy was asleep in her car seat, which sat on an overturned wooden highchair. Silver was in his glory, seated next to Perkins, who'd slid as far from Silver as he could and was nearly leaning against the wall. The restaurant was full. A lot of golfers were present, and there were obvious media types. On the way to the booth, Lisa had stopped to chat with enough former cronies to prompt Perkins to suggest she run for governor.

"Of what?" she'd replied.

"Media Nation," Perkins said, looking around and shaking his head contemptuously.

Indeed, I knew the media crush on this quaint upstate New York PGA Tour stop would only get worse. Likewise, I knew how Perkins felt about the media. He was presently dining with the only reporter to whom he spoke. For Perkins, whose job often called for anonymity, he was starting out largely disadvantaged. A reporter as skilled as Lisa, for example, never forgot a face. When the face is attached to a person the size and appearance of Perkins, it becomes even harder to forget. Consequently, being around hordes of reporters had the same effect on Perkins as putting a gun-shy dog on a rifle range.

"The new course record will likely go unnoticed," Lisa said.

"Not by you," I said.

"That's right, sweetie." She leaned and kissed my cheek. "You were the best golfer in the world today."

"Oh, Jesus," Perkins said.

"I think it's beautiful," Silver said. "What devotion."

Perkins and I were drinking beer—Heineken for me; Sam Adams for him. They had served the bottles with chilled glasses and Perkins took a long drink, beads of condensation running down his glass.

"Grant appears tomorrow at eight-fifteen, damned early, which suggests the judge is going ahead with bail."

"The evidence is so strong a judge would consider not setting bail?" Lisa said, morphing into Reporter Lisa. She had ordered iced herb tea. The drink sat before her untouched.

"Thought you retired?" Perkins said.

"You know I'm writing freelance pieces."

"We on the record?"

"Background only."

Perkins nodded. "Typically, a judge won't set bail if a guy might flee or is deemed a danger to society. Grant wouldn't fit either—he's in the middle of a tournament and the crime is considered revenge." He paused to sip some beer.

Lisa waited. Reporter Lisa apparently knew there was more.

Perkins sighed. "You're right about the evidence. It's a DNA match."

"DNA match?" Lisa looked at me. "Why didn't I know about that?"

"I just found out last night. I was up and out of the room early." I shrugged.

"Don't take it personally," Silver said. "I didn't know either."

"He wouldn't tell you," Perkins said to Silver. "Be like putting it on CNN."

Silver did something that might have been batting his eyelashes. "Are you wearing Tommy Hilfiger cologne?"

Perkins looked relieved to see the waitstaff arrive with our meals. He was having the porterhouse. I was eating pasta primavera again. Lisa had ordered pasta salad. And Silver got a portabello-mushroom-and-pasta dish.

"At eight-fifteen Grant will be arraigned," Perkins added. "He's got a heavyweight lawyer." He ate some steak.

"The FBI is charging him? Not the State of Ohio?" Silver said. When he was serious, he could utilize his master's in journalism well enough to have once been hired by Lisa to locate background material on a New Orleans mobster.

"With the FBI taking the case, the U.S. Attorney's Office is formally charging Grant."

"If the judge sets bail and Grant makes it," Perkins said, "it might be controversial. MacDonald was probably hoping Grant wouldn't play well today."

"That affects the case?" I said.

"I'm no lawyer," Perkins said, "but I think if Grant's in contention it eliminates the fear-of-flight theory, so they'll let him continue."

"To play golf?" Lisa said.

"To earn his living," Perkins said. "The guy has yet to be convicted."

"DNA is strong evidence," Silver said.

"Not unimpeachable," Perkins said. "Remember O. J. Simpson?"

"The prosecution built its case around the DNA," Lisa said.

"Same thing here—a tiny drop of blood was found when they searched the house."

"On what?" Lisa said.

Perkins detailed the search.

"So that's all they have? Just that drop of blood?"

"Yeah, just a trace."

"Grant's whereabouts at the time of the murder? When was that?"

Perkins shook his head. "They guess between eleven p.m. and three a.m. No alibi."

"Murder weapon?" Silver said.

Perkins shook his head.

"Don't you think Grant would have an alibi, if he killed Easley?" I said.

Perkins looked at me. "You're still at it?"

"At what?" Lisa said.

"Jack can't let this go—the idea that Grant might not have done it. I've talked to MacDonald about this. Grant never asked how Easley was killed. Before details were made public, Lynne Ashley and Jim Dempsey asked how Easley died, right off."

There wasn't much to say to that.

"Jack, I saw the second interview with Grant. I think he did it, too."

"You sat in on the second interrogation?" Lisa said, a hint of jealousy in her voice.

Perkins nodded and drank more beer. Next to me, Darcy began to cry. I leaned and took her out of the car seat, holding her against my shoulder, burping her gently. Lisa nudged me, and I handed her the baby.

"You have quite a rapport with the FBI agent in charge," Lisa said. She held Darcy in the crux of her arm. "That's usually tough to do."

"Why don't you eat, Lisa?" I said. "I can hold the baby."

She shook her head. "You eat first. A salad can't get cold."

"Peter Barrett," Perkins said, "the Tour commissioner, has known MacDonald awhile and has a very good relationship with him. But MacDonald's kind of grown to accept me. We're a little alike."

We ate in silence for a while, and I ate my pasta primavera and thought back to the scene in Boston, when I'd made my statement. If tough guys can have kindred spirits, Perkins was MacDonald's.

I bought Perkins a second beer since I'd opened the Grant can of worms and, unknowingly, sicced Reporter Lisa on him during dinner.

Lisa sat rocking Darcy, still thinking. Finally, she spoke. "If Grant is convicted, what will happen? Does the federal government have the death penalty?"

Perkins was chewing and raised his brows, momentarily, then swallowed. He paused as if he didn't want to say. "Remember Timothy McVeigh?"

"The Oklahoma City bomber?"

Perkins nodded. "Jury decides. McVeigh got lethal injection."

"Jesus," I said.

Throughout it all, I'd kept coming back to Grant as a kid who, in my eyes, had wanted so little—a solid career, a home, a family—and who'd lost so much. He'd been a kid who'd sought my help, a kid whom I'd befriended, much the same way I'd now befriended Kip Capers. But Grant and I were closer than I ever imagined Capers and I becoming. We were more than practice-round friends. Despite the age gap, we were ball-game–and–beer buddies. Idle chat. Putting for money on the practice green. This was a wake-up call. The U.S. District Attorney versus Grant Ashley. Execution.

"Without a witness," I said, "could they do that?"

"Do what?" Perkins said, chewing his steak.

"Kill him?"

"I'm not a lawyer," Perkins said again and shrugged. "I do know federal executions are pretty cold. McVeigh got a letter saying when the execution would take place."

"What a waste." Lisa shook her head. "All to get even with Mike Easley for exploiting Lynne?"

"There's a little more now," Perkins said.

We all waited.

"During the second interview, Grant admitted Easley was blackmailing Lynne and himself to allow Easley to caddie."

I remembered he had told me that already. Lisa, though, was taking it all in.

"Not for money?" Lisa said.

"Sort of," Perkins said. "Grant was paying him. But Grant told MacDonald that Easley thought it was a rush being around the Tour." He looked at me, eyebrows raised. "All the money and stars."

I sat silently, thinking about what Perkins had said. Dempsey and Lynne had asked how Easley died. Grant had not. Grant had motive. And Grant had Easley's blood on his sneaker. I felt the way I do when I look up from a shot to discover my ball airborne and descending over a water hazard. Darcy began to cry, so we left.

30

$\mathcal{S}$ince I'd gone off early Thursday, my Friday tee time was late, 1:36 P.M. Weekend starting times and pairings are based on standings, but Thursday and Friday groupings, typically threesomes, don't change. Therefore, I would once again play with Capers, in fourth place after round one, and Crispey, who needed a miracle to make the cut.

"So we're meeting on the range at eleven?" Silver said.

I confirmed that and headed to the fitness trailer, where I spent the next hour lifting dumbbells—bench press, triceps, flies, incline bench, decline bench, and a hundred sit-ups. A television hung from the ceiling and played *SportsCenter*, which began and concluded by updating the Grant Ashley murder charge. Halfway through my bench-press routine, Capers appeared above me as I exhaled slowly and pushed up the weights.

"What are you using?" he said.

"Fifties." I strained to finish my fifteenth repetition.

"Rugged." Capers looked genuinely impressed.

I set down the dumbbells on the rubber floor mat and sat up.

"Thought you'd just want to maintain," he said, straightfaced.

"At my age, you mean?"

A smile finally broke across his face.

"Anytime you'd like to go yard for yard off the tee."

"No thanks." He clapped my back. "Just kidding."

"I'm glad you're relaxing," I said.

He shrugged shyly as he had when we'd sat in the locker room at the Memorial discussing greens. "It takes me a while to feel comfortable."

"I understand," I said. "But relax. You've got the game to have a home here."

He stood looking at me, as if expecting a punch line.

I spread my hands. "What?"

He shook his head. "Thanks."

I took the fifties off the floor and leaned back on the bench.

"I'm looking forward to playing with you again today, Jack . . ."

Exhaling as I pushed the weights up, I saw him smirk.

". . . and trying to take the lead away from you."

I'd never had anyone kid me about taking my lead before. Maybe that was because I'd only led a handful of events. Regardless, I just smiled at Capers. I liked the kid's spunk. I'd originally been impressed by religious dedication; however, this week I was seeing another side of him—he had game, and, truth was, without a solid golf game, he'd not have the forum for his religious aspirations. So it was good to see the kid's competitive juices.

"Bring it on," I said and smiled. "I'm too old to get intimidated."

"Be hard for a skinny guy like me to intimidate you."

"Spare me," I said. "But it beats having you call me Mr. Austin. That makes me feel old."

"Well then, Mr. Austin, by all means finish your workout."

I grinned and watched him move toward a Lifecycle.

When I was done, I toweled off, wiped down the bench, and grabbed a bottle of water. I walked out into the sunshine. Eighty-five had given way. It had to be pushing a hundred now, and the prediction of 100-percent humidity looked to be on target.

"Jack."

I was drenched in sweat, moving toward the locker room for a shower, after which I planned to eat a late breakfast before finally heading to the range to loosen up. I turned to see Jim Dempsey approaching. He'd been leaning against the side of the fitness van, apparently waiting for me.

Dempsey was dressed in his usual Texan garb, although he wore no hat on this day. Instead, he had on wrap-around shades like the ones worn by David Duval. The glasses covered part of the scar Dempsey had on one cheek, courtesy of a steer, and seemed to clash with his old-time cowboy look. I knew the sunglasses offered Duval more than protection from damaging rays. I'd read of the symbolic barrier the glasses provided, of how the reflective lenses served as a metaphoric wall between Duval and spectators, opponents, and journalists. A Texas native and Houston resident, sunshine was not a new experience for Dempsey. In fact, during the ten years I'd known him, I'd never seen Dempsey wear sunglasses before.

"Got a minute?" he said.

"I need to shower, then eat."

"Talk to Grant?"

"No."

"Everything's screwed up bad now, Jack."

"What's screwed up?"

Dempsey looked around, over one shoulder, then the other. I waited. It was nearly 9 A.M. The sun was in the middle distance and felt hot on my bare arms.

"Joan told me you called."

"Yeah," I said.

"What did you want?"

I only shrugged. I'd wanted to see what the hell was going on, find out who killed Mike Easley. My gut had answered the question the night before. Now I feared confirmation.

"Well, if you need me, just call," he said. "I'm still your agent."

"You still Grant's agent?"

His jaws clenched, and the scar on his cheek rose and pressed against the bottom of the sunglasses. "I stick by my clients, Jack. I got Grant a hell of a defense attorney."

"Nice of you," I said.

"What's that mean?"

I shook my head. Pushing him here would do no good. "I'm taking a shower. Meet me in the dining room at ten. I'll buy you breakfast."

. . .

I had on my usual game-day outfit—khaki trousers, logo-bearing golf shirt, my PGA Tour I.D. (a money clip) attached to my belt, and Footjoy Dryjoy shoes—when I sat across from Jim Dempsey for a late breakfast. Food had always been an integral part of my life. It is one of the great perks of owning a PGA Tour card. At each Tour stop, players and immediate family members eat for free at on-site player dining facilities. Since Dempsey was not a family member, we were eating in a public dining room, and I was paying.

"You here alone?" I said.

"What do you mean?"

"Are Joan and the kids here?"

He shook his head.

A young college-aged guy took our orders. I was having Wheaties; Dempsey got eggs.

"How are things at home?" I stirred sugar into my coffee.

Dempsey drank his black; it smelled rich. Around us, people ate. Most were spectators there to see the event. Some were golfers I recognized. No one seemed to notice me. For a moment, I thought of what might happen if Tiger Woods attempted a public meal with his agent and considered myself lucky. As Perkins and I had discussed earlier in regards to Lynne Ashley, fame has a high price.

"Things at home . . ." He shook his head.

"What?" I said.

"No."

"'No,' you don't want to talk about it, or 'No,' it's not going well."

He drank some coffee and glanced around the room.

Many of the people had the relaxed appearance only familiarity can breed. I assumed them to be members. We were in the dining room; they must have eaten there often.

"Both, I guess," Dempsey said. He put the coffee down. "I really don't like to talk about this."

"You were waiting for me," I said.

"Because you called me, and I'm your agent."

"And you don't want to lose your only client?"

He leaned back in the chair and folded his arms across his chest. "Is that what you think?"

"Cut the bullshit, Jim. You had life by the tail—Grant as a client, marriage, kids, you were courting other clients. Now it's gone."

"You don't know that."

"I know you've lost Grant. I know players won't be lining up to have you represent them. The sport can turn on you in a moment's notice. Family and loyalty means a hell of a lot."

"I'm as goddamned loyal as you can find."

"I saw Grant and Lynne having dinner together the other day."

A simple statement of fact. Yet it stopped Dempsey, his coffee cup halfway to his mouth.

"Where?" he said.

"Hotel restaurant."

He shook his head. "They didn't think I was coming out here. But it doesn't matter now."

"What is going on?"

"You read the papers?"

"Did he do it?"

Dempsey took in a deep breath. "I'm a legal representative for the guy, Jack."

"That doesn't sound like a denial."

Across the room, a little boy sat eating with his father. The boy wore a white hat, the visor covered with autographs.

"You said, 'everything is screwed up now.' What is 'screwed up'?"

Dempsey looked at me.

"Did he do it for Lynne? Even after what she did to him?"

Dempsey set his coffee down, leaned forward, and pressed his palms to his eyes. "What she and I did to that kid. Jesus Christ."

I stood and pushed my chair in gently and tossed some bills onto the table. I went to the place I'd gone to think since I was nine years old—the driving range.

I was hitting easy wedge shots to the hundred-yard marker, when a young on-course commentator approached and asked if I might offer a brief pre-round interview. I said sure, and, as I looked around, saw Lisa with Darcy in a front carrier, standing outside the ropes. They were amid maybe a hundred other spectators, but, as is often the case, Lisa stood out in the crowd. She wore white shorts and a pale-blue sleeveless top. Darcy, asleep in the carrier, had on a white bonnet to protect her from the sun.

Lisa waved me over, her eyes running to the young reporter, who stood waiting.

"I wanted to give you a heads-up," she said.

We moved away from the crowd.

"*USA Today* is breaking the story of Lynne's past and the Web site and linking Mike Easley to her."

I didn't know what to say. Although I'd assumed the inevitable trial of Grant Ashley would uncover everything, I hadn't expected the Lynne Ashley Web site to become public knowledge yet. This would surely fan the flames.

"Does *USA Today* know about Easley's blackmailing Grant?"

"I don't know. My friend at CBS only said they got wind of the *USA Today* scoop and found the Web site and are looking into the whole thing. They know I did the Tour wives piece, so my friend stopped me for background."

"You mention the blackmail?"

"Are you questioning my intelligence, Jack?"

"No. Sorry. It's just . . ." I glanced over my shoulder to the CBS kid; he was waiting patiently.

She spread her hands. "DNA is very hard evidence. People are going to have strong opinions about this."

"And blackmail gives Grant a hell of a good motive."

"You think he's guilty?" she said.

"He's a friend," I said.

She stood waiting, head tilted slightly. Her tongue moved along her upper lip.

"Lisa," I said, "I don't know if he did it."

"I didn't ask what you knew. I asked what you thought."

"Yes," I said. "I think he did it."

We stood looking at each other in silence.

"God," Lisa said, "what a waste."

"If the *USA Today* is running it tomorrow, the story will be on television before then."

"Probably." She looked at the young reporter again. "Anyway, I wanted to give you a heads-up in case you're asked about it."

I kissed her and Darcy and walked to the reporter. If the Web site news had broken already, I couldn't tell from the scene on the range. Things were as they always were. The range was packed, the heat apparently having little effect on anyone's pre-round routine, and no players had paired off in discussion. The interview began with five or six questions about my game, what I hoped to accomplish this day, and a question about my relationship with Peter Schultz.

"You're opening round is the season's low score, Jack. Was it surprising, given your play of late?"

"Not at all," I said. "I've been out here more than ten seasons. I think I've proven I belong out here."

"Unfortunately, a lot of the talk this week has not been about your sixty, but, rather, about your friend Grant Ashley. Can you comment on his relationship with late-caddie Mike Easley?"

"All I can say is that I send my regrets to the Easley family." I paused and thought for a moment. "And that I hope justice is served."

. . .

"Capers is looking better," Silver said, when I returned. I retook my spot in the line of players beating balls. "Keeping the club on plain better."

I nodded and took the three-iron from the bag. As I swung slowly back and forth loosening up, I thought of my answer. It had surprised me, but had been the truth: I hoped justice would be served in this case. Yet I didn't think it would be. Three people were involved. I thought one person would take the fall for a scenario created by three.

The previous day's sixty seemed long ago. I took two practice swings with the three-iron, then addressed a ball, and swung. The *whoop* sound of the club head sweeping down, digging the turf, and the *click* of steel against the Surlyn cover offered brief serenity. What I'd told the CBS kid echoed in my ears. I'd known of the potential storm for weeks. When Grant had been arrested, I'd thought that would be the worst of it. Now the waves were high overhead and about to crash against the shoreline.

. . .

The back nine at Westchester CC plays to a par of thirty-five. Since I'd begun on No. 1 Thursday, I had played the back nine first Friday and had gone out in thirty-two. My opening-nine highlight had come early—an eagle at the 314-yard tenth. Driving the tenth green had allowed me to bury a year-old demon, since my second-place finish the previous year had been in large part due to the tenth hole and my conservative tee shot. The tournament had become a two-horse race, and I'd selected an iron off the tenth tee. By contrast, Phil Mickelson had hit driver and reached the green. The hole—and my conservative tee shot—led to a two-shot swing from which I never recovered, finishing second.

"What goes around comes around," Silver said when we walked to the tee box at No. 9, my finishing hole. We stood next to the tee, waiting like on-deck batters, for the group in front of us to hit and move down the fairway. "Now you've paid back that tenth hole."

"I was wondering if you remembered," I said.

"How could I forget? I wanted you to stay in the present, but we've got some time now." He took a water bottle from the bag and handed it to me. "I'm sure Lisa noticed, too," he said and nodded toward her.

Lisa had Darcy in the front pack still and stood near Perkins to the side of the tee box. She'd matched us stride for stride since the round had begun and looked vibrant in the sunshine. She was tan from the summer in Maine and long days spent outdoors. Furthermore, she looked happy and content. This was the first Tour event she'd attended—not worked—and her comfortable appearance put me at ease.

When the group in front of us had cleared, Silver handed me the driver. The ninth is a par-five, 505 yards, that annually averages less than par. It was a great way to finish. I needed a finishing birdie to secure a sixty-four, a score that had been shot by several players this day. Your drive must carry 250 yards just to reach the fairway. My tee shot landed safely in the short grass.

Capers, similarly needing birdie for sixty-four, also took the driver. He grinned at me. "Still chasing you, big dog."

"Pretty scary when you need to shoot sixty-four to keep up with the field."

"Or," Crispey said, "you can just say screw it like me and shoot seventy-five."

There wasn't anything to say to that. In fact, since the third hole, only Capers and I had spoken, Crispey opting out of the round, if not mentally, certainly orally. Capers, meanwhile, had informed me that his family owned a cabin in Aroostook County, Maine, about five hours north of Chandler, near the Canadian border, which he frequented to hunt, fish, and ice fish. I told him I, too, had a cabin in northern Maine and mentioned the Aroostook Valley Country Club, a little-known gem, where, legend had it, Sam Snead once played an exhibition.

Capers hit a solid drive. It would still be a three-shot hole for him. He stood near me as we watched Crispey hit his best drive of the day.

After the others hit their second shots, we stood at my ball.

"What did that carry, three hundred?" Crispey said.

"Jack's third in driving distance," Capers said.

"Is that true?" Silver said to me.

I shrugged. "No idea."

"Yeah," Capers said. "Hank Kuehne, Daly, and Jack."

Again, I shrugged. Stats didn't matter. I had a three-iron to the green and wanted an eagle putt. To the side of the fairway, I saw Perkins standing beside Lisa and Darcy, wearing a white golf shirt, dark slacks, and his wrap-around shades.

"Is that Lisa Trembley?" Crispey said. "She is hot, man. Just looking at her makes this seventy-five feel better."

Capers cleared his throat.

"What? You don't think so?"

"That's Jack's wife," Silver said.

"Oh, sorry. No offence. Congratulations, man."

I pulled the three-iron from the bag.

"Does she hire private security?" Capers said.

Silver chuckled.

"No," I said. "He's with the Tour. A friend of mine."

"Scary-looking guy."

"Not just scary-looking," Silver said. "Just plain scary." Then to me in a whisper: "And cute as a button."

I rolled my eyes and took a few steps back, signifying I was preparing to hit. I made two controlled practice swings, then addressed the ball. The contact wasn't as crisp at it had been for the past thirty-five holes, but I got away with it. The ball came to rest on the front left fringe. I wouldn't be able to putt, but could chip. The pin was cut in the back, on the second tier. Capers, conversely, played the hole in three shots, his third hitting the putting surface like a dart, sticking eight feet from the hole. Crispey missed the green with his third shot, although at least he'd stopped staring at Lisa.

I had an eagle opportunity but not a realistic one. I wanted to get the ball on the green and rolling as soon as I could and therefore took a seven-iron. I choked down and made several practice strokes, the club face brushing the grass. I kept the back of my left hand, and the Velcro clasp of my glove, in front of the club face as I did so, effectively taking any wrist action out of the chipping motion. My follow-through had my watch face pointing at the target. I'd once read that Chi Chi Rodriguez could play six or seven different clubs—and, thus, shots—from any spot greenside. To the contrary, I'd also read Dave Stockton, Sr. played the same club from nearly any greenside lie. I didn't have the short game of Tiger Woods or Phil Mickelson, but could play the flop shot when I had to. This lie, however, didn't require that. I used the forward press and bumped the ball to six feet for birdie.

"Nice shot," Silver said.

I shrugged. "Not great."

"Six feet for sixty-four," he said. "I'll take that any day."

He was right. I hadn't found the zone this day, but had played well, nonetheless. And sixty-four is never a bad score.

Crispey chipped his ball inside mine, so I was first to putt.

The leader board behind the ninth green had me atop, seventeen shots under par, now six clear of Woods and Grant Ashley, who were still tied. Tiger had come back from six shots to win events before. I wanted this birdie putt. I looked at it from all sides, then studied the slope from my ball to the cup intensely. My ball was beneath the hole, meaning the putt would be uphill and therefore I could hit it firmly.

I stood over the ball and inhaled deeply, held it, and blew out slowly, my putter blade hovering above the green momentarily. I checked my alignment once more, the club still not yet on the turf. An eruption came from somewhere near the clubhouse, and I backed off the putt, never grounding the club.

"What the hell?" Silver said.

I saw Perkins moving quickly toward the crowd. He entered the circle of reporters, like a running back into a goal-line stand, emerging on the other side with Grant Ashley in tow. The two of them ran into the locker room.

"Jesus Christ," Silver said. "Place is a zoo."

"Grant just finished on the eighteenth green," Capers said.

"Feeding frenzy," Crispey said. I hadn't thought him capable of empathy, but he shook his head sadly.

I ignored it all—or tried to. I addressed the ball again. The stroke was not solid. I pulled up and off the putt, pushing the ball weakly to the right. I tapped in to finish with a sixty-five, seventeen under par (125), breaking the thirty-six-hole scoring record established by Bob Gilder in 1982, by two shots.

.   .   .

The sound of the television could be heard in the locker room at 3:55 P.M. I couldn't remember the last time, this late in the day, when you didn't need to stand three feet from the thing to hear it over the cacophony of post-round energy. Typically, the locker room on the PGA Tour is open to players' sons, Tour staff, select members of the media, and (limited) tournament officials. This afternoon the room had been posted "off limits" to all but players, and with good reason. Scandals seemed always to hit other sports. The Atlanta Braves once dealt with John Rocker's outrageous racial and homophobic remarks; the L.A. Lakers had to deal with Kobe Bryant's sexual assault trial. Like all sports, though, this room, regardless of the venue, serves as our sanctuary, a place where we not only shower and dress, but have access to telephones and meals, a locale that supplies us an area to mentally prepare for a round or to wind down before an interview. Likewise, it renders a comfortable setting where card games are played or fishing is discussed during rain delays. It is a place where photos of newborns are passed around. On this day, however, no one said a word. The murder and ensuing suspicion led to a tension our locker room had never seen, and, truth be told, we weren't handling it well.

Grant Ashley sat alone, silently in front of his locker.

Padre Tarbuck, the former priest, approached Grant first. I was across the room, sitting on a bench, pulling off my Dryjoys in preparation for a shower.

"Sixty-three?" Padre said. "Great shooting, Grant. The day's low round."

It was tremendous; moreover, the score, I knew, gave Grant a total of twelve under par, meaning he had pulled one shot clear of Woods and would be paired with me Saturday.

The television was tuned to The Golf Channel, which was

now live at Westchester CC. Jennifer Mills was standing some-where on-site reporting the scene that had played out after Grant's final putt had fallen.

"Can we turn that thing off?" Grant said.

I got up and went to the television and clicked it off.

Grant's words attracted the attention of the entire room, as if no one had thought he'd speak. I hadn't expected to hear his voice, and, momentarily, was shocked to learn nothing had changed: It was the same southern drawl I'd heard over the drone of televisions previously—above the sound of ball games in bars, or chatting casually on the practice green, chiding me for making a putt to take ten bucks from him. It was also the same voice I'd heard above the slap of waves as we'd stood on the dock at my home only days earlier.

Padre seemed to stand frozen. He'd originally approached Grant, apparently, to offer a quick word of encouragement and now found himself next to Grant and thus part of the room's focal point.

"Well," he said, his whispered voice nearly a shriek amid the stillness and silence of the room, "just wanted to say nice play-ing, Grant."

Grant looked at him for several seconds, an expression that said, *That's all you've come to say?* Padre couldn't hold his gaze, turned, and walked away. Grant continued to stare after Padre, hurt, as if desperate for things to be like they had been. The still air of the room held the scent of cologne, and steam from the showers stood still like early morning fog. I went back to my locker, quickly stripped down, wrapped a towel around my waist, and headed to the showers, stopping in front of Grant's locker.

When he looked up, I held out my hand. He sat staring at it for several beats. Finally, shoulders hunching, he took it, looked up at me, and smiled broadly. We shook.

"You're my friend," I said. The remark seemed ill-placed, in-appropriate, the words seeming to leap from my mouth before rational thought could dispel them. Yet the statement seemed all there was to say.

"I don't have many left." His eyes searched the room.

I watched many players, whom I hadn't expected to do so, turn away.

I was beginning to think I'd never have a peaceful meal. To my surprise, however, the hotel restaurant didn't shut down when we entered at nearly 7 P.M. and found our party at a table in the back corner of the room. Although Lisa, Perkins, and Silver knew the man beside me—the one hiding behind sunglasses and beneath a new golf hat—they offered Grant Ashley a collective jaw-drop.

Grant took the seat next to Silver. I leaned over and kissed Lisa. She sat staring at Grant, who said nothing, offering only a tiny wave in response. Darcy was positioned next to Lisa in her car seat, sleeping. I adjusted her blanket before sitting down.

"I asked Grant to eat with us," I said, taking my seat. "A man can't live on room service alone."

Back in the locker room, when I had gotten out of the shower, I'd asked Grant if he was dining with Lynne. His response had not been what I'd expected after seeing him eating with her only days earlier. He'd looked at me the way one does when awaiting a punch line. When none came, he simply shook his head.

Then I asked: "Eating with Dempsey?"

"He'd leave me holding the bill, the son of a bitch," was all Grant had said.

So I'd asked him to join us. He had declined, but I'd persisted. He'd told me he was staying alone, just playing golf, then holing up at the hotel, ordering room service, and watching television. Television this evening, I knew, would offer nothing he wanted to see or hear. Neither would radio, nor the Internet. Now he sat across from me, fidgeting and sipping ice water.

"Too bad I'm not still working," Lisa said, smiling at Grant. "The two guys leading the event sitting here with me? What a scoop."

Grant smiled weakly.

Few people understood the subtleties of conversation better than Lisa. She was letting Grant know this was just dinner, and thus she'd not dig for a story.

"I've never eaten with the guy chasing me before," I said.

"Got to lead a tournament for that to happen," Silver said. He looked down, avoiding my stare, but couldn't hold it. His shoulders began to shake, and he started laughing, slapping his thigh.

"Glad you amuse yourself," I said.

The joke had been about even par for Silver—meaning double bogey for anyone else—but Grant chuckled. I could only guess at what was going on internally. I didn't know what the future held for the kid, but I sensed this meal offered a reprieve from evils I would never understand. I had thought about Grant, about Lynne and Demspey, and Mike Easley for a long time and concluded no one would probably ever know exactly what happened the night Easley died. Only two people had been present; one was now dead. The man I'd brought to dinner might very well be a murderer. But he was a young man who'd had his whole life ahead of him, a guy who'd treated me well for the three years I'd known him. And on this day, he'd sat in the same locker room he'd called home for the last three years and found it no longer to be one. Grant Ashley was smiling now, chuckling at Silver's sad one-liner. I sensed he'd smile very little in the future and felt like toasting Silver, in spite of his comedic failings.

"You've got me by five shots," Grant said to me. "That's a lot of ground to make up."

"Didn't you come from four back when you won the Canadian Open?" Lisa said.

"Hey," I said, "he doesn't need that kind of encouragement."

Everyone laughed. The waitress came to the table and we ordered drinks: Heineken for me; caffeine-free Diet Pepsi for Lisa; Perkins got a rum and Coke (which told me he was very uncomfortable with this arrangement); Silver ordered Diet Coke with a lemon slice; and Grant ordered Jack Daniel's and Coke. I'd never seen him drink hard liquor.

"The Canadian, last year?" Grant said, nodding to Lisa. "That was a great week. I'd met Lynne before flying to the tournament."

Around us, life seemed to go on as usual. People ate, drank, talked, smiled, and laughed. The restaurant was full. There were large rubber plants that gave the place a spacious feel. Silverware clattered. Voices blurred to one muffled rumble. I spotted golfers; some obviously recognized the man eating at my table in hat and dark glasses. Likewise, I noticed members of the media—some I picked out based on the jacket and tie or skirt suit; others, dressed casually or in golf attire, I knew from their continual coverage of the Tour. Doug Ferguson from the Associated Press sat across the room. Jaime Diaz from *Golf World* was there as well. The young guy from *USA Today* sat near the door, alone, a salad and his open laptop on the table.

"God, I'll never forget the Canadian Open," Grant said, staring absently at the tabletop, his voice carrying the flat overtone of one thinking aloud. "I was on such a high that whole week, from the flight up there, right through Sunday, when I got the trophy. Lynne and I had just met. I called her each night, and we spoke for like an hour."

"When exactly was that?" Perkins said. Nothing Perkins did was casual, and his question had certainly not been. He was running dates in his head, a fact missed by no one.

Grant looked up and took in a lot of air, then blew it out slowly.

The waitress returned with our drinks. Grant sat, elbows on the table, twirling his Jack and Coke, his stare contemplative and shifting from Perkins to the dark glass in his hands. I shot Perkins a look. He looked at me, his gaze deadpan. We ordered meals, and the waitress left.

"How many more events on your schedule this year?" I said to Grant.

Asking a man in Grant's position about the future was futile and insensitive, but it had been the first thing to come to mind in an attempt to steer the conversation from Perkins. Hindsight provides merely a mental mulligan and is useless. But I was realizing I should have called Perkins from the locker room, gotten a handle on what he was working on, then gauged whether or not to bring Grant.

"Memphis, Milwaukee." Grant shrugged. "Eight, nine more weeks." He took in some of his drink. "Supposed to play the Open Championship across the pond." He smiled halfheartedly and shook his head. "It's at Carnoustie this year. I've wanted to play that course since I watched Jean Van de Velde on the seventy-second hole. What a course."

Carnoustie Golf Links, on the east coast of Scotland, was the venue of the 1999 Open Championship (the British Open), where Van de Velde had stepped to the tee on seventy-second hole needing only six to win and had made seven, leading to a play-off, which he lost. Now Van de Velde lived forever in infamy the way former Red Sox first baseman Bill Buckner is remembered for the error that cost New Englanders the 1986 World Series. I, too, had dreamed of qualifying for the tournament when played on that course, Van de Velde's collapse having also piqued my interest. As I had done following the Memorial, I'd flown to England several times prior to the British Open to qualify. Some years, I'd gotten in; others, I had not. The expense was great, the weather typically terrible, and the odds of qualifying long. Many non-exempt players from the U.S. PGA Tour did not bother with the attempt to qualify. To me, the chance to play the British Open was worth it. I hadn't grown up playing plush country clubs, nor had I played links courses. But the tall grass, the whipping wind, and the hard, rough fairways was closer to my past than many of the manicured venues I now played. Moreover, the British Open represented the game's origins.

Grant sat staring at his drink. "Thanks for inviting me tonight." His voice was quiet, and the words came slowly, as if he were exhausted. "I made bail this morning and it's been crazy. On the fourteenth hole today, a guy yelled, 'How come a murderer is still playing golf?' during my backswing."

I didn't know what to say to that. Lisa and Silver exchanged awkward glances. Perkins looked around the room as if disinterested. I knew he was anything but.

"Seems like no one understands." Grant finished his Jack Daniel's and Coke and held up his hand. The waitress looked over, and he motioned to his drink. She nodded.

"Things have a way of working out," Lisa said.

Grant looked at Lisa for a long time. Perkins was looking at everything in the room but Grant Ashley it seemed, attempting to let the conversation flow. The waitress returned and set Grant's Jack and Coke before him.

Grant's head began to shake slowly back and forth. "You know what's funny about all this? My lawyer, the guy who's supposed to be on my side, doesn't really give a shit."

"Grant," I said, "the guy's taken an oath to do his best for you."

"No, that's not what I mean. I mean he doesn't care about me. You saw what it was like in the locker room?"

I nodded.

"When I said I had no friends left, I meant it. This lawyer comes in, tells me what to say, and leaves. I'm a number to this guy. Just feels kind of strange—my life hanging in the balance and I'm a 'case' to him."

I didn't doubt that, but didn't tell Grant. As Dempsey said at breakfast, Grant's attorney was a high-profile defense lawyer. He did, I was certain, have many cases. Thus, Grant would be a number. Grant's failure to realize this reminded me once again how naive he was. Lynne Ashley, at only twenty-one, was far more worldly than twenty-four–year–old Grant. I'd seen Lynne sit in my living room with women far more mature and not only hold her own but fire arrows. Lynne Ashley was many things, but she was tough as salt rock. And, at this point in his life, Grant, with his slow, southern drawl, could take a page from her book.

"I'm sure the lawyer is there for you," Lisa said.

Grant shook his head again. Then he turned to me. "You

asked about my eating with Dempsey? About a month ago, he'd have been the last person on earth I'd want to eat with. Yesterday, when he brought the lawyer by to meet me, and the lawyer had left, I asked Dempsey if he wanted to go eat someplace."

Across the room, I saw the kid from *USA Today* looking at our table.

"Dempsey tells me," Grant was saying, "he's got a line on two new clients, and, well, maybe we could just eat room service.'"

Lisa looked at me, so did Perkins. I'd been with Dempsey a long time, had said I'd stick by him. Grant's story, though, spoke volumes.

"He didn't want to be seen with me," Grant said. He looked down, then drank half the Jack and Coke. "I played with Ryan Sterns today. Kid won the U.S. Amateur. It was like someone told him not to associate with me."

I nodded. It all made sense, and, after the scene in the locker room, there was no denying Grant's claims. Sterns was the latest up-and-comer, rumored to be Tiger Woods's next great challenger. Upon seeing the pairings, Sterns surely would have been told by agents or the like to stay clear of Grant. After all, endorsement contracts aren't taken lightly. In defense of Sterns and the others, I'd read stories of convicts having difficulty reassuming a place in society, upon being "reformed." I, like many, read those pieces dispassionately. After all, the convicts shouldn't have committed the crime to begin with. Sitting next to Grant, though, I knew several things: No matter who did it or why, I'd never condone murder. But the public and his peers had already convicted Grant. And no one had mentioned that Grant had been blackmailed. Most importantly, Grant had treated my family and me warmly and loyally as long as I'd known him.

"This whole thing will blow over," I said. It was a ridiculous statement, but I was searching for a way to give him hope. "Next January, when we start up again, it'll be like it always has been."

"No," Grant said and looked away. "That's the thing. It won't be. That's not how it works."

No one spoke.

"Before, I thought that—that everything could go back. I thought I could win the case." His head shook slowly. "Now I realize it doesn't really matter if I do. People never forget." He took a long drink from the dark Jack and Coke.

The table fell silent.

"My lawyer is talking plea bargain." Grant looked up as if having just realized he'd verbalized his thoughts. He took another drink.

Lisa looked at me as if to say she'd heard too much. I knew she'd drawn a line with her original remark. She'd put Reporter Lisa aside. Now Grant was unintentionally tempting her. Perkins sat staring at the far wall. Silver was looking at his Diet Coke.

"Where are your parents, Grant?" I said. He had mentioned his childhood home, his parents' long marriage, in my kitchen when he'd flown to Maine.

The waitress arrived with our meals atop a large circular tray just as Grant looked up at me slowly, a tear emerging from beneath his dark glasses and streaming down his cheek. The waitress set the tray on a stand, then turned to the table, about to say something. She froze at the sight—all of us waiting for Grant to speak.

"No one forgets," Grant said. "Not even the people you love forget what you did."

.   .   .

By the time dessert rolled around, our table was silent. Perkins had left, saying he needed to call home before his son went to bed. He'd simply announced his departure, stood, meeting no one's eyes, and left. Lisa, Silver, and Grant ate dessert.

I had watched Perkins go, kicking myself again for not calling him beforehand. I'd put him in a difficult situation: He'd worked with MacDonald to investigate Grant's alleged involvement in the murder. Now I'd asked Perkins to have dinner with the suspect. It had been insensitive on my part, but we'd left the locker room hastily, my focus, at the time, squarely on getting Grant out of there.

Grant had drunk five Jack Daniel's and Cokes. The alcohol

was taking hold. He'd stopped talking, and I'd noticed several more tears. I was glad he was with us. He needed someone.

Amid the silence, and in spite of the tension we all surely felt, Lisa, eating cheesecake, chatted easily, filling gaps in our conversation as if this were an unexpected rain delay and she had three hours of network coverage to satisfy.

I had passed on dessert and sat holding Darcy, whose head rested on my shoulder, eyes open, silently focusing on a nearby rubber plant. On the far side of the room, I saw the reporter from *USA Today* looking from his laptop to us, then back to his laptop, as if describing the scene. He'd spotted Grant.

As the others ate, I continued to think of Grant's final statement: *Not even the people you love forget what you did.* His last two words seemed to spin in my mind, resonating with something I didn't wish to hear, and high-fived my gut for its previous interpretation. Perhaps Perkins had picked up the same vibe and felt the need to leave, either to call MacDonald or because he felt bad about Grant spilling his guts naively in front of him. I'd never seen Perkins express sympathy for anyone who'd committed a crime, so I doubted the latter.

Across the room, the kid closed his laptop and stood, pad and pen in hand. He approached our table. In his peripheral vision, Grant spotted the reporter and set his spoon down, his ice cream half gone.

"Not in a restaurant," I said.

Lisa turned, saw the kid, and shook her head.

It was no use. The kid was on the hunt, his game sitting squarely before him. He began to speak several feet away, finally catching up to his words when he'd reached the table. "Grant, do you know who killed Mike Easley?"

"The man is eating," Lisa said. She was on her feet and got between the reporter and Grant.

"Lisa," he said, "you, of all people, know I have a job to do."

"No," she said, "this is not doing your job. Your job was in court and at the golf course. This is invading a man's privacy. You've been sitting there staring all evening, probably taking photos to sell."

Grant's eyes ran to where Lisa pointed, his shoulders dropping when he spotted the laptop. His head shook side to side. "It's no use," he said, the words directed at no one, as if thinking aloud. "It's no goddamned use."

"You let this man eat his meal," Lisa was saying. "You treat the subject as a human. Not a story."

The reporter stepped around Lisa to get closer to Grant. In doing so, he brushed her with his shoulder, pushing her back two steps. It amounted to a shove, and I was on my feet, Darcy still resting against my shoulder. The commotion and my own sudden movements startled her; the baby began to cry. The sound pulled Lisa from the *USA Today* kid to my side, where she took Darcy.

"You don't shove my wife," I said.

"Jack, I didn't shove anyone."

"You've got three seconds to get out of here."

"Jack, you're not being reasonable."

"One."

"I've got a job to do."

"Two."

"Grant, at the arraignment, will you plead not guilty? Did you kill your caddie?"

The kid's pad and pen were airborne as he went backward, skidding on the seat of his pants, stopping near the next table, blood running from his mouth. I stood next to Lisa, took a cloth napkin off the table, and wrapped it around my right hand. Several knuckles were bleeding.

A camera flashed. Darcy was still crying.

"Come on," I said to Grant, and we all left.

. . .

At 8:35 P.M., Grant and I were in his room. "See?" he said, his voice frantic, cracking, his words slightly slurred, "things can't go back. No one understands."

We had dropped Lisa and Darcy at my room, and I had continued on with Grant.

"Relax," I said. "We're dealing with one bad journalist. That's all."

I guessed at how things would play out: Grant would continue to drink, eventually pass out, and I'd creep back to my room. Perkins would call, having heard of my assault, and offer a verbal backslap. Next, someone from Tour Headquarters would call—maybe even Commissioner Peter Barrett himself—to fine and possibly suspend me.

"You're right," Grant said, shrugging. He propped a pillow against the headboard and lay against it in his bed.

I took the room's lone high-backed chair and unwrapped my right hand. Cut knuckles bleed a lot. I'd require bandages but no stitches. I only wished I wore my glove on my right hand. As the tournament's leader, my gloveless right hand—bandages and all—would be exposed to a national TV audience.

"You shouldn't have hit that guy, Jack."

I was opening and closing my hand, examining the cut. "The guy shoved Lisa."

"It was my fault," Grant said. "You shouldn't have punched that guy. All they'll talk about after this tournament, whether you win or lose, will be how you punched that guy. And how you were with me."

"He had it coming," I said.

He clicked on the television. ESPN had the Red Sox playing the Yankees. A ticker at the bottom of the screen offered the day's scores and headlines. Beneath "PGA," it read: BUICK CLASSIC: J. AUSTIN, −17; G. ASHLEY, −12; T. WOODS, −11; K. CAPERS, −9. After the scores, a headline ran across the banner at the bottom of the screen: GRANT ASHLEY RELEASED ON BAIL. ACCUSED IN STABBING DEATH OF CADDIE. WILL PLAY BUICK CLASSIC.

Grant sat staring. The media, it seemed, were everywhere this night. "Funny how things turn out, you know?" No longer upset, he spoke as if genuinely surprised.

"This will all go away," I said, looking away as I spoke. "In January, it'll be just like old times."

"Ryan Sterns might have been right, Jack."

"What are you saying? People shouldn't associate with you because you've been accused of a crime?"

He started to speak, then stopped. He turned to the television. We were quiet as the announcer described Kevin Brown's night. Apparently, the Red Sox were losing.

"Jack," Grant said, "you're my good friend, the only one I have left. Always been there for me. You took me in as a rookie and helped me out. And you tried to help me this summer."

"That's what friends do," I said.

His face was red, and I knew it wasn't the alcohol. Tiny beads of perspiration formed on his brow.

"Do you know why I did it?" he said. "I want you to understand. I don't care about the rest. But I want your respect."

I had defended him to Perkins and MacDonald. My initial reaction had been loyalty-based, not evidence-based. Then one shoe had fallen nearly a day ago, when something inside told me the truth and made me face it. Now the other shoe hung, dangling.

I held up my hand. "Be careful. I'm sure I'll be subpoenaed to testify."

"I just want you to know why. I owe you that, after all you've done—trying to find Lynne, being there for me tonight, taking time to see me when you were home. And I need your respect."

I exhaled slowly and leaned back. For a long time, I'd hoped something would come up, something to disprove what I suspected, what my gut had told me again tonight at dinner. That wish had probably been futile—no one survives a decade on Tour without good instincts—but I'd never wanted to believe it. Now there was no going back.

I'd always believed scandals involving pro athletes were, in one way or another, the result of poor judgment. Consequently, when I read of accusations such as those leveled at Kobe Bryant or Ray Lewis, my reaction was never sympathetic. Grant, too, was a grown man; he'd associated with the wrong people. Unlike them, though, he'd fallen in love. Where most find marriage to provide emotional support and stability, Grant's wedding vows led to the opposite. As I sat looking at him, his return stare was weighted with need.

"I thought about it for a long time, Jack. About how Lynne tried to walk away, to start fresh. About what Easley did to her, how he used her, how he made her an addict."

"You should have gone to the cops, Grant."

"You saw the Web site. You know why I couldn't do that. She didn't know what people would say. This was going to be her fresh start."

He went to the bathroom and quickly returned with a drink. He motioned to me. I shook my head, and he sat down.

"We'd go places, and once in a while, someone would come up to her—say things, call her things. When I missed those two weeks early in the season? It wasn't a golf injury. I sprained my wrist hitting some guy."

I blew out a long breath.

"She tried to walk away, Jack. We had it all planned out. Then Easley wouldn't let her go. That was why she took up with Dempsey. She told me so at dinner the other night, when you saw us."

"You were both crying."

"That's why. She told me she still loved me. It was why she couldn't stay with Dempsey."

"She wanted to be an actress. He had connections."

Grant waved that off.

"She left you, Grant."

"I love her. Always will. It would've worked out. We would've gotten back together."

I ran a hand through my hair. I didn't believe much of what Lynne Ashley said to anyone.

"Mike Easley wasn't making money," Grant said. "The son of a bitch just left the Web site up so he could hold it over Lynne's head. We'd been married three months when she said she needed help."

"She asked you to kill him?"

"No. No, Jack. She'd never do that. She told me everything, said she needed to pay Easley, that he wanted to caddie."

I nodded. It was how Perkins had explained it.

"Dirtball shows up, tries to shake my hand. Says—get this— he'd feel guilty just taking my money, so he wants to earn it. Bullshit. He loved being around the money and the TV cameras. The idiot tried to talk to Greg Norman about private jets. Norman tried to be polite, but finally had to walk away. Easley comes back to me and says, 'Greg and I have a lot in common.'"

Grant's face reddened again. Anger. Then it passed. "When I saw that Web site, I thought it would kill me. She was there with Easley, with others, doing things I'd never ask of her. It was too much." He took in some air, tilting his head back, trying to stop the solitary tear running down his cheek. "I asked him to go to OSU, show me how to get pot. We drank before we went. He drank a lot more than I did, since I was driving. I never smoked the stuff in my life, so it wasn't tough to act like I didn't know what I was doing. I parked in a vacant lot."

He set the glass on the nightstand. His eyes left mine to stare at himself in the mirror, his expression blank; but his eyes were haunted.

"When we got out, I told him to lead." Grant took a deep breath. "I just—I thought about Lynne, about what he'd done to her—the drugs, the money he'd made from her, how he got her addicted to cocaine. Then, I just . . ."

His eyes came back to mine, his face still void of emotion as if speaking in his sleep.

"I just did it," he said. "Four times, quick. I couldn't look. He was drunk and just fell, straight down. After, I turned and ran to my car."

We sat in silence for maybe ten seconds, looking at each other.

Then Grant looked at the drink. "That's all I wanted, Jack. You deserve to know it all."

I sat staring, my focus on the blank wall behind him.

"It's going on ten," he said, "and tomorrow the weather is supposed to be good." He looked up and smiled slyly, the way he always had when thinking of a joke. "People are going to make moves. And I'm one of them. Better bring your A game."

My head was pounding. Now I knew it all. I never thought anyone would.

I stood and blew out a long breath. "Grant, I can't lie under oath. I want you to know that."

"I know what kind of person you are, Jack."

He stood and held out his hand. We shook. Then I walked

stiffly out, back down to my room, knowing everything but as confused as if I knew nothing.

.   .   .

I left the phone off the hook, intentionally, but didn't sleep. I lay next to Lisa with Darcy at the foot of our bed and thought about what Grant had done. I was to play golf with him the next day. Eighteen holes. Spend four to six hours with the man—and his murder confession.

Confession or not, Grant Ashley was slated to stand trial as an "alleged" killer, and I took refuge in the belief that his words and melancholy had driven Perkins from the dinner table. *No one understands* and they never *forget what you did.* Perkins had listened, worked on his mental timeline as Grant spoke, then probably went to MacDonald with it all. Those two lines would help build the case against Grant. And the DNA was the smoking gun. Unfortunately, I now had all the gaps filled in.

Lisa continued to breathe in a soft, steady rhythm. Minutes marched by like defeated soldiers. I had told an interviewer I hoped justice was served. Had it been? Mike Easley shouldn't be dead. He should be facing trial for blackmail and statutory rape. Would it be served at Grant's trial?

I got out of bed and rocked Darcy, turning a chair to face the dark night sky. Darcy, of course, knew nothing of what had taken place. But she also knew nothing of Grant's internal struggle. Moreover, she was still alien to all that drove individuals to commit such crimes. I needed to be near that, to know it existed, and to hold it close.

I would be subpoenaed to testify. Of that, there was no doubt. And I would not lie. Would justice be served if Grant were executed or sent to prison for life? Mike Easley should not be dead. But the scenario was not cut-and-dried: Grant had been betrayed, lied to, promised things. The life he sought and had found had been stripped away. Yet he had killed a man.

And I knew about it.

At 3:15 A.M., I stood before Grant's door. First thing in the morning, I would tell Perkins and MacDonald what I knew. But first, I had to be up front with Grant about that. Using my unbandaged left hand, I knocked. Grant did not answer. I knocked on the door again.

"I received three calls last night," PGA Tour Commissioner Peter Barrett said. "One from *USA Today*, one from the National Press Association filing a complaint against you, then a third call, at nearly four this morning, from yourself saying you needed to talk to me, Perkins, and Mr. MacDonald from the FBI."

It was 7 A.M. I was showered, shaved, and seated across a large cherry desk from Barrett, who had set up shop in a private office in the Westchester CC clubhouse. I only nodded.

I had the third round to play and a five-shot lead to protect—or add to. Saturday is moving day. Players would rise and fall on the leader board. But I had learned more about the Mike Easley murder than anyone else knew. Telling Perkins and MacDonald was the only course of action. The one thing tugging at me, however, was that I hadn't been able to tell Grant first. He'd either ignored my knocks or left his room.

My right hand was stiff, the knuckles still sore. Lifting weights, apparently, didn't prepare one to punch somebody in the mouth.

"I assume what you need to speak to the others about regards a legal matter," Barrett said. "Perkins and MacDonald are on their way. Let's take care of my business while we wait for them."

Efficiency seemed to emanate from him, as if everything was somehow easier for him. You trusted him, his insights, and his word, the way people do a top-dollar motivational speaker. The result, this day, was the feeling of sitting in the principal's office, when the principal is your dad.

"Tell me what happened last night," he said.

"Someone pushed my wife."

He hadn't expected that. I'd contradicted what he'd been told.

"Elaborate, please."

I told him how the reporter had watched us throughout the meal, how he'd approached, how Lisa asked him to leave. "We were trying to give Grant Ashley a couple hours of peace and quiet."

"Jack, I was told you punched a journalist for asking Grant questions. That, as your wife can tell you, is a journalist's job. And Grant must be questioned. He is in very hot water."

"Lisa was highly offended that a journalist hid like the paparazzi then made a run at our table."

Barrett spread his hands. "I'm not here to argue journalistic ethics with you. You were out of line, and your actions hurt the reputation of the Tour."

That remark cut deeply.

"But," Barrett said, leaning back, folding his arms across his chest, "in the past, you've done a lot to help the Tour. You're one of the game's good guys. Our fan base knows that. So I'm fining you ten thousand dollars."

"That's a lot of money, sir."

Money, in this game, is hard to earn, and I'd been on the cusp of losing my card enough to know that well.

"Jack, I slept on the figure fifty, but woke in a better mood. I've been told you were interviewed by the FBI and have assisted the authorities. Those things contributed to my waking in a better mood. You are fined ten thousand dollars."

Neither of us spoke for a beat.

"That's all," he said. "Your hand looks like it hurts."

"It does."

"Good luck today. I'll send for you when Mr. Perkins and Mr. MacDonald arrive."

· · ·

The range was busy. Everyone's daily routine is different. Some guys show up, hit only a few balls, then play. Others spend hours before their rounds, beating ball after ball, trying to find a groove. Some play their round, then slash range balls until 8 P.M. I was neither practicing nor warming up. Just waiting—hitting balls and thinking.

The Philip Levine poem "Ask the Roses" begins:

> Snow fell forward forever
> I heard the trees counting their breaths
> the laughter of icicles
> the rivers turning to stone
> What became of the sea's dream
> to become spirit and range the sky
> what became of astronomy
> of the gopher tunneling under the lettuce
> and the onion that died like a saint
> from the head down
> what became of the wooden heart

The poem offered questions, not answers. I had learned some are better unanswered. But what had become of the wooden heart? Grant still loved Lynne. He continued to envision her as innocent as Snow White. To Grant's credit, Lynne had indeed started with little, gone through a lot, and had been exploited. No man has ever been smart enough to fully understand women, and I sure as hell didn't. However, Lynne Ashley continued to come into clearer focus. Having been exploited, she had, I believed, in turn exploited both Grant and Jim Dempsey. Grant, though, didn't see it that way. He thought they would get back together. Denial? After all, she left him for another man—a guy Grant once trusted—and had done so to enhance her chance of an acting career. She had chosen herself, her shot at fame and fortune.

Then Grant killed Easley on behalf of his wife. And last night, when Grant had no one to eat with, once again, Lynne was nowhere in sight.

"Jack."

I turned to see Padre Tarbuck approaching. He extended his hand, and I shook it.

He glanced down at my hand. "How's that feel?"

"A little stiff. I've hit a few balls. Doesn't hurt."

Padre paused, looking uncomfortable. "Yesterday, I froze in the locker room. I should've invited Grant to dinner."

"It's okay," I said.

"No, it's not. He's been a friend for three years. The three of us have had a lot of good times. You did the right thing. I didn't, and I feel terrible about it. I should've been there for him."

"Maybe," I said. "But dinner didn't exactly go like I thought it would. And you stopped to talk to him. A lot of guys didn't do even that."

"I expect better from myself." He held a club in his hands and looked down at the grip, rubbing his thumb over it as if to scrape something away.

"It's tough. Spur of the moment."

He shook his head. "It's not that. Hell, I heard confessions for years. When Grant looked at me yesterday, I just froze."

"Why?"

Padre glanced around. No one was within earshot. Silver had arrived early and had stopped to chat with Nick Price.

"I saw something in Grant's eyes," Padre said. "I've seen it before, during confessions. I didn't like what the look told me."

We stared at each other through a long silence.

"That's why I froze," he said, his voice not defensive, just explaining his actions. "I'd seen that look before."

Padre left, and I went to work. Time to focus. I flicked a Titleist Pro V1 to the center of my stance and brought the wedge back slowly, stopping short of parallel, then dropped the club down, clearing my hips, and sweeping through the hitting area, a three-inch divot rising and tumbling end over end in my periphery. I looked up, belt buckle facing the target, to see the ball drop near the hundred-yard marker. Crisp contact. You never truly know how you'll perform until the round has begun. I'd once shot low-sixties after throwing up all night with the flu. By contrast, the best warm-up of my life produced a seventy-six. Yet now I felt comfortable with my swing. I felt something else, too, something I'd never felt before on the PGA Tour: With thirty-six holes remaining, I felt in control.

The TV network coverage had changed. USA had given way to ABC and former British Open champion Matt Baker approached. A guy toting a shoulder camera was with him and filmed me hitting several shots. Baker watched me hit a few five-irons, apparently not wishing to interrupt. When I paused to move on to the three-iron, I looked over. The Aussie was still tall and slim and, retired or not, looked lithe, as if he could still compete.

"Swinging beautifully," he said.

"Sure thing, mate."

"Nice accent, Jack. We pronounce R's in Australia." He grinned. "Can we get a couple minutes with you?"

Given my chat with Peter Barrett, I quickly agreed.

"Feel any different this week?" Baker said, when the cameraman had set up.

"My swing feels better than it has all summer. Peter Schultz helped me groove it."

"Great coach, great gentleman. Does the success you had here last year help you?"

"Oh, sure. I feel comfortable on this course. I know what I'm going to get and where to hit it on different greens. Experience is the best confidence builder."

"Jack, you know I have to ask about your hand. Will it affect your play at all today?"

Athletic tape stretched across the back of my right hand, pressing a bandage against the knuckles of my index and middle fingers.

"Not at all," I said. "The hand is fine. I'll stand by whatever score I post."

"Jack, I have to ask one more thing: Would you like to give your account of what happened last night in the restaurant? Several morning papers carried the story and quoted the journalist."

"The hand is fine," I said again.

Baker nodded, understanding I'd go no further, thanked me for my time, and moved down the line of players.

I turned to Silver, who was rifling through our bag. "What time is it?"

He told me.

Not allowed on the range, over a hundred reporters stood outside the ropes. Notepads, cameras, zoom lenses, microphones. The Buick Classic had become the U.S. Open. I was the tournament leader. Now, as the bandage signified, I was also a figure in the event's controversy. I looked up and down the range. Grant Ashley was nowhere in sight. That didn't jive with his warm-up routine, which I knew to be longer than most.

My next swing produced a snap hook.

"Come on," Silver said. "Getting quick. Straighten it out."

I nodded and was mid-swing when I heard Perkins call my name. He was jogging toward us. I handed the club to Silver, my meeting apparently at hand.

Perkins reached us and stood next to Silver. "Grant's not coming," he said. "You're playing a threesome with Tiger and Capers now. Barrett wants to meet with all of you."

Peter Barrett was still behind the desk, drinking coffee. Except now he looked like he wished the china cup contained bourbon. It was tight quarters, and the room smelled of cologne. A guy in a quiet suit sat where I had less than an hour before. A uniformed cop was there, too. Tiger Woods stood next to Kip Capers, facing Barrett. I took my place next to Tiger.

Perkins was at my side, his face ashen. Had Grant Ashley confessed to authorities?

"I don't want to drag this out, gentlemen," Barrett said. "The Tour lost a great—" Barrett stopped, as if catching himself, his eyes running to the cop.

Barrett hadn't wanted to finish the description. That didn't sit well with me. I wondered what he'd been about to say. A great what? Why stop?

"Grant Ashley died last night," Barrett said, his voice direct but soft, his eyes now directly on mine.

Tiger took a deep breath; Capers's mouth was open.

"What?" I said. "How?"

Barrett looked at the cop. The cop nodded.

"Grant took about three hundred Tylenol. Then he drank and went to sleep. Never woke up."

For the first time, Barrett looked down. He was a lot of things—the most powerful man in golf, the guy who levied the fines, and the place where the proverbial buck stopped on all PGA Tour matters—but he was also someone we respected because he cared. When he looked up again, he did so with the expression of one who'd lost a son.

"You will play a threesome this afternoon. We'll make an official statement regarding Grant Ashley after you've teed off." Barrett came as close as he ever did to a shrug. "Might alleviate the media barrage."

Kip Capers stood stunned, his mouth finally closing. Tiger was too composed in all earthly matters to look shocked, but he stood perfectly still. For my part, emotions ran from initial confusion, to anger that Grant had done it, to a sudden realization—and a jagged bolt of guilt ran through me.

"Jack," Barrett said, "these men have some questions for you, as you were the last one to see Grant alive."

I nodded, my right hand covering my face.

"Are you all right, Jack?" Barrett said.

"No, I'm not."

"What is it?" Perkins said. "Peter said you wanted to see me and MacDonald. He's on his way. What is it?"

"Grant confessed the murder to me last night."

"This is getting worse by the second," Barrett said. "Tiger, you and Kip may leave."

They did.

I heard someone sigh deeply and realized it was me. "I told Grant to stop talking, that I'd probably have to testify. He kept talking. I should have known what he had planned. But afterward, he talked about playing golf today, trying to take my lead, so I . . ."

The room fell silent as I looked from Barrett, to the suit, to the cop, to Perkins. No one spoke. "Poor fucking kid," I said.

"He murdered someone," the cop said.

"I know that," I said.

"You find that sympathetic?" the cop said.

The cop was in his twenties. Had probably gone to the Academy young and moved up the ladder rapidly. Young, with a weightlifter's shoulders. Maybe he'd never been through this before. Regardless, he was going by the book, and I'd just thrown his book out the window.

"He was a friend," I said.

"The guy was a murderer."

I took a step toward him. "He had nowhere to turn."

"Took the easy way out," the cop said.

"He saw it as his only way out," I said. "That's a terrible thing."

Perkins was more cop than golfer and remained conspicuously silent during the exchange. He had, however, positioned himself between us.

The cop shrugged. "FBI agent named MacDonald is on the way. At least the case is closed."

"Yeah," I said. "Makes it easy for you."

The cop glared at me.

I turned to Perkins. "Grant spilled his guts to me, and I couldn't help him. I was right there, then left, and he ate three hundred Tylenol."

"You tried to help him all summer," Perkins said.

"No one could've helped him," the suit said. "I was his lawyer. I know."

I remembered what Grant said about his lawyer, about how alone this man had made him feel. Everything seemed to boil inside me then. The whole thing rushed at me from all sides. Easley and Lynne. Lynne and Grant. Lynne and Dempsey. My phone conversation with Joan Dempsey.

Grant had been a friend for three years, just a twenty-four–year–old kid who called my home looking for his wife. He'd phoned when Perkins had been there. Sensing her troubles,

Grant had called full of concern, deeply in love. Then everything spiraled away from him after that—his marriage, his career, his life.

.   .   .

Kip Capers looked out of sorts beneath the mid-day sun on the par-three first tee. Tiger shook my hand, said he knew Grant and I had been tight, and offered condolences.

Hours earlier, Grant and I had seen our scores on ESPN: J. AUSTIN, −17; G. ASHLEY, −12; T. WOODS, −11; K. CAPERS, −9. One member of that foursome would not play this day, would not play again. My five-shot lead was now six, though I felt as if I'd missed the cut. In fact, I'd missed much more. Grant had told me everything. I hadn't guessed what the confession would lead to. At twenty-four, I'd played my rookie season. Grant Ashley, at twenty-four, was now gone.

I moved to the side of the tee, awaiting the customary first-tee introductions. I had long lived life on my terms, playing the game I loved and respected, trying to help people when I could. When Grant originally called my house, Perkins had been there and chased the missing woman to cyberspace and places beyond. But Perkins got paid to do so. I was paid to hit golf balls, yet I had chased, too. Had I helped? Much more than two others to whom Grant had been close. And I would address that issue later.

"I called your name two times," Silver said. He was beside me now, squinting into the sun to see the green at the 190-yard first hole. "This isn't the time to be thinking of anything but golf. You're in your element now. Get everything out of your mind. Focus on what you do best."

"I shouldn't have left him last night."

"You were there for him when no one else was. He didn't confess to you by accident, Jack. And he didn't want you to stop him either, not if he was talking about playing golf today."

I took a five-iron from the bag and made some slow practice swings. Starting at a par three can immediately jumpstart the round (an opening birdie) or set a dismal tone (a near-instantaneous dropped shot). I had a six-shot lead; yet, I knew Tiger once made up seven shots in seven holes to win the AT&T Pebble Beach National Pro-Am. I'd worked hard to get into this position. Had worked, in fact, for years. I was nervous. I was excited. But, like background noise, Grant Ashley's death hung over all other thoughts. There was no way around that. Instead, only one thing to do with that background noise: Turn the volume up, and let it play.

The first hole plays to an average slightly over par. The pin was in the middle of the green. You don't want to be putting from the back. No one wants to begin the day with a three-putt bogey. A four-iron is the safe play, but I wanted to the keep the ball below the hole, so I'd selected my five-iron.

Silver nodded at the club selection.

One can find motivation in many places. My father had given me a kick in the pants. Schultz had told of his desire to leave an athletic legacy for his daughter. I turned the background noise up to full throttle. In less than twenty-four hours, I'd heard a confession I'd long dreaded, learned a good friend died, and had been fined for conduct detrimental to the Tour and the sport I loved, a sport built on integrity. Maybe the burden I now felt was justice. Maybe I should have stayed with Grant. Or maybe I should have returned to my room and immediately called the cops. Maybe Grant would still be alive if I had done either. Maybe. Maybe. And again, maybe.

The five-iron flashed down, sunlight flickering like a camera flash off the steel shaft. I held the follow-through, belt buckle pointing down the target line.

"Never saw it," I said to Silver.

He didn't have to answer. The gallery cheered.

"Six feet, right of the pin."

The opening tee shots were challenging and foreshadowed the day's events: Tiger stuck his approach inside mine; Capers was distraught and came out of his swing, hitting the ball thin. It ran to the back of the green, three-putt territory.

.   .   .

"Can't get a read," Silver said, when we'd reached the two-tiered first green.

Capers hit his putt from atop the back of the green. The ball started at the hole, then darted right, slipping past, and running six feet by. He would have his hands full saving par. The gallery reacted sympathetically.

Woods's ball was inside mine, so I would putt first. Tiger would be able to watch how my putt reacted to the green's intricacies and play his putt accordingly. Silver's estimate of six feet had been generous. I had nine feet. The putt would break left to right, a slider. I crouched behind the hole and looked at the line from the hole to the ball. As I walked back to my ball, where I would crouch and get one final view of the line, I heard a rumbling in the gallery. Several members of the press pushed their way to the first row of spectators encircling the green. Cameras flashed and clicked and whirred. Barrett had doubtless given the press conference. I ignored the cameras and bent behind my ball.

"Cat's out of the bag," Silver said. "This will break about eight inches, left to right."

I nodded. Tiger Woods has the ability to intimidate players into dropping from contention. Before him, Jack Nicklaus had that same capability. It is an endowment one earns—from outdriving players by fifty yards, from shooting sixty-six on windswept courses that leave players saying, "Sixty-six? I didn't think there was a sixty-six to be had out there." Yet I had watched Bob May give Tiger all he could handle at the 2000 PGA Championship, finally losing in extra holes. I remember realizing May wasn't scared of Woods. They were the odd couple: May, five feet seven, a career grinder; Woods, tall, thin, and graceful, the game's Chosen One. Yet May had nothing to lose and matched Woods, shot for shot. Silver had mentioned Woods's aura before: *Like watching Mike Tyson enter the ring*, back when Tyson had been in his prime. Tyson had fallen from grace off a skyscraper. Not Tiger. This putt could send a message, let Woods know I, like Bob May, had nothing to lose and would not back down.

I brought the putter back slowly and made a good stroke. But the ball took the break, then some, sliding four feet past.

Tiger putted next, burying his ball into the heart of the hole. He and caddie Steve Williams exchanged fist taps. Capers went next, making his six-footer for par, a good three, something he could build on.

My situation was different: I had begun by sticking my approach. Then I had fumbled the birdie attempt. This putt was not to build momentum. This four-footer, straight uphill, was to right the ship. I had begun with a six-shot lead. Tiger had just cut one stroke off that. I needed to prevent an opening-hole two-shot swing.

The sun was hot on my back. My shirt felt like damp tissue paper against my skin. Thinking I could get Grant Ashley out of my mind would not have been realistic. The background noise would not go away. It should not go away. I would simply have to play through it.

"Let's go, Jack," a familiar voice called from the gallery.

I turned to see Jim Dempsey.

I crouched one last time behind the putt. Straight. Four feet. Into the grain, which meant I could give it a firm stroke. I did, and the ball fell, center cut. I extended my arm and clutched my fist— not a fist-pump, not a celebration; rather, a fierce but controlled determination. It was what the shot and the day called for.

. . .

"What's Dempsey following us for?" Silver said.

We were on the tenth tee. Our threesome had played the front nine well: Woods had shot thirty-three, Capers ran even par, and I'd scrambled to a thirty-five, one under par and a four-shot lead. The leader board now read: J. AUSTIN, −18; T. WOODS, −14; K. CAPERS, −9.

I shrugged.

"He still your agent?"

"I need you to do something," I said. I told Silver, and he walked to where Dempsey stood, spoke briefly, then returned, and nodded a confirmation.

The gallery formed a U around the tee box, and Lisa, holding Darcy, stood next to Perkins, across the tee from Dempsey. I walked over, and she kissed me. I kissed Darcy. The group in front of us had been timed once. We were waiting again.

"Hanging tough," Lisa said. "You're bringing the putter back too fast, though. Slow it down."

I grinned.

"Just a suggestion," she said.

"I will slow it down."

"Take your time out there," Perkins said. "You won't enjoy the press room much."

I looked at him.

"You're everyone's number-one interview. Barrett said a lot. Don't know what MacDonald will think of that, but there it is."

"They know I was the last person to see Grant?"

Perkins nodded. There was more. I could tell.

"What?" I said.

Perkins glanced at Silver and my clubs. "Not the time."

"What is it? I'll be wondering the rest of the round."

"The kicker is: Lynne Ashley is the beneficiary of Grant's will. She gets all his assets and a ten-million-dollar life-insurance policy he took out as a rookie, three years ago."

.   .   .

I played the back nine as well as could be expected, shooting par, thirty-five, an eighteen-hole total of seventy. I was eighteen under par and leading Woods by two. Capers finished even and remained a distant nine under par, having fallen to fifth place. Fellow New Englanders Billy Andrade and Brad Faxon were now in the mix. Faxon had climbed to minus fourteen. Andrade had moved to thirteen under par.

In the press tent, and for the first time I could remember, someone overshadowed Tiger Woods. Unfortunately, that person was myself.

"Jack, were you questioned by police?"

I said I had been, not commenting further.

"What did Grant say to you last night?"

I told them we talked golf.

"Could the Lynne Ashley Web site have been the root of his suicide?"

"I don't wish to speculate."

"Authorities are ruling the death suicide. Is there anything to make you doubt that?"

"No."

When the feeding frenzy finished, Mitch Stapleton, a gray-beard from the *Chicago Tribune*, asked if I had any final memories I'd like to share about Grant."

"Grant Ashley," I said, choosing my words deliberately, "was kind to me, to others on the Tour. He was a friend. He loved his wife very much." I spread my hands. That said it all.

"I thought his wife left him."

Before I could speak, someone yelled: *"Are you insinuating that she was the cause of Grant's death? And, if so, Mike Easley ran the Web site she was on. Would that be motive for the Easley killing?"*

"I don't know what happened the night of Easley's death," I said.

Stapleton said, "Jack . . ."

I looked over.

Stapleton was in the front row, his face emotionless. "A Tour press release said Grant confessed to you."

I had no answer for that and had been caught in a lie that could appear as a highlight on national television. No one from the Tour had informed me of exactly what had been said at Barrett's press conference. It was apparent, though, that the whole story was out. As the young cop had said, Case Closed.

"No comment," I said.

"Did Grant say why he did it?"

The frenzy began again—a cacophony of voices, camera flashes popping, recorders clicking.

It had begun with an abrasive blonde in my living room and a phone call answered at my kitchen table. Now it was over. Everyone knew everything, or nearly everything. Even the media were well informed. However, I still had one question that required an answer. I stood and walked out.

"Hey, buddy," Jim Dempsey said, sliding onto the barstool next to me. "Silver said you wanted to see me. This is about that Maxfli offer, I bet. Told Silver I had expected, eventually, you'd reconsider that one."

For the previous fifteen minutes, I had sat staring at the wall mirror, which hung across from me, behind three rows of bottles. I didn't turn to look at him. I sipped from my Heineken bottle. I had left Lisa and Darcy following dinner to be at this appointment. The barroom air felt cooler than it was, and my hands were icy holding the chilled bottle. Yet beads of perspiration lined my forehead. I'd been with Dempsey a long time.

"Now, Jack," Dempsey said, "I know I can get the Maxfli people to sweeten the deal."

The bartender appeared, and Dempsey, wearing jeans and a denim shirt, pointed to my beer. "His tab," he said, grinning.

When all this had begun, Dempsey had lied to Perkins and me, denying knowledge of Lynne Ashley's whereabouts. He'd slept with my late-friend's wife, in fact had planned to run off with her. He'd hurt his family in ways I hoped never to understand. Now he was joking. Old times. To him, nothing had changed.

"Maxfli knows you like the Titleist Pro V1, Jack. They'll compensate you well to go back to a Maxfli ball. I'm glad you're seeing the light, buddy."

I shook my head slowly, still looking at my beer. It was 8:15 P.M. Behind us, the hotel restaurant was not busy. The television over the bar played a ball game, but the Red Sox weren't on.

"No?" Dempsey said, the heels of his boots hooking the stool's

259

circular footrest. "What do you mean, no?" When he smiled, the scar on his cheek bunched.

"I'm not here to talk deals or golf balls." I turned to face him. "What then?"

This wasn't easy. We'd been together more than ten years. Maybe people just change. Or maybe life throws things at them, and they change to adapt. I didn't know. But none of it mattered. I knew myself, and that was enough.

"Jim," I said, "I'm cutting ties."

"What? With me?"

"I don't want you representing me anymore."

He leaned back on his stool and sat staring. "Because of Lynne and me?"

"And Grant."

"Jesus, Jack, you know what she went through. She was confused when she married him."

"Were you, when you cheated on your wife and two kids?"

"Don't be a self-righteous prick, Jack."

"Or how about when you lied to me? Were you confused then?"

"I've done a lot for you, Jack."

"Thank you."

"You're all I have left. I had a line on Ryan Sterns, but this morning he said he's signing with IMG."

"This morning?"

He nodded, then shook his head. "I've been counseling the damned kid for weeks."

"Advising him?" I said.

He snorted. "So much for handshake agreements. You're the last of a dying breed, Jack."

We were quiet for a moment.

"Look," he said, "I know I made mistakes. You're my only client."

I shook my head, took a drink from my beer. "So you told Ryan Sterns to stay away from Grant, after the search turned up the DNA match."

Slowly, Dempsey blew out a long breath. He raised his beer

bottle and drank from it. The pause bought him time. He turned to me, opened his mouth, then closed it.

I nodded. "Not much to say to that, is there?"

"It wasn't like that. I was looking out for Ryan."

"Were you still looking out for Grant Ashley? How about when you were in bed with Lynne? Were you looking out for him then? Or how about me? When you sat in a restaurant just like this one and lied to me? Who were you looking out for then?"

He was a broad man with thick hands, but now looked much smaller than he actually was, sitting slouched at the bar. He didn't respond. But I knew the answer. The person he'd been looking out for was himself, and beyond that, the girl with the curl, Lynne Ashley, blond and sexy.

I drank from my bottle. Then I set it down and shook my head. "I've always been standup with you, Jim. I can't have an agent who lies to me."

"So that's it?"

"That's it," I said.

He stood, turned, and walked out. I finished my beer, paid the tab for both of us, and followed.

. . .

"Have you been waiting for me?" Lynne Ashley said, walking into the hotel lobby.

"You weren't in your room, and you weren't in the restaurant. I figured you'd return, eventually." It was 9:45 P.M.

"I had a dinner appointment," she said. "How did you know my room number?"

I shook my head. Perkins had given it to me, but she didn't need to know that.

"How'd you meet Grant?" I said.

The hotel lobby was quiet. A few people moved past us. Only one woman was working the desk.

Lynne stared at me before answering. "In Atlanta. God, how I miss him."

"How did you meet?"

She was not dressed to mourn. She wore a black cocktail dress and heels. A pocketbook the size of an envelope hung from her shoulder. She reached into the pocketbook and retrieved her keycard. She looked from the key to me and paused, then looked around. We were alone.

"Let's sit down," I said and pointed to the couch across the lobby from the desk.

"I don't know," she said. "I'm leaving tomorrow and have to pack."

"I only want a couple minutes."

"I've spoken to the police and FBI. I don't see what we have to talk about."

"This isn't about legal matters." It was about something simpler, something she wouldn't understand. "I was with your husband the night he died. I thought you'd want to know about his final hours. He loved you more than anything and said you'd get back together."

"God, he was sweet."

We went to the couch.

"How did you meet him?"

She shrugged. "I had a flat. He changed it for me."

"At his apartment complex?"

"Yes. People don't choose where to break down."

"Not usually. You're a very rich woman now."

"What are you talking about?"

"I'm talking about ten million dollars. How did you pick Grant? There were others before him."

"We picked each other."

"How did you know he lived there?"

"What are you saying? I don't have to take this." She pulled her purse to her side, preparing to stand.

"No, you don't have to stay," I said. "You're in the clear. This isn't a legal issue. I just want to know."

"You're a bastard, Jack Austin."

"I was called a self-righteous prick an hour ago. Bastard is an improvement. Grant Ashley is dead. He was my friend. He killed a man for you, Lynne. And he gave up everything for you."

Her head shook, denying what I said. But her eyes betrayed her. They began to pool. I knew tears would follow.

"Grant told me the divorce papers were in the mail," I said. "I know you and Jim Demspey were going to run off into the sunset, despite Grant, despite Dempsey's wife and two kids. Then you dumped Dempsey, too."

Crying now, she was not leaving, her voice an angry whisper. "Divorce happens. Don't be so old-fashioned."

"I don't see it that way. How did you pick Grant? How did you know where he lived?"

"Don't you judge me. You have no idea what I've been through. Grant killed himself. I didn't murder him. And let me ask *you* something: Do you think you'd be with Lisa Trembley if she had a past like mine, and you knew about it? Think about that. Grant was like a fairytale for me. We had a big house, cars."

"You still have those things, probably more. You wanted fame and fortune. Grant provided both—the ten million dollars and the Easley murder made your name national news."

"I don't have the fairytale. No one can control the Internet."

"You waited for Grant Ashley at his apartment complex."

"He fell in love with me."

"But you set him up. Now he's dead."

"I did what I had to do. And I didn't make him fall in love with me."

"Now he's dead."

"I did not kill him," she said and stood. "I'm leaving."

She had taken two steps when I stopped her. "Where do you go from here?"

She turned back and studied my face for a long time before answering. "Someplace where I can start again." Then, without another word, she dropped the keycard back inside her purse and walked outside to the parking lot.

I got up and watched her. In the lingering silence, the sound of her heels clicking on the pavement grew faint, finally fading to silence, and only Lynne Ashley's failed dream remained. I was tired and went up to bed.

36

Sunday, the heat had finally passed. The yellow sun burned bright in the distance as Tim Silver and I walked from the practice green to the tee at the par-three 190-yard first hole. The air, for the first time that week, felt cool. I held a towel with my still-bandaged right hand, which served as a reminder of all that happened: Grant Ashley killed himself. Part of me would never forgive him for that. He had been wrong to stab Easley and should have faced the legal system. However, nothing could be done about that now. Now there was only the loss.

On the tee box, I casually passed the towel to Silver and shook Tiger Woods's hand, looking him directly in the eye and wishing him good luck, the customary first-tee gesture.

"Hand sore?" Silver said.

"No." We moved to the back of the tee box.

"What's with the towel?"

"Wanted to be sure my hand was bone-dry."

Silver looked at me, started to speak, then stopped. "Hold on," he said, finally, his voice a whisper, a grin spreading across his face. "You're trying to out-calm the Tiger?"

"Yeah."

"That's like trying to win the stare-down with Mike Tyson when you tap gloves, before the first bell."

I shrugged. He was right. Yet, I wasn't intimidated. I hadn't slept past 8 A.M. in years, but this day had awakened at ten, refreshed and feeling different than I had all summer. I was still reeling from the loss of a friend, and now, for the first time in more than a decade, stood agentless, with a family to support. However, I'd finally discovered the truth about the murder and about Lynne Ashley. The information provided understanding, even a vague sense of closure, although I knew I'd wonder about Lynne Ashley and her quest for self-reinvention for years to come.

"No breeze today," Silver said, drawing my five-iron from the bag. "And the pin is tucked six paces from the front right bunker."

"I thought they'd put the pin in back today."

He shook his head. "Put the flag in front and see how many suckers go for it."

The nearby leader board told the story: J. AUSTIN, −18; T. WOODS, −16; B. FAXON, −16; B. ANDRADE, −13; and K. CAPERS, −9. All red numbers. Four players within five shots of each other. Brad Faxon had begun the day fourteen under par, but opened with two fast birdies. The weather, allowing for many low scores, would not be my ally. I had to play aggressively. I looked at the five-iron. It was the safe play, but might carry the ball to the back of the green, effectively eliminating my birdie chance. I drew the six-iron. Silver was silent as I made practice swings.

I was eager to hit my first shot; indeed, I had been since waking. It's the waiting that gets you. Contending is exhausting, a culmination of emotions—excitement, tension, and anticipation. Yet it's wonderful, too—gooseflesh, the return of a childhood rush, taking you back to when you stood over five-footers on practice greens, telling yourself, *This is to beat Nicklaus*, and leaped when the putt had fallen. I'd often marveled at players like Ernie Els, Phil Mickelson, and Woods, at how they seemed to contend each week, somehow maintaining intensity. I had also vowed to see what that was like and to join the elite with a string of strong performances—beginning this day.

Apparently, Lisa had spent enough time around me—and via interviews with hundreds of Tour players—to know I wouldn't make good breakfast company, because Saturday she'd made Sunday brunch plans with Angela Davis and had taken Darcy, clearing out long before I woke. It left me with five hours to kill.

Since I began playing competitive golf, on very few occasions had I sought solitude—the day I won the Maine State Amateur; my victorious final round at the New England Amateur. Those days, I had spent the hours before my tee time alone, hitting balls, thinking strategy, and locating a quiet place inside myself where I might go to right the ship, should I begin to falter.

This day, I found myself seeking that place after the very first swing.

The-six iron was not enough club. My ball found the front trap. Tiger, meanwhile, stiffed his approach, his ball stopping four feet from the pin. The exchange set the tone for the day and rocked me to my heels, like a fighter swinging wildly, trying to battle off the ropes in the opening round.

"The swing was a good one, Jack," Silver said. "Let's go from there. Save par. You're still swinging well."

I pulled the sand wedge from my bag and walked silently to the front right bunker.

My two-shot lead would be one after the first hole. I had to count on that. I had to force myself to save par at all cost. Tiger had not held the top spot on the Official World Golf Rankings year after year by missing four-footers. In fact, he, better than anyone in history, could knock you down, then hit you again to make sure you stayed down. I knew that, going into these final eighteen holes. I'd slept on the fifty-four–hole lead once before, years earlier, and the result was not worth remembering: a sudden-death playoff loss. This time would be different, I vowed, walking toward the trap.

The lie was generous. My ball sat atop the sand, on a slight incline. I opened my stance, aiming well left, leveled my shoulders to the slope, and made a full outside-to-in swing, the club face never closing. I stood watching through the shower of sand the way I had squinted through snow squalls as a child, and saw the ball sail high and land about ten feet from me, bounce twice, and stop two feet from the pin. Lisa, holding Darcy, stood near Perkins in the first row of spectators, cheering wildly. Perkins thrust his huge arm in the air, an emotion I'd never seen him exhibit. Silver, to his credit, only handed me the putter. I marked my ball, glancing at Woods. He nodded in appreciation of the shot, then went about his business. I had not anticipated a talkative round. Woods wanted to win. So we had nothing to talk about.

Woods made his four-footer with ease, quickly going to seventeen under par.

I replaced my ball, pocketed the coin, and crouched behind the two-footer. I didn't want to take a lot of time over the putt. Woods didn't need to know I was nervous this day standing over even two-footers. I addressed the putt, made my customary two practice strokes, and firmly buried the Titleist Pro V1 into the heart of the cup. More importantly, I had moved off the ropes, countering Woods's first punch with a solid straight left of my own, maintaining a one-shot lead.

. . .

Woods and I each parred the second hole and stood on the No. 3 tee, waiting for Faxon and Andrade to clear the fairway. The third hole usually plays over par. It's a 408-yard par four that slopes left to right—not good for someone whose natural shot is a fade, as the ball can quickly find the right rough or beyond. The rough is nasty, the green two-tiered and surrounded by bunkers.

"A nice little draw," Silver said. "Three-wood will leave a seven- or eight-iron."

I took the fairway metal from Silver and looked across the tee box. Woods had his driver out. His club selection contrasted my conservative choice. Memories of my showdown with Phil Mickelson—when he had reached the green and I laid up—crept in to my mind. That was then. And that had been the tenth hole. Neither Woods nor I would drive the third green. I kept the three-wood.

Woods hit a perfect drive that carried well over 300 yards and left less than a full wedge to the green.

I hit a solid draw with my three-wood, leaving 140 yards. As we moved down the fairway, I saw Lisa standing with on-course commentator Matt Baker. A cameraman stood beside Baker. I couldn't hear what they were saying, but Lisa shook her head, pointed toward me, then to Darcy, and I knew what he'd asked her: Did she miss her work? A legitimate question, one Lisa had answered for me during our basement conversation after the

Memorial Tournament. I had a difficult approach shot waiting, but momentarily thought again of Lisa's sacrifice and wondered if I could so easily give up my profession. She had done so for Darcy, of course, but for me, too.

"One forty-three to the front," Silver said, tossing grass into the air. The grass fell straight down. "No breeze. One fifty-six to the pin."

The big Maxfli staff bag stood between us. I took off my hat and dried my forehead on my shirtsleeve.

"Use the towel," Silver said.

I looked at him. "What's the difference?"

"It's so . . ." he searched for the right word, glanced around, saw we were out of earshot, and shrugged—"*straight* to wipe your head on your shirt. Like using your sleeve to wipe your mouth."

"You complain that my truck is filthy, too."

"It is."

I grinned. "Give me the seven-iron. I'm going for birdie here."

I didn't know if Silver strategically placed his distractions, although this one had been well timed. I chuckled to myself, blew out a deep breath, and went through my pre-swing routine. Finally, I brought the seven-iron back slowly, then down, striking the ball with a descending blow, and taking a large divot, generating backspin. Across the fairway, Woods and his caddie, Steve Williams, watched as my ball hit near the pin atop the second tier.

"Inside five feet," Silver said and held out his palm.

I slapped it, and we moved to Woods's ball. Watching Woods go about his on-course business was surreal. Part of me was intrigued, the way I would be to watch Sandy Koufax pitch or Joe Montana engineer a late-game drive; yet, the other Jack Austin, the stubborn son of a bitch who knows in his heart of hearts he can beat any golfer in the world on a given day, took interest only in the man's score. I stood casually as Silver and I watched Woods and Williams review the yardage and discuss club selection. They settled on what looked like a sand wedge. Woods made his customary high-voltage slash—the club moving back slowly, pausing briefly at the top, then the brilliant flash of metal, the hips snapping back to square and beyond, the follow-through and well-documented finishing pose—Tiger staring the ball down. His Nike ball landed near my Pro V1, then spun back, stopping eight feet below the cup.

"Advantage Austin," Silver said quietly, and we moved to the green.

Silver had been right, on both counts: I had five feet, straight; and Tiger's putt was much more difficult—eight feet, up an incline, then leveling off, even breaking near the hole.

I reviewed my line from several different angles, as did Silver. We met back at my bag on the fringe.

"Straight in the heart," Silver said and shrugged.

I nodded. There wasn't anything to say. It was a big moment in the round, and I was certain Woods knew that. I watched him grind over his putt, reviewing the line several times from behind the ball and each side. Woods and Williams both studied the final break, which, from my vantage point at the side of the green, looked to be six inches or a foot, right to left.

A gallery can emit a near-tangible feeling. Since our opening tee shot, I'd felt as if the consensus was, even at two strokes back, Woods had me where he wanted, and it was simply a matter of time. After all, hadn't he once stormed back from seven shots? I knew my place in the game. I'd been called a "journeyman" in articles and television features over the years. Nothing wrong with that. The connotation spoke of work ethic and drive, qualities in which I took pride. I knew, however, the media routinely used "journeyman" in place of "one who routinely struggles." *Journeyman, Jack Austin.* I'd heard it over and again. Never *PGA Tour winner, Jack Austin,* as I was winless. Yet also never, *Talented* or *World-class.* I knew I was both. I'd played the world's most competitive tour for more than a decade, competed against the best, many weeks matching shots with heralded players.

When Woods, still trailing by one, hit the putt, the gallery seemed to hold a collective breath in anticipation of it falling. Next, the script would call for me to miss, leaving us tied. Finally, my role would demand a complete breakdown, so Ryder Cuppers Faxon and Woods could duel to a dramatic conclusion.

Except Woods's ball stopped six inches short of the hole.

Woods looked at Williams, who shook his head, neither man believing it. Moreover, the gallery was silent. What was going on here? The script had been written, a commoner found for the sacrifice.

Neither Silver nor this journeyman commoner spoke as Woods finished, tapping in for par. I went to my ball, got one final read, and made my two practice strokes. I set the blade carefully behind the ball, brought the putter back and straight through, holding the follow-through, listening for the music of Surlyn rattling against plastic.

I heard it, then what could only be described as a sigh from the gallery. I was up two again.

. . .

We had gone out with respective front-nine rounds of par. Faxon, though, had moved to seventeen under, one back of me. Tiger and I stood on the tenth tee. Behind the tee box, Baker had Lisa talking again. This time they were close enough for me to hear. Lisa, wearing headphones now, was holding Darcy in a front-pack.

"The longer Jack leads, the better chance he has to hold off Tiger," she said. "Think of Ben Curtis at the 2003 Open Championship. The longer someone plays with the lead, the more comfortable he becomes. This crowd began the day waiting for Tiger to overtake Jack. Now the gallery is reacting to Jack's shots."

It was true. My birdies and clutch par putts had begun drawing ovations. Was the gallery genuinely rooting for me, or simply happy to witness a closely contested final round? And, stay-at-home mom or not, Lisa was a journalist and had picked up on the change, too. She walked golf courses the way a great architect would casually stroll through a custom-designed house.

"Time to slay the dragon," Silver said, holding the driver out to me.

A back-and-forth front nine, Woods had made the last birdie and had the honor. I glanced to see his club selection. Unmistakable. Driver. The tees were in the front. I thought of the "dragon." The year before, on this hole, Phil Mickelson reached the green and made the eagle putt. I had hit an iron off the tee, resulting in a two-shot swing, and concluding with my second-place finish.

I took the driver.

Strategy would suggest I wait to see the result of Woods's swing before selecting a club. Not this time. I was going for the green. An eagle or birdie might provide a cushion. On the tenth, trees challenge any wayward tee shot. A severe drop-off collects balls missing left; likewise, if your approach to the green is long, your ball settles nearly thirty feet below the putting surface. The tenth hole provides a risk-reward opportunity; but you must be precise off the tee. And Woods was: He brought the big Nike driver back and hit a long, straight tee ball. The drive landed in the fairway, squirreled between the front sand traps, and onto the putting surface. The gallery exploded. Goliath had woken.

I waited for quiet. The marshal raised both arms, holding the large QUIET sign. The gallery fell silent. Energy, nearly tangible like a pungent odor, seemed to disseminate from the crowd. I teed my ball, stood back, and made my customary practice swings. One year previously, nearly to the day, I'd played this same hole, made the wise choice, and lost, coming so close to victory Schultz thought the near-miss affected me more than it had. In one sense, he was right: I'd altered my strategy as a result. However, my life and my golf career had gone on. I glanced to the first row of the gallery and focused on Darcy, who bobbed gently in Lisa's front-pack. I thought back to my ride through Portland, Maine, with Schultz and recalled his comments of his late daughter and his talk of legacy.

"Jack," Silver said.

"Yeah?"

"Everything okay?"

"Sure."

My eyes were on Lisa, who stood smiling into the camera. She leaned away from it, offering me a thumbs-up. I nodded and looked at Darcy once more. She slept silently—soft dark hair, closed eyes showing long lashes, smooth fair skin.

It was time. I addressed the ball, brought the driver back slowly, stopping just short of parallel at the top. Then I began the descent, rotating my hips, firing down and through the ball, wrists snapping, my hands registering the sensation of the club face striking the ball crisply. I looked up, well after contact, and watched the Pro V1 rise against the blue sky, level off, then plunge, land and roll onto the green, stopping very near Woods's ball.

The gallery's reaction was not one I'd have predicted. There was a moment of silence, as if all spectators sat staring in disbelief, then a loud eruption, as if the crowd had thrown its collective hands in the air, shrugged, and said, *To hell with it,* before cheering wildly.

"Been waiting a year to hit that shot?" Silver said.

I didn't answer, only held out my fist. He tapped it with his own.

At the green, my mindset was firmly in the present. I had to look at this as must-make. I had forty feet. Woods had thirty-five. My putt would show him the speed and highlight the breaks. Woods made these putts. I knew that. Holes like this— the drive and this long putt—defined his career. Not merely for their degree of difficulty, but because they shifted the momentum of a golf round. Timing. Good players hit great shots routinely. Great players hit great shots at the most crucial moments of golf tournaments. I had a two-shot lead. It had taken most of the day, but the gallery had begun to warm to me, finally accepting the idea that I wasn't going to roll over for Tiger. The momentum, for the moment, was mine, and I wanted badly to build upon it. We had eight more holes, two full hours. Crowd support would be a tremendous advantage for either of us.

"Double break," Silver said, leaning over my shoulder as I crouched behind the ball. "Not a lot of break in each, but there're two of them. You see the line?"

I nodded.

"Stage is yours, Jack," he said and moved away.

It was a putt I had hit before. In practice rounds, I always dropped a ball or two near this spot, and slapped it toward the hole, in case this very scenario occurred. I selected my line, choosing a spot several inches away over which to roll the ball, assuring it would start on line. It did, rolling slowly, bending several inches, then sliding back, narrowly missing on the left side, and leaving a tap-in birdie.

As I putted out, Woods reviewed his line again. He'd seen something and was adjusting. He consulted Williams, the two nodding and pointing as they spoke, then finally Woods was over the putt. He started the ball several inches outside the line I'd selected. His Nike ball bent back and wove its way closer to the hole, catching the left lip, and dropping. He'd made two, to my three, cutting the lead to one.

. . .

We traded birdies like heavyweight boxers standing toe-to-toe, slugging it out, finally arriving at the 374-yard par-four seventeenth tee in the same position: I had a one-stroke lead over Woods; Faxon had fallen back. One dragon—the tenth hole—had been slain already this day.

"You've never birdied this son of a bitch," Silver said, "in all the time we've played here. I'd love to go to the eighteenth with a two-shot lead."

There was nothing to say to that. You couldn't wish a birdie onto your scorecard. In fact, it was probably more likely to occur if you didn't think about score at all—simply took the hole a shot at a time. However, Silver was right. I was a single shot ahead of Woods. The gallery was now gigantic. If fifty thousand had come out this day, forty-nine thousand now followed us.

"A lot can change in this game in two months," I said.

Silver looked around. "Stopping to smell the roses?"

"Just taking it all in," I said. "Doesn't get any better—a crowd ten rows deep, stretching a hundred yards, the world's best right on my heels. . . ."

And Lisa was there, too, holding Darcy. She still wore the headphones. Perkins was nearby, his ever-present scowl nearly gone. If he were anyone else, I'd have even said Perkins looked nervous. Baker eyed Perkins the way every stranger seemed to, with trepidation. The sun was behind them. It was 5:20 P.M. Lisa smiled at something Baker said. I had to hand it to ABC Sports. The opportunity to cover her husband attempting to win his first tournament offered Lisa a unique journalistic experience, one she couldn't refuse. It was also genuinely interesting: *How would Jack Austin handle the day?* And, given that, how would she handle it, on-air, no less? Clever.

For me, though, that wasn't the most important aspect of having Lisa there. Darcy was awake now, blue eyes wondering from face to face, seeming to observe it all. Only weeks old, Darcy would, of course, recall none of it. But she was there with me on the journey. Schultz's attempt to leave a legacy had been negated by daughter June's untimely death. She would never outlive him, never tell her own kids stories of Granddad Schultz's best days in golf and life. Yet, June had no doubt lived to an age where she saw the trophies, heard the stories—from Schultz, but, more importantly, from others—of her father's storied career. Thus, she had known of her father's successes. Knowing Schultz, she'd been told of his failures, too, and, as would be Schultz's hope, had learned from both. I thought of my own father, of his phone call at the Memorial. I thought of all he had given me, the lessons I'd learned watching him conduct himself, the pride that rose inside me as a child—and even now—upon hearing him praised.

"Leave it to Lisa to find a way to get front-row access all day," Silver said. "And I love those shoes, too."

I looked at him. "Shoes?"

"Those flats. They're killer."

"You killed the moment," I said.

"A moment? We were sharing a moment?"

"Forget it."

"Well, Lisa does accessorize very well, Jack."

We waited to see what Tiger would do. He had the honor. At 376, the yardage is deceptive because the hole plays uphill. Likewise, your tee shot must be straight to avoid fairway bunkers and to set up an approach that, first, carries the fifteen-foot sand trap in front of the green, and, second, stops short of a steep drop-off awaiting any overcooked approach shots. I had the three-wood in hand and leaned against it.

Woods pulled the driver from his bag. Williams said something and offered an iron. Woods considered the iron, they talked, and he slid the driver back. He started to the tee with the iron. Then he stopped, shook his head, gave Williams the iron, and took the driver out again.

"Going for it," Silver said.

"Can't reach it," I said.

"No way."

"Trying to put it just short of the bunker."

Silver shrugged.

In 2003, Woods had searched most of the season for a driver. Poor tee shots had cost him several tournaments that season, and his driver had become the talk of the golf world. Now, standing on the seventeenth tee, he had the driver out. Uphill, the 376 yards would play 425. Clearly unreachable. But Woods never played for second place. I knew he'd rather attempt a miracle shot and finish third than play safe and finish second. Every guy on the PGA Tour plays to win. Period. But, in this scenario, Woods had an additional luxury: a lifetime exemption. So even if he knew I had three of a kind, he could stay in the game, try for the full house, gambling, essentially, with house money. Also, the strategy was logical: If Woods could hit his drive to pitching distance, surely he could make birdie seven of ten times—and he needed to make up a shot.

Truthfully, I had expected the miracle. I'd seen too many from Woods to bet against him. But it was not to be, at least not at the seventeenth hole. The golf gods called his bluff, the drive sailing wildly right of the fairway. A resounding *Ooohhh* echoed from the gallery, and Tiger slammed his driver into his bag and stood glaring down the fairway.

"Put the ball in play," Silver said, "at all cost."

"You the man, Big Jack," someone called. Then: *"Grip it and rip it, Jack."* And *"Don't back off, Jack."*

"And you thought I was the only one who thinks you're cute," Silver said.

"Three-wood is the play," I said and went about my pre-shot routine, finally hitting a solid drive to the left side of the fairway.

Next, Woods punched his ball back to the fairway. Then it

was me again, from 116 yards. The drive left me a full pitching wedge. The hole was cut at the back of the green, seven paces from the left fringe.

"Conservative off the tee," Silver said. "Safe play is to the center of the green. Hit it a hundred and ten yards, right at the middle."

I shook my head.

"No?"

"Pin sheet says it's one-sixteen from here."

"That's to the pin, Jack."

"I know."

Silver started to speak, then stopped, and nodded once. "Your show, boss."

I stepped away with the wedge, made two practice swings, then I addressed the ball. I didn't look around. Nothing seemed to move. No noise. I felt no breeze. I brought the club back slowly, then down. The contact felt crisp, the divot flaring up, momentarily entering my vision, then gone. I watched the ball hit on line with the flag, bounce once, then roll, and, finally, stop. I couldn't tell how close it was. Nevertheless, the gallery exploded.

Then Perkins's voice like a thunderclap booming above the cheer: *Three inches, Jack.*

. . .

At the eighteenth, I was up two strokes. Woods had saved par in near-heroic fashion at No. 17 but had slapped my back, congratulating the approach shot to tap-in birdie range. Thus, on the eighteenth tee, I had the honor. The eighteenth is a true "finishing hole." Many Buick Classics are decided there. It plays 526 yards, a par five, dogleg left. Deep rough always guards the fairway, and a greenside sand trap, front right, entices many second shots. Consequently, from that bunker, it's thirty-five yards to the multi-tiered green with a steep drop behind the putting surface. That wasn't what I was thinking about on the tee, though. My natural shot is left to right. Due to the dogleg, this hole called for a draw, meaning I had to shape my tee shot right to left. Fighting your ball's natural tendency is difficult any time. On the seventy-second tee, protecting a lead, the challenge becomes grueling.

The hair at the back of my neck stood, the sun seemed hot on my back, and I had sweat through my shirt. Gooseflesh lined my bare arms. Golf is not a reactionary sport. It's what makes it so challenging. You don't try to hit a pitch or intercept a pass. Therefore, you have plenty of time to think. It's why it is often said more golf tournaments are lost than won.

Silver held out a water bottle. When I took it, my hand shook. He stared at my hand through an awkward pause, then moved silently to our bag. There was nothing left to say. I was no longer playing against Tiger Woods. The round had reached another level. I'd never been in this position before. My playoff loss had been long ago, back when I'd been naive enough to believe I'd have many more chances. The game had grown exponentially in the decade I'd played the PGA Tour; subsequently, the Tour now had a worldwide flavor, swelling its talent pool greatly. This was clearly my best chance to win a tournament in a decade. The fact that I was wise enough, at thirty-six, to understand that made it all the more difficult.

I walked to Silver and pulled the headcover off the driver.

"Not playing this in three shots?" he said. "You stung the three-wood on seventeen."

"Tiger will reach the green in two," I said. "You think I want to sit back and watch him roll a putt for eagle? Stand there watching, as he tries to push this thing to extra holes? No, thank you." I pulled the driver from the bag. "Game plan has been play for birdie, when we can. It's worked."

"That it has," Silver said.

I moved away and took my two practice swings. Neither Woods nor Williams spoke. Lisa, still wearing headphones, stood behind the tee. Her face was pale. For the first time I could remember, her eyes held no hint of laughter. I teed the ball and addressed it, my right toe parallel with my left arch support, the standard set-up for a draw. With the club head resting just off the turf behind the ball, I momentarily squeezed the grip with as much force as I could, my knuckles turning white. Then I released. Tension seemed to drain not only from my hands, but from my shoulders, neck, and upper back. I inhaled deeply, then let it out and brought the driver back slowly, pausing at the top, and made a good swing.

The Titleist started down the right side, then bent left, hitting in the center of the fairway, and running past the corner, out of sight.

I walked to Silver and heard Lisa: ". . . one of the best shots of his career."

We watched Tiger hit a similar shot. He was going for eagle, hoping I would three-putt. It was all there was left for him, but it was enough.

Arriving at my ball, in the fairway, it was clear I had all of 230 yards to the green. Woods's tee shot had bounded past mine, so I would hit first. Woods and Williams stood maybe twenty paces away, watching intently.

"How do you feel?" Silver said, his hand on the three-iron.

I looked at the club and nodded. "Enough adrenaline to lift a house."

"Rip this son of a bitch," he said. "Flag's on the back tier. Land it on the front, and she'll run all the way back."

I took the three-iron and moved away. We were the final two-some. Spectators lined the fairway on both sides and had also moved behind us now, forming a huge U. Silver was smiling ear-to-ear.

"What?" I said.

"Just fun, man. That's all."

"Better than missing cuts?"

"Slightly."

Two hundred thirty yards with a three-iron was the outer limit of my range, and my mis-hit at the Memorial, where I'd dumped the five-iron short with the tournament on the line, loomed large. Yet instinct whispered three-iron, and I sat up and listened to her with every fiber of my being. No time for second-guessing now. No time for recollections of bad shots. Only here and now.

Lisa had Darcy out of the front-pack now. The baby was awake, drinking from the bottle. Lisa spoke to Baker, motioning to Woods, then back to me, pointing with her chin, as her hands held the baby. The sun burned bright behind them, an orange streak against a sea-blue backdrop. My hands still felt shaky. I didn't want to think about what was at stake. For my family, a win meant security—a two-year exemption and, agentless or not, calls from sponsors. For me, much more—the work of a lifetime fulfilled, a trophy of inestimable personal value on my mantel.

I completed my pre-shot routine, because I felt I had to. Physically, practice swings would add nothing now; however, I had remained loyal to my pre-shot routine all day. The results had been positive. No changes. I had hit three-irons off patches shoveled from snow-covered fairways on twenty-degree January days in Maine. As a kid and, later, as a struggling Tour player, I'd hit three-irons at driving ranges until my hands bled.

Now, I stepped into the spotlight, set the club face behind the Pro V1, and let muscle memory take over.

The ball never wavered, landing on the front of the green, rolling to the second tier. Not the approach I'd hit on the seventeenth, but twenty-five feet and two putts away from a birdie.

The gallery exploded—*You the man, Jack! Keep Tiger hunting, Jack! This is your day, Jack!* I didn't feel like "the man," as I stood next to Silver, watching Tiger. If I'd hit three-iron, I knew Woods would use a five-iron. And, of course, the shorter the club, the more precise Woods could be, making eagle still very likely. As if on cue, Woods hit a shot that swung the momentum back to him. The ball stopped five feet from the pin.

Now I had to make birdie.

·   ·   ·

The walk to the eighteenth green was not the champion's stroll. No waves to the crowd. No mouthing *I love you, Mom* at TV cameras. The champion's stroll occurs when somebody has a five-shot lead with his ball fifteen feet from the hole and Tiger in the clubhouse watching television. By contrast, I faced a long putt that would rise over an undulation before settling on the third tier and breaking two feet right to left near the cup. If that putt didn't go in, I would then have to stand back and watch Tiger hit a five-footer, attempting to momentarily tie. Finally, assuming Woods made his five-footer, if I missed my long first attempt, I would then have one putt to win.

Accordingly, I walked to the green without speaking to Silver, my mind firmly on my ensuing twenty-five–foot putt.

"Jack," Silver said.

I looked at him.

"The crowd's cheering for you, man. Do something."

Embarrassed, I waved in acknowledgment, then headed to my ball. I marked it and flipped it to Silver. He wiped it, and I returned the Pro V1 and pocketed my coin. Silver and I read the break from all sides. We discussed the final right-to-left swing near the hole, although it felt futile. The whole experience seemed to fade to surreal. Break no longer mattered. Distance and speed no longer mattered. The ball simply *had* to lag within tap-in range. There was nothing else now.

I squeezed the putter's grip, as I had my three-iron. I inhaled and exhaled. These were putts Tour players practice over and over. Jack Nicklaus once said a great putter doesn't make them all; a great putter leaves himself sure-thing two-putts.

I brought the putter back slowly and made my slow, three-second stroke. The ball climbed to the back of the green.

Then, however, it slowed, stopping two feet short of the break, four feet from the hole.

I heard the gallery's reaction. Unmistakable. A sigh followed by a scattering of applause. The sigh spoke volumes. I had left the door open. Woods had a five-footer for eagle and a momentary tie. If he made and I missed—resulting in respective eagle and par finishes—we would be deadlocked and facing extra holes. I thought back to the Mercedes Championships in Hawaii in 2000. On the first extra hole, Woods needed one swing to essentially decide the tournament, sticking his tee shot on the par three to six inches. Clearly, he wanted that scenario to replay here, as he and Williams spent a lot of time analyzing the five-footer.

Finally, Woods addressed the ball, glancing once from it to the hole, and refocusing on his Nike ball. Then he pulled the trigger. The ball followed the line they had selected, covering the five feet of green, breaking hard, right to left, and entering the cup, dead center. Woods made his legendary fist pump, and the place erupted.

I moved to my coin, replaced my ball, and stood stoically, waiting for the crowd to settle. I looked at Lisa. She had taken the headphones off now. Darcy's head rested gently on Lisa's shoulder, eyes closed, sleeping peacefully amid the havoc. Perkins pointed at me, then to his chest, a gesture saying, *You've got heart. Use it.*

Heart meant everything. Heart led me from a tiny nine-hole municipal course in central Maine to the PGA Tour. I'd witnessed more talented competitors come and go but had out-worked many, earning a decade-long career and affording my-self the opportunity to compete against the world's best. Like golf and its transitory players, life, too, had brought many people into and out of my world. Lynne Ashley had entered with roar, then simply walked away in unforgettable fashion. Jim Demp-sey had fallen from view, as if blown from a shelf and shatter-ing. Grant, though, still lingered the way wisps of smoke from a crushed cigarette spiral through empty light.

And through it all, golf remained the lone constant. Now there was family, too. As a golfer, I was winless. Family, though, had championed me. I stood over the ball and looked one final time at Darcy and Lisa. Then I glanced at the hole, then back to my ball. I exhaled deeply and made my stroke.

This time, the ball fell, center cut.